Sterling STREAK

L.B. DUNBAR

www.lbdunbar.com

L.B. DUNBAR

STERLING STREAK
Copyright © 2024 Laura Dunbar
L.B. Dunbar Writes, Ltd.
https://www.lbdunbar.com/

Cover Design: Lori Jackson Designs
Photographer: CJC Photography
Cover Model: Dominic Calvani
Editor: Nicole McCurdy/Emerald Edits
Editor: Gemma Brocato

Other Books by L.B. Dunbar

<u>Sterling Falls</u>
Sterling Heat
Sterling Brick
Sterling Streak
Sterling Clay

<u>Parentmoon</u>

<u>Holiday Hotties (Christmas novellas)</u>
Scrooge-ish
Naughty-ish
Grouch-ish

<u>Road Trips & Romance</u>
Hauling Ashe
Merging Wright
Rhode Trip

<u>Lakeside Cottage</u>
Living at 40
Loving at 40
Learning at 40
Letting Go at 40

<u>Silver Foxes of Blue Ridge</u>
Silver Brewer
Silver Player
Silver Mayor
Silver Biker

<u>Sexy Silver Fox Collection</u>
After Care
Midlife Crisis
Restored Dreams
Second Chance
Wine&Dine

<u>Collision novellas</u>

L.B. DUNBAR

Collide
Caught

<u>The Sex Education of M.E.</u>

<u>The Heart Collection</u>
Speak from the Heart
Read with your Heart
Look with your Heart
Fight from the Heart
View with your Heart

A Heart Collection Spin-off
<u>*The Heart Remembers*</u>

BOOKS IN OTHER AUTHOR WORLDS
<u>Smartypants Romance (an imprint of Penny Reid)</u>
Love in Due Time
Love in Deed
Love in a Pickle

<u>The World of True North (an imprint of Sarina Bowen)</u>
Cowboy
Studfinder

THE EARLY YEARS
<u>The Legendary Rock Star Series</u>

<u>Paradise Stories</u>

<u>The Island Duet</u>

<u>Modern Descendants – writing as elda lore</u>

A famous center fielder. A country music darling. He needs to get away.
She needs a break. They both might find more than they bargained for
in the small town of Sterling Falls.

DEDICATION

For the Chicago Cubs and Wrigley Field.
Thank you for the memories.
#baseballislife

L.B. DUNBAR

Playlist

If you'd like to follow along with the music selections for this book, here is the playlist. You can also find the playlist on Spotify.

"Heartache on the Dance Floor" – Jon Pardi

"Songbird" – Fleetwood Mac

"Save Me the Trouble" – Dan & Shay

"Thank God" – Kane Brown, with Katelyn Brown

"Thought You Should Know" – Morgan Wallen

"Lady" – Little River Band

"Ready For It" – Taylor Swift

"Chasing After You" – Ryan Hurd, Maren Morris

"Craving You" – Maren Morris and Thomas Rhett

"White Horse" – Chris Stapleton

"Fast Cars" – Luke Combs version

"Good Time" – Niko Moon

"Delicate" – Taylor Swift

DISCLAIMER

Let's have a repeat in reading this paragraph.

This is a work of fiction, created without the use of AI technology. Any names, characters, places, and incidents are the *products of the author's imagination and used in a fictitious manner*. **Any resemblance** to any actual people, living or dead, events, or locales **is entirely coincidental**.

But let's be honest, in the years 2023-2024 (when this book was written and copyrighted), a world renown singer dated an equally popular professional football player, and their romance was covered in the regular news, pop culture news, and sports entertainment news. I'm not pledging any allegiance for or against either the relationship or the individuals. A girl loves a boy. The end, as far as I'm concerned.

Any resemblance to them, however, felt impossible to avoid, especially when *this author's active imagination* created a fictitious country singer in January 2023 (the real-life romance began, rumor has it, in July of that year) along with a fictionally famous baseball player (who, while not a football player, is still considered a professional athlete/star in one of the greatest sports out there – we can debate that later). So, while I did everything I could not to resemble or replicate this real-world romance, having, of course, no immediate knowledge or access to either the musician or the football player, there might be a very small (teeny-tiny) incident that mimics real-life actions.

Let's add another disclaimer, please. Despite a certain app believing they've invented everything and anyone famous under the sun since roughly 2019, the concept of friendship bracelets goes back to the 1960s, if not earlier. Sharing said bracelets is nothing new in the 21st century, thus some fifty years later for those who can't math. So, again, resembling real-world, but in a fictional manner, these made-up characters do something very real (and quite popular in more places than just music concerts).

If you wish to call foul ball on what I'd done, take a deep breath first. One thing that appealed to the masses for the real-world romance was the fantasy of it. Escape in the fantasy here as well. Remember it's fiction, created by the imagination of this author.

Read on and enjoy.

- L.B.

Chapter 1

Offseason

[Ford]

I wake with a raging hard-on in an empty bed, although I'm certain I went to sleep with someone beside me last night.

While my head thumps to a wicked beat, I roll it on the hotel pillow. The space beside me is rumpled. The sheet tossed back. The extra pillow creased. Someone else was definitely in my bed. But who?

Candy? Cassidy? Something along those lines.

Lifting my hand to squeeze my forehead takes effort. Thinking is more difficult than it should be this late in the morning.

Then again, the purpose of last night was to *not* think. To shut down my recall of what I'd seen yesterday afternoon, moments before I was scheduled to leave my home in Chicago for my brother's wedding.

Closing my eyes, I press my finger and thumb into my lids as if I'm able to scrub from my vision what now resides in my mind.

Nope. Not going to go there yet.

Instead, I'm going to lay here and try to pull up an image of the woman I'd met last night. The one singing to herself in a corner of Randy's Bar, hosting a private concert for one. She peered at me under half-lidded eyes, the brim of her cowboy hat working as a shield for her face and covering her hair.

I didn't need to fully see her. I didn't have to remember her. There was just something about her. A recognizable sadness resonated around her.

I'd had a disguise of my own last night. A baseball cap pulled low. My head down; my collar up. I could have gone to Milton's Roadhouse in the center of Sterling Falls, but I'd have been recognized by everyone in this town. My hometown.

Randy's was the place a man went when he wanted to get lost and didn't want to be found.

For once, I didn't want to be noticed.

Later tonight at my brother's wedding rehearsal dinner, I'm not going to have a choice. My brothers will give me that look. The one that's a lethal combination of sympathy and I told you so. Vale, my sister, will be the one filled with concern. I love my family but there's a reason I stay away from them. There's also a reason I need them now more than ever.

Rolling to my side, I slide my hand over the cool, vacant hotel sheet beside me.

Did we fuck?

What I do vaguely remember is she matched me shot for shot last night. In a game of who can drink the most tequila, she won. And I hated losing.

Every inch of me demands I be a winner.

In my profession.

In my personal life.

And yet, I'd been on a losing streak lately. One I needed to turn around before I lost everything important to me.

With a heavy head and a stiff body, I press on the mattress to sit upright.

Jesus. If I didn't know better, I'd say I was roofied. My brain is foggy. My memory wiped clean. However, something tells me, the woman from last night wouldn't do such a thing.

Suddenly, my phone buzzes beneath my pillow.

"Fuck," I cry out. The sharp reaction hurts my head as much as the annoying trill blasting through the room. As I answer, I snap, "What?"

"Daddy?"

Shit! "Hey, Zelle." I hold the phone outward to read the caller ID. Vale's number.

"Daddy, you sound funny."

"I . . . I have a headache." I massage my forehead again, scrubbing at my skin as if I can cleanse my mind. "What's going on, Zelly?"

"Aunt Vale asked me to call you. Where are you?"

Good question. Glancing around the room, I find an unmarked pad of paper on the bedside table, which offers no clue as to the name of the hotel I'm in, if I'm even in a hotel, and not some seedy rent-by-the-hour motel. A phone number is written across the top sheet.

Fuck. Am I any better than my ex at this point?

"I'm getting coffee and donuts," I announce a little too hopeful I'm not too far outside of Sterling Falls to make my excuse legitimate. There's no way I drove last night.

Is my Escalade still at Randy's? What a clusterfuck.

"Give me a half hour, Zelle. Tell Aunt Vale I'm good."

"Okay, Daddy." My eight-year-old pauses a second. "You're coming back, right?"

Fuck, again. And fuck Felicity for putting doubt into our children.

"Yeah, baby. I'll be back to Aunt Vale's soon."

What I need is a liquid IV, something instant and deliverable, but being that I don't know where I am or how I got here, that's out of the question. Coffee it is this morning, a gallon's worth and stat.

Shifting my legs off the side of the bed, I balance on the edge a second. Even with my feet firmly planted on the floor, my knees bounce. My hand holding the phone shakes. My left arm feels worthless.

"Be a good girl for Aunt Vale, baby. I'll be there in thirty."

"I'm counting backwards, starting now. Thirty, twenty-nine—"

"Love you, sweet girl." I hang up and bitterly chuckle.

Guilt hits me like a ninety-seven mile per hour fast ball to the elbow. I wanted so much more for my girls. More than a cheating mother and a losing-it father.

Tipping back my head, I stare up at the ceiling a second.

Just one bat at a time, Ford. I could swing and miss as long as I learned from each misstep.

I'm not certain what lesson there is to be learned when one finds his wife—correction *ex-wife*—with another man from your team. A fellow player. A brother in sport.

Shaking my head because I don't have the bandwidth for Felicity this morning, I notice my SUV fob and wallet on the desk across the room. Over the back of the chair are my jeans, neatly folded in half, along with my T-shirt and jacket from last night. Glancing down at my briefs, my dick is still pitching a tent in the material.

I didn't fuck anyone last night.

I couldn't have, right?

It's been so long since I've had sex I'd remember the act.

But I don't.

+ + +

Thankfully, I was outside Sterling Falls and quickly able to make good on my promise of donuts before returning to my sister's home soon. As I stand inside Curmudgeon Bakery, the bake shop owned by my youngest brother, a female presence stands too close to me near the counter while I wait on my order. I do not have the energy to encounter a fan. Not yet.

Turning only my head, the bluest eyes meet mine and a wide, lush feminine mouth curls in recognition. "Hey you."

I cringe at the cheerful familiarity in her voice. I also notice she's wearing a Chicago Anchors baseball cap. Wisps of light brown hair dangle from beneath the hat around the long column of her neck.

I grunt in response.

Staring back at me, her eyes dance like little blue flames. Like she holds a secret or is about to let loose a laugh. Her head tilts the slightest bit, like she's waiting on more than a disgruntled noise from me.

"Look, I don't really want to sound like a dick, but I don't want to sign any autographs today. I'm here for a family thing. Can you respect that?" My tone is a bit sharper than necessary, but my point is made. While everyone in this town might know me, I don't want to be acknowledged this weekend.

Her dancing eyes dull. The crooked smile on her face falls, but I bury the guilt because I just want to be left alone.

I want to be Ford Sylver, brother to Sebastian Sylver, who owns the Curmudgeon Bakery. Not Ford Sylver, center fielder for the Chicago Anchors baseball team, otherwise known as The Streak. Rookie of the Year when I started fifteen years ago. A two-time Golden Glove recipient and countless times an All-Star player.

Quickly looking away from her, I sigh as I reach for my wallet in my back pocket and pull out my credit card for the bill.

The woman beside me continues to stare, standing a little too close and smelling a little familiar. Something citrusy. Grapefruit, maybe?

I wrinkle my nose as if I can distinguish the scent. *What the hell am I doing?*

As the bakery clerk tells me my total, I snort. "What happened to the friends and family discount?"

"It doesn't apply to dickheads." The deep masculine voice has me turning toward the back of the shop where my younger brother is exiting his office.

Fuck! I'm not ready to see Sebastian, especially when I'm wearing yesterday's clothes, sweating out tequila, and this woman is still standing too close to me.

"Hey, man." I open my arms, and Sebastian and I embrace in an awkward one clap on the back motion that doesn't allow our chests to meet, before pulling apart like we singed one another. "Should you be working today?"

"I work every day." His gruff voice suggests there's something more he wants to say on the subject of working, but at the same time, he's smiling a goofy grin. My little brother is getting married tomorrow. He's in love and I've heard his future wife is a treasure. I haven't met Enya, the woman who changed Sebastian's life, yet.

I huff but Sebastian is already looking around me at the woman behind me.

"Hey, Cadence," he states.

Cadence? Fuck, why does that sound . . .

Slowly, I turn to glance over my shoulder. The spark in her gemstone blue eyes has shifted to the iridescence of a blow torch, and she wants to incinerate me. Reaching for a napkin in the holder on the counter, she snatches one free. A bright purple marker appears in her other hand, and she leans forward, signing something on the flimsy paper.

When she stands upright, she slaps the napkin against my chest with a hard pat.

"Here. How about taking my autograph as you clearly lost my number?"

My mouth falls open.

Sebastian lets out a choking cough.

"Cadence," I repeat the name like it is foreign on my tongue but familiar in my head.

"C-A-D-E-N-C-E. Seven letters like the number of digits in a phone number *and* the number of shots I drank to your . . . what was it?" She taps her chin like her memory needs a minute. Then she stands straighter. "Oh right, your four. Alliterative with your name, Ford. Or is it four, as in the number of inches in your . . .?" Her coolly amused eyes flicker to my crotch, those lush lips of hers kicking up on one side again in a wicked grin.

Harsh. Closing my eyes a second, my foggy memory clears a little. A woman singing in the corner of the bar. Her voice somber and sad. My offer to buy her a drink. She bought me one instead.

The thought of alcohol makes my stomach roll.

When a strong pat comes to my shoulder, my lids pop open. Sebastian rounds me and Cadence.

"Yeah, I'm not gonna touch that." He chuckles harder as he walks around the glass bakery display case and steps behind the counter.

"Met your brother last night," Cadence announces, looking away from me and toward Sebastian. "Pity party of one."

Wow. Way to spill my secrets.

Wait? Did I tell her my secrets?

I don't ask. I can't do anything but stare at her, taking in the brightness of the acorn-colored hair curling in subtle waves along her neck and the smoothness of her skin.

Did I fuck her? Please say I did.

No . . . don't say that.

Still, my body jolts like some kind of awareness is happening. Or maybe that's the fact she boldly took the napkin she wrote on and is now tucking it into my front jean pocket.

Fuck. I'm such an idiot.

"And how do you know each other?" I question, pointing between my brother and this woman, giving away how lost I am in this encounter.

Sebastian glances from Cadence to me and back. His chin lifts in her direction.

"This is Cadence Calloway. Enya's sister."

Her sister? Did I know that Enya had a sister? Did Cadence mention the relation last night? Does she know who *I* am to Sebastian?

"That's Cadence only to you, my friend." Acidic sass fills the command as she steps toward the counter, picks up a to-go cup of coffee from my order of three and pops the lid. Taking a sip, her plum-colored lipstick marks the paper mug. She grimaces.

"What self-respecting American drinks their coffee plain?"

My mouth falls open, ready to argue that I do, and many others as well, American and otherwise.

But she wiggles her fingers at Sebastian who absentmindedly hands her four sugar packets. I watch as she pours the sweetener into the cup, stirs it with the bottom half of her purple marker, and then takes another sip.

"Better." She sighs, smacking her lips before holding up the mug in salute like she's thanking me for the coffee I didn't offer her. "See ya 'round, cowboy."

Cowboy? I'm no fucking cowboy, which has me glancing at her cap again.

My baseball hat on her head.

Before I can demand she give it back, she's already turning on the heels of her eggplant-purple boots, forcing me to notice her long legs peeking out from a short denim skirt. As she walks away, I can't seem to take my eyes off her. The flexing of her toned legs. The sway of her hips. The way that skirt hugs her ass.

"What the hell, man?" Sebastian grouses.

Only I don't drag my gaze from Cadence's exit. My heart continues to thump. My body leans forward as if I'm drawn to her, being pulled to follow her. Like a ball connects with a bat. *Crack!*

Instantly, I stand taller, holding myself back and mentally shaking my entire body.

Fuck. I think I slept with my future sister-in-law last night.

Chapter 2

[Cadence]

"Where are you?" My older sister's concern rings through the phone as I cross the quaint small-town street and slide into my BMW. I'd arrived in Sterling Falls yesterday evening when I'd originally told Enya I wouldn't be here until this morning. I'd planned to surprise her by arriving a day early. Last second, my plans changed.

"Getting coffee." What I hadn't planned on was running into Ford so soon. Or having him stare at me like I was a blank music score.

The heavy pause between Enya and me hints my sister wants more details. More like, where was I last night? And who was I with?

My reputation isn't one that surprises Enya. Being the best between us, she's never judged me for my lifestyle or my decisions. I live large. Over the years, I've sometimes thought she was jealous of me, but I've learned through therapy I'm more envious of her.

I want to be a better person. I *tried* and made the biggest mistake of my life.

"Don't you worry your love-swollen head," I tease.

Enya sighs. She does worry because she knows the error of my ways. Again, she's not passing judgment on me, she's just concerned, no matter how many times I've tried to reassure her that I'm fine. It's over.

I straighten my shoulders, take another sip of the coffee I stole from Ford, and repeat the mantra in my head.

I'm fine.

It's over.

A broken heart is good for a singer's soul. I could write an entire album based on my experience. I should be writing, or at least fiddling with my guitar, but somehow my head and my heart aren't getting the memo. I've hit a dry spell. It could also be that I'm exhausted. A world tour isn't for the faint of heart.

"I'm leaving town now, and I'll be to your house in ten," I wistfully announce.

Sterling Falls is a cute mountain town in West Virginia with two main crossroads and a green square just off the small business district. The community is perfect for my sister and her future. The one that includes a gorgeous husband and her beautiful baby girl, Adara. A few months ago, Enya moved here as a single, new mom, and her world flipped upside down when she met the curmudgeon baker, a local reformed bad boy from a huge family.

I haven't met every Sylver, but I know who Ford Sylver is. Who didn't?

The tall, lean, six-foot something machine was a looker. With hooded eyes full of ghosts and cliff-like cheeks, he's a study in edgy masculinity. Not to mention, he does this jaw tick thing, like he's clenching his molars, biting back his feelings. Or he wouldn't mind taking a nip of me.

Either way, he's as tense as they come.

Not that I know anything about him coming.

We might have played a little drinking game, and he told me a thing or two about himself last night, but I don't have sex with married men. Or newly divorced ones.

With a full-body shiver, I take another sip of my coffee. Unfortunately, the liquid gold doesn't dull the sudden chill of Evan's memory.

"See you soon," Enya's voice breaks into my wandering thoughts, and I nod as if she can see me.

"Soon." With a more genuine smile in my voice, I click off the phone, set my coffee in the drink holder, and start the ignition. I'm a shaky driver. Being driven everywhere when I'm on tour has had the residual effect of diluting the practice, but I wanted to drive to my sister's house like any good sister might. The distance from here to my home in Nashville is only five hours. Five blissful hours of alone time.

Right foot accelerator. Left pedal is brake. Hands at ten and two. Glance over your shoulder to reverse and . . .

I slam my foot on the brake as my gaze catches on Ford in the review mirror. He is exiting the Curmudgeon Bakery with a drink carrier full of coffees and a bakery bag on top of a box of donuts.

He is such a good-looking man with his short dark hair and artfully-scruffed face. A hint of his fragrance wafts through my nose. Worn leather and fresh fields. Strange, as he's all the way over there and I can't possibly smell him from here.

Still, a woman learns these things when she tries to undress a drunken, shattered man. For the first time in my life, a man wasn't trying to grope, fondle, or get me into bed in a strange hotel room. And I didn't need, nor want, to go anywhere sexual with Ford either. If anything, I simply wanted to help. To take away his hurt and sorrow. To erase the heartache that seemed to be permanently etched into the furrows of his face. He wasn't at the I'm-fine-It's-over stage with his relationship.

Since neither my company nor tequila did the trick, I laid down beside him on the bed until I was certain he wouldn't be sick. It was a very strange, decidedly unsexual, yet oddly intimate experience. And I didn't know what to make of it. Shaking my head, I turn back to the task at hand—driving to my sister's place.

Only, my gaze flits to the screen on the dash where I wirelessly programmed my phone. A text pops up, mechanically read to me in an eerie monotone voice.

"Did you sleep alone last night?"

Forgetting all that I'm supposed to do, my foot slips from the brake pedal, I release the steering wheel, and the car rolls backward. Before I can react, I see Ford Sylver through the rearview mirror again, eyes wide and tight, shouting something before my car rear-ends an SUV parked across the road.

Chapter 3

[Ford]

"Jesus fucking Christ," I holler, stepping back as my vehicle shudders from the collision of a BMW rear-ending the Cadillac.

Only, it wasn't someone.

"Cadence!" Can I not escape this woman today? Or the mistake I clearly made last night?

Setting the coffee carrier on the hood of the Escalade, along with the bakery bag and box of donuts, I step toward the back of the SUV. The vehicle is a beast, but the impact of Cadence's sporty little sedan shook the hell out of this thing.

Inspecting the spot where her back bumper still kisses mine, I stare at the dent made on her vehicle. Thankfully, there's hardly a scratch on mine. While inspecting both vehicles, I hear the slam of a car door and footsteps racing toward me, sensing her approach before she even speaks.

"I'm so—"

"You're a fucking hot mess," I yell, glancing up at the woman who has not only intruded on my night and stolen my baseball cap but has now backed into my ride.

Her eyes widen, bright and blue as the October sky overhead before narrowing to slits.

"I'm okay. Thanks for asking." She waves toward me. "And clearly you're well."

Am I okay? It's only a car with nary a dent but my head is still pounding and my heart racing as I consider she could have hit the SUV harder, or worse, plowed into me. I've just gotten off the injured list and despite the Anchors' season being over, I don't need some mindless woman running into me with *a car* to place me back in physical therapy.

"What were you thinking?" I counter. "Oh, wait, you must not have been. Texting and driving, perhaps?"

Her eyes widen again, expressing guilt in her angel-like face.

Dammit why do I have to notice how innocent she looks even with remorse written on her cheeks?

And why was she texting and driving?

And why are we still staring at one another while her car blocks the street?

"Are you guys okay?" Sebastian asks, suddenly standing beside Cadence, inspecting his future sister-in-law.

"I'm great. Thanks for checking," I holler, watching as Sebastian visually assesses Cadence before sparing me a glance. *I'm* his fucking brother. But then again, Sebastian and I are as different as apple pie and orange juice. Of the two, believe it or not, I'm the sweeter one but I'm still standing here, fists formed, heart hammering, wondering what kind of alternate universe I must have entered to spend the night with a woman I don't know and then have her rear-end my Escalade in the morning.

Sebastian glares at me a long minute before shaking his head and glancing back at Cadence.

"You okay to drive?"

With a quiver to her lower lip, Cadence nods. Her shoulders fall, as if her confidence is waning.

"I doubt it," I mutter.

"Ford," Sebastian growls, his tone a warning.

Cadence lifts her head higher. "I suppose we should exchange insurance or something like that."

A car horn honks and we all glance toward the small line of traffic caused by Cadence's BMW blocking the road.

"Do you even have insurance?" I snap next.

"I—" She glances at the car like she isn't certain.

"Great. Just great."

The car beeps again, and Sebastian holds up a hand, then he curls his fingers so only one remains upright.

"Nice," I mutter while I watch Sebastian slip into Cadence's car. He pulls the vehicle forward, back into the original parking space across the street and parks the BMW before returning to my side of the street where

Cadence hasn't moved more than a few feet closer to the back of my Cadillac.

She licks her thumb and leans forward, rubbing at the scratch on my bumper. Standing upright, she inspects her work. "Looks good as new."

"It better be," I mutter, clenching and unclenching my hands at my side, shaking my head at the audacity of her.

"Don't be such a dick," Sebastian states, standing next to Cadence and glancing down at the scratch.

"Why are you taking her side? *She* rear-ended *me*," I state for the record.

"It was an accident," Sebastian clarifies.

Although I know he's right, and thankfully no one was hurt, I can't help what comes out of my damn mouth next. "And you're still sticking up for anyone but me."

Sebastian peers up at me, eyes narrowing in a familiar sneer. His facial features instantly go blank, yet remain rigid, mirroring mine.

"What does that mean?"

"You know what it means, always taking the underdog's side." I wave toward Cadence, who glances between Sebastian and me.

"The underdog?" He slowly draws out the word, side-eyeing Cadence a second with an expression that reads: *can you believe this guy?*

"You always want the other person to win. To best me."

Sebastian's brows lift, eyes the same color as mine widening. I don't even know what I'm saying or why I'm arguing with him. Why are we even talking to one another? We don't talk. We're complete opposites. He fucked up. I succeeded.

Guilt slams into me at my unkind thoughts. My brother has worked hard to turn his life around. He owns the bakery. He loves a beautiful woman. He has her daughter. He has everything he always deserved, and legitimately earned this time around, so why do I feel this clawing inside me? This feeling of incompetence as I stand before him.

Maybe it's because my own life is crumbling.

Or maybe, I'm just angry . . . about everything.

"Fuck you, Ford," Sebastian finally says, cupping Cadence's elbow and guiding her to the sidewalk to re-enter his bakery.

Yeah, well, fuck you too, Sebastian, and your perfect new life in our shitty old hometown.

Just like before, I can't wait to exit Sterling Falls.

+ + +

Forty-five minutes later than I promised Zelle, I arrive at the Sylver homestead, a white clapboard house with a green roof that's much improved from what I remember of the place. With my baseball schedule and Felicity's social calendar, plus the girls and their activities, my visits here have been few and far between.

But a month ago, I heard a strange whisper in my head telling me to come home.

Home.

What a strange word to call this place? A house once full of kids, raised without a mother and despised by their father. The dysfunction in our family came gradually. Older brothers leaving home. Younger siblings left unprotected. Knox and Sebastian, the brothers above and below me in the family lineup took the brunt of Dad's wrath. I found if I stayed out of his way, practicing all day, I could avoid his hits.

His words did more damage.

Think you're bigger than you are? Better than me? No major league team will ever want a scrawny mountain rat like you. You'll be a nobody like the rest of this lot.

Demeaning me only drove me harder. To be better than the rest. To be the best. I'd show him.

Standing in the driveway with a still-pounding head and the coffee carrier in one hand, Dad's damning words feel like they've come to fruition.

My worst fear is to be insignificant.

"Daddy," Zelle yells, rushing through the screen door of the house now owned by my eldest brother, Stone. My eight-year-old looks like a mini-me with stick straight, dark hair, and bright blue eyes.

On Zelle's heels is Winnie, a child in complete opposition to her sister with thickly curled, lighter locks and wide brown eyes.

Finally, Vale exits the house with June on her hip. My three-year old has her own look with wild blond curls and blue eyes like her mother, too often narrowed and suspicious of the world instead of being full of childlike laughter. With her thumb in her mouth, she glares at me, saying everything while saying nothing. *Get your shit together, old man.*

Worse than being insignificant in my career would be if I proved inadequate as a father, as I feared was possible. I'll never be like my dad when it comes to my girls, but I'm still scared I'll fuck up as a parent.

"Are you okay?" Vale asks, reaching the bottom step of the front porch and approaching me. "You look like you've seen a ghost."

You have ghosts in your eyes.

The statement comes to me like a flashback. Cadence with her elbow on the bar. Her body positioned toward mine. Her cowboy hat pushed back, staring at me like no woman has ever looked at me.

Sure, I've had my share of one-night stands and short-term relationships before I met Felicity. She'd been my biggest fan, greatest cheerleader, and my wife, and still, she never looked at me as intently as Cadence had been looking at me last night.

Strange.

I shake the thought and meet Vale's gaze. "Yeah. Just a little fender bender in town."

Her eyes widen. "Are you alright?" She glances toward the back of the SUV.

"Yeah. Just . . . shaken." But was that the right word? I was stirred up and left to spin with my ill-placed anger. "I got in a fight with Sebastian."

Vale chuckles. "Well, that didn't take long. What happened?"

He breathed. The childish excuse was one I'd have used at ten years old when Knox would try to break up fights between my younger brother and me. Or worse . . . when Vale tried to intervene. Being the youngest of our brood of seven, and the only girl, I didn't envy her position in our family. She was no better off than most of us in the younger set who lost our mother when we were too little to have a memory of her.

I shrug. "Just a misunderstanding." There was nothing to misunderstand. I'd lost my shit when I pride myself on keeping my cool.

Vale continues to eye me, not believing a word I've said.

"Daddy, did you bring the donuts?" Winnie asks, drawing my attention to my middle child.

"Yeah, baby, I got the donuts." I gaze back at Vale. "And I'm sorry I'm late." *I'm sorry about last night, too.*

Vale nods, jostles June on her hip and nuzzles her neck. "We made do. Plus, I love my girl time."

Growing up with brothers and now a single mother to a nine-year-old son, my sister isn't lacking for testosterone in her life, so she'd gobble up my girls whenever she came to visit me.

"Did you got a pink frosted one with sprinkles?" Winnie asks.

"They didn't have pink frosting with sprinkle ones."

Winnie places her hands on her hips and stares at me. "What kind of donut shop doesn't have pink frosting?"

"Uncle Sebastian's apparently." I sigh before handing the box of donuts to Winnie and the bakery bag of additional treats from my brother to Zelle.

"Here," I reach out for June, holding out a coffee to Vale as a peace offering in exchange for my baby girl.

Vale tugs June tighter to her and presses a kiss to her temple. "No deal."

Yeah, my sister just bested me, sensing I wanted a snuggle with my youngest in hopes of erasing my foul mood.

Suddenly, the screen door screeches open and out steps our eldest brother in his sheriff's uniform. "Heard you were in a little fender bender this morning? You okay?"

"Yeah." I will be.

"Want to make a report?" My brother is in full officer mode in his sharply pressed shirt and dull brown pants.

"How did you hear so quickly?" The accident only happened about ten minutes ago.

"Scanner."

"Does he ever stop working?" I mutter out the side of my mouth.

"Do you?" Vale laughs while I stare at my brother, feeling all the respect in the world for him.

Stone taught me how to toss and catch a ball. He supported my drive to practice and my need to succeed. He found the means to get me new baseball equipment when I was growing faster than he could keep up with my too-large feet and long skinny legs once I finally hit fourteen. He sent me to sports camps and helped me apply for college scholarships.

The man on the porch was more of a father than the one legally on my birth certificate. He taught me hard work and determination pay off, and for him, I wanted to be somebody. For all he'd given up for us, I wanted to make him proud by hitting the big league.

And I'd done it.

Stepping toward the porch with my girls in tow and Vale following, still holding June, I take the stairs two at a time.

"Been a rough morning," I admit to Stone, holding out my hand to shake his. I hadn't seen him yesterday when I dropped off the girls.

He stares at me a while, assessing me, knowing it's more than a few hours this morning that have been difficult. I've had a tough year and choppy waters lay ahead of me.

Slowly, Stone nods and tugs me toward him for a deeper hug. "Can stay as long as you need." He isn't asking what happened a few days ago. He isn't asking me what my plan is for the future. He's just here for me, the rock he's always been.

I don't offer more details. I'm still processing everything myself. "I appreciate it, but we'll only stay the weekend."

When we arrived yesterday, I'd promptly dumped my girls with Vale, left her a hundred bucks for some pizza, and told her I needed to be alone for a while.

Only, I hadn't been alone. I'd met a woman in a cowboy hat, singing a sad song, and eventually outdrinking me, whom I'd then spent the night with.

Like the slam of this old screen door, another memory from last night comes back to me.

Cadence's laughter. Deep, low, and rich. She didn't giggle but guffawed hard. I don't remember what I said. Or maybe she said something and the expression on my face made her respond. Still, that laugh.

When was the last time *I'd* really laughed? Hands on my hips. Bent at the belly. Tears in my eyes.

Staring back at Stone, I wasn't certain laughter was a trait among us Sylvers.

Chapter 4

[Ford]

As we sit around a large wooden kitchen table, one that looks new compared to the nicked one I remember as a child, my girls regale Stone and Vale with random stories.

Despite Winnie not getting a precious pink frosted donut, she eats a cake one with white icing.

"Come here, you little mess," I tease, reaching for the crumbled stash of paper-thin napkins I'd grabbed at the bakery and shoved into my pocket. I swipe over Winnie's mouth and pull back the napkin with a sticky purple smear on it.

"What's that, Daddy?" Winnie asks, noticing the coloring of the napkin in comparison to her mouth.

"Oh, it's nothing." Still, I unfold the rumpled mess and silently read off the smudged name. "It's an autograph."

"C-A-D-E-N-C-E," Zelle reads over my shoulder as she stands beside me, leaning into my arm, physically telling me of her fears through her closeness. She was afraid I wouldn't return.

"What's that spell?" Winnie asks.

Vale and I meet eyes over the table, and she speaks. "Cadence." Her brows pinch, questioning the word.

"Cadence?" Zelle squeaks. "As in Cadence?"

"The singer?" Winnie's awe-filled voice echoes her sister's.

"What singer?" I ask, running my hand up Zelle's thin back.

"Daddy," Zelle drones. The number of eye rolls I get from my eight-year-old has me truly concerned about her future teenage years. How am I going to handle that time—*alone*—as a single father of three girls?

Puzzled, I glance at my sister again, wondering what I'm missing.

"Certainly you've heard of Cadence."

"Enya's sister," I confirm. Long-legged girl in cowboy boots, plum lipstick, a woman who can down tequila like it was water. *That Cadence?*

Then, I think back to the Cadence I saw outside the bakery only an hour ago. Wide-eyed, pale and panicked—and wearing my baseball cap—as I growled and stomped, worrying about my damn car. A flicker of remorse sloshes in the pit of my alcohol-soaked stomach.

However, Vale doesn't know the details of the vision I saw this morning, or the woman I met last night.

"Well, she's that, too."

"What do you mean, 'that too'?"

"Daddy," Zelle's voice squeaks even louder. "Did you meet Cadence?"

"I met Cadence," I answer, certain I'm still not understanding something.

"*You. Met. Cadence.*" Winnie drags out as she leans on her elbows on the table, her dark eyes as round as the donut she just ate.

"I met Cadence," I repeat, looking back at my sister. What the fuck? She's Enya's sister. Big deal.

"I bet your daddy has met lots of famous people in his profession," Vale counters.

"What's a profession?" Winnie asks.

"His job."

"Daddy doesn't have a job. He's a baseball player."

"Winnie, baseball is my job," I correct.

"Mommy says you play a game for money."

"I—" My gaze meets Vale's once more and I shake my head, dismissing my counterargument. I'm not having this kind of discussion with my five-year-old. "Let's get back to Cadence."

"*When I look at you, all I see is pink. And I think. Could you love me?*" Zelle sings.

I choke. "What the—"

"It's a Cadence song," Vale explains, watching me as understanding slowly dawns.

"Cadence," I whisper. As in *the* Cadence. *That's Cadence only to you, mister.* A singular name. A singing sensation. I stare down at the napkin now on the table. Her autograph since I forgot her number.

"Shit," I mutter.

"You said a bad word, Daddy," Winnie points out.

"I know." But I didn't know. I didn't recognize her. Cadence. Doesn't she typically have blond hair? The woman I met had light brown hair. But the cowboy hat and the boots. The sway of her ass last night and the song she was sing—

Another flash of memory comes to me. *Songbird*. Both the name of the song and the sound she made while singing it. I'd called her a songbird when she'd approached me and gone into a diatribe about whether the song was a funeral tune or a wedding anthem.

"Shit," I mumble again.

"Daddy, you said it again," Winnie chastises with a giggle.

"Your daddy is lucky Hudson isn't here. He charges a dollar per word."

Zelle's brows lift. "A dollar per word?"

"For swearing," Vale explains about her son and his famous swear jar.

Zelle's mouth falls open as she glares at me. "We need a swear jar. I could be a billionaire."

I glare at my sister before dropping my gaze to June sitting on Vale's lap. With her thumb in her mouth, her eyes narrow at me once again. *We've needed a swear jar for a long time, buddy.*

I don't typically swear—much—in front of the girls, but right now I'm off-kilter. Ignoring the swear jar request, I look back at my sister, almost begging her to clarify what I'm missing here.

"She's Cadence," Vale explains, reading my desperation. "*The* Cadence. As in Country Artist of the Year, and Grammy award winning darling of country music."

Darling of country music?

"And Enya's sister."

I scrub my hand down my face, certain all the color has drained despite the heat in my cheeks.

"You're a nice shade of pink, brother," Vale teases.

All I see is pink. And I think. Could you love me?

How many times has Zelle played that song?
I'm so screwed.
I'm just going to have to avoid Cadence.
How difficult could that be?

Chapter 5

[Cadence]

When I finally arrive at my sister's house, under the escort of Sebastian driving my car, Enya holds off on questioning me until Sebastian returns to the bakery.

"Are you okay?" Her concern runs deeper than just this morning's fender bender.

She knows about Evan.

"I'm fine." If I keep telling myself the lie long enough, I might believe it. Evan was an expert liar; not me.

My older sister watches me, as if looking for signs of meltdown. When everything fell apart months ago, I turned to her. Typically, I try to restrict my outbursts to my music manager and my therapist. For my sister, I pretend life is grand. After all, I stole her dream.

My sister once wanted to be a singer, but her songbird's wings were clipped by our parents, and Enya's need to be responsible. She went to college and earned a degree in accounting, worked nine-to-five, and had a perfect boyfriend for a while. Then her superman turned out to be a dud, nine-to-five became a grind, and Enya admitted after one too many margaritas that she always wished she'd followed her dream to be a singer.

At thirty-nine, her life has taken another turn: motherhood and marriage. The rhythm of love is the song in her heart. Somehow, I think she's happier than me. Enya didn't need fame, like I'd once craved it. She needed stability and love. I've been sensing for a while I might need the same thing.

My sister has never resented me for becoming a famous music star. For her, I wasn't an icon, I was just her little sister with a big dream, and she had become my biggest cheerleader. Always encouraging. Always supportive. She never criticizes my business decisions or my reckless directions. She doesn't chastise me for one-night stands, and she never judged me for Evan, even though there were plenty of reasons to cast stones.

My father liked to say I was a loose cannon. I prefer wild streak. My trajectory easily diverts, thus the reason one-night stands used to appeal to me. No commitment necessary. Plus, I have a reputation for being unobtainable. I liken myself to Queen Elizabeth I. A rather grandiose comparison, but the virgin queen had a reputation, although she wasn't a virgin. She was the poster-woman for I-don't-need-a-man to rule my *queen*dom.

Then I met Evan.

He wasn't after my queendom. He only wanted me, or so I'd thought. How I'd missed the signs about him is beyond me; however, he was an actor, so pretending was in his repertoire.

"You're here earlier than I expected," Enya states.

What my sister doesn't know is that I'd planned to arrive here yesterday as an overdue apology. A few months ago, I'd planned to be her plus-one when her daughter Adara was born. Only, my sweet little niece had other plans and arrived a month early. Still, my calendar was marked off for that time with Enya and her new baby girl. Two weeks off the tour. Fourteen glorious days to disappear, help my sister, and meet my new niece.

My manager and Evan had other plans for me. Everything fell apart within days of my arrival in Sterling Falls, and I returned to London with a heavy heart and guilt eating my gut.

I'd hurt Enya's feelings, although I'd also learned about a gracious stranger named Sebastian Sylver who my sister had recently met, and I had a sneaky suspicion he'd take care of her and Adara. Who wouldn't want to love both of them? They are amazing.

The sudden need to depart then also hurt me. I'd wanted that time to regroup with my big sister. I'd needed her.

My surprise timing this round had been a fail because I stopped at Randy's Bar outside of town to take a call from my lawyer. Upset by the news, I ordered a drink, headed for the classic jukebox in the corner, and . . . my night was full of shots from there.

Deciding not to mention Ford, I state, "Just eager to get this party started." I clap my hands once. "Now, what can I do to help?"

Being that Enya is the most capable person I know, and I once tried to convince her to be my manager, I have no doubt she has everything under control. The rehearsal dinner is tonight at the Sylver homestead. The wedding will be tomorrow afternoon in Enya's backyard. A casual breakfast is being held at Sebastian's bakery on Sunday morning.

And through every moment of my sister's wedding weekend bliss, I'll have to face my latest blunder—Ford.

My sister slowly smiles, as both our thoughts fill with her joyous occasion. "You don't need to do a thing. I'm just happy you are here."

I have three days dedicated to sister-time, or so I thought until I got the text message this morning. The caller ID read unknown, but the message had to be from Evan.

Lifting up my phone, I dramatically swipe it off and announce, "I'm here."

I plan to *be present* for everything.

No thoughts of Evan.

And no thoughts of the hot-under the collar, and seriously hot, Ford Sylver.

+ + +

At the dinner following the wedding rehearsal, it becomes further evident Ford Sylver has no recollection of last night.

The Sylver homestead is located outside of Sterling Falls on a parcel of land bordered by woods and overgrown meadows. The space is picturesque with a rickety old barn that once housed horses and a beautiful white clapboard house that screamed *The Waltons*. I swear I could hear the whisper of voices calling out goodnight wishes as I stood outside the house before entering.

Sebastian will be spending the night here and I'll be sleeping at my sister's house in keeping with the archaic tradition of the groom not seeing his bride after midnight on their wedding day, even though Sebastian and Enya already live together.

As for Ford, he wasn't at the rehearsal as he is not part of the wedding party. Enya mentioned something about Sebastian and Ford having a rocky relationship which left me curious about the Sylver family dynamics. If Sebastian was the black sheep at one time, does that make Ford the prodigal son?

As for the wedding lineup, the unusual formation includes Sebastian's older brothers, Stone, Clay, and Knox, plus Sebastian's sister, Vale, and me as maid of honor for Enya.

I was already on edge when I arrived at the dinner because I'd seen my mother and father at the rehearsal. Enya was more forgiving than me and had invited our parents to her wedding despite their recent behavior toward her. Rightfully, she has decided to walk herself down the aisle. She didn't need our father giving her away. She was a thirty-nine-year-old woman who had been responsible for herself for quite some time. She didn't see walking down the aisle as giving anything about herself away but gaining the man at the end of the carpet runner.

I'd been caught off-guard by my parents' presence at the rehearsal when they were not involved in the actual wedding ceremony. Neither spared me a glance.

So, when I see Ford standing in the kitchen purposely ignoring me as well, I snap.

Walking right up to where he leans against a large kitchen island covered in alcohol bottles and a variety of glasses, I bump my shoulder into his arm and say in the sugary-est voice I can muster, "Hey you." Like we're familiar with one another. We *did* spend last night together.

"Hey. . . uh, Cadence." His eyes shift right a second and I notice a man on the other side of the island. The bartender I presume. For a man who understands limelight as a major league center fielder, the awkward shift of Ford's eyes and the tension in his suit-jacket covered shoulders sets me off even further.

"Now, sugar lips, you can do better than that. How about a kiss, cowboy?" I pout my lips more than pucker them as I turn to face him.

His narrowed eyes flit left and right, as if making certain no one heard me. Or maybe no one sees him lay one on me. Not that I expect him to actually kiss me.

"I, uh—"

"Now, cowboy. Nothing to be ashamed of." I lean in as if I'm about to share a secret with him. Or plant my lips on his. "Would be rather innocent compared to what we shared last night." I wink.

The poor man turns a deep shade of red, and for such a tall guy who exudes confidence, the color is almost endearing compared to the cockiness he effervesced last night. I recognized a man on the verge of a mistake yesterday evening. He offered to buy me a drink afterward.

Ha. I can buy my own damn drink, told him as such, and then bought him that first shot. He looked like he needed it more than me.

"What should we drink to?" he'd asked, eyes already half-mast.

"Marital bliss," I'd countered in a bitter tone.

Something in his eyes registered my sarcasm or maybe he sensed my envy. He tapped my shot glass with the edge of his and downed the first wallop of tequila. His lips puckered in a cute way before he motioned for a lime and sucked the citrusy wedge dry. Watching him then, my thoughts ran rampant, wondering how those lips might feel against private places on my body.

Having sworn off men, I instantly shook the thought.

"Look, I'm sorry about last night." His voice strengthens from the stammering mess he was seconds ago.

"What exactly are you apologizing for?" Watching him squirm almost makes me feel sorry for him, but the deal is, I thrive on recognition. I'm not psychotic enough to demand I not be ignored, but I hate not being acknowledged. And Ford Sylver needs to recollect we shared a moment last night.

There was something about his sad state, sitting at that dimly lit bar, and my somber mood which drew us together. Like magnets attracting. More like a warm blanket wrapping around us and tugging us tighter to one another. Without him explaining all his painful secrets, I felt them.

Strange. But true.

He glances nervously over his shoulder before turning back to me. "I don't exactly remember much about last night."

My mouth falls open, appearing insulted a second before I decide to forgive him.

Leaning even closer to him, I tip up on my toes and bring my mouth to his ear. "Darling, if we'd spent the night together, four shots of tequila wouldn't have erased your memory of me. I'm unforgettable."

As I pull back, a vibrant shade of red creeps over his face again. His blue eyes brighten but his jaw ticks, a hint of tension.

There he is. The man I remember watching me, giving off vibes like he'd devour me if he were free to do so. But here's the thing about last night, I'd learned what happened to him and his newly-ex wife.

"So we didn't—" His gaze drops to my chest, the girls perfectly positioned and a little cleavage peeking out the edge of my square-cut plum-colored dress.

I chew at my lower lip and shake my head.

"Oh, thank God." A deep exhale relaxes his shoulders a little, and he swipes his hand down his face. When his eyes meet mine again, the bright blue diminishes a bit.

Now, I *am* hurt.

"Really?" I fist my hand on my cocked hip. I might not have slept with the man, but he doesn't need to look that relieved.

"I mean, of course, you're beautiful and—" He waves a hand up and down my body, but I hold up my palm, already cutting him off. I'm tired of weak comebacks and even weaker compliments.

"The sentiment goes both ways, cowboy."

Ford tilts his head to the side, eyes narrowing in that way I'm already familiar with. His jaw clenches again, making his cheeks more prominent, almost sculpted as if by a master. "What do you mean?"

"I'm relieved as well. *I mean*, I can't have you falling in love with me after one night." I wink.

Ford's face pinkens and his mouth twists as if he's fighting a smile in response to my quip. He thinks I'm ridiculous. Maybe even cutely quirky, but still ridiculous.

"Cadence."

The sharp masculine reprimand comes from my right, and I twist to see my father standing too close to me. I'd wonder how much he heard or how long he'd been standing there but it wouldn't matter. The man takes everything out of context. Making assumptions about me is his favorite pastime.

"Daddy." My tone is equally edgy and direct, as if I'm holding my breath for more from him. Stupidly wanting him to accept me for who I am and praise me for what I've become. Ford stiffens beside me from the mention this man is my father, but I release my lungs, knowing pride in me from my dad isn't going to happen.

His cool, dry hand comes to my upper arm, and he leans it to press an equally cold, distant kiss to my cheek.

"Want to introduce me to your friend." The implication is clear. He heard enough to assume Ford is a *special* friend.

No. "Daddy, this is Ford Sylver. Sebastian's brother." I point at Ford, who reaches out and shakes hands with my father. I purposely don't mention my father's name.

"Which one are you?" Dad counters.

"I play baseball, sir."

Dad's brows lift. "The center fielder for Chicago Anchors." My father's face softens, impressed by this Sylver. Fame. Fortune. Sport.

Strange how he can be in awe of Ford's accomplishments but not mine. However, I'm growing less tolerant of a world where men are revered for their achievements and women are belittled for theirs, as if we women didn't work twice as hard, if not harder, for our success.

"And how long have you two been together?" Dad addresses me, his expression creasing in measured increments of severity as he tries to piece together who Ford and I are to each other.

"We met last night." Ford's answer is innocent enough, and truthful, but Daddy takes it as he always does.

"Well, she certainly works fast, doesn't she?" His suggestive tone has my shoulders falling while I steel my spine.

Lifting my head, I speak out the side of my mouth. "Can we not do this here."

"Always jealous of your sister. Have to have what she has. Next, you'll tell me you are pregnant."

"Dad!" The exclamation is a little louder than necessary but what he's said is so uncalled for. My face flames with embarrassment. However, my humiliation is quickly replaced by ire. *How dare he?* This type of insult only reinforces the years of unfortunate hope I'd put on my parents and their continued disappointment. We both know I'll never be Enya. I'll never be good like her. I'll never be good enough, period.

"Not certain it works that fast, sir," Ford interjects, not correcting my father with the explanation that nothing happened between us and even if it did, we couldn't be certain in twenty-four hours if I was pregnant or not. "But we can keep working on it."

My jaw drops. Ford is acting like we did sleep together when I've disputed it, and he's now given my father the idea we will continue sleeping together in hopes I get pregnant. Neither of which I want to happen. Not the man nor the babies.

As I've explained numerous times to my parents, I don't need a man, a child, or a family. I have a career. A lucrative, awe-inspiring, extremely successful career. I take care of me. *I* define myself.

I glare at Ford whose cliff-like cheeks give nothing away. He's clearly teasing but his hardened face suggests otherwise.

"Ford," I mutter.

Further surprising me, Ford slips his arm around me, palming my lower back and drawing me closer to him. He kisses my temple and my father's mouth falls open.

Slowly, something registers in my father's eyes. "Aren't you married?" Dad's once-impressed expression tightens in slow increments to disapproval.

"I'm separated."

Lord, have I heard that before.

"Well, I see you're still on the path of homewrecking, Cadence. I couldn't be prouder." Sarcasm drips from my father's mouth like a vampire after a succulent blood-fest. However, there isn't a chance my father knows anything about Evan Lauer.

Ford's fingers on my lower back tighten in my dress. Whether to hold me back or keep him from lunging at my dad, I can't be certain.

"Maybe you should write a song about it." Dad continues. "Oh wait. You already did."

I could be impressed that my father knows the name of one of my songs. What would be more remarkable, though, is if he knew the song was about a father emotionally abandoning his children, wrecking them.

Too stunned to speak, I stay silent. I've learned it's often best not to correct my dad. You can't change the opinion of those unwilling to listen.

Also, for Enya's sake, I'm trying to be on my best behavior. I don't want to get off on the wrong foot with her future family. She loves these people and by default I want to love them as well. As for the Sylvers, I want them to at least *like* me.

Biting hard on the inside of my cheek, I watch as my father nods once at Ford before stepping away from us.

He's the homewrecker. Not me.

Chapter 6

[Ford]

"Well, that was intense."

Everything vibrant and flirtatious about Cadence vanishes in a flash at both the sudden presence and then abrupt absence of her father.

"It's nothing," she mutters, turning toward the man on the other side of the kitchen island. "Bartender, shot of tequila please."

I turn as my brother Judd's brows lift and, from behind his thick rimmed glasses, his eyes flick to mine. Unfortunately, he'd been present to this shameful debasing of Cadence by her own father. I don't think Cadence even noticed Judd, but thinking she needs a drink, she's fully conscious of him now.

"Actually, make it two. I don't want my left hand to be jealous of my right."

Sweet Jesus, who is this woman?

Judd continues to stare at her. "I'm not the—"

He cuts off when I reach across the large countertop and pick up the tequila bottle from the array of alcohol. While Sebastian doesn't drink, he wasn't opposed, or offended, that the rest of the family does. He actually encouraged celebrating this occasion, and I was starting to think I'd need liquid reinforcement to make it through this entire wedding weekend.

"Two," I warn Cadence, pouring a sliver of the Mexican devil into two separate disposable cups. "That's your limit tonight."

"Okay, *Dad*." The sarcasm in her voice is almost as rich as her old man's had been. I could make a comment that the apple didn't fall far from the tree. However, Cadence doesn't look anything like the man who just publicly insulted her, in front of me, a stranger no less, and a future family member.

Instead, I'd like to take her over my knee for that sassy mouth and see how she pleasantly responds to the punishment.

As for a man like her father, it would be a cold day in hell before I called someone like him family.

Glancing at Judd, I take in his pristine suit and neatly parted hair. He's an accountant, like Enya. A little stiff. A little nerdy. He'd been quiet as a kid, keeping to himself as much as he could. Of all of us, losing our mother seemed to affect him the most. Not that losing her was any less tragic for the rest of my siblings, but the younger set—myself, Sebastian, and Vale, being four, two and newly born—don't have much recollection of our mother.

I've been told Judd was especially close to our mom. Watching him lack confidence and cower from our father, I'd often imagine our mom protected him from our dad. I'd also been told that once upon a time, our parents loved each other deeply, and my father wasn't the evil man he'd become after her death. Without mom present, it was evident what our father thought of Judd. Weak. A geek. A loser.

I'd disagreed with his assessment of Judd when we were kids. He was as lost as the rest of us, but I didn't have a way to stand up to my old man other than step out of his way, and prove I was the opposite of everything he said about me.

No one will want a scrawny kid from nowhere on a major league team.

Even if our father was dead before I could show him what I'd become, his words motivated me to prove him wrong.

I blanch, suddenly remembering my family doesn't know of the situation between Felicity and me, although her absence sends a strong message. I might have told Cadence's father I was separated but that isn't even half of it.

Turning back to Cadence, I watch as she picks up both cups, taps them together and then shoots each one back. She slams the plastic containers to the countertop in unison while her mouth puckers from the biting alcohol. Without any prompting, Judd is already extending a lime wedge in her direction.

"Thank you, kind sir," Cadence chokes, struggling to fight the burn and accept the fruit offering. She sucks hard at the juicy inside, squeezing the bright green flesh between her lips, and causing a drop of juice to trickle down her chin.

Damn, if I don't want to lap it off that angular edge.

The relief of finding out we didn't sleep together took hold and was instantly followed by deep regret. However, I wasn't mentally where I needed to be yet to dip into another woman. While I'd been certain I wouldn't be interested in any woman anytime soon, there was something about Cadence that had me questioning everything. My sanity. My desire. My life goals.

She was hot, I'll give her that. In a purple dress that hugged every curve of her body, leaving not much to the imagination as it outlined her hips and clung to her legs, I was suddenly sorry I didn't remember more about last night. Did she undress before me? Did she sleep naked beside me?

"Did you sleep with me last night?"

Cadence's mouth falls open, dropping the lime she held between her lips and awkwardly catching it in her hand before the fruit hits her cleavage.

From the opposite side of the island, Judd coughs once. "I think I'm going to—" He points toward nowhere in particular and turns on his heels, heading away from the island.

Slowly, Cadence's blue eyes narrow. "I thought we already clarified that point." Gone is the flirtatious tension, in which she strung me along for a hot minute, thinking we'd had sex.

"Yeah, but you stayed the night, didn't you?" Something lingers in my memory. A warm body pressed up against mine. She hadn't dumped me in a motel room and deserted me. She'd stayed.

"Would it matter?" The question is laced with a razor-sharp edge, or maybe a shield of protection. She wants to appear untouchable.

"You're not answering my question and after leading me on, making me think we fucked, the least you can do is answer the question."

We glare at one another.

"Well, songbird?" I finally demand, reminding us both that some moments from last night were not forgotten.

"Fine. I stayed, okay?"

I tilt my head, curious, confused. "Why?" If we didn't have sex, why would she remain in the motel room with me?

"You were really drunk, and I was . . . worried."

Beer before liquor, never sicker. "And do you often worry about drunk strangers you just met and sleep with them in seedy motel rooms?"

Cadence's gaze narrows again. If her eyes had the power to shoot darts at me, my face would be a bull's eye and she'd hit the mark every time.

My accusation sounds vaguely like her father. What did he mean she was jealous of Enya and why would he suggest Cadence wants to get pregnant?

"Once you told me your name, we weren't strangers," Cadence clarifies.

I'm surprised I told her who I was. Maybe I told her because she was the only person in the bar who didn't know me. I must have asked her name, but her status didn't click in my brain.

"Baseball fan?" I arch a brow, aware of my own popularity in the sport.

"Hardly." She snorts. "And clearly you aren't a country music buff."

"I never said that."

Cadence glares at me. If I was a fan, I apparently hadn't shown it. Then again, I hardly remembered my own name last night and that was the point of doing shots with a woman I thought was a stranger in a bar. Dangerous game I'd been playing, though.

"Besides," Cadence interjects, "you looked like you needed someone to save you."

"I don't need saving," I counter.

"Yeah, but there was a woman in the bar last night who acted like *she* wanted to handle you, and I didn't think you'd want that. Or need it." Cadence purses her lips and tilts her head. "Maybe I misread the situation, though."

No. No, I'm certain she read it correctly. I wasn't interested in sleeping with someone random, especially after adding infidelity to the list of infractions against Felicity.

"What do you mean there was a woman who acted like she wanted to handle me?" I don't remember another woman in the bar.

"Oh, come on," Cadence drones as if I'm oblivious.

Like a lightning strike, I realize I might have only been concentrating on one woman. The same woman I can't seem to drag my eyes away from now.

"You can't be that clueless." Cadence's gaze rolls over my body, taking in my tailored suit and tall height, lingering on my face when she finishes. "You're fucking hot as sin and give off this edgy vibe which just draws women to you, like a fast ball to a catcher's mitt."

"Nice analogy," I mock. "And I do not." I might have had my share of women before Felicity but once I put a ring on my finger, I never looked at anyone else. Didn't notice them. Didn't notice them noticing me. I'd been faithful to a fault because that's what my vows required, and I believed we were forever. I belonged to Felicity. She's the one who misread the memo.

"*Pfft.*" Cadence snorts and reaches for the tequila bottle, but I'm quick to snatch it upward and tuck it to my chest.

"Hot as sin, huh?"

"And don't you know it, darlin'."

Maybe. Still, the compliment is nice to hear. I don't remember the last time Felicity said something nice to me. My mouth slowly crooks. I might not have had sex with Cadence, but she would have been good for the ego if I had.

As I refuse to set down the tequila bottle, Cadence's shoulders slowly lower and she turns back toward the countertop. Placing her hands on the surface, she glances down at them, and I notice how slender and fine they look. Delicate even. She plays the piano and guitar. This information came from my girls and their love of the country superstar.

"Why'd *you* do it?" Her voice drops, quiet and soft. Gone is the sugary sweetness. In its place is a vulnerability I hadn't expected and don't understand.

"Do what?"

Cadence turns her head, keeping her hands braced on the countertop. "Why'd you tell my dad we were working on getting pregnant?"

Because he was an asshole talking to his daughter like he was. "I was joking, but I'm sorry if that ruined your reputation."

Cadence snorts and turns her attention back to her fingers, splaying them out against the polished counter. Slowly, her fingers start to move, like she's playing the piano. Like a tune has come to her head. I'm reminded of her swaying before the jukebox in Randy's last night.

"What reputation?" A shield barricades the vulnerability in her question.

"America's darling," I tease, hoping to lessen the tension slowly swirling around her.

She lets out another dismissive exhale that doesn't settle well with me, and I watch as her fingers continue to tap against the counter in a steady pattern.

"Daddy, Zelle won't let me have another cupcake!"

With Winnie's whining voice, I turn toward her. A stern looking Zelle follows closely on her heels. Behind both girls is Halle Reynold's teenage daughter, Violet, who has become self-appointed keeper of my girls. The slim redhead with long legs and a wide smile looks exactly how I remember her mother when Halle was in high school and dating my older brother, Knox. As high school sweethearts, they recently reconnected and love struck a second time for them.

"Actually, *I* didn't think it was a good idea," Violet interjects, hiking June higher on her hip, protecting Zelle's older sister authority while gently chiding Winnie. "Three should probably be the limit until we get you some dinner."

Fuck. I'm being a negligent father. The entire family was waiting on the arrival of the bridal party before eating. Stone didn't want anyone touching the buffet before they returned from the rehearsal at Enya and Sebastian's place. As the grill master, he planned to do the honors although Enya had the rest of the meal catered. Sebastian made all the desserts, thus the cupcakes, and a set of lemon baby-bundt cakes specifically for Enya.

"Violet's right, baby. Let's get some dinner." I reach forward for June who tucks herself tighter into Violet's side, ducking her head into the teen's shoulder. My youngest misses her mother and tells me at every turn by clinging to other women and glaring at me with those wisdom-filled eyes. *You're fucking up, Pops.*

"So, you're a dad?"

Cadence's question has me giving her my attention once more while Winnie wraps her arm around my left leg, and I place a hand on her head.

"These are my girls. Zelle." I nod at my oldest. "Winnie." I stroke my hand over her hair. "And June."

"Me bug." June corrects with her thumb in her mouth. My older brother Knox started calling her June Bug, and now my daughter wants to be named after a beetle.

"Girls, this is Cadence."

"She is not," Zelle argues, like she doesn't see the woman she fangirled over only yesterday morning. "Cadence has blonde hair."

Cadence arches a brow but Winnie whines again. "Daddy, I need dinner so I can have another cupcake."

I glance at June and catch her staring at Cadence. And Cadence can't seem to take her eyes off my youngest. Slowly the singer's smile returns. She almost transforms in front of me again, back to the performer. The flirt. The superstar.

But I'm curious about the woman who took care of me last night.

The one who *thought* I needed taking care of, and then took it upon herself to do so.

I hadn't answered her question about her father. I don't know why I wrapped my arm around her or leaned in to kiss her temple. I just didn't like how he spoke to her. He could fuck off.

"June," Cadence whispers. "What a beautiful name." Then she blinks. "Well, June, how do you feel about hot dogs? I bet there is one somewhere around here with your name on it."

June's eyes widen and she lifts her head from Violet's shoulder. She kicks her legs signaling she wants to be set down and Violet accommodates. Then Cadence is holding out her hand and June easily takes it, spiking that fear I have that she'll wander off with any woman as a replacement for the one who abandoned her.

Cadence leads June toward the dining room where the buffet is set up, and for a ridiculous moment, I wonder what it would be like if Cadence was actually June's mother.

She'd probably do a better job caring for my girls than Felicity ever has.

Chapter 7

[Ford]

I don't know how Felicity and I ended up like we did. Hell, I no longer know how we even ended up together in the first place. When she told me she loved another man before she met me, I thought it was a simple explanation of her relationship history. When she told me she loved me, I believed her. Why wouldn't I? No one else had ever told me such a powerful thing, and all I'd wanted was my person. That one woman who had faith in me, believed in me, and loved me.

When her love for me stopped, I have no idea. Or maybe it was never there. When she suggested we get married, I agreed. I was ready for a family. Felicity had not wanted to be a mother so soon in our marriage, but I was nearly thirty at the time. I wanted kids. After talking it through, Felicity seemed to change her mind quickly. She appeared more excited and eager to be a mom. But I didn't know it had all been an act, until it was too late. Our entire marriage had been a sham.

Zelle came along rather easily. Winnie was a surprise. June a bit of a how-did-that-happen. But I wouldn't trade my girls. I'd grown up in a large family, and despite the troubles with our dad and the loss of our mother, I had siblings to commiserate with me.

Our oldest brother, Stone, had stepped in as guardian of the Sylver clan when our father was gone, and I garnered a lot of positive attention from him. He was full of encouragement. If I wanted to play baseball professionally, I had to work hard and take every opportunity I was offered to put myself in front of the right people. Most of all, I had to be kind and grateful for chances.

Stone knew what he was talking about. He'd given up all his professional football dreams to come home for Knox, Sebastian, Vale, and me as we were minors when Dad died.

I'd done all my brother had advised and more. Then I met Felicity.

"You can't be Cadence. She has blond hair," Winnie parrots her older sister, breaking into my thoughts after I'd followed my brood, led by Cadence and June, into the dining room.

My gaze wanders to Cadence's hair, the color definitely more acorn than gold, and falling in long, loose waves around her shoulders. Her blue eyes flit upward meeting mine, hesitating a second, like she's worried she'll spill the truth about Santa Claus. Then her expression shifts.

"Well, a woman has a right to change her hair and her mind." She bops Winnie on the nose. "Remember that, darlin'."

Winnie continues to watch Cadence, skeptical she's the superstar Zelle and her admire. With Cadence's makeup lighter than what she wears on stage and her hair darker, a second glance is needed to register that she is indeed the woman behind the music sensation.

"Here you go, June Bug." Cadence holds out a bun with J-U-N-E written in mustard on the dog. "Told you there was a hot dog with your name on it."

June beams up at Cadence. Her thumb slips out of her mouth in awe. Zelle smiles as well, staring at the rudimentary dribble of mustard on the dog like it's a masterpiece.

"Unfortunately, she can't eat that bun and all. It should be cut into little pieces." I motion with the side of my hand, chopping the choking hazard into fine slices and then divided into quarters.

"Ah." Cadence nods with understanding. "I'll eat this one then, so I'll always have a little piece of you inside me." She drops down to a squat before June and tickles her belly.

"What will happen when you poop it out?" Zelle asks and Winnie giggles.

Cadence looks to me once more for guidance on this one, but I simply shake my head. "Zelle, no poop-talk tonight."

If someone told me boys were the ones with creative imaginations, I'd say they hadn't met my girls. Zelle's question wasn't so much because she wanted to be surly but that she's fascinated with numbers and the human body. She's my future scientist.

Cadence stands back to her full height and I take her in again. The purple shade of her silk dress. The way it curves along her body, like wine being poured into a glass. My mouth waters, wondering if she's crisp and dry or bold and flavorful.

Then I jolt because something hits me just above the kneecap. June bumped into me, hot dog in hand, and mustard smeared the knee of my suit pants.

"Sow-wy, Daddy." June whimpers. Zelle and Winnie hold their breaths.

If I had been Felicity, there would be sharp reprimands for messing up the expensive clothing. Her demeaning tone often made *me* cringe. She didn't need to spoil our children, but she should have given them more grace. Now, she wasn't even interacting with them.

"It's okay, June. It will wash off." Or not. I don't care about the damn pants. I care more about the tears welling in my youngest's eyes, and the stark fear on Zelle and Winnie's cheeks a second before their shoulders loosen and the tension fizzles out like air released from a balloon.

Scooping up June, hot dog and all, I pepper her cheek with kisses before leaning forward and taking a bite out of the offending sandwich.

"That mine." June's little voice scolds me and the tears are forgotten.

"Mmm. Tastes like a June Bug, too." I chew fast, swallow quick, and nibble at June like she's a delicacy.

June giggles, and Zelle and Winnie laugh. Situation defused.

All the while, Cadence watches me. Again, our eyes meet, and the corner of her mouth slowly ticks upward.

"Want to take off your pants, cowboy." She winks.

I swear my face flames. *This woman.*

"There are children present," I chide prudishly.

"Keep your clothes on." She dismissively waves. "I only meant I could help with the spot."

Glancing down at the drip of mustard on my knee, while holding onto June, I huff-laugh. How did my life get so chaotic and why is it that this woman is the one smiling back at me like I hung the moon?

Straightening, my shoulders tense. My jaw clacks. I cannot be flirting with her, *especially* in front of my girls. I have no idea yet what they've seen of Felicity's antics with my teammate, but I won't be replicating that behavior.

My dad never put his children above all else, but I won't follow in his footsteps.

My girls will always come first.

Chapter 8

[Cadence]

The man was like a *bolang gu*, a Chinese pellet drum on a stick with balls on string attached to the side. The faster you spun the stick, the harder the balls bang the drum. And Ford was that *flip-flip* motion.

Bang. One second sweet. Boom. One second closed off.

I wasn't certain what happened between teasing nibbles against his youngest's cheek and my joking suggestion to remove his pants, but Ford went into that stiff jerk phase, like he'd been this morning in his brother's bakery. Distant. Aloof. Uptight.

I'd have offered to take his daughter so he could treat his suit pants that probably cost him a pretty penny and happened to be the exact same shade of blue as his eyes. However, he was suddenly looking at me like I might kidnap his kid or steal his soul. I did not need that kind of glare in my life.

Thankfully, I was saved by the sudden appearance of my sister at my side. Enya is beautiful in a brown-eyed girl way wearing a white dress to signify she's the bride, something we all know.

While Ford exits the dining room with June on his hip, my sister draws my attention to her with a light grip on my upper arm. "I heard Dad got to you. Are you okay?"

While I had been the wild one, acting like I had second-child syndrome, I was actually the third in our clan. Our older brother had been the troublemaker, putting Enya in the middle, but somehow, she ended up with attributes often seen in the first kid. She'd been the perfect child growing up. Not until she was thirty-eight did she have a streak of rebellion, and then she absolutely glowed. She got pregnant without giving anyone a hint of who the father might be. Our parents went ballistic, so Enya is aware of our parents unwavering opinions. She also knows they hold a long list of dissatisfaction in me.

"And hello to you, too, bride-to-be. You look radiant as always," I tease, trying to lessen the concern on her pretty face.

"You look radiant as well," she grouses, but deep down she means the compliment. My sister and I adore one another. Her sternness comes with concern. "Now cut the shit and tell me what he said."

"You seem to already know Dad approached me."

"Judd told me, but Dad's stiff upper lip confirms he said something."

"Which one is Judd again?" I glance around Enya's shoulder as if I can distinguish anyone behind her.

The Sylvers are quite a brood of lookers. Stone and Clay are silver-haired, having gone gray relatively young. Knox has silver at his temples. Sebastian has small speckles within his dark locks, prominent mostly when his beard grows out. Ford's hair is still solidly deep brown while Vale, the only sister, has cornstalk-colored blond waves.

That leaves Judd, who I don't recall meeting.

"He's right there." Enya turns to her side and inconspicuously points toward another good-looking future brother-in-law in a crisp white shirt, sleeves rolled to his elbows, wearing a long, slender black tie and thick glasses on his nose.

"I thought that guy was the bartender." I giggle.

"Bartender?" Enya laughs. "No, he's an accountant."

Right. Enya told me how she met Judd when she came to Sterling Falls to audit their family business, Sylver Seed & Soil. He could be the reason she fell in love with this town and decided to purchase the worst house on a big piece of land because she met him before Sebastian. However, anyone looking at Enya and Sebastian knows my sister only ever had eyes for one of the Sylver siblings.

"I can't keep up."

Enya sternly scowls back at me. "Quit trying to distract me. What happened with Dad?" Her brows pinch. "Judd said something about you getting pregnant by Ford."

"And that's how rumors get started," I jest, knowing well how quickly and easily gossip grows. Sometimes, it holds hints of truth. Mostly, it is hyperbole that hurts.

"Cadence," Enya impatiently groans.

"Fine. Dad walked up to me, wanted to be introduced to Ford, and then accused me of sleeping with him when Ford said we met last night."

The comment came out salacious and a bit humorous, as if Ford and I shared a private joke, but my dad wouldn't have ever interpreted the situation that way. Nope. He had to jump to conclusions.

"You met Ford last night?"

Oops. "Yeah, well . . ." I pause, caught in a trap of my own making. "I planned to surprise you by being early for once in my life and show up here yesterday. But I stopped at Randy's Bar outside town to take a call." Then I went inside for a drink.

Enya watches me, not doubting my story. "Who called you?" New concern fills her voice.

"My lawyer."

After Evan, Enya encouraged me to contact a lawyer as a means to protect myself. I hadn't called Maggie for Evan reasons, though. I had bigger issues that I needed resolved.

Not asking for further information about my call with my attorney, Enya questions, "So, how were you with Ford?"

My sister *isn't* accusing me of anything. Nothing she hasn't heard me admit to doing say a hundred or so times. One-night stands. Reckless relationships. The truth is that rebellious streak had died down a long time ago, but *Cadence* has a reputation to uphold. The unobtainable woman. The one who won't settle for anything less than what she deserves—the best. Which is why the Evan situation was all the more confusing.

"We only slept together," I tease, turning toward the extensive display of food on the dining room table and reaching for a plate.

"You slept with Ford?" Enya speaks a little too loud and a little too harshly in her need for clarification.

Quickly I glance around us. Eyes motionless, fake smile in place, I respond. "Will you keep it down. We didn't sleep together, like *sleep together* . . . " I use tongs to scoop up some salad and drop it on my plate. "We *slept*."

Enya leans against the table, waiting for more details.

"I went into Randy's to use the bathroom after the call and had a drink." To settle my nerves. "And some woman was trying to get Ford's attention. I recognized a guy who didn't want to be noticed. When the bartender said his name, I simply put two and two together as to who he was. As in your future brother-in-law, not just the hot center fielder for the Chicago Anchors, and I didn't think he'd want the trouble that woman was offering, so I intervened."

"What did you do?" Enya whispers, following me as I circle the table, eyeing each bowl and tray for something my personal trainer would allow me to eat.

"I bought him a drink and pretended he was mine."

Maybe Ford doesn't remember but that's how things played out. I acted like he was my guy, and that other woman could fuck right off. Just for a little while, I pretended he belonged with me, as we shot the breeze and a couple tequilas. After swearing on my life I'd never tell a soul anything about him, I learned some dark truths about Ford. As I had my own secrets to keep, his were safe with me.

Still, Enya eyes me suspiciously. "Tell me nothing happened."

"Nothing happened," I mischievously repeat.

"Now say it like you mean it."

When I look at my sister, her anxious expression tightens. She lowers her voice and says, "He's married."

I could tell her the truth, but Ford's story isn't mine to share. Plus, his secrets are under lock and key with mine. So, I can't argue with her on a valid point of concern.

"Nothing. Happened." I stress each syllable because nothing did. "I took him to a motel because he didn't want to come here. I didn't know he had kids. Maybe he didn't want them to see him shit-faced. I tucked him in, laid down beside him to make sure he didn't vomit on himself, and drifted off."

I'm so tired lately.

And my sister knew better than to accuse me of being with a married man.

"I'm sorry," she quickly states watching me, sensing my suddenly irritated disposition. "It's just . . . I don't want another Evan situation for you."

"Evan situation," I snark, setting my plate on the table with a little more force than necessary.

"You know what I mean," she quickly amends.

I did know. The shame. The guilt. How could I have been so stupid? How could I have believed his lies? How could he have done such a thing to me? To *her*?

Standing taller, I stare back at my sister. "I need some air."

"Cadence," she whispers, more motherly than my own mother has ever been.

Enya and I are opposites in many ways, but there was one thing I could count on with her—she wouldn't pass judgment on me. Still. I felt judged and juried on the Evan situation.

Without a glance back at my sister, I turn and my gaze snares on Ford. From just inside the kitchen, he's watching me with that clenched jaw I'm growing to both like and loathe. The last thing I need is him questioning my intentions with him.

I helped him out last night, and that was that.

I didn't need him to like me or appreciate me.

I have hundreds of thousands of adoring fans to rev my boss-lady engine.

Straightening my shoulders, I head for the front door and step out onto the large wrap-around porch, inhaling the crisp fall air with a hint of rain in the forecast. Breathing deeply, I close my eyes, and wish away my guilt.

No one judges me harsher than I judge myself.

A crackle of thunder booms off in the distance and I slowly open my eyes. I'm not a fan of thunderstorms. Never have been although I can't explain why. There's something so powerful about them, an out-of-control energy, like chaos personified. I should feel right at home among a storm, but I don't.

As I also want everything to be perfect for my sister's wedding, I don't want it to rain. *She* deserves the happily ever after she's about to receive, not the disorder of a sudden downpour. I don't want anything to mess up her day, including me.

With that thought, I step down the porch and walk around the house, stopping when I hear two men arguing in the dark yard behind the house.

Chapter 9

[Ford]

The tension coming from the corner of the dining room where Enya followed Cadence around the table rippled through the air. Cadence's demeanor shifted again, like the crackling energy before a storm. A strong need to intercede tugged at me, but I reminded myself it wasn't my place to step in with anything pertaining to Cadence.

Which is what made my response to her father's demeaning behavior toward her so baffling.

Glancing around the kitchen where I found a stool for June to sit at the kitchen island and eat a cut up hot dog, my gaze catches on Sebastian, who was watching his future wife before turning toward me.

His eyes narrow in a way I recognize. Pointing at me, he mouths *Outside. Now.*

An invisible friction existed between Sebastian and me, like a batter trying to draw a balk from a pitcher with his windup. When Sebastian and I were kids, we often disagreed. While he was a little rebel when we were younger, I just wanted to stay out of trouble. I found hitting a baseball, giving it a good smack took away any tension brewing inside me. *Eye on the ball, Ford.* The continual stress of not knowing when my dad would be too drunk to notice he had kids or drunk enough he forgot we were his children was a churning constant. I buried myself in baseball because I needed a way out of Sterling Falls.

As for Sebastian, I'd simply ignore him when he tried to pick a fight with me. Like his comment about always rooting for the underdog, always wanting someone to best him. He couldn't be further from the truth. However, tonight, his command has me following him with pent-up anger. He wants a fight; I'm ready to fight.

I've got a backstabbing ex-wife.

A three-year-old who glares at me.

An eight-year-old afraid I'm going to leave her.

And a five-year-old who seems indifferent about everything, which scares me the most because it's so like me when I was a kid.

Don't let it get to you, Knox would coach me after unwarranted insults from our dad. I'd built a shield around myself to not anticipate praise from Dad for my accomplishments nor be astonished when insults flared instead.

"Hey, Violet, would you mind watching June for me a second?" I'm going to owe this kid a year of college tuition by the time this weekend is finished.

"Sure," she eagerly agrees.

Sebastian has already turned toward the screen door that exits the kitchen and is pressing forcefully at the edge. As the door swings back at me, I catch the frame with my hand before it collides with my face. Following Sebastian into the back yard, thunder rumbles overhead. The smell of rain mingles with the damp, cool mountain air.

"One day." Sebastian rounds on me. "One fucking day, and you can't let me have it."

"What the fuck?"

"You just had to make a scene." His voice grows louder. "Had to be the center of attention."

If he'd punched me, I'd have been less surprised. I have no intention of being center stage this weekend. In fact, I'm not certain I even want to be here.

Lies, whispers through my head.

"It's *my* wedding, man." Sebastian swipes a hand down his face as if to calm himself, but the rest of his body language says he's ready to pounce like a hungry mountain lion. A scrapper as a kid, I remember him rushing our dad a time or two, trying to get Dad away from Vale.

Stunned by this outburst, I admit, "I know it's *your* wedding weekend."

"Still, you had to fuck Cadence and make a scene."

"I didn't fuck her," I quickly defend.

Sebastian sighs, giving me a look like he doesn't believe me. "Enya is my world, Ford. My everything. I cannot have you fucking with that. Her sister is important to her, and I do not want Enya upset."

"Why would she be upset?"

"Because you fucked her sister."

"I. Did. Not. Fuck. Her." My voice rises, echoing off the trees on the edge of the property and hurling back toward us. "I didn't touch her."

Maybe an hour or so ago I wouldn't have known any better, but now the facts are clear. Cadence and I did not have sex. The thought we hadn't is like a second sucker punch that I'm still trying to catch my breath after, but the question—*why not*—will have to wait for another day.

"You just can't let me have a moment, can you? You always have to be on top."

"What are you talking about?" I argue, sensing a shift in this discussion and a return to his comments about me cheering for anyone against him.

"*Look at me, Stone. Do you see me, Stone. Are you watching me?*" Sebastian mocks.

"I never said those things." Sure, Stone was my biggest fan, coaching me through both the good and the bad. Correcting my stance at bat. Hitting endless balls to me to catch. But I never asked Stone to focus on me in the manner Sebastian says.

"Just stop it," Sebastian fires back as if I didn't contradict him.

Then he shoves me. Like an eleven-year-old boy, he pushes my shoulder for emphasis.

And I push back.

Before I know it, Sebastian's arm is cocked at an angle, fist raised and aimed, and I'm prepared to take the punch but not before I get in a good shot myself. Lifting my fist, I'm positioned to go off on my little brother, wedding day be damned.

"Sebastian." The feminine cry is sharp and quick, like the clap of thunder overhead.

"Not his face," warns a second female.

At the anxious tone in Cadence's voice, I turn, wondering if her concern is for me or my brother.

Then, a hard punch connects against my jaw, and I stagger backward, catching myself before I fall to the ground. Standing taller, I aim for Sebastian again.

Suddenly, a large mass is between us, a hand on both of our chests, pressing Sebastian and me apart.

"What is wrong with you two?" The strong masculine tenor triggers a flashback to my childhood. Stone stepping between us. Stone keeping us separated.

You're brothers, he'd say. *We're all we have.*

Sebastian is huffing and puffing, eager to continue the fight. I don't know what I ever did to him. Being brothers did not make us friends.

And for all his crazy talk that I demanded attention from Stone, he was wrong.

Sebastian is the one who was constantly in trouble as a teen, and Stone was always bailing him out. Getting called to school for Sebastian issues. Getting calls from his fellow deputies for illegal actions.

"He started it," I argue, sounding like the children Sebastian and I once were. Shifting my jaw side to side, Sebastian's hit is going to leave a bruise.

Sebastian takes a reluctant step backward and Enya slides between him and Stone, placing both her hands on her fiancé's chest to capture his attention.

"I can't do it," he mutters.

A collective gasp occurs. Cadence and I meet eyes.

Sebastian wraps his hands around Enya's upper arms, lowers his head and closes his eyes. "I can't be without you tonight."

Jesus. Way to scare a man.

Enya and Sebastian already live together, sharing Enya's daughter, Adara; however, they planned to sleep apart tonight with Sebastian in our old room here at the house. I shiver at the thought. I didn't exactly want to stay here either, but Vale insisted there was room for me and the girls. Stone owns the house but Vale lives here with her nine-year old son, Hudson.

"I want to wake up with you tomorrow and make breakfast for you and Adara." He quickly flicks his eyes open, pleading with his soon-to-be wife. His gaze holds on her, as if he's afraid she'll disappear.

I recognize that feeling. The need to have one person in your life who won't let you down, who won't leave you.

"You're going to be okay," Enya coos, cupping his jaw. "I'm right here. And you'll have all the days after tomorrow to make us breakfast."

"But I want tonight." Sebastian grows petulant while lowering his voice. He drops his forehead against Enya's.

"And we will have all the tonights . . . tomorrow." Enya tips up on her toes, but Sebastian is already bringing her to him to kiss her.

I glance at Cadence again, who is watching with rapture as her sister makes out with my brother.

However, I can't pull my eyes from Cadence. Her lush mouth. Her fit body. That dress flowing over her shape, makes me a thirsty man. For the first time in my life, I'm envious, jealous of what my little brother has tonight and all the nights ahead of him.

Cadence slowly turns toward me and sets her small, delicate hand gently against my jaw. The coolness of her skin a welcome balm. I want to lean into that touch, let her soothe me. For once, I want someone to take care of me.

Softly, she says, "Let me clean you up, cowboy."

"What the hell happened?" Stone mutters, giving his back to our brother and his bride-to-be, as if shielding them from us, the audience to their kiss. He also breaks the spell Cadence has me under and I draw back from her.

"Just a little anxiety," I mumble, before turning for the house. Shifting my jaw right to left a second, I gingerly cup it, missing the tenderness of Cadence's hand. Fuck, that hurts.

"Not cold feet but pent-up nerves, I guess," I add a little louder, walking toward the back door.

"Do not cover for him," Stone grumbles as he follows behind me.

Cover for him? That's something I've never done for Sebastian. He'd sneak out of the house at thirteen years old and I wouldn't question where he went or what he was doing. I knew what he did. He sold drugs at the middle school and infiltrated the high school once he entered. Jocks and junkies didn't mingle. Being two years older than Sebastian, I'd been ashamed of who he was, and I kept my distance back then.

Within another two years, I was off at college, hardly looking back at Sterling Falls.

"Honestly, I don't know what that was." Sebastian's words were a rush of drivel, making no sense, just like this morning.

As I open the back door, I step aside, allowing Cadence and Stone to enter first before I walk into the kitchen, hoping to go unnoticed so I can inspect my jaw.

Unfortunately, Vale sees me. "What happened?"

"It's nothing," I dismiss, passing the refrigerator and heading down the hallway toward the bathroom.

I sense someone following me, but I don't glance back until I enter the powder room and attempt to close the door. "What are you doing?"

Without an invitation, Cadence pushes me deeper into the small space and shuts the door behind her. "Taking care of you. Again." She winks.

Cadence motions toward the toilet and I close the lid to take a seat. She helps herself to a basket of rolled washcloths, then soaks the material with cold water from the sink. Like wringing out a washcloth takes great skill, I watch Cadence's slender fingers work the cloth. When she turns toward me, I spread my knees allowing her to step between my legs. She tips back my head by gripping the short hairs on the back of my head and our eyes meet.

"This might hurt," she whispers.

My brain fogs for a second. *Does she mean touching my jaw or her in general?* The hammering in my chest grows stronger, and I fist my hands on my thighs, so I don't reach for the backs of her legs and tug her closer to me.

When Cadence presses the cold dampness against my jaw, I wince.

"You took that punch like a champ, cowboy." Her hand on the back of my head gently slides forward to cup the opposite side of my face.

I grunt, wincing once more as she presses the cool fabric to my jaw.

"Been in a fight before, have ya?" Cadence continues, giving me a knowing glance. When I don't answer, she adds. "I saw that fight with Romero Valdez from a few years ago."

Romero. Fucker called himself Romeo, playing into the rumors he was a major manwhore. When the fight occurred, he was the shortstop for Florida, and a damn good one. A year ago, he became a Chicago Anchor, and we buried our grievances because I'm a team player. He became a friend. Or so I thought.

"Didn't think you were a baseball fan."

"I'm good at stalking Instagram."

I chuckle sharply, a guffaw that causes me to wince once again at the pressure on my jaw. "He had it coming to him."

"Care to share with the class," she teases.

The physical fight with Romero happened on a day when I'd already had an argument with Felicity. With my mood sour, my adrenaline was heightened. After hitting a potential double to left field, the fielder fumbled the pick-up and overthrew the ball intended for second base. I rounded to third, hoping to steal another base, when Romero obstructed my run, which isn't legal when he didn't have the ball. I tripped, or more likely he tripped me, and I went skidding in the dirt feet from the third base bag. Romero had time to get the ball and tagged me out as I stood up. I turned on him, spouting off about his illegal position. He took the argument one insult too far.

"He'd made a derogatory comment about Felicity." Pausing, I avoid her eyes and correct myself. "Or maybe it was more about me."

Maybe your wife could use a man who can keep himself up. Romero motioned toward his dick, and I lost it. Two quick steps and one fist later, the tension boiled out of me. He deserved it. No one would talk about my wife like that, even if she and I were fighting all the time. I hadn't known then that Felicity and Romero had history.

"What happened with you and Enya?" I ask, desperate to change the subject. "Things seemed a little tense in the dining room."

Cadence dismissively waves a hand, but I catch it with mine, feeling how delicate her fingers are compared to my big palm. Stroking my thumb over the inside of her hand once, our hands shift like we intend to shake them. Only we're both holding on and my thumb draws circles on the back of her hand while I wait for a real answer.

"Just a little misunderstanding. Rumor has it you and I slept together," she whispers as if scandalized.

I don't like the teasing tone. Hurt lingers beneath the surface.

Cadence is a superstar. She understands being in the limelight comes with dark moments. Her superfans are triple any fanbase I might have. Her enemies are just as many. Rumors and gossip should ping off the armor she needs to protect her head and her heart. She should know how to deflect lies, but I'm well versed in mind games and know how hard it can be to let that shit go.

Additionally, I don't like that gossip has started about us among family.

"Nothing happened, right?" I remind her, hoping to soothe any worry she has that family meddling will go any farther than our backyard.

Cadence watches where my thumb circles around the back of her hand, pressing gently into the delicate bones leading to her fingers. Fingers that play piano and produce songs that become major hits.

"Nothing happened," she softly confirms.

Another memory from last night comes to me. A body pressed against my back as I slept on my side. Delicate fingers caressing my bare back, at one point tapping out a tune.

Was she trying to hold me upright or was she leaning into me, needing support?

The idea is ridiculous. Cadence is a strong woman, confident and carefree. She could have any man she desires and the last thing she's going to want is a newly divorced, father of three, professional baseball player near the end of his career.

The thought is sobering.

Her kindness is appreciated.

Stretching up, I cup her face and tip it downward to press my lips against her forehead, lingering against her soft skin. Grapefruit. She definitely smells like grapefruit. However, I'll never have the answer to the burning question of whether the scent comes from her hair or her flesh.

Cadence relaxes, like hidden tensions float out of her. Between her father's accusation and the misunderstanding with her sister, she's had quite a night as well.

In another lifetime, I would suggest we get out of this place, get lost in each other. But I have three little girls on the other side of this bathroom door counting on me not to leave them behind.

"I should check on the girls," I mutter against Cadence's smooth forehead.

"Of course." Her voice is rough and low before she clears her throat and pulls away. Her eyes are so blue.

And it's true, I could love you. The line from her song is a whisper in my head.

Cadence licks her lips and my gaze drifts to the movement.

It could have happened.

In another lifetime.

Chapter 10

[Cadence]

After helping Ford in the bathroom, he excused himself. Needing a minute to collect my thoughts and calm my racing heart, I exited a few moments later.

For half a second, I thought he might kiss me.

Please collided with *not again*.

The Evan situation my sister did not want repeated was something I'd promised myself would never, ever happen again. Fool me once and all that.

Eventually, I whisk my sister away from the Sylvers' home, sans Sebastian, like she's a blushing bride about to embark on her first night of debauchery. He wasn't happy to let her leave and kissed her once more like they were in the front seat of a car minutes before curfew. Or maybe that was just my experience.

I, on the other hand, wasn't kissing anyone when I left the Sylver homestead. Instead, small waves and soft smiles were given to Ford's adorable girls who followed their self-appointed babysitter Violet like they were little ducks in a row. The only thing missing were yellow dresses and big bows in their hair.

Once Enya and I returned to her house, with baby Adara, the silence was overwhelming after the rousing Sylver siblings reunited in one place. The cacophony of sounds among a collection of adult family members had been music to my ears. I'd learned the local family members get together every Sunday for a mandatory dinner.

I wanted what they had.

The quiet of Enya's space was a reminder of all that Enya and I had endured as children. Our household involved non-speaking dinners in the years our brother caused trouble, and more silent meals once he ran away from home.

Standing outside Enya's bedroom door, I softly rap on the wood.

"Come in."

With relief, I enter. As much as I crave alone time, I find I don't know how to be alone with myself, especially after Evan's betrayal.

Enya sits upright in her bed with the blankets pulled up over her lap. She holds her phone, smiling at something that lights up the screen.

"Sebastian?" I climb onto her bed and lay down on my side, facing her.

"Yeah." Her wistful voice pierces my heart, not in jealousy but envy. I'm beyond thrilled for Enya and Adara because no one deserves a happily-ever-after more than them. However, I want what my sister has. The love of one good man, who is dedicated and true to his word.

"He loves you so much," I whisper, afraid to break the silence that's haunting me. Tucking my hands beneath the pillow, I clasp my fingers like I intend to pray.

"I know." Her smile widens. "And I love him."

"Remember when you questioned everything last summer," I ask, reminding her of a conversation we had when Adara was newly born, and my confident sister was panicking that she'd made the wrong choice. Not wrong in having her daughter, just mistaken in how she went about her pregnancy. A momentary lapse in her judgement about raising her daughter on her own. Enya needed our mother then, more than any other time in her life. Instead, she had me, and I wasn't able to offer any encouragement other than I believed in her.

Enya glances at me, her brows pinching in question.

"And look how everything turned out. Happily-ever-after." I smile up at her from my pillow. This is technically Sebastian's pillow and his side of the bed, but I'm claiming it for a little while. I'm a little like him, in that I don't want to be without my sister tonight.

"Happily-ever-after," Enya whispers, a thoughtful grin curling her lips. "Who knew it would come to this?"

"Who knew?" Strangers become friends, become lovers, become partners. Right there is the basis of every romantic song. In my thirty-five years, I've lived bits and pieces of that music. However, I don't think I'll ever find my equal. My other half to complete the equation of love.

As the owner of a lonely heart and the queen of broken heart harmonies, my image has sold millions of albums, garnered millions of fans, and made me millions of dollars. And still, I'm stuck in the one place I'd rather not be. Alone.

"It can happen," Enya says, as if reading my thoughts. She softly sings, "*One day my prince will come*, right?"

She really does have a pretty voice, but I scoff. "Who needs a fucking prince when I already own the queendom?"

Enya eyes me. "It's lonely in a glass turret, though."

She's right, so I don't argue.

"Ready for tomorrow?" I ask, wishing to change the subject.

"It's going to be like any other day, except for a big party."

"What do you mean?" I ask, shifting my head on the pillow.

"Sebastian will be home tomorrow night. We'll laugh and sleep together and raise Adara."

"And have all the good sex," I add.

Her cheeks pinken. "We'll love each other and our little family. No different than any other day."

"But you'll get to wear a beautiful white dress and awesome shoes and be center stage."

Enya gives me a soft smile, one that's sympathetic, not chastising. "That's your dream, Cait. Not mine."

The use of my given name startles me, reminding me I'm more than Cadence, the musician. I'm just a woman, living a grand life, looking to take care of myself . . . and fall in love with someone who understands me.

I could tell my sister I don't know what my dreams are anymore, but I don't want to turn this night into my sob story. Tonight isn't about me. Tonight is about her.

"Tell me more about your future plans," I beg, like a child eager for a story.

Thankfully, Enya grants my request, telling me a grandiose tale of what it means to be a family.

+ + +

Wedding day.

My sister looks more beautiful than ever, but it isn't her light makeup or the complicated updo of her hair. The love radiating around her makes her practically glow. She's been welcomed into this big, loving, loyal family of the Sylvers, but most importantly, she has the heart of one hunky brother, Sebastian.

If only it would stop raining, the day would be perfect.

"Seems apropos," Enya sighs, staring out the window of her bedroom, overlooking her backyard. A giant white tent covers a portion of her two acres, protecting both the ceremony and the reception from the elements. Enya had hoped to stand beneath the autumn-changing leaves on the edge of her property, but the weather is not cooperating.

"I met Sebastian during a rainstorm." The smile lighting up my sister's face suggests the weather is forgiven, maybe even appreciated.

"It's a good sign," I offer, standing behind her as we watch the final guests being ushered under umbrellas to the tent. Sebastian has already called Enya four times with concern. She isn't worried in the least.

By the end of this day, I'll be your wife, she told him each time, followed by *I love you*.

After Sebastian's display of aggression last night, I could be worried for my sister but I'm not. He loves her and Adara fiercely and he'd never hurt either of them. He'll protect them both, forever. Their love is swoon-worthy, and I can only hope to have a spoonful of something similar one day.

When the ceremony is finally set to begin, the entrance march shifts. Instead of each groomsmen meeting a bridesmaid at the start of the aisle to walk her down the carpet, he greets each of us at the backdoor of the house to escort us beneath an umbrella to the tent.

Sebastian's brother Clay escorts Vale.

His brother Stone is best man and walks beside me.

Knox is in charge of six-month-old Adara, carrying her down the aisle and responsible for holding her during the service.

My sister was to proceed on her own, giving herself away, however Judd met her with an umbrella and walked her to the tent. When the flaps finally open, exposing my sister and blowing Judd's umbrella backward, Sebastian's impatience catches up to him, and he charges down the aisle. When Sebastian sweeps up my sister, she squeals as she loses a shoe. He doesn't bother picking it up.

Instead, he carries Enya down the aisle, stands her on her own feet, where she steps out of her other shoe and faces her Sebastian to the sounds of clapping, whoops, and hollers from the amused guests.

As the ceremony starts, my gaze wanders to Ford. He looks immaculate again in another suit, this one dark but no less expensive, and obviously custom fit. The large bruise coloring his jaw is covered by the new growth of hair on his face but does nothing to detract from how good looking he is.

However, I could not be attracted to him. I *would* not. Ford has a difficult path ahead of him and three little girls to take care of. The last thing he needs is the hurricane of America's country singing darlin' and her lifestyle. The tour schedules, the legions of fans, the multitude of paparazzi.

The thought would make me melancholy if it weren't for the joy emanating from my sister. I'm struck with wedding fever.

After the ceremony, the bride and groom pose for photographs and then disappear for a while. I don't want to think about what they might be doing. Eventually, they return to the tent to mingle with guests before dinner is served.

Ford keeps his distance from Sebastian while I keep my distance from Ford. His little girls have been running wild throughout the tent, followed good-naturedly by Violet. The teenager has developed an aspiring fan club. There is something most endearing about June, who seeks me out in the crowd while bashfully hiding whenever I wiggle my fingers in a wave at her. Then she'll peek her little head upright to make certain I am still looking in her direction and we play the game again.

"She likes you." The strong masculine voice behind me sends shivers up my spine. "And you're avoiding me today."

"I wouldn't say avoiding, I was just—" Words falter as I turn toward Ford . . . who is holding Adara. Something happens to my ovaries, and I almost double over with the sharp explosion in my lower belly.

"Avoiding," Ford confirms, pressing a soft kiss to Adara's little head pressed against his shoulder.

Dear God. He's minus his suit jacket with his shirt sleeves rolled to his elbows, exposing strong forearms, which are holding a baby.

Is it hot in here?

"It was a beautiful ceremony," I stammer.

"Beautiful," Ford counters. "But I hate small talk."

"Oh, are we small talking?"

Ford chuckles as we remain side by side, watching Violet jiggle June on her hip while Zelle stands like a shadow nearby. And all the while I'm hyperaware of Ford's closeness. His leather and fresh grass fragrance. Him cuddling Adara.

Definitely hot in here.

"I should probably check on Winnie. She's my troublemaker."

"Ah, a girl I can relate to."

"You? A troublemaker, songbird?" Ford arches one brow while his jaw does that clenching thing. "I cannot imagine."

"Sarcasm does not become you, sir." But that nickname becomes me and the heat I'm feeling from a hot baseball player holding a tiny baby has turned into an inferno beneath my skin.

Ford laughs, a deep guffaw that makes his blue eyes spark brighter. Adara's little eyes jolt open as they were momentarily drifting closed.

"Your suit, however." *And that baby.* "Very fine." I hum as I roll my gaze up and down his body. He looks like he walked off a men's magazine titled *Super-Hot Single Dad.*

A faint blush creeps over his face.

"How's the jaw today?"

Ford slides his mouth awkwardly side to side. "Better. And you're not so bad yourself. Purple becomes you." Ford appraises me in another plum-colored dress, this one floor length chiffon with spaghetti straps. Not exactly conducive to a chilly, rainy, autumn mountain afternoon, but still a lovely shade for this time of year and a cut that hugs my body in a manner I like, highlighting all my assets.

He should check on Winnie.

I shouldn't be admiring him.

And still, we stay put.

Someone taps a spoon against a glass and people turn their attention to a sweetheart table set for only Sebastian and Enya. The wedding party and family will sit in collections on either side of the table for two while remaining guests have assigned seats. Thankfully, Enya placed our parents far from me. My father has graciously kept his distance today while my mother continues to eye me, as if willing me to her when she could just as easily cross the room and speak to me.

Sebastian and Enya are announced as a couple as if they haven't already been working the room and the two walk to their table, kissing every few steps before standing behind their seats. A wireless microphone is handed to Sebastian.

"There are traditions established within weddings, and then there is Enya and my way." Sebastian holds my sister's hand and brings it to his mouth before adding, "Like carrying your bride down the aisle."

Everyone laughs.

"So bucking tradition because I'm good at that . . ."

More laughter, especially from his family.

"I'm giving the opening speech."

Typically, the father of the bride would speak, welcoming everyone to the dinner and thanking them for sharing in the celebration, but Enya didn't want our father to talk. He hadn't paid for the wedding. He hadn't even been supportive of Adara's birth. Our parents had been invited as a courtesy, and I'd wager their attendance only came from curiosity. They hardly see Adara and haven't interacted with her, to my knowledge, yet this weekend.

"First, I'd like to thank Enya." Sebastian turns to her again. "For having faith in me, in us, when I didn't see what was right in front of me. And the thing I wanted more than I imagined. You. Adara. A family."

Enya smiles wide, her gaze loving as she looks at her new husband.

"Thank you to my family who helped us pull off this party. Stone, Clay, Knox, and Judd for setting everything up."

Ford is conspicuously left off the list.

"But mainly, I want to thank my best man, Stone, who as we all know is a great man. More father than our own."

Many Sylvers lower their heads and from the corner of my eye, I watch Ford dip his to press another kiss to Adara's smattering of hair.

"Stone is also the best brother and friend, and we all know he's been there for me more times than I can count. That's where Judd comes in, the accounting."

"Bah-dum-dum," someone calls out and a few people laugh.

"I also want to thank Vale, who has equally been there for me." He squeezes Enya's hand, lifting it within his own. "For us. And for giving me the kick in the head I need sometimes. I love you."

Vale swipes beneath her eyes, watching her brother, as she mouths that she loves him, too.

For some reason, my own eyes well up. Sebastian continues talking, thanking a few others, and eventually even gives a shout out to me, for checking out of my busy schedule to be present for my sister. However, I notice that Ford is left off the thank you list entirely, and I glance at him surreptitiously to gauge his reaction to the slight. If he's resentful or hurt, he doesn't show it outwardly other than that tick of his jaw, marked now by a bruise from the brother who didn't mention him. Ford's stiff indifference doesn't keep his secrets from me, though. The lack of acknowledgement stings.

"Finally, I want to circle back to Enya, who gave me the best gift this morning." Sebastian doesn't publicly share what that gift was while gazing at Enya, but I already know what it is. Enya has officially made Sebastian the father of Adara on paper, as he's already Adara's dad in every other way.

I glance at my parents again, watching as they stare at my sister, wondering, maybe already knowing, that Enya considers Sebastian Adara's father, and nothing will change her decision.

Sebastian concludes with a final thank you and more tapping on glasses begins. I doubt my new brother-in-law needs an excuse to kiss my sister, and when their mouths lock, I excuse myself from Ford and slip out of the tent.

The rain has dissipated. The sky is dark and still heavy with clouds. The air is cold and damp. I cross my arms, rubbing my hands up and down them to warm my chilled skin.

"You okay?" Ford's low voice startles me.

"Just needed a minute."

Ford has passed off Adara, and suddenly regained his jacket. He gently slips it over my shoulders, and I'm instantly hit with both the lingering warmth within the silky material and the sharp scent of Ford again. Worn leather, cut grass, and something masculine.

I press at the corner of my eyes uncertain where the tears have come from. A warm hand squeezes the back of my exposed neck, as my hair is also in an intricate updo.

Ford doesn't say anything, but I feel the need to speak. "Enya and I had an older brother."

Ford remains quiet.

"And it just sort of hit me how Sebastian and Vale sound close from what Enya tells me. Enya and I never had that kind of relationship with our brother." I lower my head and my voice. "And he's dead now."

How many men have I thought were in my corner yet weren't? My older brother, who only ever wanted money from me. My father, who shunned me for deciding to pursue a career in music, and equally upset with my life choice to be a free-spirited woman, independent and sexually carefree. My manager, who has suddenly turned from the father-figure I'd grown to rely on to a money-grubbing thief. And then there was Evan.

"I'm sorry for your loss," Ford says.

"You can't lose what you didn't actually have," I counter, a bit too bitterly. "Plus, I thought you didn't like small talk."

"Is giving condolences small talk?" Ford softly chuckles.

"It's a filler."

Ford hums, squeezing the back of my neck once more before releasing me. Instantly, I miss the feel of his fingers against my skin and the comforting warmth they provided.

"They're about to serve dinner," Ford states.

"Why didn't you help with the set up?" The question surprises both of us.

Ford sighs. "I was supposed to be here a few days earlier but then . . . and that's when . . ."

The stammering blanks in his explanation can be filled in from what he told me the other night happened between him and his ex-wife.

"I'm really sorry she did that to you." The short version is his wife left him and the girls for a fellow teammate.

"Now who is filling the space." He bitterly laughs, slipping his hands into his pants pockets.

"I'm serious. You shouldn't have been treated like you were. She shouldn't have been with someone else." Marriage vows are sacred. Even if I'm not married, I respect the hell out of the promises couples make to one another and the fact I was *the other woman* once still makes me sick to my stomach.

"Yeah, well. It happens, I guess."

"It sure does," I whisper.

Ford scratches under his chin, while staring up at the cloudy sky.

"But you're going to be alright, Ford Sylver. You're a catch."

Ford laughs. "For someone not interested in baseball, that was a good euphemism."

"Who ever said I wasn't interested in baseball?"

"You. When we met."

"You said you don't remember anything about the other night," I remind him.

"My memory is slowly coming back to me." Ford faces me and our eyes lock.

"Oh, yeah, and what do you remember?"

A loose hair blows across my face and Ford gingerly brushes it off my cheek and around my ear. The backs of his fingers sweep down the side of my neck. "I remember you pressed into my back. You kissed my neck, didn't you?"

"I don't know what you're talking about," I mutter, rolling my lips inward a second, locking in the lie.

"Seven shots of tequila, and now you're telling me *you* don't remember anything. I'm offended."

"Somehow I doubt that." I slowly grin at him.

"I'd be offended if you forgot me, Cadence Calloway."

Will he remember me?

"Caitlin," I correct him, swallowing around the name I hardly say and the reminder of a girl I no longer recall. "My real name is Caitlin. Cait for short. My manager thought it was too Irish for an American darling. Cadence is more lyrical."

I'm not certain why I tell him my real name, other than I've been curious lately what it would be like to be seen as a regular girl meeting a normal boy. Cait was not a brand; she doesn't belong to the masses. *She* could be any woman meeting a hot, small-town single dad and nothing outside these town limits would exist. Not Evan. Not cheating ex-wives. Not fame nor scandal or a world that loves to see the famous fail. Unfortunately, there wasn't anything average about either Ford or me.

"K-a-t-e-l-y-n," Ford spells, questioning the connection.

"C-a-i-t-l-i-n." I explain and pronounce phonetically. "Cate. Lynn. See, complicated."

"Cait. It suits you." Ford bumps his elbow into my arm. "Brings you down to earth where the rest of us peons reside."

"You're hardly a peon, cowboy."

"I'm definitely not a cowboy," Ford laughs.

"You might be more country than you think." I wink, knowing he came from this small mountain town and something about him still hints at grass stains on his knees and strong roots.

"I doubt it." Ford shivers.

While I've been tucked cozily into his coat, he's been braving the cool night.

"Here." I shrug out of his jacket and hand it to him. "We better get back inside before someone thinks we've run off together."

"Or thought I've gotten you pregnant."

"Yeah, we wouldn't want that to happen." I shiver, both from the sudden loss of heat from his coat and the thought of having children. I'd be a terrible mother.

"You don't want kids?" he questions, hooking his finger in the collar of his jacket and slinging it over his shoulder, model-worthy style.

"Nah. I'm better as the aunt. I plan to be the best aunt Adara has."

Ford watches me while smoothing a hand down his tie. "You'll have stiff competition with Vale. She loves my girls."

"Maybe I can add your girls to my list. I can be the aunt-in-law or something weird like that."

Ford tips up his chin, a crooked smile on his lips, before waving out his hand, motioning for me to lead the way back to the tent. "Yeah, something weird like that."

Chapter 11

[Ford]

Once we return to the tent, Cadence and I separate, as I spot Winnie suspiciously close to the cake table.

"What are you up to, little monster?" A blob of frosting on the tip of her finger gives her away.

"The cake wanted me to taste it."

"Uh-huh," I groan, picking up my five-year-old and meeting her dark, round, guilty eyes. "I don't think Uncle Sebastian would be too happy to find a finger poke in his wedding cake."

"Especially before he gets a slice." Sebastian's rugged voice startles me, and I spin with Winnie pressed to my chest. The sudden clenching of my jaw accentuates the sting from the punch my brother landed.

Despite the roughness of his tone, Sebastian offers a crooked smile to Winnie. My girls hardly know their uncle. Part of that is my fault. The other part is his. Sebastian has never been to one of my games. I don't come home often.

Winnie sticks her offending finger into her mouth and sucks at the sugary icing as if she can hide the evidence with one swallow.

"This one has a sweet tooth." I jostle Winnie in my arm before setting her back on her feet. Placing my hands on her delicate shoulders, I reroute her toward our table. Winnie breaks free of my grasp and scampers toward our seats.

"Girl after my heart."

"Yeah," I scratch at the back of my neck, a nervous tick when I don't know what to say and hate trying to fill in conversation. Small talk avoidance.

"About last night," Sebastian starts.

"Don't worry about it." Still, I shift my jaw, emphasizing where he hit me. We have a bushel of shit to unpack in all he said last night but now isn't the time. In true Ford-Sebastian form, there might never be a right time to discuss all he said.

"I'm different now," he states.

"I know." While we have a family group text, I don't often respond in it and assume a separate group chat exists for those who live closer together. I'm the outlier.

I should tell Sebastian I'm proud of him, but I don't.

He's never said he was proud of me, which makes me sound petty.

We're just different breeds despite being from the same gene pool.

Enya makes her way over to us and I'm grateful for the distraction.

"Did you apologize?" she playfully scolds him, slipping a hand against his chest as if steadying him.

"I'm working on it, sugar."

Hearing my brother talk sweet to his wife conflicts with all my memories of him. I hear the difference in him, but I'm still having trouble disconnecting who he was to who he is.

Then again, people change. Felicity is a prime example. My father another, although I don't remember him much different than how I knew him. If people can flip from good to bad, they can go from worst to best, and I should give Sebastian more credit.

"No need to apologize," I state. "Just pre-wedding jitters, right?"

Enya's head swings, glancing up at Sebastian like he actually might have changed his mind last minute. Like that moment last night when he said he couldn't do it and we all thought he was canceling the wedding.

"I wasn't jittery," Sebastian quickly quips, snapping at me while trying to reassure his wife.

I've said the wrong thing again. Clearing my throat, I try a different tactic. "You look beautiful, Enya. Congratulations." I step forward and she accepts the kiss I press to her cheek. I expect my brother to push me away, act possessive and caveman, and he might have behaved that way if Enya didn't have her hands still on his chest.

"We're very grateful you could be here, Ford."

I hadn't met Enya prior to this weekend. Again, Sebastian didn't come to me; I didn't come home. Still, I'm happy for him and his happiness is almost radiating around him. A fist to my jaw or not, he's still my brother. I want the best for him. Enya seems like the best. Adara as well. The three of them will make a great family.

"I better check on Winnie. The cake looks safe for now, but who knows what else she's getting into. Just wait until Adara is five."

Sebastian groans, but a small smile curls his lips once again. From what Vale tells me, Sebastian is an amazing dad. With a father like the one we had, fatherhood can be extra frightening. The fear of being like him because we don't know differently is real. Except we did know better. Stone made up the difference, patching the holes and filling the empty crevices.

"You'll be great." Taking a risk, I place my hand on my brother's shoulder and squeeze.

If Sebastian is surprised by my touch, he doesn't show it. He also doesn't shrug me off like I thought he might.

"Thanks," he mutters.

Enya gently smiles, suggesting that's all Sebastian might give me. I nod once and remove my hand, knowing I might need to do more myself to heal the divide between us.

For now, I need to find my girls and set them up for dinner before more damage is done to the cake or anything else.

+ + +

Dinner passes in chaos. Zelle is a picky eater, Winnie eats everything in strange combinations, and June could use a highchair but instead she sits on my lap. Food is everywhere. Thankfully, Knox and his girlfriend, Halle, sit at my table with Halle's twelve-year-old son and the angel that is her daughter.

"Where do you want to go to college, Violet? I'm giving you a full ride scholarship."

Knox chuckles while Halle's eyes widen.

"I'm only a freshman, so I haven't decided yet." Violet blushes. I'd been told there was a little trouble with her when Halle and her kids first moved to Sterling Falls this summer, but I haven't seen a hint of defiance in her, and if my girls can be half as patient as Violet in their teens, I'm going to be a lucky dad.

"I don't even know what I want to be," Violet adds.

"There's no rush," Knox interjects, giving her an encouraging smile. He's another brother who stepped into the role of fatherhood, or in his case more like a stepdad, but he eats up his position. He's proud of Violet and he adores Tim, whom I'm told is a shadow to Knox.

With all the changes in my family, I'm struck even more with the disconnect between me and them. I've missed so much. Do I dare say I might have missed them all?

"Hey Tim, do you like baseball?"

Tim shrugs. "I'm more of a soccer fan." He wears a blue clip-on tie with soccer balls on the fabric.

For a few minutes, we discuss his favorite team and players.

"We have a professional team in Chicago. You guys should come visit me and I can get you tickets."

Tim's head swivels toward his mom but he questions Knox. "Can we go, Knox?"

Knox sits with his arm casually around Halle who leans toward him. "If it's okay with your mom, we can definitely go to Chicago. All four of us." Knox's answer includes a glance at Violet, making certain she'd like the trip.

"My girls would love to see you again, if you aren't sick of them after this weekend," I reassure Violet, who is already smiling. Her fan club will be counting down the days, especially Zelle.

"I've never been there, so I'd love to go."

"We'll pick a date after the wedding," Halle adds, and something inside me swells.

It feels good to have invited them and even better that they'll actually visit Chicago. As Felicity was the one who normally handled everything related to the girls, their schedules now need to be juggled with mine.

I'm going to need a nanny.

"We're also having a sort of house-warming Halloween party next weekend. If you're still around we'd love for you to attend," Halle says.

"We're probably only here for the weekend but thank you for the invitation."

A sharp, loud laugh draws my attention to the table opposite mine. With her head tipped back, and her mouth wide, Cadence is laughing. From the position of her hand on Stone's arm, he must have said something funny; however, something inside me rumbles. I don't like her touching him.

Suddenly, she's looking at me across the room and her laugh slowly dies but her smile expands. Her lips are a deep plum shade, complementing the color of her dress. I wonder if she tastes as ripe as her lips look.

The thought surprises me and I blink once and look away, turning my attention back to June on my lap but my mind is still across the room.

Is Cadence attracted to Stone? He's a good-looking guy with his silvery hair and thicker beard. He's also a good man and deserves a woman in his life for balance. She'd be a lot for him to handle, but he tackled raising six siblings when he was only twenty-something. He's made of strong stuff.

Still, I'm unsettled by the thought of Stone and Cadence together.

She didn't have sex with me, but would she sleep with Stone?

"You okay there, man?" Knox draws my attention to him, but not before I catch him glancing over his shoulder at the other table. He chuckles as he looks back at me. "I heard that growl all the way over here."

"What growl?" Zelle says, perking up on her chair.

"Your daddy sounded like an angry bear," Knox teases, giving Zelle a wink.

"He can be a grizzly some days," Winnie adds, not even looking up from stacking green beans into a teepee. "He even looks like one when he has more hair on his face."

Violet giggles from the other side of me.

"A grizzly, you say," Knox encourages, playfully poking Winnie in the side before snagging one of her green bean poles and popping it into his mouth. He growls as well.

Winnie giggles. Her legs swing beneath the table, jostling her a bit in her seat. "You're so funny."

There's competition among my brothers to be Adara's favorite uncle, even though she's only roughly six months old. Knox claims he's in the lead. He's clearly working on Winnie as the next member of the Uncle Knox fan club.

Hearing a squeal of delight, I glance at the other table in time to see a man leaning toward Cadence who quickly pops out of her chair to hug him. Tall and burly, the man wraps his arms around her back and lifts her, causing her to kick her feet up behind her. Once she's set back down, she turns toward her table and introduces the man.

"Is that Daggett Ryan?" I question, narrowing my eyes.

"Where?" Violet perks up, twisting in her seat and glancing in the same direction I'm looking.

Standing way too close to Cadence, the famous country singer keeps his hand on her lower back while leaning over the table to shake hands with Stone, Clay, and Judd.

"I think it is." Knox lets out a low hiss, expressing how impressed he is with the rugged master of country music.

Felicity loved his music and I'd paid an ungodly price for tickets to see him in Chicago when he performed at Anchor Field. Plus, we had backstage passes. He seemed like a genuine guy from all I could learn in a ten-minute conversation with him.

"I didn't know Cadence had a date for the wedding." I grumble.

Halle gazes at Knox before both of them look across the table at me.

Knox clears his throat. "I didn't know either."

With Daggett's hand still on Cadence's hip, she leads him to Enya and Sebastian, who stand and greet him in a similar friendly fashion with kissed cheeks and back-slapping hugs.

"Are they friends?" I question aloud.

"Daddy, you sound like a grizzly bear again," Winnie giggles.

Zelle is watching me, and I clear my throat before casting a glance at Knox once more. His brows pinch but he doesn't say anything further.

Eventually, dinner is cleared away. I'll owe the cleanup crew extra for the mess my girls have made.

Cadence has disappeared with Daggett Ryan. I fight the urge to twist in my seat, wondering where they went, what they're doing. Visions of them kissing haunt me for half a second before my girls notice Sebastian and Enya are cutting the three-layer cake. My brother doesn't specialize in wedding cakes, but he made his own. The top layer is lemon flavored.

"What is the deal with lemon flavor and Enya?" I ask Knox.

Halle answers. "They met when she went into his bakery for a lemon baby-Bundt cake."

"They are so good," Violet adds.

"Their story is rather romantic," Halle continues.

"So is ours," Knox interjects and leans over to kiss Halle's shoulder.

"If you call reuniting by getting locked in a bathroom during a funeral luncheon romantic." Halle laughs.

Honestly, a wedding is the last place I should be with my headspace and heartache. Love is oozing inside this tent, between Sebastian and Enya, and Knox and Halle. I glance again at Stone, noticing Cadence has returned to their table. My breath catches when she pats his arm again before glancing up at me.

Anger strikes like the flick of a lighter. How many men does she need? Daggett? Stone? Is she stringing them all along like she did me, making them think there could be something between them? Is she hoping to take one of them back to that motel outside of town?

Shaking my head, I scold myself for thinking such things. Cadence is *not* Felicity. However, my thoughts are a strong inkling of how I'm going to view women in the future. I'm not going to trust so easily, if ever. And I will never give my heart away again. Distrust and suspicion will hound me at every turn and that wouldn't be fair to someone else.

Lowering my eyes, I press a kiss to the top of June's curly-haired head. My girls are all I'll ever need.

"Hey you." Cadence's voice startles me, and I don't respond to her greeting. "How's it going over here?"

She squats down, despite her long dress and tickles June's belly. To my surprise, June opens her arms and leans toward Cadence. I hold her back before she gets her sticky hands on Cadence, but Cadence also has her hands up and open as if she'll catch June.

"I can take her."

"She's a mess."

"Just the kind of girl I like." Cadence stares at June, wiggling her fingers for me to hand my daughter over.

I don't release her, but I do reach for a napkin and struggle to wipe June's fingers while she squirms on my lap. From the sudden shift in her little body, she's eager to be released to Cadence.

"No, June," I admonish.

Zelle's head picks up at the sharpness in my tone. Fuck, I'm never going to be able to reprimand my girls or correct their behavior without them holding their breath. However, I'm not Felicity, and June needs to sit still on me.

When I don't release June, Cadence stands tall again.

"Did you lose your date?" My voice is edgier than it needs to be.

Cadence's eyes narrow as she gazes down at me in my chair. "Daggett is not my date." Her hands come to her hips. Her voice just as rigid as mine.

"Cozy greeting," I counter.

"We're friends."

"Bet that's what all the boys think."

"Ford," Knox groans from across the table.

Fuck. I don't know why I said that. I don't know what I'm saying at all. I don't like this feeling crawling over my skin. This woman took care of me the other night and I don't know why I'm reacting like I am to her hugging another man.

She's nothing to me. We aren't *even* friends.

But I watch as Cadence's stunned expression slowly melts to liquid-filled eyes that drop their gaze to the floor. Her teeth dig hard into her lower lip. Then her shoulders straighten, and she lifts her head up high. With those blue eyes, now clear, and lasered in on mine, the fire in them lets me know exactly what she thinks of my retort. No man is ever going to make her feel small, least of all me. And I'm being a dick.

Abruptly standing, awkwardly lifting June, I hold her out to Cadence.

"Here, take her." My tone isn't contrite like it should be. I'm still too riled up and I don't know why. "I need some air."

The second Cadence grips June by her sides, June reaches up for Cadence's hair and wiggles her fingers into the sides of the intricate updo.

Cadence laughs. "Your fingers might get stuck in there, baby girl. I have so much spray on this thing I'm going to need more than wash, rinse, and repeat to get it clean."

Knox coughs into his fist. "More like repeat, repeat, repeat."

My eyes narrow at him and the innuendo in his voice but he gives me a knowing grin. Suddenly, an image of Cadence in the shower, washing her hair, water sluicing down her tight body has my own humming again. In a different manner.

Cadence carefully unwedges one of June's hands from one side of her hair and kisses the tips of her fingers. June watches where Cadence is playfully acting like she might bite June's fingertips.

"Whatcha got inside you, June Bug? You're as heavy as a load of bricks," Cadence teases, jostling June on her hip.

I said I needed air, but I can't seem to move. I'm not certain I'm breathing watching this superstar powerhouse let my daughter mess up her hair. Felicity would have been pitching the biggest fit.

"I'm the only brick around here," Knox counters, speaking of his nickname from Halle.

"Got good bones." Cadence taps June's nose. "And strong fingers." Cadence good-naturedly laughs, distracting June by rubbing her nose against my baby's and using the tactic to unwind June's other hand from the other side of her hair. A clump on each side now sticks out, making Cadence look like she has an extra set of ears.

The image brings back Cadence's remarks about being the cool aunt versus a good mom. In her bridesmaid gown, hair askew, and giving my daughter a laugh despite me hurting her feelings only seconds prior, this woman is a pillar of strength, and I doubt she'd be terrible at anything, motherhood included. The thought sends a strange rush through my gut.

"Your hair," I whisper.

Cadence's eyes meet mine. "It's only hair."

Felicity would have never said such a thing. She would have yelled. She might have even cried. Then again, she wouldn't have let the girls get so close to her if she'd been all made up. The dress. The makeup. The hairstyle.

I can't breathe again, and this time I really do need some air.

Chapter 12

[Cadence]

As Ford retreats outside, my gaze follows like a toy on a pull string. Watching me hold his daughter, he suddenly looked so stricken, so puzzled, and I wanted to solve all his pieces.

I set June down, glancing at Violet for assistance, while I reach for my clutch.

"I got her," the young girl states, reading my desperation. I didn't want to let go of June, but I had to chase Ford.

Those ghosts in his eyes had returned.

Once clear of the tent opening, Ford spins as if he senses me behind him. "Ever feel like your entire life has been one big fucking lie." His arms flare out from his sides, until bending one to reach for the back of his neck. He tips his head and stares up at the cold autumn sky. The clouds are clearing. Stars speckle the velvety midnight blanket here and there.

His question sounds vaguely reminiscent of our night together.

"Ever feel like what felt like the right life has gone wrong?"

I haven't felt *right* in a while. But Pre-Evan, life was good.

"I don't think my wife ever loved me." Ford sighs, still gazing upward. His voice is low, pain lancing through the roughness.

Clearing my throat, I say, "I'm not really an expert on love, but she must have loved you. She married you and gave you three beautiful daughters."

Ford huffs.

"What?" I whisper, truly confused.

"Felicity didn't want children. She'd told me, but I hadn't believed her." Shaking his head side to side he explains. "Zelle was all my idea. Winnie came along as a consolation. Felicity thought it would help us as a couple." Ford closes his eyes. "I don't even know how June happened."

When his lids flip open, the blue inside them is molten heat. "But I'd never change one minute of having those girls. And I'm not giving them up."

I'm not certain if he's trying to convince me or himself. While their divorce is final, I have no idea what their custody arrangement is, if there even is one.

"My father gave my mother seven children, and he hated every one of us," Ford continues.

My mouth falls open. "That can't be true." Enya hinted that Sebastian had a rough life growing up, but he also had the love and care of his siblings, especially Stone and Vale.

"That's the only truth I know about my upbringing."

A heaviness falls between us, as oppressive as the earlier clouds.

Finally, I ask, "Are you still in love with Felicity?" The question comes out like a record player needle scratching over vinyl. The accusation reminiscent of the last fight I had with Evan.

You will not *leave her. Contrary to your actions, you still love her.* There was no way I was going to ask him to leave his wife. *His* child. I hadn't known they existed.

"No." Ford grunts, turning his head away from me. "No, absolutely not. Infidelity is a hard limit for me."

Understandable.

I'm not clear if Felicity cheated before the incident the other day or if what Ford witnessed—and what a thing to see—was the first time. Regardless, he'd been divorced at the time, if only days old.

"Cadence." My name is a soft call by my sister from just inside the tent. "It's time."

Ford stares at me. "Time for what?"

"I promised my sister I'd sing. One song." I hold up a finger emphasizing the number. I did *not* want my sister's wedding to turn into a Cadence concert. However, Enya really wanted one particular song sung. As the tune is a duet, I couldn't have pulled it off on my own, so I was fortunate Daggett was in the area. We've been friends for years, acting as plus-ones for each other on several occasions.

"Your date," Ford mutters, closing his eyes.

I'm not the bad girl here and Ford's earlier words still stung but I recognize a hurting soul, and his is flaming with pain. Still, he shouldn't have said what he said about all the boys thinking I'm their friend. Or sound so snarky about a *non*-date.

Stepping away from him, I head toward the tent but then I turn around again. Ford is pacing, head tipped back as if he's lamenting his troubles to the sky. With measured steps, I walk back to him, watching as he slowly stops moving, his gaze turned on me, flickering to my mouth. My eyes visually trace the tightness of his lips before darting up to those ghost-filled eyes. He doesn't speak. Doesn't move. Just watches me.

When I take the final steps forward, each punctuates my command. "Apologize. To. Me."

When the tips of my shoes are kissing his, his nostrils flare. His jaw is tense and locked. His hands ball at his sides like he's restraining himself. Then, like the snap of fingers, his stoic expression breaks.

His hands are on my face, and I'm tugged toward him. Our mouths collide. The kiss is hard, biting and desperate. His mouth eager to capture mine, and we fight for control. Him. Or me.

Too quickly, I find myself giving in, losing the battle to keep a wall between Ford and me. He's broken. I can't fix him. Still, this kiss is everything. Flames of desire surge up my legs, igniting a part of me that's been cold for too long. I lean into Ford, dropping my clutch to fist his tie in my hand and pull the thin length forward as if I can draw him closer to me.

But just as quickly as we crash, we fall apart.

Ford steps back, his eyes wide. His lips parted. His chest heavily rises and falls, like he's run an entire baseline in under thirty seconds. Still, he looks at me like he could devour me. Everything within me crackles and tingles, like the air before another storm.

Ford is that storm, only I can't get caught out in the rain again. I've already had my hopes and dreams washed away, and I won't risk my heart again.

He is practically family now and we need to behave.

"I'm sorry," he whisper-chokes, brushing the back of his hand over his mouth and glancing down at his skin where my lipstick has surely smeared. "I shouldn't have done that."

I want to reprimand him. I want to tell him he's correct, he shouldn't have. But everything in me fights the urge to lunge for him, demand he repeat what he just did.

Repeat, repeat, repeat.

Fool me once, shame on me. Fool me twice. Nah, not gonna happen.

Without a response, I turn away from Ford and head toward the tent, wondering if my sister witnessed what happened. I need a second to fix my hair and touch up my lips, erasing the kiss Ford just gave me that stole my breath but pierced my heart.

I cannot afford to be hurt again.

With fisted hands, I charge around the tent, knowing Daggett pulled his truck up to one side. He'd excused himself earlier to set up his guitar and an amp he travels with.

"Hey, darlin'," he calls out to me but as I near the smile on his face lowers. Daggett is a good-looking man with chin length hair and a trim beard. The once dark strands on his head now hold threads of silver that match the smattering of chrome speckles in his beard. He's going to make one sexy silver fox in a few years.

"You okay?" he asks as I stop beside his truck.

I shake my head, not certain I can stop the vibration of my body or the pulse between my thighs but those needs will have to wait.

"Mind if I use your truck to freshen up." I don't have my purse, but I refuse to double back to where I'm certain I dropped it near Ford. I can work away the smudges and maybe pull a few hairpins from the back of my head to fix the stray clumps on the side.

Daggett opens his passenger door, still watching me. He's been a good friend over the years. He can read when I need to talk; knows when it's best if we don't. He's one of the few men I haven't slept with when we were touring together, and he was once an opening act for me. Now, he headlines his own shows.

Stepping into Daggett's truck, the leather seat is warm, and a reminder of how cold it actually is outside.

"Here."

I jump at the sudden sound of Ford's voice.

"I thought you might need this." He holds out my clutch, and I'm grateful while still shaken. His eyes remain lowered. He quickly steps back, allowing me space or maybe giving himself the distance. We don't need a repeat of what just happened on this front seat.

I'd never make it to stage to sing for my sister.

Because there's one thing I'm certain about amid the chaos rumbling through my head. If Ford kissed me again, I'd be kissing him back like I just had.

Repeat, repeat, repeat.

+ + +

Within a few minutes, I have my hair fixed and lipstick reapplied, and Daggett and I clasp hands to enter the tent through a side opening.

Enya gives me a relieved look, mingled with a questioning one. I've taken too long to get here.

"Good evening, everyone," I say into the microphone.

While I'm used to playing stadiums, and faceless crowds that span hundreds of yards, I'm almost more nervous to sing amid such a small gathering. This is family. These are Enya's friends. I do not want to disappoint her.

"I'm Cadence."

Eager clapping and a loud catcall come from a table to my right and I catch sight of Zelle and Winnie eagerly standing on the edge of the dance floor.

"This is my good friend, Daggett Ryan."

Louder clapping occurs. A sharp whistle pierces the space. My eyes seek Ford, who stands behind his designated table, hands in his pants pockets. He's looking back at me and I'm not certain I've ever been so anxious to sing before anyone.

"My beautiful sister asked me to sing a song for y'all. Being that it's a duet, I asked my good friend Daggett Ryan for a little help tonight." I glance over at Daggett while clutching at the microphone on the stand, needing the support to still my suddenly quivering limbs.

"Enya tells me it's her song with Sebastian."

My new brother-in-law's head swings to look at my sister. She holds out her hand for his and he leads her to the center of the parquet floor.

Daggett strums the first few chords and Sebastian tips his head as if knowing what we are about to sing. Then, Daggett starts in on "Thank God" by Kane Brown, a duet with his wife, Katelyn.

As we sing about thanking God for that person in our life, about hands fitting together, and the gratitude of love, Sebastian and Enya dance in their own little bubble, seeing only each other.

As for me, I can't take my eyes off Ford, knowing I'll never have that one person. The place where my hand will fit, and my heart will feel complete.

Chapter 13

[Ford]

As Cadence sings, I'm starstruck. In front of me isn't someone in a glittering costume with a dance crew behind her and enough gyrations to make a man dizzy. Instead, a sultry woman sings a beautiful song accompanied only by a guitar.

She's mesmerizing on her own.

When she finishes, Daggett and Cadence are approached by Sebastian. After a few words are exchanged, Daggett begins "Thought You Should Know" by Morgan Wallen. The range is more in Daggett's wheelhouse. Suddenly Sebastian is dancing with Vale and Stone is dancing with Enya. Not exactly a mother-son and father-daughter moment, but still a moment. As Sebastian said earlier, Enya and he aren't following a script. Vale and Sebastian are close. Enya's parents have been invited to the wedding, but they aren't participating in it.

Neither Daggett nor Cadence fall into the wedding singer category, so once their two songs are finished, Cadence excuses herself. Daggett is coerced into singing one more song and Cadence heads toward me.

Apologize to me. Her tone almost had me dropping to my knees and begging her to let me please her. I'd have done anything she asked of me. What I should be doing is giving her space. Put some distance between me and her. I shouldn't have kissed her like I had. So harsh. So angry. So desperate.

But I can't seem to fight this crazy pull toward her.

And she's approaching me. Only once she nears the table where I've been standing off to the side, she scoops up June. Hitching my baby girl on her hip, she takes June to the dance floor and starts spinning in slow circles. Other couples pair up and join the dance.

Enya somehow ends up dancing with her father who is a little too close to Cadence for my liking, so when the song switches to another one sung by Daggett, and Cadence's father starts for her with June, I find myself moving forward.

"Cadence," her father begins. "Don't make a scene." He's cupping her upper arm as if he's about to lead her off the dance floor. Only, Cadence is good at subtly pulling her arm free from his grasp as I reach her.

"Dance with me, if you must dance," he chides.

"Sorry, sir. The next dance was promised to me." Wedging myself between Mr. Calloway and Cadence, I grip both her arms and gently move her away from her father. With June still on her hip, I wrap my arms around them both and awkwardly we sway.

Cadence drops her head to my chest a second before June kicks her legs, signaling she wants down. After Cadence sets June on her feet, Cadence straightens, and I stop the potential of her retreating by catching her hand.

"Dance with me."

With weary eyes, she agrees, and I slip my arms around her better without the hinderance of June between us. With her body lined up against mine, I'm hyperaware of every curve and dip of her shape. Her bare arms circle my neck and I fight the urge to kiss her forearm.

Cadence is dangerous for me and not who I need. She's famous in her own right, understanding the life of living in hotels, traveling often, and missing out on family time. Her touring life isn't much different than my season. The lifestyle can be glamorous and tiring.

I wonder if she's lonely like I'd sometimes been during road games.

"You sing beautifully," I tell her.

Her head lifts and her eyes narrow, suspicious of the compliment.

"I mean it. Your voice . . ." Her voice is like a seductive siren singing to a lonely sailor.

Sensing my sincerity in my lack of words, she slowly smiles. "Thank you."

I clear my throat. "Also, I should apologize. A real apology. I don't know what came over me."

"Just couldn't resist me, huh?" she teases, her body tensing beneath my hold as she slips into performance mode. The walls are going up. She's shutting me out.

"Something irresistible about you."

"That's the reputation," she jokes.

However, I'm not kidding. I shouldn't have taken advantage of her like I did. I'm surprised she didn't slap me on my bruised cheek.

"Anyway, I'm sorry," I repeat. For getting drunk on tequila and spilling my secrets. Running hot and cold. Kissing her. "I'm a mess right now, Cadence."

"Aren't we all?" she mumbles, reaching for my tie and sliding her hand down it.

I'm instantly reminded of how she fisted the material earlier, tugging me toward her. I might have kissed her fast and furious, but she kissed me back. Was she as hot and hungry for me as I'd been for her?

"Darlin'?" Both our heads swivel toward Daggett, who is no longer singing but standing beside us. I hadn't even noticed the song had finished. A disc jockey has taken over.

"Daggett," Cadence stammers, stepping out of my arms.

"Been fun, girl, but I've got to go."

"Of course." Cadence pauses, glancing from him to me and back. "Let me walk you out."

Daggett looks from me to Cadence. "No need. Keep dancing with your man."

"Oh, he's not—"

"We're not—"

Daggett holds up a hand to stop us both.

Cadence clears her throat and tips up to kiss his bearded cheek. "Thanks again, Dag. I owe you."

"You know I'll be callin' in the favor." He winks at her before holding out a hand to shake mine. Then he steps over to Sebastian and Enya for a farewell.

Cadence and I remain on the dance floor. "You two seem close."

"All the boys consider me their friend." Cadence rolls her lips together, eyes dimming.

I scratch underneath my chin. "Yeah, I shouldn't have said that." The accusation came purely from envy. She'd never be my friend, even if I did want more with her.

As my leg is knocked into, I glance down at Winnie wrapping her arms around my thigh, and she's reason number one reminding me why I can't be with someone like Cadence. While our worlds are similar, they are also vastly different.

"Dance with me, Daddy," Winnie whines as I reach down to pick her up under her arms. She squeals and giggles before I hitch her on my hip and take her little hand in mine.

"Thanks for the dance, Ford." Cadence's appreciation comes with a farewell in her tone.

"It was my pleasure, Cadence." Along with kissing her.

She exits the dance floor and I spin with my middle child so I don't have to watch another woman walk out of my life.

+ + +

The morning after the wedding, breakfast is held at the bakery. The gathering is more of a public affair for those not invited to the wedding who want to wish the newlyweds well. Sebastian isn't exactly an exemplary citizen of Sterling Falls, so the people present are probably here out of curiosity and for the free coffee, like Trudy Wallace and Emory Milton, two of the biggest busybodies in this town.

Conspicuously missing is one famous singer.

"Have you seen Cadence?" I ask Stone, as I lift a coffee mug to my lips. The night ran late once again, but I steered clear of tequila. Clay and Knox were the instigators this time around, keeping me out when Violet suggested she take the girls back to Knox and Halle's house for a sleepover. I swear that teen is a saint.

"You seem a little preoccupied with Cadence," Stone counters. He slipped out before the shenanigans with Clay and Knox, leaving with

Hudson, Vale's son. My eldest brother and I haven't had much time to talk since I've been home.

"Not preoccupied. Just curious." I set my mug down and glance away from my brother's assessing eye. Rubbing my hands along my jean-covered thighs beneath the table, I attempt to dry my sweaty palms. Stone is making me anxious because it's time to tell my family the truth.

"Where's Felicity?" he asks outright.

Lowering my head, I lean against the table and admit, "I can't talk here." The place is too public and despite Sebastian and Enya being the focus, I don't want to risk nosey old neighbors or little ears hearing this tale. Not to mention, I'm embarrassed by my failure. I never want Stone to be disappointed in me, and I've been pushing this conversation off as long as I could.

Stone isn't letting it go, though. "Meet me in the truck." He doesn't mean take my time or get there when I can. He means now.

My girls won't want to leave the bakery and when Stone and Vale exchange a glance, she's suddenly volunteering to watch my kids again.

I'm really going to need help with my girls once I leave Sterling Falls, but that's a thought for when I get home.

Picking up my ceramic mug, refilled with the complimentary coffee, I exit Curmudgeon Bakery and follow my brother down the street to his pickup. Once inside, Stone fires it up and drives.

Our positions remind me of countless rides when Stone would pick me up from baseball practice or drive me home after a game. We'd assess how I'd done. The good and the bad.

Now it was my life we'd be deliberating.

"What's going on?" Stone lazily rests his wrist over the steering wheel, heading nowhere fast and abiding by the speed limit as he's the local sheriff.

"Felicity and I . . ." I swallow hard. "Are divorced."

Stone's head jerks toward me, the truck swerving with the directional shift, and he grips the steering wheel to straighten our course. "When did that happen?"

"Apparently in the Dominican Republic about two weeks ago."

"What do you mean 'apparently'?"

In order to spell this out, I'm going to have to start at the beginning. "Felicity and I have been struggling for a while. Fighting all the time. I thought it was normal marriage stuff. She's married to a baseball player who has an erratic schedule, that doesn't include nights and weekends off, but does include loads of travel for a good chunk of the year. She understood that when we married."

Stone patiently waits for more details.

"But with the girls, it's been a lot." Especially when my wife would have preferred we did not have children in the first place, and then when we did, they cramped her style.

Stone's fist tightens on the steering wheel, perhaps sensing where I'm already going with my tale.

"I never knew she was in love with someone else."

Stone slowly shakes his head, and suddenly I realize my story might be a little too close to his own history.

"She'd been in a relationship with him before me. I hadn't known it was that serious. I mean, she told me she loved him, but it was over, right? She was dating me, acting like my biggest fan, and we got married." At her suggestion. "Only she didn't really want kids, and I did, and I didn't see the signs."

"What signs?" Stone stiffens.

"She didn't want to be a mother. She hired a lot of sitters. Went out when she could. Didn't like the kids messing with her stuff or her." Felicity never would have allowed June's little fingers to touch her hair like Cadence had last night, and then to walk around with her hair sticking out in clumps . . . never.

"She hurt your girls?" Stone's gruffness was endearing.

"Only by leaving them."

"Get back to the divorce."

"*Apparently*," I emphasize. "She reunited with the guy. He wanted her back. *They* fell in love again."

Stone nods once. His lips pressed tightly together while he drives us outside of town.

"He's from the Dominican Republic and she'd learned she could obtain a divorce in a day by going down there."

"Wouldn't she have needed you present?"

"Not if she had an affidavit with my signature."

Stone's brows crease together, and he risks a glance at me while driving. "So, you signed off on the divorce."

"She forged my signature."

Stone's creased brows shift from a deep divot between them to folds of his forehead layered on top of each other. "That is not legal."

"I know." I sigh, staring out the side window a second, watching as the trees slip by. The leaves are a variety of golds, crimson, and burnt orange at this time of year. The rain last night removed some of them from the trees but enough remain for an autumn rainbow.

"What will you do? Press charges? Contest the divorce?"

With heavy shoulders, I turn back toward Stone. "I might have considered a reconciliation if I hadn't seen her having sex with him."

Stone's nose wrinkles. "How'd that happen?"

"Felicity was still in the house. I caught them in our shower." I snort. "Celebrating, I guess."

Stone side-eyes me once more, hard expression softening. "And you found out about the divorce then?"

I shake my head. "Certified mail. Came to me at the Anchors' clubhouse. I'd gone in for weight training and got served, so to speak." There was a formal letter of divorce approval along with a copy of documents with my 'signature' in the attachments.

Felicity and I were officially divorced.

"I don't want her back. Not if she doesn't want to be with me or the girls. It just—" My throat thickens.

Silence falls between us a moment, and I'm afraid to look at my brother. Afraid of what I'll see in his eyes. Finally, Stone sympathetically states, "It fucking hurts."

I hear compassion in his words. He feels sorry for me, not with pity, but because of the pain. He might know a thing or two about losing someone he *thought* was special.

My eyes begin to burn. The woods blur around me. My wife not only left me, she snuck behind my back and stabbed me. She could have simply asked for a divorce. Waited out the process.

I blink a few times before pinching my eyes with my forefinger and thumb. "She told me she didn't want the house or the girls."

Stone's forehead furrows once more. "Who the fuck is the guy?"

"Here's the additional punch to the balls. Romero Valdez."

Stone's head spins once more toward me, and the truck does a swift swerve. "The shortstop from Florida."

"Yep."

"Same guy who was traded to the Anchors last year?"

"Yep." I let that sink in a second before adding. "That's how Felicity and he reunited."

"Fuck." Stone hissed along with the word, scrubbing down his face with a beefy hand. "That is just . . ." He pauses because what words best describe the situation? "So messed up."

"So now, I'll return to Chicago and want to burn the house down, especially that shower. Need a nanny. And have to explain to the girls that Mommy is never coming back but she'll be at all my games . . . for *him*."

"Ford. You can't keep playing for the Anchors."

"Why would I quit? He's the one who came after me." Plus, I have two years left in my contract. I wanted to squeeze out playing until I was forty but making it to thirty-nine will be a stretch.

"How's the shoulder?"

"It's fine," I lie. Throwing balls anywhere from seventy to a hundred miles an hour toward home plate has taken a toll on my left shoulder over the last fifteen years.

Stone doesn't say more. He knows how hard I've worked. How long I have remaining. I'm *not* quitting my team because my wife quit me.

"Any chance he'll get traded again?" Stone asks.

"I doubt it. We've got a new manager coming in. Things will already be rocky enough."

"Heard about that," Stone says. "Ross Davis is a good guy."

Not that Stone knows Ross personally, but Ross has a reputation in baseball for being fair and well-liked. He played for the Anchors years ago. Tragedy hit his family and he left the pitching mound to coach instead. He recently managed in Philly, but he'll be returning to the Anchors for the next season.

"I don't envy his position. There isn't enough space in all of Illinois for Valdez, let alone having to share the diamond and a locker room."

Stone shakes his head once more and pulls into a parking lot. I recognize the space. Trails lead from here into the woods toward Sterling Falls, the namesake of our town.

Stone puts his old truck in Park but keeps the engine running. "Want to hike?"

I lean forward, and glance up at the sky, heavy with clouds once again. "Looks like rain." I'm also not dressed for a hike, plus the girls are waiting on me.

I can't keep disappearing on them. I won't be going anywhere without them ever.

Silence fills the cab a minute as we both stare at the woods before us. After a grueling practice or a tough loss, Stone would bring me here to walk it off. He'd learned after our dad was gone how tough the man had been on us. He knew I kept a lot inside me, and he never pressed me to talk. But he also knew keeping anger or bitterness inside me wasn't smart, and I had to let out the energy, even if I was already wiped from hours of playing baseball. I had to let that bad practice or lost game go, because I wasn't the failure that I'd once told Stone our father had called me. Actually, on more than one occasion Dad called me a variety of names. Loser. Piss poor. Weak link.

"You didn't fail," Stone graciously states, as if knowing where my head has gone.

"My marriage didn't work out." I squint at the windshield.

"Doesn't make you a failure, Ford. Sometimes things just happen."

I huff to disagree, but Stone knows better than the rest of us.

Sometimes mothers die, and good dads turn bad. Sometimes you're the only one left for six siblings. Sometimes you lose the love of your life to someone else. And all you can do, as Stone would say, is pick up the pieces. Make a mosaic. Repurpose what remains.

To use a baseball euphemism, he'd explain: sometimes you get a new position on the team. You aren't always comfortable with that spot, but you learn it, you practice it. Like I'd once been first baseman, but now I played center field. You might never perfect the position, Stone would say, but you don't quit on the team.

Stone never quit on us.

I won't be quitting on my girls.

And I won't be leaving the Chicago Anchors.

Chapter 14

Spring Training

[Cadence]

Back in October, I left Sterling Falls the night of the wedding. I couldn't spend another night with my sister because, *duh*, new husband. The newlyweds planned to take a few days during the week after their wedding for a short honeymoon, and Knox and Halle had volunteered to watch Adara for them. Once more, I'd been a failure to my sister.

I also didn't have the energy to face Ford again. After our dance, we kept our distance the remainder of the night by mingling with his family and enjoying his girls. When the disc jockey played a Cadence song, his three daughters and I *danced, danced, danced* while I lip-synced my own tune. His daughters were a riot, and they knew the words as well as I did.

Another reason I needed to leave Sterling Falls: the number of text messages blowing up my phone.

Where are you?

Is your bed cold?

Are you alone?

Fucking Evan. As if it wasn't enough he broke my heart, he had to string along the pieces. In text messages, tone and inflection are difficult to interpret, but there was no questioning Evan's cadence. His angry voice rang through my head.

He had no right. We were over.

Last fall, my tour had been a godsend. Evan couldn't get to me. There were planes to catch and busses to ride, plus rehearsals, parties, and of course, the concert performances. In the mix was my manager and his demands which I was patiently ignoring.

My attorney told me to play nice for a little longer. Papers needed to be drawn. Injunctions made. Jerry wasn't going to be happy, but I'd been complacent for too long. My songs were my songs, and he'd manipulated the system and me. My loyalty rested with my fans. I wouldn't disappoint them by canceling a world tour or hashing out my history during one, but I was done being a darlin' behind the scenes.

Jerry Septor was a music-managing god at one time. He worked production magic, harvested talent, and recognized a sure thing when he saw one. He'd told me I was all three—a magically talented sure-fire success. He'd done a lot for me as I grew in the industry, but he'd also done his share of secret sales and backdoor deals at my expense. Roughly seven years ago, I hired a new assistant. Lana Barclay learned quickly, had a better attitude, and knew the right people in the industry. She'd been heaven sent.

I'd wait, as Maggie recommended.

Still, time moved slowly. I'd been in the studio, but I couldn't embark on what I wanted to do. Yet. I'd missed Thanksgiving and Christmas, as I always did, with my sister and her new family, opting for my traditional Friendsgiving and then spending the winter holiday with Jerry and company.

By January, I was coming out of my skin.

+ + +

By mid-February, football season was over, and baseball was headlining the sports channels. Not that I cared about sports, but I found myself looking for stories about Ford Sylver. Since October, I'd thought of Ford and his three little darlings constantly, wondering what they were doing, how they were doing. That kiss played on repeat in my head. His mouth against mine. His fingers in my hair. The instant attraction to him in a way I couldn't explain to myself. Months of distance did little to settle my thoughts, but time had been my friend. With Ford's divorce no longer so fresh, I was curious if the ghosts in his eyes were less. I wondered if we could be friends.

I'd been in California laying low when the news app on my phone mentioned the upcoming spring training season for the Chicago Anchors and fourteen other teams that made up that league in Arizona. While hundreds of miles away from me, I felt close enough, and bold enough to reach out to Ford after all this time.

Me: Hey you.

To my surprise, a response came quickly.

Cowboy: Who's this?

Me: I'm offended you don't recognize our secret greeting.

Cowboy: Because 'hey you' is so original?

Me: Seeing as you lost my number before, I thought I'd ship it right to your phone.

Cowboy: Who says I want your number?

Me: I've got you in my favorites as Cowboy. You can put me under TQ.

He could also put me under Songbird, but I wasn't certain he'd thought of that night as often as I did.

Cowboy: For totally quintessential?

Cowboy: Terribly quirky.

Cowboy: Talented quacker.

I could almost hear Ford laughing across the miles. Or maybe he was doing that endearing jaw clench, fighting back a smile that would crook up the corner of his lips.

Me: Talented quacker? *duck emoji*

Cowboy: I was running out of Q words. I'm too tired to think.

Me: I was thinking more along the lines of Tequila Queen but being five-times essential works. Quirky is never a bad thing. *Quack, quack, quack.*

Cowboy: Tequila Queen. Why would that be? My memory escapes me.

Me: Ha.

Had he really forgotten me? We all had blackout moments in our history but had the memory of me really escaped him? Was that kiss forgettable for him? Maybe reaching out hadn't been the best idea. I didn't have a reason to speak to him. Strangely, though, I've missed him. His mannerisms with his girls. His edgy expression. The way he claimed me with only a kiss.

Cowboy: Still there TQ?

Me: Why are you tired?

Cowboy: Long practices. Juggling three girls.

Me: Goodness. I realize you're a talented center fielder so catching is your thing but juggling little girls? Mad skills. *baseball emoji* *smiley face tongue out emoji*

Cowboy: Haha.

If he wasn't laughing before, I'd hoped he was laughing now.

Me: Good to hear you still have a sense of humor.

Cowboy: Still? I'm always funny.

Now I laughed. I couldn't remember Ford really yucking it up at our siblings' wedding.

Me: With your brother and my sister married, that doesn't make us anything weird like in-law siblings, does it?

Cowboy: Sometimes I think you're just weird. *smiley face emoji*

Me: Talentedly quacky. *smiley face emoji* *duck emoji*

Cowboy: JK.

Me: See, you totally get the initial thing.

Cowboy: Speaking of girls. I've got to get them to bed. Our first game is tomorrow.

Me: No doubt you're eager to be greeted by adoring fans cheering for you from the stands.

Cowboy: Just a sea of nameless faces. *shrugging emoji*

My breath catches at the seemingly blasé tone in his text. Because there's something in those few sparse words that is indicative of loneliness which he tries to cover up. I know all too well what it's like to look out over thousands of strangers, wishing only one of them was a familiar face; that one of them was present for me in a way no one else has ever been. Someone there for Caitlin Calloway, a woman who has been successful, not turned into a brand. Certainly, my parents would never be there.

I glance at the time on my phone—it's only seven—and then reach for my laptop.

Me: Break a leg. They probably don't say that in baseball. You couldn't run the bases if you did.

Cowboy: Totally weird. *smiley face emoji* And I thought you didn't know anything about baseball.

Me: Never said that.

My screen lights up and then dims. Three dots appear as if he's typing, then disappear.

As I type away on my laptop, another text comes through.

Cowboy: Thanks for reaching out.

The response sounds like I was checking in with a grandmother or something.

Me: Now that was just weird. But get some sleep. And knock one out of the ballpark. << See baseball reference.

Cowboy: Thanks.

Cowboy: Oh, and Tequila Queen. Never said I lost your number.

Cowboy: Night.

Me: Night, cowboy.

I could question why he never called me then, but I don't. Instead, I smile to myself and stomp my feet on the floor like a giddy girl, because his statement suggests he remembers me. Or thought of me. Or at the very least, didn't forget me.

Chapter 15

[Ford]

A week after my brother's wedding, I'd returned to Sterling Falls for some unknown-to-me reason.

I could argue it was to get out of my house which I'd immediately put on the market when I'd returned to Chicago. Felicity had demanded half the proceeds from the sale after all. Thus, the battle began. Her true colors were starting to show, and they weren't loyal to the red and royal blue of the Anchors, or even the metallic shade of my namesake. No, Felicity's favorite color was dollar-bill-green, and she wasn't getting more than she deserved from me.

I could also argue that I'd returned to my hometown in hopes of seeing Cadence. This argument was a fight I contended with, and lost, repeatedly.

Cadence had a life that wasn't in Sterling Falls. One bigger than my own career. She'd returned to her glamorous experience of touring the country and performing for others. I would never be able to compete with that glory. As a newly single dad with three little girls, my priority had to be them while I finished out my contract with the Chicago Anchors. I couldn't even picture my life two years from now when the contract ended.

While I had Cadence's phone number, neatly written on a blank piece of motel pad paper, I hadn't reached out in all the months that had passed. I hadn't known what to say.

Speaking of reaching out, what a nimrod I sounded like when I said such a thing to her.

"Daddy!"

That cry alone was the reason I had trouble focusing despite being pleased to hear from Cadence.

"Coming, June Bug." I'd given into the nickname when she refused to respond to her given name. That little one is stubborn. And speaking of stubborn, she's struggling to go to sleep.

"Junie, Daddy really needs you to go to sleep."

"Want Ru-bee." Ruby was the girls' latest nanny. We'd had three already in as many months. The latest was someone I found in Arizona from a caretaker service willing to babysit at odd hours. As a grandmotherly type, she'd been my best so far, because she didn't spend her time trying to hit on me. Married thirty-five years, and having raised five children, she was perfect, but she wasn't here tonight.

"Dah-dee," June whines and I pick her back up from the bed, sit in a glider chair in the corner of the room, and set her on my lap. The position reminds me of when June was a baby. She was so easy-going until she learned to hitch her leg over the crib railing and toss herself out of the thing. She was going to be my adventurous one someday.

With her settled on my thighs and her head tucked against my shoulder, I press my feet on the floor, launching the chair into a soothing glide.

She already had a drink of water, been read three stories, given a second drink, used the bathroom, and finally I'd set her down hoping she could settle in on her own.

"Where Ru-bee?" she says around her thumb.

"Ruby went home tonight, like she does every night. She has her own family." With her husband plus one daughter and son-in-law, and their three kids, along with a single son living in the same house, Ruby tells me coming to watch my three girls is a reprieve from the chaos.

During spring training, players often brought their wives or girlfriends to Arizona, renting places, or in the case of some, owning them outright. Living near one another forms a family village of sorts. Without Felicity present, Ruby had been entertaining and educating my girls while I had practice, training, and meetings. I hated taking Zelle and Winnie out of school, but I also wasn't ready to leave them for six weeks with a stranger. Ruby had worked in an elementary school as an educational aide and helped the girls with their learning.

"My fam-wee."

"Your family is Daddy, Winnie, Zelle, and you."

"Mom-mee, too."

Mommy, too, while technically I disagreed. Felicity will always be June's mother but walking away from our sweet girls strips Felicity of the magnitude and importance of the title. She's mother in name only.

"Where Mom-mee?"

Jesus. I tip back my head. I cannot have this conversation tonight. However, our situation is only going to become more difficult when the girls attend a game and Felicity is present. I could steel myself to the speculative gossip and the too-personal sports news articles, but I couldn't always protect my girls, especially if they *see* their mother in the WAG section for wives and girlfriends, as *Romero's* girlfriend.

Because Romero Valdez is also here. As our key shortstop, he was valuable to the team. As a fellow teammate, I didn't need to like him. I didn't want to speak to him. Such negativity sucked because that wasn't typically my philosophy. The team should be a second family; however, some guys were just closer than others. I wouldn't say that Romero reminded me of my relationship with Sebastian. My dislike of Romero was nothing in comparison and when I saw Felicity in the parking lot waiting for him one afternoon, my anger grew triple-fold.

Most of the Anchors had my back. They saw Romero as a shit-stirrer and not a team player. He was out for himself only when, as the saying goes, there is no 'I' in team. As both a veteran of the red and blue, and a team captain, they followed my lead, and as a leader it was damn difficult to quell my dislike for one of us.

I hadn't pressed charges yet for forgery, but I did worry that the quick divorce in the DR wasn't legal and binding without *my* express permission. I'd had to hire a lawyer, especially with the sale of the Chicago house, and Felicity's verbal demand she deserved half the proceeds. The girls and I had been fortunate to find another house near our original neighborhood to rent for the time being. In the midst of this legal battle, some days on the field helped as a distraction. Other days, catching sight of Romero, were a constant reminder of what I'd lost.

I don't miss the fights with Felicity. What I missed was the idea of us. A family.

I couldn't believe I'd been so easily seduced by her and then swindled. As for Romero, I didn't give him a thought one way or another. He could fucking fuck off right back to the Dominican Republic for all I cared. My only qualm with Felicity was the girls. She didn't want to see them. She couldn't face what she'd done.

Qualm. Q.

Ha. Instantly I think of Cadence. Tequila Queen replaces Songbird as her contact in my phone.

"Mommy is—" What do I say? Not coming home. Not with us anymore. Never going to act like a mom.

I didn't even know exactly what a mother should act like. I'd grown up without one, and the one woman who tried to be motherly, Trudy Wallace, our father had shunned, stating he could raise his own children without her meddling. Trudy had been our mother's best friend.

He might have said he'd raise us but lifting us up had not been his calling. Most of us took to raising ourselves, finding our own niche, until Stone returned. I've always been grateful for sports and the generosity of coaches. Stone was especially giving when I was fourteen, purchasing new sports equipment when I went through a growth spurt.

I'd do everything I could to prove that my girls did not need Felicity. They had me.

As my mouth falls open in hopes some explanation will follow the deep exhale, June's thumb falls out of her mouth and I glance down to see her eyes closed, her head heavy. I lean forward and kiss her blond curls, inhaling her baby shampoo scent before tipping back my head again, continuing to glide in the chair and hold my youngest girl.

+ + +

Sometime in the middle of the night, I wake with a start, clutch June to my chest and take a deep breath. I'd fallen asleep holding her and I thank all the gods I didn't drop her. Gingerly standing, I creep quietly to her bed and lay her down, bringing the covers up and over her little body. After a soft kiss to her forehead, I exit her room, double checking that the nightlight is on, and the door is open just enough but not too much for her.

After a peek on Zelle and Winnie, I head to my room and collapse on the bed. Sitting upright again, I tug off my shirt and slip off my shorts, then lay back down on top of the comforter. Suddenly, I'm wide awake after the four-hour nap I took while holding June.

I'd like to call Cadence but when I reach for my phone, I note the time. I also read back through our messages. I sound stupid. My flirting game is literally in left field. At one time, I didn't have to work to get a woman in my bed. Then I met Felicity and I thought we clicked.

Holding my phone against my forehead a second, I sigh, wiping away thoughts of my ex.

Instead, a vision of Cadence appears. That purple dress hugging her body. The column of her neck. Her lush lips.

I might have stalked her Instagram. Taken note of various outfits. Sought out any images of her with someone. Thankfully, there's no evidence of anyone in her life.

Cowboy.

I chuckle at the nickname. Nothing is further from the truth, but I still like how the nickname makes me feel special.

Closing my eyes, I run my fingertips down my chest, stroking up and down my sternum. Cadence *is* quirky, like I said. A lady-boss at other times. I recall her stern tone telling me to apologize to her.

What if she told me to touch myself?

I slide my hand further down my body, noting the rise already in my boxer briefs. I can hardly remember the last time I was this wound up. Might have been the morning I woke up to an empty bed, absent of Cadence beside me.

What if she'd reached around my body and cupped me that morning?

I shove down my boxer briefs, setting my dick free from restraint and take a deep breath. Opening my legs a bit, I slip my hand up my cock, giving the hard length a tug before fisting myself. I should use lotion or spit but I'm already stone stiff.

What if she climbed over me in that purple dress, letting the silk material kiss my skin before tugging it upward and exposing herself to me. Showing me glistening folds and her perky tits.

A deep grunt escapes me, and I squeeze harder at myself.

Then I stop.

How many thousands of creeps jerk off to images of her. Fantasizing about her just like I am.

"Fuck," I groan, releasing myself and rolling face down on my bed. The position doesn't help as I envision her beneath me. The friction of my cock against the firm mattress makes things worse. With a rapid push upward, I spring from the bed.

If Cadence had really been present, I'd take my time with her. Learn every curve. Memorize every gasp. I'd know for certain if she was pink. *And think. Could she love me?*

I rid my brain of the impossibility and head to the shower for an ice-cold dose of reality.

Chapter 16

[Ford]

Our spring training park isn't nearly as big as Anchor Field back in Chicago. Seating roughly fifteen thousand fans from left field to right, there is also a berm lawn section that mimics our bleacher area back home. In this smaller-scale stadium, there is no way for Felicity to avoid the girls, or the girls not to see their mother. I've suggested Ruby take the girls to the lawn where they'd have space to stretch a bit, plus keep their distance from Felicity. Zelle, Winnie, and June won't attend every game, but I want them here today on opening day.

As the game begins, I force thoughts of Romero and Felicity out of my head. The task isn't difficult with the spring training stadium packed and the love of baseball in the atmosphere. I don't risk a glance at the WAG section despite its proximity to the dugout. Instead, I find my girls sitting with Ruby and her husband, Javier, on the lawn seats just off center from left field.

Ruby rushed me off this morning. The girls aren't allowed to bring snacks into the stadium. A backpack isn't even allowed but I wanted to make certain the girls had blankets and layers of clothing. While it's Arizona, the weather has extremes. The sky is bright blue, but a desert chill ripples over the field. The day is perfect for a baseball game.

The game is going well until the third inning. We're playing our hometown rivals from Chicago, and their star second baseman hits a pop fly to center field. The ball arches high but drops midfield, causing me to run forward and our shortstop to back pedal on quick feet.

"I got it," I call out at the same time Romero calls "Ball, ball, ball."

Neither of us gets the ball as we collide with one another having our heads focused up toward the sky. In the collision, I'm knocked in my left shoulder with his right one before I'm falling. In a not so graceful drop, I extend my left arm to catch myself before I hit the ground. I hear the tear and feel a jolt from wrist to shoulder.

"Fuck," I cry out rolling into my hurt arm until I'm flipped onto my back. With deep inhales, I try to breathe through the pain radiating over my shoulder and along the back of my neck.

"You okay?" The team trainer hovers over me.

"Just give me a sec." Another exaggerated inhale. Another sharp exhale. I focus on the sky.

"Ford?" Ross Davis says my name.

"I'm good," I lie before jackknifing to a seated position. I take another deep breath, wincing while rolling my left arm.

Our team trainer holds out his hand, and I take it with my right one, appreciating his assistance to hoist me upward. The crowd applauds as I stand, after the quiet hush of concern that I'd been hurt.

"Need to sit?" Ross asks.

"Nah. I'm good," I repeat, not quite confident in my answer. I roll my left arm again. *Fuck.* As team captain and the oldest member of this team, I refuse to go down during training season.

Romero stands a few feet away with our left fielder and second baseman watching me.

Ross Davis watches me, too, noticing where I'm glaring. His gaze follows my line of sight before turning back to me. "Let's get through this game." He smacks me on my good shoulder and heads back toward the dugout.

"You got this," the trainer adds. "Fuck him," he mutters underneath his breath, side-eyeing Romero, before walking away.

While it isn't public knowledge, the team has slowly gotten wind of my marital situation. Felicity and I are no longer together. I have no idea who knows that she's now with Romero.

Hodge Porter is our left fielder, and he jogs over to me as the trainer walks away.

"You got this," he says tapping his mitt to mine. As one of my best friends on the team as well as another long-timer with the Anchors, he knows everything about Felicity and Romero. He glances over his shoulder at our shortstop who has given us his back and returned to his position.

"Head in the game, man." He pats my good shoulder and hops once before racing back to his spot.

The game goes on.

Once the bottom of the inning ends, I head back to the dugout, taking my time, swinging my shoulder gingerly to keep it loose. Fucking hurts like hell. Still, I scramble into the dugout and collapse to my seat, sneaking a glance at the lawn section. A commotion occurs near my girls. A woman in an Anchors ball cap pulled low approaches Ruby and her husband. Instantly, Winnie jumps up and the woman catches her.

I narrow my eyes in hopes to better identify who she is. From this distance, she could be anyone, wearing jeans and some kind of Anchors T-shirt. Her hair is tucked up in the cap.

Standing, I approach the edge of the dugout, squinting as if it will help me more clearly see the woman .

Felicity? I've been fortunate not to catch a glimpse of her today, and I'm wondering if some sliver of kindness has entered her heart, keeping her away from the stadium during the game.

The woman sets Winnie down and bends at the waist to hug Zelle. Then she hitches June upward, notching my youngest on her hip and shifts so she's pointing toward me. June waves. I wave back. The woman wiggles her fingers at me.

Cadence? My pulse kicks up.

Cadence is at the game? I fist my hands, finding my palms sweating.

Then, the truth hits. *Cadence came to* my *game.*

A slow smile curls my lips. My heart hammers with . . . surprise? Joy? Panic even?

"Sylver," the batting coach calls out and I jerk myself back into the dugout. "On deck."

Shit. I reach for my helmet and pull my gloves from my back pocket. Finding my bat, I head to the deck and take some light practice swings, watching the timing of the opposing team's pitcher. My shoulder screams but I focus on the pitcher's delivery.

After our new prized hitter, Caleb Williams, cracks one to left field he races toward first and rounds to second, sliding into the base.

With a cheer from the crowd for Caleb, I take my position in the box, tap home plate twice and square my stance.

No one will want a scrawny kid from a mountain town, boy.

Don't shoot the messenger, the mail courier said after I ripped open the envelope telling me I was divorced.

I'm in love with Romero, Ford.

Fuck them all. I swing and miss. My arm cries out in pain.

"Strike one," the umpire calls.

Clutching the bat harder, I rub my hands around the base of the neck and reposition.

The ball races toward me again.

Fuck them. I swing again, hissing as I do. Another miss.

"Strike." The call echoes around me.

I will not go down without a fight.

A final ball curves toward me. The bat connects with a resounding crack. And I watch as it soars between left and center, heading out of the ballpark.

Homerun! With a single clap, I take off for first base, round to second, and pull at the bill of my cap as I head toward third, then point toward the lawn seats where my girls sit.

All four of them.

+ + +

Anchors win 6-4 and the crowd sings our winning song. Entering the dugout, I gather my things. There's no elaborate tunnel that takes us to a clubhouse but a short walk to the path leading to a second building on the property with locker rooms and a training center.

In this area, Ruby waits with the girls. Cadence holds June once more.

"Daddy, you won!" Winnie cries out and leaps for me. I hike her into the air by her shoulders, planting a kiss on her nose and setting her down. My left shoulder screams through the motion.

"Did you see my homerun?" I ask, knowing she did.

"Sure did."

"Congratulations, Dad." Zelle leans into my hip, side-hugging me.

I curl my hand around her ponytail and slide it down the length. "Thanks, baby."

"And what about you?" I reach for June, whom Cadence angles toward me.

June falls into my arms and I toss her into the air, feeling my shoulder extra when I catch her and bring her to my chest.

"Daddy do guwd." I kiss her cheek and she's quick to restore her thumb to her mouth. Tugging at her little hand, I act like I'm going to bite off the appendage.

"No," she whines, pulling her hand back and tucking her head into my right shoulder. As a left hander, I'm used to carrying her on my left side but awkwardly I hold her against my right.

"Hey you," Cadence finally says, watching me, with some distance between us.

People are slowly starting to mill around us, taking second glances at her wearing my cap and an Anchors T-shirt.

"Who's T-shirt you wearing, songbird?" Recognizing hers is the graphic kind with a player's name on the back.

She turns around, giving me a view of her firm ass and my name on the back of her shirt. When she turns back, she leans forward, and whispers a little too loudly, "Figured if you were going to get me pregnant, I should be wearing the name of my baby daddy." She winks.

And I laugh hard. *This crazy woman.*

"You came to my game?"

She shrugs, her smile sweet. "Figured your ego could handle another fan."

Does she really mean she came to support me? She'd been on tour since last fall. Her personal time must be limited and precious, so it's hard to believe she flew all this way to see me play ball. And yet, here she stands wearing a T-shirt with my name on the back, and I'm liking it a little too much.

Looking around me, she narrows her eyes. "Any sign of the ferret."

"Ferret?"

Felicity, she mouths.

"No ferret. Not today." Who is even looking? I have my girls here. And Cadence. "You met Ruby and Javier."

Cadence smiles at the couple lingering close by but giving us space. "We're best friends already."

"Of course you are." I laugh again, jiggle June against my chest and then set her down, flinching once more.

"I'll take the girls home now," Ruby says. "We've had enough popcorn and hot dogs. I think an apple or two might be in order." With her hand reaching for June's, she adds, "Good game, Ford."

Javier pats my left shoulder and I try not to recoil from the sharp sting.

Zelle takes a few steps forward but then turns back. "When will you be home, Dad?"

"One hour," I say. "Sixty minutes."

"I'll be counting." Then she takes a step. "One." Another step. "Two." Her voice drones on as she moves forward and my chest aches from her fear.

"Better make it one hundred," I call after her and I hear Zelle start all over again.

"You okay, cowboy?" Cadence asks as I watch the girls walk away and reach for my bat bag, hiking it up and over my right arm.

"Yeah. It's just my shoulder." I roll my left again, the pain more than a pinch. I'll need ice and lots of it.

Cadence walks with me toward the training facility, and I'm hopeful of pulling her away from the prying eyes. Within a few feet, we reach the path leading to the second building and most people respect our privacy as if an invisible line in the pavement is drawn once the team reaches this spot.

"So, why'd you really come?" I bump my elbow into her arm.

Cadence grabs the bill of her cap—*my* cap—and tugs it downward. "I heard baseball players are superstitious and I worried this hat might be special. I thought I'd bring it back to you, but I was running late, and the game had already started. Some guy wouldn't let me near the dugout even though I explained I had your lucky cap."

"Lucky cap, huh?"

"Of course. It's what you were wearing when you met me." She smiles wide. Her mouth full. Those blue eyes dancing.

I shake my head. "Which guy?"

"Don't know. A silver fox wearing an official jersey."

Silver fox? What the fuck is a silver fox? An old guy with gray hair? "Half the coaching staff might qualify under that description."

"Seeing as I know who Ross Davis is." She exaggerates her heart throbbing by patting her chest with both hands three times. "It wasn't him."

"Got a thing for silver foxes?"

"Nah. Just hot center fielders."

I stop short and Cadence takes a step forward before turning to face me. We stare at one another a second before I clear my throat. "How long are you in town?"

She sighs. "I need to fly out first thing tomorrow morning." She holds her hands upward and spreads them apart like a headline as she says, "Breaking news in the music industry."

"Care to share with the class?"

"Maybe over a drink?" Her brows hitch.

"Not tequila."

She flirtatiously pouts before straightening her lips.

"How do you feel about milk?"

Her eyes widen. "I don't drink it. Why?"

"It's what I'll be serving with dinner."

Cadence's mouth falls open and her head nods once before she tilts it the slightest bit. "Ford Sylver, are you asking me over for dinner?"

I think I might be. My cheeks flame and it isn't because of the hot Arizona sun. Holding out my hand, I say, "Give me your phone."

With a huge grin on her face, Cadence hands me her phone where Cowboy is indeed listed as a favorite right after Enya. I add my address to the contact so she has it with the number and can easily map a route to the condo.

"How about six?" I need time to ice my arm and shower. And maybe tidy up my place a bit.

She smiles wide. "What can I bring?"

I bite my lip before suggesting her fine ass is enough.

"Just you, TQ." She's going to be more than I can handle.

"See you at six." Nodding once, she steps aside so I can pass for the training facility but once I pass her, I turn and walk backwards.

"Hey, Cadence? Did you see me knock it out of the ballpark?"

"Really?" She tips her head back as the bill of the cap is covering her face too much. "Hadn't noticed," she teases. Her gaze lowers slowly, taking me in from top to toe. "I was too busy objectifying you in those pants. No one told me baseball pants were so sexy."

My face flames a thousand watts again.

"I'm turning around now, Cadence. See you at six."

"I'm going to objectify you again as you walk away." She laughs and I swivel for the training center as I give her a backhand wave.

While smiling all the way to the building.

Chapter 17

[Ford]

Suspicious eyes watch me as well as whispers follow when I enter the locker room.

"Was that Cadence?

"Is he dating her?"

"She's so fine."

"Is that a smile?"

I smile wider at Hodge's question, but the grin is wiped clean from my face when Romero speaks.

"I'd tap that."

I'm dropping my bat bag and rushing him so fast it takes three guys to hold me back so my fist doesn't connect with his face. My shoulder screams. I'm typically not so aggressive but everything about this guy rubs me the wrong way.

"Valdez. Sylver. My office now."

There is no way I'll enter the coach's office with Romero beside me. Sensing my opinion, Kip Garcia, a pitching coach, steps in and tugs Romero in the opposite direction.

Shrugging off the guys holding me, I lower my head and follow our manager to his office.

I collapse into a chair in front of his desk while he rounds it and takes a seat facing me. He removes his cap, tosses it on the desk, and swipes both hands down his face. Leaning forward, he crosses his arms on the desktop and looks to his right, taking a deep breath before he speaks.

"This isn't an ideal situation."

I snort. *He's got that right.*

"But we're a team." He redirects his gaze to me.

With my heart still racing, I hear what he *isn't* saying even if I don't want to accept the words. Team. We play like a machine.

With another exhale, his shoulders lower. "I get it, though. I have three kids." He unfolds his arms and stretches them to fold his hands on the desk. "And when Patty died, I was beside myself."

"Felicity isn't dead," I grouse, feeling sympathy for my coach, though. He'd been roughly my age when he lost his wife.

"But she might as well be, right?" He pauses, letting it sink in that he hasn't missed her absence for me and her presence for someone else on our *team*. "Perhaps you have it worse."

Because she's still alive and purposely absent from my children's lives.

"I told Valdez she wasn't allowed to attend today. Strangest conversation I've ever had with a player." Ross sits back, defeat in his body language. "But we don't need that kind of media circus. Your personal life is yours. And while privacy seems to be a privilege the press doesn't always respect, I was still trying to spare your feelings."

Saving face wasn't up to my coach. We had a publicity department for those things, and I had an agent to help as well, but I am not ready to make a statement or publicly announce my marital status, as if explaining I'm divorced and why is necessary.

"However, when that personal life interferes with the team, I have to make a decision."

My attention piques and I lower my elbows to my thighs, holding my breath. Ross could go several directions with his decision. Release Romero. Or worse, release me.

"You've been a valuable player and a valued member of this program."

Fuck, he's letting me go.

"As a veteran and a captain, I need you to keep your head together and your heart in the game as best you can. Step up like the man I know you to be."

Silence follows, but I'm certain my coach can hear my heart thundering. I lower my head for half a second, taking a deep breath of relief that I'm not getting canned.

"When I lost Patty, I thought about quitting."

My head pops up, fingers against my mouth. Is he asking me to quit instead? I can't do it. I'm not a quitter. My heart sprints once again.

Ross exhales. "In my grief, losing baseball would have been the last thing I needed."

Same. I couldn't lose my team.

"Instead, I left the field and accepted a coaching position. I went home."

I sit up again, knowing coach's story. A native of Philadelphia, their program welcomed him, and he joined the coaching staff there, working his way to manager in a few short years.

"Are you saying I should quit?"

Ross's eyes narrow, leaning forward once again. "I'd never say that."

"I can't exactly put in for a trade to a team in West Virginia." The state doesn't have a professional baseball team. Or any professional ball teams for that matter. The closest I could get to home within the Anchors organization is a double-A team in Knoxville, and I didn't want to be sent down a level. Or three.

"You have two years left in your contract and I plan to honor the time." Ross's eyes drop to my left shoulder. "How's the arm?"

"I'm good." My coach narrows his eyes once more and I amend my answer. "It hurts like a mothertrucker, but nothing a little ice won't help." And a shit ton of ibuprofen.

Ross nods once and clasps his hands together again. "That's what I thought. I want a full examination. I know there have been issues in the past and physical therapy helped. You might need it again."

"But PT will put me on the IL." Injury list.

"And I can't have an injured player during the regular season. Get that checked." He nods once more at my shoulder. "I also need someone with a clear head. I'm recommending a talk with the team shrink."

"Coach," I groan.

"Head and heart." Ross touches each before pointing at me. "And a fully working arm."

I place my hands on the arm rest of the chair, think better of the position for my shoulder, and lower my hands to my lap again. "What about Romero?"

Ross watches me a long second before saying, "Let's try to make Romero *not* your problem."

I don't understand how that can happen, but I nod and stand. Holding out my hand to shake Ross's, he stands as well.

"One more thing." He keeps my hand clasped in his. "Was that Cadence? My children are fans."

I chuckle lightly without directly answering his question. "You want an autograph or something."

"Want to know if you knocked the snot out of that ball to impress a girl?" he asks, still holding onto my hand.

I laugh harder. "Actually, I was envisioning Romero but if it worked on the girl, I wouldn't be upset."

Ross finally releases my hand. "I don't think you'll have any trouble impressing her, Sylver."

I turn and take one step away before Ross calls my name once more.

"Oh, and Ford? Remember us baseball players have our superstitions. Who knows? That girl might bring you a little luck."

I might agree.

Chapter 18

[Cadence]

I arrive at Ford's condo with a minute to spare when I've never been on time in my life. Wiping my sweaty palms against my jeans, I lift my fist to knock just as the door flies open.

"Hey you," I greet him, fighting a too-goofy grin.

"Hey. I thought you might be the pizza guy." Ford lifts his phone. "The app says he's arriving."

"Nope. I come bearing cookies." I lift the store-bought package and wink. "I heard they go well with milk."

Ford smirks and reaches for my wrist, tugging me forward. "Get in here." A smile mingles with the command but if I wished Ford might pull me in for a hug, he doesn't. Instead, with a press at my hip, I'm moved out of the way for the man standing behind me.

"Someone order a pizza?" A Velcro closure rips apart, and two pizza boxes are removed from the warming bag.

"I didn't think anyone said that anymore." Most deliveries I receive leave the food on a stoop or in front of a hotel door and rush away with hardly a knock.

"At Homer's, we do it the old fashion way." The comment sounds like a sales slogan, but as long as the food is decent, what do I care?

After Ford takes the boxes and closes the door, I follow him deeper into the condo. "Milk and pizza?" The combination doesn't sound appealing.

"I'm a growing boy." He smirks over his shoulder as he leads the way to his kitchen.

I let my eyes roam his body, taking in the strength of his back despite a loose-fitting T-shirt and the outline of a firm backside beneath his jeans, which looks almost as good as it does covered in baseball pants. *Almost.*

"Ladies, look who I found?"

All three girls' heads pop up, two of whom scramble from the table. One tackles my leg while the other wraps one arm around my hip.

God, these girls have burrowed into my heart somehow and I love how they hug with individual personality. Winnie just grabs on. Zelle leans in. Then there is June.

Once released by the other two, I approach the cutie with riotous blond curls and lean down for a kiss to her sweet head. She's seated in some kind of toddler chair, strapped into the seat pulled up to the table where the older girls had been coloring. June was scribbling over a paper with the outline of a baseball cap on it.

"Coloring? I love coloring." Helping myself to a kitchen chair, I glance through the pile of pages with cartoon characters and bold objects before picking one that strikes my fancy.

"How about food first?"

I playfully pout at Ford. "Spoil sport." But then I stand and clear the table of the papers and crayons.

"Wash up, ladies," I say, sounding too much like my mother for a half a second before clearing my throat.

Ford sets the pizza boxes on the counter and reaches into a cabinet for paper plates. His T-shirt rides upward and I catch a hint of a tattoo on his lower left side. I'd noticed the ink the night I undressed him but didn't take long to inspect the art. Cautiously, I catch the hem of his tee and Ford twists his neck to look over his shoulder. Our gazes lock only briefly before I continue to lift the soft worn cotton and trace over the design with a hovering fingertip, afraid to touch his skin. The design includes a baseball bat crossed with an anchor to form an X and a baseball over the intersection drawn like it's coming at me. In the angle of each cross are the initials Z, W, J. Zelle, Winnie, June.

"All the things and people most important to me." His voice is rough with the explanation.

Could I ever be someone special to him? Would he mark his skin with something just for me? Do I want that? Should I want that?

The girls return to the kitchen like rolling tumbleweeds and I drop the corner of Ford's shirt, stepping back to give us space and a moment to calm my racing pulse.

Before setting the table, Ford wets a paper towel and wipes off June's hands. I go for the plates he set on the counter and set the table while he finishes with June and then tosses the used towel in the trash. We rotate around one another in his small kitchen like a well-oiled machine.

"Bet you're used to something fancier than this," Ford mutters.

When I look up, Ford has stilled, hands on his hips, watching me.

"I can set a table, Ford," I state, a bit disgruntled that he doesn't think I can do something so mundane.

"I just meant, you're probably more used to five-star restaurants and fine dinnerware with takeout. Not paper plates."

I pause, holding the last plate against my chest. "Are you suggesting I'm a snob?"

"No, I just mean . . ." The blush on his face implies he didn't intend anything hurtful. He just thinks I'm better than delivered pizza on paper products.

I sigh and lower my shoulders. "Ford, let's pretend I'm just a girl whose sister happens to be married to your brother, making us weirdly related and possibly friends."

Not a superstar. Not even a country singer. Just a woman wanting to spend time with a man and his little girls.

Ford nods once and steps forward, taking the final plate from me. His hand runs down my arm, as if he couldn't help touching me, as if he didn't notice he had. My skin pebbles from the caress, but when I turn toward June, a shiver runs up my spine.

Her little eyes are watching where her dad just touched me, giving me a stare like: *I see what's happening here.* What I can't read is whether June would approve or not? She's only three, but I'd never want to do anything to hurt this little one's feelings or give her the wrong impression about Ford and me.

We're friends. Or at least, I want us to be.

Ford points toward a seat for me and steps over to his fridge. He pours milk for his girls then sets the jug back inside the refrigerator. Then he pulls out two beers. "I should have stopped to buy wine."

"I love a good beer." While some women adore wine, I've just never acquired the taste. I like something a little harder, thus tequila and an occasional beer.

Ford pops the tops while Zelle and Winnie scamper to their seats. He squeezes into the fourth spot at the table. The space is cramped but I love the chaos that quickly starts with Zelle complaining about the sausage topping and Winnie demanding her sister give her the unwanted dollops. I'm grateful for the vegetable pizza Ford probably wanted all to himself.

"Should have asked what kind you like?" Ford says as he plucks the sausage off Zelle's slice and places them on Winnie's plate.

Ford appears to be beating himself up over a few things tonight; however, it can't possibly be all about me. I don't need fancy plates, fine wine, or specialty topped pizza.

"Hey you," I whisper and he glances up at me. My brows pinch, questioning what's going on in his head.

He simply shakes it, forces a smile, and watches as Winnie tries to pick up a piece of pizza with too many sausage balls on top.

Winnie's mouth falls open as one ball drops from her slice and bounces off her plate to the table. When she reaches for the rolling sausage clump, she knocks over her glass of milk, and a pool of white covers the table.

"Dammit, Winnie." Ford shoves back his chair, and with a long stretch, reaches for the paper towel roll on the counter, without leaving his seat.

The situation didn't call for Ford's tone. Winnie's eyes water. Zelle sits perfectly still.

I'm quick to grab the few napkins on the table and toss them over the spillage. Then I sing.

"On top of my *pizza*, all covered in cheese, I lost a sausage ball when Winnie sneezed."

June watches me but Winnie timidly smiles.

"Milk spilt on the table, when somebody coughed." I exaggerate coughing.

Ford stares at me, so I grab the roll of paper towels from him and swipe up the milk.

"And now my sausage ball and the milk stain have run off."

June claps when I finish and I stand, bowing with a flourish before dropping the pile of soaked towels into the trash.

Winnie still has her head down when I take my seat, and while her legs swing beneath the table, her little heart still aches.

I see myself in her expression. Disappointing her father. Thinking she ruined this meal.

"Cowboy," I whisper, grabbing his attention. "Apologize."

Ford stares at me a second. Then he seems to snap out of whatever is happening in his brain, and he snags Winnie from her chair. Tugging her tightly to him, he holds her longer than I expected. For some reason, my eyes sting.

He apologizes quietly to her then pulls back to cup her face, so she focuses on him. When he tells her he loves her, spilled milk and all, a hard-fought battle to prevent the sob crawling up my throat ensues.

This is a good man. A great dad.

"It's been a rough day," Ford admits.

"Why Daddy? You won." Winnie reminds him.

"And you hit a homerun," Zelle adds.

Around her thumb in her mouth, June says, "And Cay-Day here."

Cay-Day? I glance at Ford who is watching me. "Yeah, Dad. Cay-Day here." I wink.

Ford lets out a snort-laugh, kisses Winnie on the cheek again and holds the back of her chair as she climbs onto her seat.

Spilled milk is forgotten, and dinner returns to questions about what other foods the girls like, what's their favorite kind of cake, and Winnie mentions how she wants purple cowboy boots. A random comment, causing the conversation to swing in a different direction.

All in all, the time was amazing.

Once dinner is complete, Ford tells the girls they have one hour with some cartoon program before bath time. After they settle on the couch, Ford and I return to the kitchen table where we can easily see his daughters from our seats. Ford's knee brushes mine beneath the table and I don't bother to move my leg.

"You're so good with them."

"No one else but me here," Ford grumbles.

I glance back at him as he picks at the label on a second beer.

"Things with Romero Valdez looked rough." While I still don't know all the details, I know enough.

"Told you about him, didn't I?" Ford states, reminding me he doesn't fully remember our conversation at Randy's Bar.

I shrug. "Might have mentioned a detail or two." He'd told me about being divorced while not knowing he was divorced. How he was served and then what he saw. Eventually, I'd stalked the social media of Romero Valdez. He looked like a dick. I had stronger words for Ford's ex.

Ford lowers his gaze and shakes his head. "I shouldn't have talked to you then. I hadn't even told my family."

"But we were on the verge of being family. Within forty-eight hours, we were hitched as this weird siblings-in-law thing, like stepsiblings." I laugh, knowing these comparisons bug Ford. Wiggling my brows, I continue, "Some people find that hot. Step-brother and step-sister sneaking into each other's bedrooms."

Ford shivers. "We are *not* the same thing. And I do not find that hot."

"Being step-brother-step-sister?" I lift my beer for my mouth. "Or sneaking into each other's room?"

Ford's ears turn a light shade of pink, and I don't know how I hadn't noticed that phenomenon before. I'm always concentrating on his face instead, but I'll definitely be checking out his ears in the future.

He shakes his head. He's always shaking his head at me but he's also genuinely smiling.

"What happened earlier today?"

Squinting in the direction of the living room, watching his girls, Ford tells me what happened on the ballfield with his teammate, in the locker room afterward, and then his conversation with his coach.

"That is rough." Placing my hand on his forearm, I add. "Thank you for defending my honor."

I know better than to be bothered by some random jackass saying he'd tap me. *Gross.* But I'm certain comments like that, and more, happen behind my back often. Ford cringed when he told me what was said, but I wanted to hear what set him off. I'm flattered he was sticking up for me.

"You know, him saying that is also disrespectful to Felicity." I have no feelings for the woman who has fucked up with Ford, but being that Romero said what he said means he isn't one to be trusted with Felicity's feelings. A cheater cheats on repeat.

"I don't care about Felicity," Ford says, lifting his beer and taking a heavy pull.

"But you should. She's the mother of your girls, and they are watching." An unhealthy relationship between their mother and another man could mean lasting damage for his daughters. I know. I watched my mother cower and give in to my father too often. If she wanted to correct his insults to me, she didn't. She played into them instead for his approval, but she often looked chagrined afterward. *Couldn't play it both ways, though, Mommy.*

"What they see is a mom who walked away from them. Choosing to fool around with a player instead of sticking with their dad."

"You're a loyal man, Ford. A man doing the right thing, even when it feels like you've been wronged." And he has been wronged. He's also still hurting.

Ford lowers his head another second before shaking it. "Let's stop talking about me. You mentioned you fly out tomorrow, but what brought you here?"

"Besides chasing a hot center fielder?"

Ford tips his head, his jaw tight. "I'm serious." His eyes say cut the shit, giving off June-glare vibes. The deepening blue also suggests he knows there's something more than wanting to attend a spring training game.

Sitting up straight, I take an exaggerated breath and tighten my hold on my beer bottle. "I needed a break," I admit. "Just twenty-four hours to be . . . Caitlin and not Cadence."

"Why?" A crease forms in his forehead. Then he adds, "Does this have anything to do with the *breaking news in the music industry*?" He waves his hands in the air like I did earlier while dropping his voice.

"Something like that."

"You can talk to me," he offers. "While I'm clearly a blabbering drunk, I'm also a good listener. And I can keep a secret."

Everything in me says to trust Ford. He doesn't have anything to gain from me. He's successful in his own right and has more than I'll ever have with his three girls.

"I'm opening my own production company. Taking back the rights to my earlier music and re-recording it."

Ford stares at me, perhaps not knowing how big of a deal this is.

"My manager wanted me to flip from country to mainstream. More pop. More funk. And while I have a few songs that cross genres, I'd prefer to stay in my lane." I didn't need to be someone I wasn't even if being Cadence somedays felt like I was pretending all the time.

"Weren't you just nominated for a Grammy?"

"You stalking me, Ford Sylver?"

"It's not like you don't make the news." The tops of his ears pinken again, and I smile, knowing he's been keeping tabs on me, at least a little bit.

"But I didn't win that Grammy, and as much as it would be nice . . ." I already have a few. "The Country Music Awards are more important to me. I want to be recognized among my immediate peers."

Ford continues to watch me.

"Think of it like the Golden Gloves. You're recognized by the baseball league for your skill."

Ford nods but still says, "So what does owning your own production company entail?"

"I'll re-record and re-produce my earlier songs, then re-release them, and cross my fingers my followers will like the new rendition." My new production team is banking they will, forcing the owners of the contracts I still have to surrender my rights due to competition. "Essentially, I'll be the boss. In charge of where my music goes and what it earns."

"My music manager has been with me for a long time, and he disagreed with my desire for this venture. But I didn't know he was skimming off the top and making deals behind my back." Costing me millions I couldn't allow myself to consider. I'd lost so much, but I'd earned plentifully over the last fifteen years.

"I consulted with my music entertainment lawyer, and hired a new assistant who is about to become my manager. Jerry has been forewarned. I'm breaking up with Alba Records, and I'm separating myself from him. I'm taking back control of my music. They're *my* songs."

Riding the high of my future while working through the low of severing my past, I needed a moment to regroup. I couldn't think of a better way to do such a thing than something mainstream and out of the ordinary for me, like attending a baseball game. Which happened to include one hot center fielder.

"Sounds like a huge venture."

"It is," I say, both overly excited and a bit overwhelmed. "But it's what I want."

"You're always striving, aren't you?"

I tip my head, questioning what he means.

"You're a damn big success as you are, and yet you're taking names and cashing checks, and advancing your career in a new direction." Ford's tone is both praise and awe, mingled with a touch of melancholy.

Why, though? He's just as successful as me, and major league players make millions. He's only thirty-seven, although he can't play baseball forever. For me at thirty-five, I feel like I'm finally hitting my stride.

"Well, if this is what you want, congratulations, boss lady." Ford takes his empty beer bottle and taps the neck against my half-full one.

"Thanks." While proud of myself, I'm also nervous, and suddenly, I'm wondering what it would be like to talk to someone like Ford every night about my concerns and decisions. The highs. The lows. And everything in between.

I wonder if I could tell him about Evan and how the texts have continued even after all these months of separation. No longer daily like they had once been, they are still steady enough that just when I think Evan has forgotten me, the nagging questions return.

Did you sleep alone last night?

Who was with you?

Where are you?

Looking at Ford and then glancing toward his girls, now isn't the time to blurt out my history. Not after sharing my good news about the future. I want my visit to be a happy memory.

"How's the shoulder?"

Ford hitches it but can't hide the strain in his face as he lies, "I'm good."

"What you are is terrible at lying. Is there something I can do? I can give a mean massage." I lift my fingers and squeeze the air.

"Those fingers are probably insured for billions, not a backrub."

"I can spare the change," I tease.

Ford laughs. "Actually, a massage might hurt more than help right now, so I'm good." He glances at his watch. "And I need to get the girls in the tub."

"Want help with that?"

"I got it." He stands with his empty beer and tosses it in a bin for recycling. Then he reaches for my bottle and gives it a shake. "You done with this?"

"I'm finished." What I'm not finished with, though, is spending time with him. I don't want to leave yet.

I stand as well. "Sure you don't want help with the girls? I can comb wet hair. Maybe French braid it." I glance at the girls with a need to linger.

"Help with June after her bath *would* be nice. And Zelle needs a reminder to rinse her hair when she's in the shower."

Being a girl dad can't be easy, and the job will only get tougher when they reach puberty. Still, Ford seems like the kind of guy to handle those awkward moments like a champ.

Watching me, his expression suggests he's puzzled why I'd want to help him out. His bum shoulder isn't the issue. It's me. I'm the problem. I don't want to be alone.

"Deal." I hold out my hand to shake Ford's, because if we don't shake, I might leap at him for a hug.

He stares down at my extended hand a second and then takes it, shaking it awkwardly once before holding on a little longer. "You're so weird." But he smiles like being quirky isn't such a bad thing.

"Quack, quack, quack."

Ford bursts out laughing.

I haven't heard Ford with a belly-rolling laugh and the sound is mesmerizing. Deep and rich, and a grand slam out of the ballpark. I want to do a cartwheel with how happy it makes me that I made him laugh like he is.

He rubs his thumb over the back of my hand like he did last October when I helped him with his bruised cheek in the bathroom. Then he squeezes once before releasing me.

"Bath time," he calls out to his girls.

Someone groans. Someone else asks for five more minutes. Ford pauses the program before shutting down the television and his little ducks file off the couch for the bathroom.

For the first time ever, I wonder what being a mother duck might be like.

Chapter 19

[Ford]

Cadence had no idea what she was getting herself into with the bath time routine. Zelle was too old and too big to be in the tub with her sisters, so she'd switched to showers a while ago. Shower skills had been Felicity's area, and she hated how Zelle didn't always get the shampoo out of her hair.

Cadence knows a trick to teach Zelle.

With the other two, tub time could either be five minutes or forty-five. June liked when her fingers turned pruny, but Winnie hated cold water. Either way, June could be a bear to dress afterward as I didn't always get her body entirely dry and wrestling her clothes against damp skin drove June crazy. She'd flop down in all these crazy positions, and it could take another twenty-five minutes to dress her.

Cadence tackled June's pajamas and the octopus within my youngest who suddenly only had four limbs instead of eight.

Then, a hair salon overtook my living room with brushes, combs, and colorful hairbands when I wanted these girls in bed.

However, Cadence had mastered combing June's curly hair, and June was almost comatose by the time it was Winnie's turn for braids. June didn't have enough hair for a braid, but Cadence was able to do a mini one near the side of her sweet, round face. While I read June a book in her room, Cadence's chattering with the other two girls, and the giggles they share, makes my chest ache.

I can't braid hair. I won't know all the girl things to talk about. I don't giggle, and I wasn't going to pull off being a girl dad.

But as Stone said, I'd learn. I'd practice. I might never be perfect, but I'd also never quit.

With June down in bed, I cross the hall to Winnie and Zelle's room. Winnie enters with two long lines of twisted hair down her head and dangling off her shoulders.

"You look pretty," I tell her, still feeling guilty that I lost it over her spilled milk. When anything was broken, stained, or spilled, my ex would blow up at the kids, and I swore I wouldn't ever sound like her, react like her. Be my old man, essentially, which meant never demeaning my girls in any form. My nerves got the best of me earlier, thinking I needed to be better in front of Cadence when all she seemingly wants is to spend time with us—the girls and me. I'm still baffled by the attention, but I'm not complaining. My girls love Cadence. Not the superstar but the woman singing silly songs, coloring pictures, and braiding their hair.

Winnie picks a book off the shelf and climbs onto her bed. I join her by sitting on the edge and reading a story about a girl who saves a village, which reminds me of Cadence. Always striving for more while surprisingly down to earth at the same time.

For twenty-four hours, she just wanted to be Caitlin, not Cadence.

Just like she wanted to be a faceless girl in a bar, singing a tune in the corner until she saved me from a potential mistake.

Even having her here tonight brings an easy quiet after an emotional day.

Within seconds, Winnie is nodding off and I whisper the remainder of the book although I'm not certain she hears me. Scooting her down the bed when I finish, Winnie immediately rolls to her side, and I drag the covers over her tiny frame.

With a kiss to her head, I exit the room and hear the end of a conversation between Cadence and Zelle.

"Sometimes it's better to have one whole, great parent than the half-hearts of two," Cadence says.

I stall at the end of the hallway, staring into the living room. With Cadence on the couch and Zelle between her legs, getting her braids finalized, my girl is quiet.

"Your daddy is going to be the best girl dad ever."

"He can't braid hair, like you." Zelle doesn't lie.

"But he can learn. Or you can learn. My older sister taught me how to do my hair because she learned on her own. That's what big sisters do. Sometimes, they need to be the teacher." Cadence finishes wrapping a band around the end of Zelle's braid and turns Zelle to face her, inspecting her braid work. Then, she bops my eight-year-old on the nose. "You're beautiful. And perfect."

To my surprise, Zelle wraps her arms around Cadence and holds tight for a second. Her hugs with me have slowly dissipated to the one-arm embrace which includes her arm around my lower back and the side of her body against my hip. My girl is pulling away from me. I assume one part of the pull is her growing up, establishing independence, but I'm worried another part is her concern about *us*. Our new unit as a family.

My throat is thick as I watch her with Cadence. "Zelle, baby. Time for bed." I can't have my girls getting attached to another woman who won't be in their lives. And Cadence *will* leave. She's a female powerhouse with a new company to run on top of all her other accomplishments, including writing and performing music. She isn't going to have time for three little girls and their dad. She's an exemplary woman for my daughters, and I hope she continues to be a role-model for them, but she isn't going to want the role of mother or friend or weird aunt-in-law, as she calls it.

Zelle pulls back from Cadence and Cadence gives Zelle's braids a final tug before standing from her seat on the couch.

"Just give me a minute," I softly say to Cadence, as Zelle passes me. Despite my fear that Cadence will disappear from my girls, I'm not ready for her to leave tonight.

Within minutes, I return to the living room, finding Cadence still standing in the middle.

"I should probably go," Cadence states, hitching her thumb toward the door.

"Are you staying nearby?" I don't want her to travel far.

"I have a hotel room in Scottsdale."

The drive will be forty minutes or more, and it's already dark outside. She's a capable woman who can navigate the area on her own, and still, I don't like the idea of her driving by herself.

"I just need to call a driver."

"A driver?" I gasp. "How did you get to the game?"

"A driver." Her brows squeeze in an adorable way, like, *duh*.

"And the store for cookies? And here to my place?"

"A driver."

Cadence isn't the best of drivers as evidenced last fall when we first met but I'd mistakenly assumed she had a rental car now. And now some random person is going to return her to her hotel room some forty minutes away?

"You could always stay here." I have no idea what I'm saying or where that came from. This place is a furnished rental for long-term stays, and all I can offer her is my bed that has a suspicious divot in the middle compared to a lush hotel bed.

With my suggestion, Cadence's eyes widen. "And where will you sleep?"

"On the couch." Then I consider my shoulder. The cushions will be hell on my arm, but I'll make do.

"I need to leave early." Cadence speaks more to herself than to me, like she's ticking off a mental list. Return to her hotel. Grab her things. Catch a flight.

And still, I don't want her to leave.

"We could watch a movie." The offer sounds weak even to me. I don't typically watch films. I'm more a binge-watch series kind of guy, but who has eight hours for a season of *Leverage* tonight?

Cadence wrinkles her nose. "How would you feel about listening to music? Or watching a concert?"

"One of yours?"

"Um, no. I'm writing off this visit as a work trip. There happens to be a music festival in town to kick off the opening day of spring training and I was planning to check out the talent. Being that I'm not there, I have a friend filming it for me, and I can tap into a live feed."

"Do you need to leave?" Maybe she should go if she has plans.

"I don't *have* to do anything." Cadence slides her hands into the back pockets of her jeans.

With a smile, I respond, "Then, concert it is."

Within minutes, Cadence has her phone wirelessly connected to my television and a live stream appears. I'd heard of the two-day festival, but I'd never been. The older I got, plus with Felicity, and then the kids, attending wasn't something I had considered.

"I don't really get to go to concerts as an ordinary fan anymore. I kinda miss being in the mayhem of a crowd, all sweating and singing in unison, gathered for one reason. The love of music and a great performance," Cadence says, settling on the couch. "There's a unity that transcends you with that feeling."

She writes the songs people want to sing, that brings them together in the way she's described, so I struggle to relate to what she said. Then, I recall her wanting her fifteen minutes to be average over fifteen minutes of fame.

A few minutes into the first song, Cadence lowers the volume a little so as not to disturb the girls. I don't know what perimeters she's using to evaluate the performance, and I worry I'll interrupt her concentration, but I still have something to ask.

"How'd you get June into her pajamas without a fight? And Zelle to rinse her hair? Even Winnie was calm while you combed her hair which she hates."

Cadence softly smiles. "Maybe it was easy only because I was someone new. Your kids are comfortable with you. They can let all the bad hang out. But with me, I'm shiny, and they aren't going to be ornery in front of me."

She watches me a second. "As for June. I made it a game, counting her body parts as we went. For Zelle, she just needed some inspiration. She's on the cusp of caring about her hair and her body, and she needs to know how to take care of it. I just told her to count to thirty, brushing back her hair with her hands as she went."

When did Cadence notice Zelle likes to count?

"As for Winnie, any girl likes to have her hair brushed. Girl tip, when someone takes their time to comb through our hair, we melt." Cadence exaggerates by fingering through her own long locks.

With a flick of her wrist, her hair tumbles over one shoulder and she slowly looks up at me over the curved edge of her arm. She's temptation personified and I bet men fall at their feet from that glance.

Quickly, I look away, fighting the pull to reach out and touch her hair, curl my fingers in the ends, fist the rest, and tug her to me. The memory of her mouth still lingers on mine on occasion. Admittedly, I want to taste her again.

"This guy is good," I say, nodding toward the television, although I'm not really listening to the singer who struts from side to side of the stage.

"Oh yeah? Who is your favorite artist?"

The next hour flows fast as we talk music and musicians, then binge-able series before drifting into random topics, like how I like pineapple and she's eaten a pinecone salad.

Eventually, I stifle a yawn.

"I should let you get some sleep, and I should probably check in with my new manager." Cadence almost looks giddy when she speaks about a woman named Lana Barclay.

"Let me just change the sheets." I stand, preparing to lead Cadence to my room but Cadence's hand on my forearm halts me.

"Don't fuss, Ford. I'll be fine." She steps around me and stops at the entrance to the hallway. Turning toward me, she pauses. "Since we're doing that weird siblings-not-siblings thing, does this mean we can sneak into each other's rooms?"

Her blue eyes sparkle with mirth, and she rolls her lips inward, as if fighting a smile.

"Good night, *Caitlin*." I chuckle.

"Night, cowboy."

Chapter 20

[Cadence]

When I close the door to Ford's bedroom, I lean against the barrier a second, tipping back my head, fighting a grin.

Ford Sylver is so easy to rile up and so cute when his ears turn pink, or his face flushes.

Lowering my head, I step away from the door and observe his room. The place is rather non-descript. An average extended-stay rental space with a king size bed and matching side tables plus a large dresser. On the stand beside the bed is a charger and a black and white photograph of his three girls in a silver frame. Taking a seat on the edge of the bed, I pick up the frame and stare at the photo. June is sitting on Zelle's lap. Winnie sits beside them, head tipped and leaning on her older sister's shoulder.

Poor Zelle has a weight of worries on those shoulders. Concerns for her dad. Conflicted emotions about her mother. I worry I've added to the pressure by suggesting big sisters learn things and teach younger siblings. Enya put that kind of stress on herself, trying to take care of me, trying to keep me out of trouble. But trouble and I go hand in hand.

With that thought, I set down the frame and pull my phone from my bag. As I suspected, the screen lights up with notification after notification. The only calls that concern me are from Lana. She's more of an I-can-tackle-this-on-my-own manager than someone who would call me with every little issue, so seeing four calls from her and a few anxious text messages has me contacting her immediately.

"Cadence?"

"What's up?" I casually ask. There are less than a handful of people who have access to this number. I'm the only one to ever answer it.

"Where are you?" She takes a deep breath and exhales. "Not that every step you take is my business, but I got a call from the hotel that you hadn't checked in. They mentioned in that call how a Mr. Burt Chimneysweep was inquiring about a Mary Poppins in the hotel."

"Evan?" My throat thickens as I whisper-choke his name.

While the pseudonyms were not terribly original, many actors and actresses are known to check into hotels under aliases that are fictitious character names. Evan liked the idea of being the chimney sweep in a famous nanny tale. He had numerous sexual innuendos about pipes and channels that I once considered humorous and now wish I'd never heard. I shiver at the reminder Evan once touched me in private places. His sudden appearance in this random location is a serious red-flag.

"What is Evan doing in Scottsdale?" The question comes out shakier than I expected when I intended to sound harsh, reprimanding even. I do not want him near me. I also wouldn't want him to learn I'm concerned about him being in the area. I never want him to know I'm growing afraid.

A heavy pause follows my question before Lana says, "I suspect he came to see you."

"How does he even know I'm here?"

Lana laughs bitterly. "How does anyone know anything these days? Social media."

I sit with the thought a second, realizing that anyone with a phone might have snapped a photo of me today at the ballgame.

"How is Ford?" The shift in her tone suggests she's smiling. Lana heard about my escapades during Enya's wedding weekend. She also knows Ford, as a center fielder for the Chicago Anchors, is now family of sorts.

But not the kind to sneak into a bedroom where I'll sleep.

I sigh and chew my lower lip. "He's good." The breathiness gives away how I really feel. I *like* him. A lot. And I adore his girls. Tonight was fun and unique. I can't remember the last time I went to a man's house for dinner. A pizza dinner no less. And then just hung out like a normal person might, although being normal is all perspective. Still, being with Ford and his girls had accomplished my mission. I was able to get out of my head and pretend. But pretending was dangerous and just like I'd believed in things Evan said, I couldn't project ideas about what Ford didn't say.

We were friends. And family by association.

"But let's get back to Evan. What happened at the hotel?"

"Registration called me after the inquiry because you hadn't checked in and they were confirming you would still be staying there. They also wished to know how to proceed with the chimneysweep-wannabe who was lingering in the lobby."

I'm about to ask what Lana said but she continues. "I told them you'd still be a guest under the name Tatia Quack."

A laugh bursts out. "Good one, Lana."

"I was concerned you'd go to check in before I reached you, though, and find Mary Poppins wasn't on the registry. Or that you'd run into Evan before you crossed the lobby. I told the desk that security should usher Mr. Burt out. They could even state that Mary Poppins would not be staying at their hotel, which wouldn't be a complete lie." Lana is a treasure for her quick thinking.

"Either way, I'm safe from being a fake nanny and staying in that hotel. I'll be staying here tonight."

"Oh, and where is here?" Her salacious tone is followed by a giggle. Lana is a romantic, but she can also be a realist. She's the formula I need within my new company.

"I'm at Ford's," I whisper as if breaking a code of silence or sneaking into someone's home. As I tell Lana my location, a soft knock occurs on the bedroom door.

"I've got to go," I whisper again.

"But you'll still make your flight in the morning? We have the announcement."

"I'll be there."

We say a quick goodbye before I hang up and rush toward the door. Opening it, Ford stands outside with his arms stretched wide. Each hand holding onto the edge of the frame.

"Forget something?" I quip.

"I need a pillow. And I wanted to suggest you could sleep in one of my T-shirts."

I'm still wearing the shirt I purchased at the game. His hat is safely tucked into my tote as I shook out my hair before coming here.

Ford doesn't move from his position, holding onto that door frame like he's restraining himself when I want him to lose control.

For one night, I want to just be a girl who is attracted to a boy, for reasons she can't explain.

"Let me get you a pillow." My voice is low, the sound strange before I move toward the bed and lean forward to retrieve a set of pillows from the four against the headboard. Only when I turn back around, I collide with Ford who has entered the room and stands directly behind me. The pillows between us are a layer of cushioning I wish wasn't present.

Ford takes the pillows from me. The backs of his fingers brushing my inner forearms as he does and an electric sizzle runs up my arms, jump starting my heart.

"T-shirts are in the second drawer." His voice is quiet, the tone rugged.

I slip by him in the narrow space and open the drawer he mentioned, rifling through the tees when a long, strong arm comes around me, plucking a shirt in his fist. With my back to Ford's chest, I can almost feel his heartbeat thundering along my spine. *Can he hear mine?* The drumming in my ears suddenly sounds too loud. I'm also inundated by his leather and fresh cut grass scent and the heat of his body is like sunshine on a perfect Arizona day. I want to melt into that warmth. Could he keep me safe?

"Don't be snooping through my things," he teases, his voice close to my hair, tickling my ear.

His warning is almost an invitation to scavenge through everything. Only, I want to respect Ford's privacy like he's been respectful of me. He's not treating me too much like a superstar and he took my scorn earlier when I told him to apologize to his daughter. He's let me invade his home and insert myself into their nightly routine, and he'll never know the night was the balm I needed before a huge bandage is ripped off and a relationship severed.

The thought brings me to images of Evan, pacing a hotel lobby, expecting to see me. My body stiffens.

"Hey. You okay?" Ford places his hand on my shoulder, his thumb massaging into my skin, and I want to melt into his touch.

I glance over my shoulder at him, wishing I could tell him the truth. Wanting to tell him everything. How Evan hurt me. How his recent actions are starting to scare me. I wish Ford could kiss away all that prickles and aches inside me.

"I'm good," I lie, sounding exactly like Ford.

He watches me a moment longer, like he doesn't believe me, but he doesn't pressure me, either. Instead, he wishes me goodnight once more and leaves the room.

I could leave the door open, suggesting he return, but instead, I shut it and take another deep breath. I'm safe tonight. Evan would never find me here. I still have hours to be free before my world implodes.

+ + +

Sometime during the night, a hand comes to my shoulder, and I jolt awake.

"Ford?" I breathe heavily. "Are you okay?"

"That couch is shit for sleeping and my shoulder is screaming."

I sit upright and take in Ford's form in the dark bedroom. He's wearing dark boxer briefs, and nothing else. His body is insane, and nothing I haven't seen as I undressed him on that drunken night when we'd first met. Still, he's so close and he smells so good. My pulse stumbles a beat.

"We can trade," I groggily state, flipping back the sheet and blanket covering me. The ones awash in Ford's leather and fresh grass scent, which overwhelmed my senses as I drifted off to sleep, imagining Ford was holding me. The strange comfort—his bed, his sheets, his scent— had me slipping into unconscious bliss faster than I ever thought I could knowing Evan was near.

I stand but Ford catches my hip.

"Or you could stay?"

Blurry eyed, I blink at him. "Why, Ford Sylver, are you asking me to sleep with you?"

He shrugs, tightening his hold on the pillows tucked underneath his other arm. "Wouldn't be the first time we slept together."

An obnoxious honk escapes my nose and I cover my mouth, as the sharp sound in the quiet condo could potentially wake the girls.

"Did you just snort?" He bites his lip, fighting a laugh.

"I was quacking."

Ford lets loose a quiet chuckle, while shaking his head. "Get in bed, Cadence."

He has no idea the effect that tone, those words, and the touch of his hand has on me. I not only scramble back to the bed, I want so much more from him in it.

But I understand his shoulder hurts and an athletic man like him needs his sleep. Once I'm settled beneath the sheets, Ford rounds to the other side of the bed, tugs back the top layer and builds a pillow wall between us. After he folds down to the mattress, he lays on his side and drapes his arm over the support.

"I can't lay on my back. The pain radiates along my neck. If I lay on my right side without support, my left arm dangles at an angle that makes it feel like it could tear off me."

"Ouch," I whisper, facing him.

"Sleeping on my injured shoulder is the only way I feel comfort but even then, a constant tingling down my arm happens, so back to sleeping on my right, hitching my arm over pillows like this works best."

"You should probably get that checked out," I chide.

"You sound like my coach. And the team trainer." Ford is a quiet a second. "But I can't be injured again. I had some issues with my arm last season. Physical therapy helped. I just need to start the exercises again."

A few stretches don't sound like they'll fix his level of pain, but I didn't know anything about being a professional athlete. I worked out and stayed in shape for dancing on stage which is often compared to the level of athleticism a professional athlete exerts, but still, Ford's ache sounds serious.

"Promise me you'll get that checked, Ford."

"On it, TQ."

I softly smile, unable to see his face in the dark room.

"Disappointed I won't be able to spoon you?" Ford teases.

However, my response is a bit more serious. "I'm more of a knife and fork girl."

"Knife and fork?" Ford's chuckle is subtle.

"You know, to signal a meal is finished, you slide the knife between the fork tines. That's how I like to sleep. Face to face, bodies entangled." I didn't need to be cradled. I wanted to be cuddled. I wanted to inhale the scent of my partner and feel his heart pulse beneath my hands on his chest.

It'd been so long since I've slept in that position, I've forgotten how it feels.

"Hmm," Ford replies, the vibration sleepy, but I'm suddenly wide awake, wondering how his mouth might feel making the same sound between my legs. Discreetly, I rub my thighs together, hoping to dispel the sudden pulsing at my core.

I stretch my hand across the mattress, hovering at the edge of the pillow wall between us, and whisper, "You're going be okay, Ford."

Ford's fingertips brush the tips of mine as if he was searching for me. When our fingertips touch, Ford wedges his fingers between mine and tightens his hold. Like the tines on a fork, spearing fresh fruit.

And I drift back to sleep imagining I'm a pineapple, Ford's favorite.

Chapter 21

The Season

[Ford]

Divorces happen every day in this country. Why some make the news, and others don't is a matter of sensationalism. The average person couldn't care less that a sport figure got a divorce, or married, for that matter. The only thing a fan cares about is the athlete's performance on the field. Could he or she win a game?

But when you are a musician or an actor, the stakes seem to rise higher the greater your level of stardom. So, it wasn't that people cared so much that I was divorced; they cared that Cadence had been to a Chicago Anchors game and was "seen lingering close" to me afterward, implying something nefarious. Even adulterous.

Within a day, news broke in the sports-centric arena that I am now single. Our PR firm handled the details. I was a proud family man and had sole custody of my three daughters. I'd been warned questions would soon arise, asking for more of an explanation than irreconcilable differences with Felicity, but the inquisition shouldn't be too invasive.

Instead, speculation focused on Cadence.

Are we dating? Are we an item? How long have I known her? When did this happen?

Did I cheat on my wife with her?

I hated everything about the shitshow spiral, but nothing bothered me more than this question.

I didn't feel the need to defend myself. And I certainly wasn't interested in protecting Felicity, but I had the girls to consider. It was no one's business what went down in my personal life. I also didn't like the implication for Cadence. It reminded me of when her father accused her of getting pregnant after meeting me only the night before. Not an impossible feat but still uncalled for.

Within hours of my divorce making sports news, Cadence's story had broken. She was going to be the mogul of her own production company, taking back her songs, and breaking up with her management team. If unable to reclaim her rights, she'd then re-produce the sounds of her music. This woman was accomplishing a major achievement and yet the only thing making video reels and audio clips were questions about me.

Are you dating Ford Sylver? Will he be the topic of your next album?

People had even been cruel enough to suggest we break up—when we weren't even together—as inspiration for her next round of heartbreak songs.

Cadence remained poised and controlled when she explained in a statement that her sister was married to my brother. We were friends by family association. Her visit to Arizona was in support of her sister's brother-in-law, nothing more. She tacked on that she attended the spring training music festival. Not exactly a lie; but not the whole truth.

Thankfully, she skipped the sneaking into each other's room fantasy, which was something I'd had trouble wrestling from my head as I lay on my couch that night, fighting through the surges of pain radiating along my arm and across my upper back, and struggling with my dick that wanted Cadence.

I had no doubt she'd be a handful, both in and out of bed, but I wanted her quirkiness and the quack.

I'd chuckle to myself when I thought of that riotous snort coming out of such a beautiful woman, reminding me she's just a girl and I'm a guy attracted to her.

I wanted to reach out to her. See if she was okay with the unnecessary chatter surrounding us when there wasn't an us. As she eloquently stated, we were friends. Circling back to that concept, I decided, as a *friend,* I should check in on her.

Me: You okay, TQ?

Me: Checking in on you this round.

Me: Cadence?

Me: Caitlin.

For three days I struggled to not let the news surrounding us unsettle me. I also tried to dismiss the fact that Cadence had ignored my text messages. After those three days, though, anxiety got the better of me and I called her number.

"Cadence?"

"She's not available. May I ask who is calling?" The stern Southern voice was not my songbird.

Making an assumption as to who might be answering her phone, I'd asked, "Lana?"

"Who's calling, please?" She almost sounded like an old switchboard operator. Formal. Direct. And a real hard ass who wasn't going to put me through to Cadence.

For a second, I'd hesitated. I should have simply said my name but not knowing who *I* was speaking with, I didn't want to add to the rampant speculation about *us*. I didn't need the headache. Cadence didn't deserve the distraction our *friendship* was taking from her new venture.

"No one," I'd replied, deciding not to leave a message.

If Cadence had wanted to speak with me, she'd have responded to my text messages. I wasn't going to jump through the hoops of a gatekeeper to get to her. I had my own issues to battle and three little ones to protect.

"Lose this number," the female voice warned. "It's being disconnected anyway."

The line went dead, and I was instantly embarrassed by a gift I'd left for Cadence after she'd spent the night at my place. Knowing she'd sneak out early in the morning, leaving me to wake in a cold, empty bed again, I'd left her a note and an item. In hindsight, the gesture seemed silly, and I cursed myself.

I don't know why I thought we were actually friends. Cadence burned too bright and too fast, and perhaps it was better to keep my distance. Only my heart had lost the memo. Once again, I'd been disappointed that someone I was starting to care about had walked away without a backward glance. She'd wanted a reprieve for twenty-four hours. The game was over and so were we.

+ + +

Spring training ended in March.

The girls and I survived the six weeks in Arizona. We missed Ruby, especially June, but we had a new au pair as I needed round the clock care for the girls. Fighting off the advances of a nanny was not on my bingo card for the new season. Thankfully, Blake was a decade older than me and not interested in men. She had more Trunchbull than Ms. Honey vibes about her. Sometimes she was even stern with me, but she fit my needs.

Through physical therapy, I'd worked out most of the pain in my arm, but my range of motion was still off. I couldn't extend my arm backward without twisting my body, which could help leverage a ball, but it also hurt like hell. Athletic tape and ice packs were my friends.

The regular season officially started at the end of the month. We had an away series first, so the official opening day in Anchor Field was in April. Stone, Vale, and Hudson made the trip to Chicago for the game. Knox and Halle promised to bring the kids in June after school was out for the summer. Even Enya asked if she and Sebastian could visit.

In our call, I'd been foolish enough to ask how Cadence was doing.

"Busier than she's ever been, which keeps her out of trouble," Enya had laughed.

As team captain and a starter, I was pumped for the new season despite my arm and the animosity with Romero. Things had not gotten better as I'd filed a lawsuit against Felicity for forgery. The suit was the only way to solidify our divorce, although the Dominican Republic's day-divorce was legal and binding pending the correction to my signature. Felicity was countersuing me for money from the sale of our house and alimony, claiming motherhood and her lack of employment earned her the right to my finances in the future.

Hell could freeze over first.

When the umpire calls "Play ball," we take our positions on the field. The stadium is alive with the excitement of a new season. *This will be our year*, as the saying goes in hopes of making it to the big game in October. I already owned a championship ring, but I wouldn't mind ending my career by earning another one with a team I loved.

I brush away any hope of finding Cadence's presence in the stands to cheer me on.

Standing in center field, I focus on the first smack of a bat against a ball that sends a resounding crack over the dirt. The ball projects in a sweeping arch toward me, but I sense it falling short. I race forward. Romero is moving backward. We both call *ball, ball, ball*. The moment is reminiscent of our first day out for spring training.

Only this time, I stop short.

So does Romero.

And the ball drops between us like something you'd see in a little league game.

We both stare at the round object with red stitching on the grass before I look up at my nemesis.

"Why didn't you fall back?"

"Why didn't you pull forward?"

Before I know it we are nose to nose with each other, a scene not unheard of in baseball but unseen between teammates. On the field. During a game.

"You're fucking up, *amigo*." Romero scowls.

"You are not my fucking friend." I point at him.

Wrong move as he grabs my finger and twists my bad arm. An ugly pop accompanies a strange ripping sensation in my shoulder.

And I know I'm done.

Chapter 22

[Cadence]

The chaos of two teammates getting in each other's face on national television was unbelievable.

I'd originally planned to attend the opening day game and surprise Ford. Then I hadn't heard from him in the months following the night I'd spent with him in Arizona.

As much as I'd hoped we were friends, we really weren't, I guess. Too often I'd reread the note he'd left me along with the silly, sweet gift I'm certain he stole from one of his daughters, and assumed there was more to the gesture. However, I'd been the aggressor, reaching out to him and showing up at his game. He'd obviously taken pity on me and invited me to his place for dinner. Touching my fingers while we slept meant nothing more than touching fingers. He'd never even made a media statement when all that bullshit started about his divorce and a relationship between us.

Still, I'd gasped when I saw the way Romero Valdez twisted Ford's arm and took him down in something you'd see in a wrestling match, not on a baseball field. Releasing Ford almost as quickly as he grabbed him, Romero stepped back holding up his hands as if he were innocent. Ford remained on a knee, gripping his left shoulder.

I could only surmise he hadn't gotten the physical therapy he needed, or he hadn't healed from the previous injury. Either way, when Ford finally was standing, his arm dangled precariously for a second before he supported it with his other hand to exit the field. The silence was deafening as fans processed what they'd seen. Then a slow clap began for their captain.

"Lana," I'd cried out. "I need a flight to Chicago."

From Enya, I was able to learn where Ford lived. While he'd conveniently lost my phone number— again—I needed to know he was whole. I had to see him in person. And a quick flight to Chicago was faster than an eight-hour drive from Nashville.

With Evan still an issue, I didn't have a choice but to travel with a bodyguard. The situation of a burly man following me around with a wireless earpiece and a dark suit stretched over bulky muscles caused a scene despite my hope to go unnoticed in jeans and a sweater with an Anchors' ball cap on my head and dark sunglasses.

Following a sharp knock against Ford's door, Stone answers.

"Cadence?" His broad brow creases in surprise.

From my call to Enya, I'd learned that Stone, Vale, and her son, Hudson, were in Chicago for the game.

"Would you believe passing by and saw the game?" I sheepishly ask, knowing the lie isn't believable in any way. I'd been in Nashville, frantically re-recording my first album.

Stone glances over my shoulder, noticing the man leaning against a black SUV, hands folded before his crotch. I partially turn before glancing back at Stone. "Don't mention it. Please."

Confusion crosses Stone's face then compassion forms in his rounder cheeks. He steps back allowing me entrance.

Ford's home is best described as narrow and tall. Like many city houses, one can practically reach out a side window and touch a neighbor's place. In Ford's case the three-story dwelling looked like any other home on the block with a steep climb to an elevated front porch, giving the home a raised effect.

From the entryway, I hear the chatter of the girls and a response from Vale.

"Where is he?" I whisper, not wanting to draw attention to myself.

Stone tips his head toward the stairs. "Last door on the right."

"Thank you," I mouth.

Slowly, I walk up the staircase, making quick note of the black and white photos lining the wall. On the second level, I find the door Stone had mentioned, softly knocking before turning the knob and entering without permission.

Ford sits on his bed, gingerly shifting, glancing down at his arm which rests in a canvas sling and propped up by pillows. He winces, the pain clearly etched in his sharp cheeks as he tries to adjust.

"Let me help you," I quickly offer, rushing around the bed as Ford's head snaps upward.

"Cadence?"

Once I'm at the side of the bed, I'm afraid to touch him, hovering my hands over his bent arm, uncertain how I could possibly assist him.

"Looks like you're in a pickle, cowboy."

"What are you doing here?" The question is harsher than it needs to be, but considering the pain he must be in, I dismiss the tone.

"What happened?" I'd love to sit on the edge of the mattress, cup his cheek and look him directly in the eye, but the way Ford is looking at me, jaw clenched, face tight, I hold my position, awkwardly standing beside his bed.

He huffs before tipping back his head and staring at the ceiling. "I don't even know." The lie is evident. Words were exchanged. He drew first. Or pointed in the face of his teammate, whom he considers the enemy. Romero reacted.

"How are you feeling?"

His head snaps forward again, eyes focused on a large screen television across the room playing another baseball game. "Like shit."

"Will you need surgery?"

Ford's head swings once more like the release of a ball. "What are you doing here?" he asks again with just as much irritation as the first time. "And why do you care?"

I step back as if the curveball he just tossed might hit me. "Whoa." I hold up both hands and narrow my eyes. "Why would you say that?"

"I—" He stops short, as if thinking better of explaining himself. Glancing back at the television, he picks up the remote and changes the channel like I'm not standing here waiting on his reply. "It was nice of you to stop by. I'm tired."

He's dismissing me? "What the fuck, Ford?"

I have his attention now. I don't need a prize because I dropped everything and flew here as fast as I could, but he could at least give me a little more than this brush off. "I know we haven't talked in a while but—"

"Yeah, I got the message loud and clear."

"What message?"

Ford huffs like I don't know what he's talking about *when I don't*.

"Your assistant told me you changed your number."

"I didn't change my phone number." I have several phones, but the one consistent number was the one for people I cared about most and roughly five people had that number, Ford being one of them.

He watches me, his mouth falling open slightly. His expression changes from argumentative to inquisitive to resignation. He looks away again as if the damn game on his television set was more important.

And I hate being ignored. "Ford—"

He continues to stare at the television.

"Is this because of what happened at spring training?" The gossip. The accusation. The implication that Ford and I were more than friends and he had cheated on Felicity with me when she'd been the adulterer.

"No." He doesn't blink.

Reaching over him, he hisses in my ear as I grab the remote from his right hand. Aiming the device at the television, I shut it off.

"I was watching that."

"And now you're *talking* to me."

Only Ford doesn't turn his head. His lips tight and pursed, he takes a deep breath through his nose. His chest heavily lifts and falls. The irritation coming off him could melt a weaker woman, but not me.

My gaze falls to his shoulder. *Shit.* "Did I hurt you?"

Ford closes his eyes a second but quickly reopens them and glares directly at me. "You shouldn't be here. I don't need you. And it isn't good for the girls."

"The girls?"

"I can't have another woman flit into and then out of their life."

"I . . . I am not *flitting*." I sling the word like it's a dirty rag. "I know I've been busy, but . . ." I'd put the ball in Ford's court. Or rather, I'd tossed it to him, and I was hoping he'd toss it back. I'd gone to Arizona, and we had a good night. I was hoping he'd call me next. But once again, I'd misinterpreted the signs.

Ford peers back at the blank television screen, our positions reflected in the black. I don't understand what's going on here, but the sling on his arm glares back at me.

The fight tumbles out of me.

I reach into my tote and pull something out, setting it on the bedside table. "Hope you have a quick recovery, Ford. Here's to watching out for you."

He doesn't even bother to look at the yellow rubber duck on his nightstand, a match to the one he'd given me.

When I'd left Ford's place back in Arizona, a note waited for me on his kitchen counter with a yellow rubber duck.

"Congratulations again on your new venture. It's a good luck duck. Here to watch out for you." He'd signed it with 'quack'. The gesture was silly and cute, and my romantic heart took the gesture to a higher level.

A foolish level.

When I hadn't heard from Ford, I accepted that we were both busy people. He had his career and the girls, with an ugly situation streaming in the background, and I'd been drowning in the directional shifts in my work. Still, I'd thought a friendship, if nothing else, had begun between us.

I'd been wrong. Again.

A sinking feeling in the pit of my stomach weighs me down. The desire to cry wells up. But I'd learned how to be stronger than this. *Never let 'em see they hurt you* was the most valuable lesson I learned from my former manager. Ford was physically hurting, and I wouldn't let him see he'd upset me.

I'd missed him. I'd missed the girls. But I wasn't taking this attitude from him.

Without a glance back, I hitch my bag higher on my arm and head for the door. Over my shoulder, I mutter, "Take care of you, cowboy."

+ + +

By the time I reach the bottom of the stairs, sneaking back out isn't the plan. I couldn't do that to the girls. Plus, I'd wanted to see them as much as I was worried about Ford. As for flitting through their lives . . . well, fuck Ford.

These three girls were new nieces to my sister, and by default, I was adopting them as my own.

Aunt Cadence was not a flitter.

Entering the kitchen at the back of the house, June is the first to look up, a smile forming around her thumb in her mouth which she promptly removes.

"Cay-Day."

Cay-Day. I had my own nickname with her. A little squeal went off inside me. "Hey, June Bug."

The three-year-old rushes for me and I bend to pick her up. With June on my hip, I tickle her belly and she sucks in the toddler pudge before wrapping her arms around my neck.

God, I needed this hug.

Setting June back on her feet I get additional hugs from Winnie and Zelle before looking up to find Vale watching me. The youngest sister of the Sylver siblings might appear quiet but beneath her is a storm of sisterly protection. She doesn't verbally question my appearance any more than Stone did. Instead, she hugs me in turn like the girls, but her language suggests she's still wondering why I'm here.

I've been asking myself the same thing for the past few minutes.

"What are we doing today?" I ask instead, looking from the girls to the smattering of ingredients on the counter.

"We're making cookies," Winnie proudly announces, returning quickly to the stool she was kneeling on to lean over the island counter.

Zelle holds up the bag of chocolate chips for further confirmation before dumping the entire bag into the mix.

"Stir it up, Zelle," Vale encourages.

"Mind if I watch." I don't want to get in the way, but I need a Sylver darlings' moment before I storm back to the airport and return to Nashville. No point in lingering in Chicago but I can spare a few minutes for these ladies I've been wanting to see for months.

Vale glances up and offers a warm smile. "Take a seat." She points to a vacant stool.

As Zelle struggles to blend the thick mixture and baking chips, I pepper the girls with questions.

How is being back in Chicago? How is school? Did Zelle learn to braid hair? Did Winnie learn to write my name? Something she had been practicing when I was in Arizona. When was June going to give up that thumb?

Good-naturedly, I tug at the slobbery, red digit and lean forward like I want a bite of it.

While Vale explains how the girls can scoop out the dough and plop it on the baking sheet, I turn to Stone who has been leaning against a counter, quietly observing the chaos.

"How's he really doing?"

Stone's casual position of crossed ankles and folded arms does nothing to lessen his concern as patriarch of his family. "He'd displaced his shoulder. Something that's happened before and it was an easy fix. But he officially tore his rotator cuff and he's been ignoring it. Today solidified that he'll need surgery."

"Surgery means recovery, though." Look for the positive.

"Four months at the least. Six months would be best."

I cringe. "Ford probably does not like the sound of that." With the season starting, he'd miss almost half of it, before he could return. *If* he can return.

"Probably not." Stone huffs but a smile curves his mouth.

The creak of the oven door opening, and the glide of a baking sheet draws my attention toward Vale, the girls watching raptly at the tray that will convert the blobs of dough into delicious treats.

"Sounds like a party down here."

Everyone glances at Ford standing with defeat weighing down his shoulders and his arm in the sling. With a ballcap backward on his head, he looks good. Too good. His voice is tight, though, gritting through the pain.

"Ford, you should be resting," Vale admonishes.

"I'm not an invalid," he counters sharply.

"Yeah, but sometimes, you're an idiot." Her eyes track to me and hold a second. Ford doesn't look at me, and that's my cue to leave.

"Well, my darlins', it's been fun, but Aunt Cay-Day needs to fly."

"No," Winnie whines.

"Why?" Zelle asks.

June struggles to lower from the stool she climbed up on, and Ford and I nearly collide as we each reach for her. With his bum arm, he shouldn't catch her.

"I got her," I mutter, helping the toddler to the ground.

Ford finally looks at me, right at me, his typically piercing blue eyes dull. "Or you could stay." There's no enthusiasm in the request. No apology for his behavior upstairs or genuine desire for me to remain.

Shaking my head, I turn away from him. I answer Zelle instead. "Must be flitting off." When what I want to do is flip off her father.

With a tight hug, I embrace each of the girls. "Enjoy your cookies."

"If you wait three more minutes you can take some with you," Vale suggests after twisting to glance at the timer on the oven.

I smile hard, the falseness almost cracking my jaw. Three more seconds in Ford's presence and I might implode. "Nah. More for you all to devour."

"When will we see you again?" Zelle asks as I reach for my bag. The room goes very quiet.

"I don't know, darlin'." I could explain how I'm busy with my production company and re-recording songs, but none of that is going to be worth a hill of beans to a little girl wanting to see me. "When does your summer break begin?"

The question buys me some time to think.

"June second," Zelle announces as if she's already counting the days.

"Me Wune," June states.

"Lucky you, girl. You have an entire month named after you." This makes June beam. Her little curls askew on her head. Those blue eyes looking at me. *Gah, my heart.*

"Okay, Zelle. Let's check our social calendars and maybe I can come see you in the summer." I hate to make a false promise, but Enya is their aunt and maybe there's some way to swindle a visit through her.

"I don't have a social calendar," Zelle counters.

Ford tightly laughs, reaching for her ponytail and curling it around his fist. "Dance lessons. Softball. School. Your calendar is full."

"Me want cawendar." June announces, thumb back in her mouth.

Ford groans, insinuating he's overwhelmed with Zelle's. Winnie probably has a calendar as well. He's outnumbered and I'd like to know more. Did he find a new nanny? How is he managing? Has he ever thought of me after Arizona?

Not until I'm back in the car does the most important question hit.

Why did Ford think I changed my number? *How* would he think that unless he did call me?

I shift in my seat, glancing out the rear-view window as if Ford might have rushed down the front porch stairs to answer my question.

Silly fantasy.

I twist toward the front seat when we turn left at the end of Ford's street.

The only man chasing me is the one I don't want.

Chapter 23

[Ford]

Surgery in mid-April meant four months recovery at best. Time ticked painfully slow. I'd been constantly irritable and, at times, irrational about how quickly my body should heal. And as much as I wanted to lay on my bed, down pain pills, and sleep away my days, I had three little girls counting on me.

Vale stayed in Chicago after that fateful game. She'd been a huge personal help, tending to me while Blake minded my girls.

By the end of May, though, Vale had missed a good portion of Hudson's baseball season and had put off her own physical therapy clients long enough. She needed to return to Sterling Falls.

"You should come home," she says only days before she is scheduled to leave.

"I can't."

"Can't? Or won't?"

Such a simple question left me puzzled.

There wasn't any real reason to stay in Chicago for the next few months. Ross Davis had come to visit me.

"You need a break. I'm putting you on the IL, indefinitely."

"You can't do that." My arm throbbed. My head ached. I couldn't be cut from the team.

"I can and I am. You need help here and here and here." He'd pointed to my chest, my shoulder, and my head. "You're in a fucked up position but it's fucking with the team."

Mental therapy sessions were mandated on top of my injury list status, since professional sports teams no longer took emotional health for granted. As Ross said, I'd need my heart, my arm, *and my head* in the game, and my head was still messed up when it came to Romero and Felicity.

With all that had happened, Romero had only gotten a three-week suspension for our fight. He started all of this bullshit. With Felicity. With me. But Ross had made up his mind. Between Romero and me, I was the loser.

Thankfully, my divorce was legitimized. I dropped the forgery charges when Felicity dropped her countersuit for extended alimony. Any alimony for that matter. She'd been given a considerable settlement upon the sale of our home last winter. With no contest from Felicity, I had full custody of the girls. One day, she might change her mind about that decision, and I'd leave it up to the girls whether they saw her or not, *if* Felicity requested a visit. For now, that concern was on the back burner. We were free and clear of one another, but my ex-wife was still Romero's girlfriend, and he was still my teammate and that made for one helluva an awkward hate-triangle.

"The girls have school," I remind Vale. I'd already taken Zelle and Winnie out of their school during spring training. Zelle had missed her friends and we'd made it back in time for a new softball season for her. Not that I'd get to see many of her games. The disappointment was a constant conflict.

With summer staring me in the face, I didn't have a plan, and suddenly I had the summer months off. Originally, I thought our au pair would handle everything with the girls and I'd do my thing as I'd always done, but I've also accepted I need to be more present for my girls. I *want* to be more available for them.

"The training center at the team's clubhouse is unparalleled," I continue, as if arguing only with myself. Where would I work out in Sterling Falls? "And my physical therapy sessions are with the team trainer."

"Really?" Vale lifts her head from where she's folding my T-shirts. I hate that she's doing my laundry because she doesn't want me lifting a basket of clothes. Her sarcastic question comes with a stern look, because, *hello*, she's a physical therapist, but I'm a shit patient, or so I'm told, and I don't want that kind of burden on her. However, watching Vale fold my shirts, I accept I can't do it alone. I can't manage the house and the girls without risking a wrong move and injuring myself all over again.

I'm going to need more support.

"But . . ." I sigh heavily. "Maybe we *could* use a change of scenery."

While the girls and I recently moved into this new place, I was getting tired of looking at the four walls of my bedroom. And one yellow rubber duck on my nightstand that I refused to let the girls have.

He was mine.

And I was an idiot.

When Cadence left my place in the beginning of April, I didn't have the mental bandwidth to process her sudden appearance. Her concern. I didn't understand the whole lose-this-number, she-didn't-change-her-number situation, and I didn't question it. I'd pushed her away because otherwise I'd have pulled her too close. I was lonely and frustrated. The team. My girls. My arm. If I couldn't play ball, I had too much time to think. And when I thought, the fantasies consisted of something that could only ever be one sided. My side.

Or so I'd thought.

Because Cadence came to me. Again. She'd taken care of me that drunken night. She flew to Arizona on opening day to support me. She'd changed her busy schedule in a blink when I was injured. And all I had done was sulk, rage, and hurt her.

The basic rules of baseball apply. Three strikes and you're out.

Now, I am riding the bench, dragging my feet in the dirt like a sullen player who struck out and lost his chance at a homerun—Cadence.

"How does June third sound, Vale?"

The day after the girls exit school, I'll be returning to Sterling Falls.

+ + +

The transition wasn't smooth. Vale had returned home as scheduled. Blake quit as my au pair, and I couldn't drive, so Judd flew to Chicago to drive us to Sterling Falls.

"Thanks for volunteering, man," I say, once the SUV is packed and we are loaded within it.

"I was volun-told."

Crap. "Sorry, man."

Judd shrugs and fires up the Escalade, then maneuvers out of the city. Once we've hit the highway, the girls drift off to sleep. Judd and I are relatively quiet after small talk about my arm and his accounting business.

But an hour in, he breaks the silence. "I'm thinking of asking Heather Remington to marry me."

Eek. Heather is one of those small-town beauty queens whose daddy is rich and mean. He runs Remington Autos, a series of car dealerships in the Milton Peak area, and he's successful because he's sneaky. A while back, Judd and Heather connected somehow, although I don't see the appeal from either side. Judd is too good of a guy for her.

"Why?" The question is sharper than it should be.

Judd purses his lips. "Not too many other prospects for me. Plus, she's rich and beautiful."

There is no way my brother is that shallow. "Money and looks shouldn't be the only thing to recommend her. What about love?"

No one in our family was convinced he loved her, or she loved him. Not that we didn't think Judd was lovable, but Heather didn't seem capable of understanding or appreciating our brother. His quiet reserve. The pain he'd suffered from our father. The deep loss he'd felt when our mother died.

Judd is quiet another second before saying, "I'm not certain love is really in the cards for me, and I'm tired of being alone."

"Is she good to you?"

The silence tells me everything and I don't like the empty sound. Judd deserves better.

Eventually, he clears his throat. "Speaking of beauty and cash, I heard you had a visitor."

Cadence. Even being some seven hours from my family, the gossip circulates. Judd's trying to flip the topic, but I'm flipping it right back.

"Judd, do not marry Heather if you don't love her. Without love, there just isn't anything." He must know love is the most important element of a marriage. He remembers it from our parents before Mom died and Dad turned into the monster he'd become. "Take it from me, if you don't have that, you don't have anything of value."

I'd been convinced I'd loved Felicity, but hindsight has opened my eyes. She was a major-leaguers wife, and a certain notoriety follows that status. I hadn't realized how much she valued the position until she moved on to Romero. Being the adulterous girlfriend doesn't quite have the same ring to it, though, neither does abandoning your children.

Judd is silent another second, letting my advice stew. With one hand on the steering wheel and the other elbow perched on the window, his thoughtful pose has me thinking our discussion is over.

"I'm not certain I know what love looks like," he quietly admits.

"Me neither." After my marriage and subsequent divorce, I did not trust myself to recognize love, but I had this weird inkling in my gut it came in the form of a yellow rubber duck.

And a woman pressing into my back in a motel room, and stealing my lucky cap.

A woman who surprised me at a baseball game, wearing a T-shirt with my name.

A woman flying to my bedside when I'm injured.

Weeks have passed since Cadence's soothing grapefruit scent invaded my senses. Months since we joked and laughed together. Time has moved slowly since I've felt something other than anger and loneliness, guilt and inadequacy. I missed her. God, did I miss her. She wasn't just another person flitting in and out of my life, like I had accused to her face. No, like a self-fulfilling prophecy, I had pushed her out, slammed and locked the door. Now, I was living one of her country songs, drowning in regret and longing for a second chance I didn't deserve.

Once we reach Sterling Falls and pull up before the rented house, the summer evening is just starting to fade. The two-story house just outside of the business district is a few blocks from Halle and Knox, though not nearly as big as their place. Violet is my backup sitter this summer and going to make a nice chunk of change for someone almost sixteen.

Nannies: 7. Number of months needing one: 8. I was a failure at keeping childcare.

Within minutes of Judd parking the car, Knox and Stone arrive to help unpack my SUV. I could have stayed in the big house, but my girls and I were going to need some space and time. Being here was just one of the changes coming their way.

With the final snick of the SUV doors, I stare at the house before me, with its two dormers and large covered front porch, and wonder how I ended up back here.

Home. The place that always felt so wrong, and now, might be very right for all of us.

Chapter 24

[Cadence]

"Ford?" I stare at him across Stone Sylver's backyard.

"Cadence?" Ford takes a step toward me and then stops.

In the movie *Grease*, Sandy and Danny reunite for the first time after a summer fling at the high school bonfire, and for about thirty seconds, they are both excited and relieved to see one another again. Then Danny looks over his shoulder at his friends and his demeanor shifts.

This is Ford and me. Only, I'm the one looking behind me at my sister.

Sundays are family day at the Sylver's home and on a beautiful June afternoon most of them are present for the weekly cookout. Enya invited me as I'd arrived unannounced last night. I needed somewhere to unwind, and Sterling Falls sang to me. Kind of like a whisper of home when you don't really have one. I came to the one place people might think I'd gone, and then decide, I couldn't possibly.

I've already explained to Enya that I don't need to stay at her home. She's still in the honeymoon phase months out from her actual wedding, and she informed me last night, she's pregnant with her second baby. I'm so excited for both Enya and Sebastian. Their amazing little family is growing. So, I don't want to intrude on their happy bubble, but I did want to be closer to my sister. She is the only person I consider *my* family.

Originally, the plan was to snag the apartment above Sebastian's bakery in town. I could be alone but still have the comfort of people below me in the busy business location. Plus, the interior entrance was an extra safety precaution, and the exterior one had a triple lock. I had no intention of imprisoning myself, but I needed a barricade between me and, well, everyone else.

Seeing Ford in Sterling Falls was not part of that plan.

"*Sister*," I hiss, quirking a brow. "Did you forget to tell me something?"

"I didn't realize this"—she nods toward Ford—"was something I had to disclose."

My sister knows I flew to Chicago on a whim when I learned Ford was hurt. Stone told her. She also knows I'd been in Arizona. The media informed her. But reading me herself, she'd guessed I have a huge crush on her brother-in-law, which concerns her. Her argument has two sides. She worries I can't commit to someone, and that I'd get hurt again.

What my sister didn't seem aware of was that beneath the songstress reputation was a woman desperate for a commitment like hers. One full of love and loyalty; support and sensual energy. I didn't crave sex as much as I wanted companionship. I'd avoided commitments in the past because I feared the pain falling in love could cause. But in the last year, my need for more outweighed being afraid.

"I didn't know you would be here," Ford says, interrupting the stare down between my sister and me.

Swinging back in his direction, I bite my tongue before snarking that if I'd known he'd be here I wouldn't have attended. This was *his* family.

"Who needs a drink?" Ford's brother Clay cheerfully interjects, clearly not missing the tension between Ford and me. He claps his brother hard on the shoulder.

"Ow," Ford snaps at his brother turning toward him. "Wrong shoulder."

Suddenly, my shoulders fall but the heaviness of concern hits. Enya kept me informed about Ford's surgery and recovery.

"Cadence!" Winnie yells and my focus shifts to the slam of the back door where Winnie is rushing toward me.

"Cadence?" Zelle's voice squeaks as she follows her sister.

A stumbling June presses through the door, catching it before it slams back on her and then pushes it hard again as if the wooden frame offended her. Once free of the door, she calls out my name. "Cay-Day."

That sense of home hits me so hard, tears well in my eyes, and I blink rapidly as I'm tackled around the thighs by Winnie and a hip hug is given by Zelle. When June finally toddles over to me, I'm a pile of Sylver girls. I can't look at Ford.

Finally, he clears his throat and attempts to pull June from my arms. "Let's give Cadence some space, yeah?"

I scoff. The last thing I want is space from these darlings, but I defer to their father as Winnie unwraps herself and Zelle steps back. I hand over June, whom Ford kisses on the cheek and sets back on the ground. He slips both hands into his back pocket, then winces and removes his left arm.

"How's the arm?" I ask at the same time he says, "How have you been?"

Weakly, I smile as he bites his lower lip. "I hate small talk."

"Me too."

That short conversation says it all. We don't need to do this. I'd made a mistake in going to see him. He set me straight on my error.

"Who wants a burger?" Stone calls out and a chorus of *I dos* follow.

"Any chance there's a hot dog with my name on it?" I tease Stone.

"Whatever you'd like, sweetheart."

Stone and I hit it off during Enya's wedding. The tough guy exterior is a front I recognize. He also happens to be the only one who knows about my current situation. I wasn't stupid. Well, at least, not all the time, and my bodyguard service insisted I inform the local sheriff department *in case* anything new develops. I didn't trust an entire department, so I called Stone myself.

Risking a glance at Ford, I notice him glaring at his eldest brother. His jaw clenches, the edge of his cheeks becoming more pronounced. His eyebrow quirks upward just the slightest bit.

If I didn't know better, I'd swear Ford thought something was going on between Stone and me, and Ford looks jealous. But that makes zero sense, and I swipe away the thought.

The next few minutes are a well-oiled machine of grilled meats served on a plate and a family digging into the bowls of chips and side dishes.

"When did you add the second picnic table?" Ford asks about the two bench-style tables butting up against each other, one looking newer than the other.

"When my family finally started trickling home."

Ford stills with the mustard in his hand, holding onto a hot dog in a bun with the other. He looks up at his brother who has already turned back to the grill. Ford sighs with guilt, then he returns to the mustard and dog, while I take a seat next to Zelle, wrapping my arm around her and tugging her into my side for another hug.

"How's my girl?" I whisper. "Learn to braid yet?"

She slowly shakes her head, picking up a potato chip. "Blake tried to teach me, but she didn't do it like you."

"Blake?" Something spikes my chest. Does Ford have a girlfriend? That certainly happened fast. I glance up to find him watching me.

"She was our au pair. *Not a nanny*," Zelle emphasizes the distinction. "She lived with us."

"Did she now?" I glance from Zelle to Ford who watches me.

The corner of his mouth curves and those blue eyes sparkle.

Instantly, I envision a bubbly, young girl sneaking into Ford's bedroom at night to administer her own form of nanny-naughtiness to the hot single dad. Give him her personal *touch*? Was she careful of his shoulder?

I see red, not the blue of his eyes still focused on me.

"She quit us," Zelle adds, suggesting something deeper than an employee leaving her employment.

Ford clears his throat. "We have Violet helping out this summer." He reaches across the table and holds out the hot dog he'd been slathering with mustard to me.

I don't really want a hot dog from Ford, but I won't be petty. Taking it from his hands, I hold the sandwich like I'd been offered Aladdin's golden lamp. The hot dog has my name on it, written in mustard.

I glance up at Ford but he's already turning toward Stone, holding open a second bun for another hot dog fresh off the grill.

"Are you staying here for the summer?" Zelle asks me, sitting straighter and lifting a burger that looks bigger than her mouth.

"I am," I announce a bit too cheerfully. I am excited about my visit but I'm also leery about my decision. I don't want to do anything to harm those I love but I want to be closer to them. Enya. Adara. Even Sebastian.

"Where are you staying?" Ford asks, his inflection raising.

"I'd hoped to stay above the bakery. But *somebody* rented out the place." I point two fingers at my eyes and then pivot them toward Sebastian. He simply shakes his head. Zelle chuckles beside me. "But I'll find someplace else."

"I told you, you could stay with us," Enya whines from beside her husband who isn't seated facing the table but with his side to it, his legs straddling his wife from his position on the bench. The look he gives her tells me, while the invitation is earnest, he'd prefer their privacy and I don't blame him. I also don't want to *hear* their love through the walls of their house.

"You could stay with us," Zelle innocently states. "We have an extra bedroom." She doesn't even look at me while picking up another chip. *Out of the mouths of babes.*

"That's not a bad idea," Stone adds.

"That's a terrible idea," Ford protests immediately, glaring at his brother with that pinched eye look I've come to simultaneously adore and dislike on Ford.

Hurt and disappointment flicker inside me as Ford didn't even take time to mull over the idea. He wasn't even pretending to be happy I was in town.

Stone glances at me. I wouldn't ever do anything to put Ford or the girls in danger, so I don't know why he'd suggest such a thing. Still, his gaze locks on me, holding firm.

Ford's eyes narrow, shifting his glare from his brother to me and back. His jaw ticks again.

I clear my throat, gaining Ford's attention and zeroing in on him. "Of course, I'd never want to stay anywhere I'm not welcome."

Ford flinches at my words. Those continually half-lidded eyes open wide for a second as if surprised by what I've said when he so adamantly dismissed the thought of me staying with him.

"You're welcome at our place." Enya affirms.

Sebastian grunts before adding, "Yeah. Our place."

Looking at them, I roll my eyes. "I cannot be at your place and listen to you two—" I glance at Zelle, reach up and cover her ears, and then mouth back at them, "Afternoon delight." I wink.

"Are you talking about sex?" Zelle says a little too loud because of my hands over her ears.

Ford turns bright red. Stone chuckles, and Sebastian chokes on a laugh.

"You could stay with me," Clay offers.

I've heard about this brother and his damsel in distress ways. However, I am not a damsel even if I am a little stressed lately.

Ford's head snaps in the direction of another brother. He glares again.

Boy, he really does not want me staying with his family.

"Thank you for the offer," I demurely reject. "But I'll figure something out."

Ford reaches over the table with a second hot dog in a bun aimed at me.

"I'm good." I wave off the offer as I already have the one on my plate that I hadn't been able to eat. I might take it home and pour liquid gold over it, placing it beside my prized awards.

Ford exaggerates bending his arm and forcing the hot dog back in my direction.

"Fine." I huff taking the bun and noticing a word once again written in mustard over the meat.

MINE.

My head snaps up and I stare at Ford, tilting my head as I wonder if I'm reading this right. It is written on a hot dog after all. And the stoic, calm expression on his face gives nothing away, but that jaw tick of his hints he's waiting on an answer. Maybe even holding his breath for one.

"Ford Sylver, are you asking me to move in with you?"

A chorus of strangled laughs and fisted coughs follow my question. The pink tips of Ford's ears give him away.

"Winnie, Cadence is coming to live with us," Zelle announces before Ford answers.

"Not live," Ford quietly corrects.

"Hurray!" Winnie cheers, wildly waving her arms in the air, almost whacking Knox, who sits beside her, in the face.

"Just stay," Ford continues.

"Stay in me woom." June mouths.

"Room," Ford corrects. "And no, Cadence can have her own room."

When our eyes lock, I bite my inner cheek, fighting the flirty question on the tip of my tongue. *Can we sneak into each other's rooms?* Instead, I glance at Stone who fights a smile and nods his head once, giving his approval of this plan.

Looking back at Ford, I say, "Okay. But I intend to earn my keep. I can help with the girls. And anything you need." Another sharp cough and a strangled laugh at the other end of the table has me amending myself. "With your arm."

Ford's face tightens but a simple nod seals the deal.

I'll be *staying* with Ford for a while.

$+ + +$

As I open the bathroom door, I'm met by a hand on my belly and gently pushed back into the small space. The door closes behind Ford with a snick.

"Well, this feels strangely déjà vu," I state.

His hand doesn't leave my stomach.

"Why'd you come see me in Chicago?" His body is coiled with tension, his features carefully blank but his eyes burn with need. Need for answers and something more. There's a slight tremor to his hand, and I cannot attribute it to a bum shoulder.

His question was not what I expected him to ask, and for a second, I couldn't think. Those eyes blazing. His body so close to mine, the nearness causing shivers along my arms. The leather and fresh grass scent of him plays havoc with my nerves.

"And hello to you, too, darlin'." I swallow hard, to calm my nerves. "It's been a while."

"Cadence," he growls, the bear coming to life.

"Why'd you immediately say staying with you was a bad idea?"

His jaw ticks again but his gaze lowers, looking slightly contrite. "Answer me first."

I sigh. "Because you were hurt," I remind him, fisting my hands at my sides so I don't pull him closer to me.

He shakes his head. "Why'd you really come?"

We glare at one another. His demand ratchets up my heart rate. I glance away from those prying eyes a second before flapping out my arms and looking directly at him, huffing. "Because I care about you, okay?"

The hand on my belly slips down to my hip and Ford steps closer to me. "Then why did you change your phone number?"

"I told you, I didn't change my number."

"I called you after you left Arizona. Someone answered and said the number would be changed, so lose it."

What? When did this happen? And why? And who didn't tell me Ford had called?

"And you never thought to call the number again?" I snap.

"I got the message the first time. I do what I'm told." Ford continues to stare at me, but his gaze drops to my mouth. "Outside, I panicked. I don't know what to do about you." The rugged waver in his voice and the nearness of his body suggests he has some ideas, though.

"Ask me nicely to live with you?" My own voice struggles, strong while raspy.

Ford leans closer, his face dipping toward my neck. On instinct, I tilt my head, allowing him access to my skin. His nose runs along the column of my throat, then curls around the shell of my ear.

"Cadence," he hums. "Will you come…"

I swallow hard, suddenly squeezing my thighs together.

"And *stay* a while with the girls and me?"

The disclaimer does nothing to settle my racing heart or calm the pulse suddenly flaring to life down low. Turning my head, my cheek rubs against his, his beard rough. My mouth finds his ear.

"Quack," I whisper.

Ford lets out a sharp laugh and pulls away, the moment shattered . . . as it should be. Because Ford Sylver was about to kiss me. Every atom in my body felt the connection, the pull, but I can't trust that Ford won't toss me out again. Not yet. He needs to prove himself to me.

"Is that a yes?"

With a shaky breath, I reply. "Yeah, cowboy."

And while everything in me says this might be a horrible idea, nothing has felt so right in months.

Chapter 25

[Ford]

Just like that I have a roommate.

Cadence was like an unpredicted blizzard during a spring game and every bit the lady boss I had expected. She had the girls registered for summer art camp and found a softball team Zelle could join despite having missed a month of the local season. She even had me on a workout regime, including physical therapy sessions with a person in Vale's healthcare group and video calls with the team shrink.

Whether Cadence did all this with the help of her assistant or on her own, I have no idea. I also don't know why Cadence is in Sterling Falls. I hadn't missed the eye-conversation between Cadence and Stone, and while I'd assumed there might be an attraction between them, the thought disappeared when Stone didn't invite Cadence to stay at the house. There was plenty of space in the old place.

However, I'd been pushed far enough when Clay spoke up, offering his home. No one was getting to keep Cadence in their house except me.

I care about you.

Not a declaration of love, but enough to help me better understand where I stood with her. She'd been right about the phone number. I should have tried to call again. I could have asked Sebastian about Cadence, but Sebastian and I weren't close like that. Simply put, I hadn't further investigated the issue.

The months I'd missed out on building a friendship with Cadence were my fault. And I wanted to be friends. Her quack when I intended to kiss her spoke volumes. Cadence didn't need the complication of my life in hers and I shouldn't want what I couldn't have—her.

However, lines blurred every day she lived with me. There were lingering looks between us, along with accidental and not-so-accidental touches. The sexual tension coiling around us had my libido wanting to steal third base and round for home plate. Most days, I was wound up, like waiting on the perfect pitch—afraid to swing too soon, anxious to let one rip.

But her presence was also a calming balm. The way she was with the girls. The casual ease she felt around us. Wide-legged pajama pants, appropriately covered in yellow ducks, never looked so adorable.

Laughter had never soothed my soul after a hard workout at PT like hers did.

Silence never felt so comfortable as when she sat on the opposite end of my couch each evening.

We circled one another each day, and I skirted the issue at hand. I wanted to be more than friends with her.

+ + +

Within days of living with me, Cadence seemed to understand me like no one else. She sensed I was restless, and it wasn't just the building tension between us. Seven weeks had passed since my surgery, and I was anxious to be more mobile.

"Field trip, my Sylver ducklings," she announces as she's serving breakfast to the girls. She'd warned me she wasn't much of a cook, but she could pour a mean bowl of cereal. I didn't need her to cook for us. I just enjoyed her presence, probably more than I should.

"Field trip?" Zelle perks up from her seat as the four ladies surround the breakfast table.

"Field trip? Field trips only happen during school, and it's summer," Winnie groans, like school is torture when she's only completed kindergarten.

"What field trip?" I ask, noticing a mug has been set out for me beside the coffee pot. Helping myself, I pour a cup.

"I want to see the legendary Sterling Falls." Cadence smiles at the girls before glancing up at me.

I lean against the countertop and stare back at her over the rim of my mug. I scoff. "Legendary?"

Cadence wiggles her brows. "I've heard there's mystery and murder, and love surrounding those waters."

"What's murder?" Winnie asks.

"When you kill someone," Zelle explains.

Both Cadence and I glance at Zelle. I shouldn't be surprised that my girl knows the meaning of the word but I'm still sad that she knows *the meaning of the word*. How am I going to protect my girls from the evils of this world?

"Well," Cadence clears her throat. "I'm more interested in the romance."

"What's romance?" Winnie asks next.

Cadence glances back at me and I twerk a brow. She started this conversation.

"Romance is when two people love each other." Her eyes drift to mine. "It's the feeling you get of excitement and wonder when you spend time together, or you do nice things for each other." Her gaze drops to the girls. "Like when Uncle Sebastian makes lemon cakes for Aunt Enya. He does it because he knows it'll make her smile and be happy."

"Daddy said you gave him a rubber duck." Winnie says. "It makes him smile when he looks at it. He says it's his lucky duck and watches over him. Is that romance?"

Cadence lowers her eyes, and for the first time, a pale shade of pink dusts her cheeks. For such a strong woman, who knocks out flirtatious quips like she has a 1.000 batting average, I've never seen her look so sweetly embarrassed. She's such a beautiful woman but even more beautiful with her acorn-colored hair in a messy bun on top of her head, no makeup on her face, and wearing pink pajama pants with bright yellow ducks on them. Even sexier is that she's in my kitchen, talking to my girls, and hinting with that soft flush on her cheeks that exchanging rubber bath toys might be romantic to her.

Before she can answer Winnie, Zelle speaks. "Henry gave me a Tootsie-Roll every day last year, but I never gave him any back." Zelle shrugs, nonchalant and uncaring that she didn't reciprocate the gesture. Curiously, I'm wondering why this is the first I've heard of anyone named Henry or the Tootsie-Roll treats. The eight-year-old has game, but Zelle is not having a boyfriend. *Ever.*

"Well, wasn't *he* romantic. That's definitely a gesture that says, I want to be more than friends." Cadence teases, placing an elbow on the table and cupping her chin. "How do we feel about Henry?"

"He's annoying." Zelle blushes as she speaks giving away how much she appreciated his daily gifts.

"Boys can be like that sometimes," Cadence glances back at me. "But when you're older you might find that behavior endearing."

I snort.

"What's endearing?" Winnie asks.

I cough, hoping to cut the vocabulary lesson short. "Let's get back to the field trip. It's a hike to the falls. To really experience the location, though, one needs to climb an unofficial trail up the boulders."

"But I've heard there's an easy walking trail. Nothing strenuous." She eyes my shoulder. "But enough to get us out of the house and moving." She lowers her arms to her sides and shimmies her body like she's strutting in her chair.

"Me walk," June mutters.

I glance at Cadence. "I can't carry her, and I don't think the trail allows for a stroller." It's been so long since I've been to the falls, I honestly don't know what the public trail might offer visitors.

Cadence shrugs and waves dismissively. "We'll figure it out when we get there."

And within an hour, we're headed on a family field trip.

+ + +

The public trail is part paved and part gravel, so we opt out of using the stroller and saunter at a slow pace for June. The day is gorgeous, with bright sunshine and dappled shade provided by the trees. The temperature threatens to be warm but the canopy of foliage over us keeps us cool. Cadence packed a picnic for after our walk. The slowed pace cannot be called a hike. And while I'd typically like to hoof it, I appreciate the lingering steps.

"This was a good idea," I admit.

"I've been known to have them on occasion." Cadence knocks her elbow into mine and I over-exaggerate a reaction, cupping my shoulder.

"Fu…dge." Her gaze shifts to the girls quickly before flitting back to me. "Did I hurt you?"

I huff. "Hardly." I straighten my arm and then bend my elbow again. Then I lift my arm as much as my shoulder will allow. "I'm not there yet but physical therapy is helping."

The sessions have been grueling, and my arm screams most days, reminding me it's still there but healing slowly. My fear is, I won't heal enough to return to the team.

As we walk, June toddles in front of us, attempting to keep up with Zelle and Winnie who are picking up their pace.

Cadence leans toward me. "Too bad you're on the mend. I would have looked good in a little nursing outfit."

She has played nursemaid in some ways, constantly asking if I need anything. Tucking extra pillows under my elbow while we sit on the couch. Fluffing the bed pillows in my room.

Walking beside me, she runs her hands down her sides like she's wearing an antique white uniform.

I laugh once, hard and deep. Visions of Cadence in a sexy little outfit, buttons undone at her breasts and a skirt exposing all that leg like the shorts she's wearing right now . . . I inhale deeply trying to wipe away the thought. She'd give a man a heart attack.

"If I hadn't been a musician, I would have been a nurse."

"Really?"

Cadence shrugs. "Probably not. I mean, I've thought about what else I might have done, but I think singing is in my blood. The stage. The lights." She waves her hands through the air for emphasis.

"I'm not really like that. The lights and shit." I quickly glance at my girls, hoping they are out of hearing range. "But I get what you mean. Playing baseball is in my blood. I don't know that I *could* do anything else." Which is another reason I need to get back to my team. I'm not ready to retire or quit.

"You and I are a lot alike, Ford Sylver. Fame runs in our bloodstream."

Glancing back at the girls, I watch as June stumbles, but Zelle stops and helps her little sister before I've even taken a faster step forward. I mull over what Cadence has said.

"I don't know that fame was ever on my roster but getting out of this town had been. I needed to get away from this place."

Cadence nods once. "I get that, too. Although sometimes I feel like I'm still running away."

With the amount of times I've seen her phone light up with notifications over the past few days she's stayed with me, I imagine disappearing can be difficult for her. Her fame is on a different level than mine.

"What were you running from?"

"Family."

I huff, relating to her on that. Although, the person I really wanted away from was my dad. Then I wanted Stone to be proud of me.

"Zelle is so good with June and Winnie," Cadence states as we both watch my girls, falling into a single file to allow people to pass them on the trail. As the other trailblazers draw closer to us, Cadence dips her head despite the oversize sunglasses and floppy sun hat she wears. I tug my baseball cap lower over my face as well.

Once they pass, Cadence adds, "Zelle reminds me of Enya."

"You and your sister seem close."

Cadence shrugs. "As close as we can be." Behind the frames of her sunglasses, wrinkles appear on the edge of her eye as she squints.

"Meaning?"

"As much as I love my sister, I also keep my distance." Cadence glances downward a second. "Sometimes, I feel like a failure around her."

"A failure? How are you a failure?" I scoff.

"I didn't do what my parents wanted." Cadence shrugs. "Enya did."

"Has anyone?" I counter.

"Your parents didn't want you to be a baseball player?"

"*I* wanted to be a baseball player." I emphasize by pointing at my chest. "And Stone. He believed in me."

Cadence softly smiles. "Enya believed in me, too. But I'm still a disappointment, at times. I'm not a great sister." She looks toward my girls again. "But I want to do better. Be better."

"If you haven't noticed, Sebastian and I aren't terribly close."

"Well, at least you have other siblings to choose from." Cadence lightly chuckles while teasing me. "But you should really work on repairing your relationship with Sebastian."

June has stopped walking, and Zelle and Winnie pause, turning back to make certain we are still behind them. Scooping up June, Cadence hitches her onto her hip and jiggles her up and down while tickling her belly.

"Sometimes, your siblings are all you have."

Don't I know it. "That's one reason I'm home." I'm slowly realizing family is much more important than fame or fortune. Family *is* home. "And why exactly are you here, superstar?"

I still don't know what Cadence is doing in Sterling Falls. She told the family she was here for a break. As the new lady-boss of a music-production conglomerate, I don't know how she can afford the time off, but I also don't know anything about the music industry. And I'd bet my current contract deal, there's more to her story than vacationing in our small mountain town.

"Still trying to figure that out myself," she laughs with her focus on June, her fingers spider walking up her belly once more.

I'd love to know what she means but Winnie announces, "I hear the water." She cups her hand around her ear.

June kicks her little legs to be set down and Cadence accommodates, then she follows my three-year-old with her own excitement building.

Meanwhile, I take my time to follow all of them, wondering what my temporary nurse slash nanny could still be running from.

And if she'd consider running *to* me instead.

Chapter 26

[Ford]

Days after our field trip, I'm running late from physical therapy to pick up Winnie and Zelle at art camp. A local art studio, appropriately named Art's Studio, was run by a friend of Knox, and hosted daily art sessions in the mornings for kids. Apparently, I'd missed a call from the studio, so I was not only late, I was also anxious there was an issue.

Within seconds of my arrival, I see Cadence seated in a chair beside Winnie, her hand on my daughter's curled back. Zelle stands nearby, head lowered. All three of them have their backs to me. My mouth pops open ready to demand what happened when Cadence speaks.

"We don't ruin someone else's artwork just because they said something mean to us."

Who hurt Winnie? What did he or she say? My step falters and I pause feet away from where Cadence glances up at Art, the owner of the studio, and an amputee in a wheelchair. Art's face is weathered skin, full of wrinkles, and he smiles encouragingly at Cadence.

"She said my project was ugly. Like me," Winnie explains.

What the fuck?

Cadence brushes back the loose hairs sticking out from Winnie's braids, the ones Cadence made this morning.

"First," Cadence begins. "You are beautiful no matter what that other girl said." She tenderly swipes down Winnie's nose and adds, "You're perfect."

My throat thickens at the affection Cadence gives to Winnie along with the encouraging words. Cadence is gentle and calm in this moment, which is completely opposite my ex-wife. Hell, even more opposite than my father. Cadence is patience personified with my girls.

She takes a deep breath, pausing the soothing stroking she's doing around Winnie's ear to clasp the back of Winnie's neck and make certain my daughter's attention is on her before she continues.

"You're beautiful on the outside and in here." Cadence taps Winnie's temple and then pokes at her heart. "And here. You're thoughtful and wonderful with a family who loves and supports you."

Cadence offers a reassuring smile but her forehead crinkles. Just the briefest waver before she continues. "Sometimes people who don't have what you have feel bad about themselves, and in turn want to hurt others to make them feel the same way. Which might be why the other girl called you and your painting ugly."

Cadence leans her forehead toward Winnie and continues in a compassionate but puzzled voice, like there's no explanation other than the truth for what she says next. "And other times people are just awful for the sake of being awful."

Winnie's eyes are downcast, but Cadence must gently squeeze Winnie's nape to regain her attention. Heck, Cadence has my full attention. I'm in awe of how she's handling this moment.

"When people are mean, it's okay to feel upset. You feel how you feel, but how you react towards that person determines the type of person *you* are." Cadence gently points at Winnie. "You be the bigger person."

"She was bigger than me," Winnie argues, sitting straighter in her chair, her legs swinging below it.

"You be the *better* person, then," Cadence corrects. "That means, you hold your beautiful head up high and smile despite what she said." Cadence imitates her suggestion.

"You'll stun her with your beauty and grace." Cadence swipes her hand along one of Winnie's braids.

"Kill them with kindness," Art adds, pumping his fist in the air.

"Daddy didn't smile when his teammate said something not nice to him."

What the fuck?! How does Winnie know what happened with Romero? Worse, how do I explain my reaction to her? I've been careful to explain my injury came from having a bad shoulder, but the girls had been present at that game. They saw Romero and I get in each other's face. They saw Romero take me down.

Cadence glances up at Art who offers an encouraging smile and nods before his watery eyes meet mine over Cadence's head.

Cadence wraps her hand around Winnie's braid, gently tugging so Winnie meets Cadence's gaze. "Your daddy is sorry you saw him get upset with a teammate. Sometimes, it's hard to hold our feelings back. But holding them back prevents us from being reactive. Ruining the other girl's project was reactive, Winnie. Your dad wouldn't want you to be that way. Think before you act. Take a deep breath. Did ruining her project make you feel better?" Cadence pauses for effect, letting Winnie consider an answer but before she speaks, Cadence continues, "I bet it didn't. I know you *are* better than that."

Cadence's reprimand is said with delicate honesty. I don't want Winnie thinking she can damage someone else's belongings because someone called her a name. I don't want someone calling my girl names, but Winnie needs to learn that those hurtful words, that mean person, isn't relative to who Winnie is. Strong. Beautiful. Resilient. Most of all, Winnie needs to know Cadence is right. She needs to be the better person in an altercation. It's a difficult lesson to teach a six-year-old, and I'll need to do better myself.

I'm worried once again I'll fail at fatherhood. But I'm also completely enthralled by Cadence. With my arms crossed, I bow my head a second, softly smiling to myself as the warmth of Cadence's tone envelops her message. She's pure magic, and it isn't just with the girls. Her compassion and empathy are a gift, along with her huge heart.

Glancing back up, my own heart swells with how she's focused on Winnie, softening the lesson but still imparting its importance. Cadence has become an integral part of our lives, and watching her play fondly with Winnie's braids, I feel myself falling deeper under the Cadence spell. A star that shines so bright, you just want to bask a little longer in the light.

Winnie shifts in her chair, finally noticing me. She presses off her seat, races around Cadence and rushes toward me. Squatting down to meet her level, I catch her in my arms. She immediately nuzzles her face into my neck, and soft tears dampen my skin.

"Hey baby. What happened?"

"I'm in trouble."

With me on my haunches and her on her feet between my bent knees, I shift her, so we make eye contact. "You aren't in trouble, Winnie. You're learning. And as long as you learn a lesson, there's no trouble. Understand?"

She nods, but I don't know if she does.

"I think you're beautiful. So does Cadence." I gently wiggle Winnie's body.

She plucks at the sweaty collar of my tee. Her eyes lowered to her fingers. "She told me."

"Well," I glance up at Cadence before looking back at Winnie. "We matter most. Along with Zelle and June. *We* love you."

Winnie's gaze drifts to Cadence, who has turned in her chair, hand poised on the back of it as she watches us. She nods once, her smile wide, encouraging me or reassuring Winnie, I'm not certain which, but I'm pleased either way.

I'm happy she's here and I don't want her to ever leave any of us.

"Can you show me your project?"

Winnie nods and runs back toward Cadence who apparently was holding the object. When Winnie brings it back to me, I hate to admit I'm not certain what it is. Something made with chicken wiring, an orange clothes pin on the front, and a bunch of yellow feathers stuck to it. Thankfully, Winnie explains.

"I wanted a lucky duck, too, Daddy. So I made myself one. It's romance, right? I'm giving it to me because I love me."

Fuck. My. Heart.

"Yeah, baby. It's romance. I love it, and I love you, too, Winnie."

With pride on her face, and a beautiful smile no one should ever insult, my girl beams.

And I catch the glint of tears in another beautiful set of eyes staring at both of us.

+ + +

That night, my body is tight, my mind a mess. Physical therapy earlier in the day was a bitch, and I'm sore but restless. My brain can't turn off the scene at the studio with Cadence soothing Winnie. Cadence getting to my girl before me and taking care of things. Cadence rushing in once more to help us.

My bedroom might be air-conditioned but the room feels stifling. I've been laying here for more than an hour and decide to refill the water glass I keep beside my bed and head for the kitchen.

"Cadence?" I whisper, finding the refrigerator open, and her body illuminated by the light within. She quickly shuts the door as if I'd caught her stealing my prized Kerry Wood autographed baseball.

"Couldn't sleep?" she asks. I could ask her the same thing.

"Thirsty," I admit, suddenly scanning her body from her toes to her head. Her hair is loose. Her tank top reveals she isn't wearing a bra. Her silky pajama shorts expose her long legs where her bare feet are highlighted with bright-purple polished toes. The color reminds me of the pen she used to autograph a napkin.

"You really like purple." Not the strangest thing to say, but something that feels awkward to mention in the darkness of the kitchen. Only a nightlight plugged in near the stove illuminates the space.

"It's my signature color." She lays the Southern drawl on thick and tosses her hair over her shoulder with flare. *Violet* was also the name of one of her albums. I might have done a little research on her.

"My mother's name was Violet." I swallow a lump in my throat. "And I have no idea why I just said that."

She slides away from the fridge, her hands gripping the edge of the countertop behind her. Her breasts lift, stealing my breath. Her head tips to the side. "Do I remind you of your mother?"

"I don't remember her."

"I'm sorry," Cadence whispers.

"Let's not small talk about family tonight, though." My mother isn't someone I want to discuss. Not with the way Cadence is looking at me as I lean into the center island with my backside. My position mirrors hers, as I hold onto the counter behind me.

Cadence bends forward a little and conspiratorially whispers. "Okay, cowboy, what should we discuss?"

After a moment of awkward silence, she speaks again. "Maybe we could discuss that attitude you gave me back in April when I came to see you in Chicago."

With my backside against the kitchen island, I scan her body again. The length of her legs. The subtle flare of her hips. The swell of her breasts. Why is she so tempting? Why do I want her so much?

When I don't say anything, Cadence speaks again. "Apologize to me."

That tone. That spark in her eyes. I drop to my knees at her feet.

A sharp gasp overshadows the hum of the fridge.

With my eyes on hers, I reach for the hem of her tank top and press it upward, exposing her stomach. However, I don't lower my gaze from her eyes.

"Cadence," I whisper, my voice rough. "Please forgive me." With my eyes still locked on hers, I lean forward and kiss her belly.

Another gasp escapes her, this one closer to a quiet moan.

Still holding her gaze, I lean back but quickly return to her stomach, pressing soft kisses along her waist. When her fingers gently comb through my hair and circle my ear, I hum.

"Ford." Her voice cracks, but her fingers return to my hair. The combing becomes more insistent.

"Tell me to stop and I will." I'll immediately pop back up to my feet and pretend I was never on my knees, wanting her to beg me for more.

"I can't." She swallows, eyes meeting mine. "I won't."

My lips open, sucking at her cool flesh. With my hands at her hips, I tug her lower body forward then pin her to the cabinet behind her. I kiss her stomach again and again, blazing a trail along her waistband before tucking my fingers into the hem of her shorts and giving a little tug.

When she doesn't protest, I pull harder at the material, easing it over her hips and giving me a peek at what I've dreamed she'd look like. *No underwear.*

Running my nose around her belly button, I lower her shorts to her ankles before dipping down to her coarse curls and inhaling her scent. Grapefruit, everywhere.

"I want a lick," I tell her.

Cadence spreads her legs a little wider. "Yes," she hisses, and I dive between her thighs, hitching one of her legs over my good shoulder.

"Your shoulder," she quips, gripping my hair and tipping back my head.

I care about you.

As she struggles to pull her leg away, I clap my hand on her outer thigh. "It's my other shoulder." Although I'm not feeling any pain in this position. In fact, I've never felt better and with my face between her thighs, I lick her long and soft.

Cadence's throaty groan has me glancing up to see her tilting back her head. Her eyes close. Her fingers smooth through my hair again.

"Watch me," I command.

Her head snaps forward, gaze dropping to me. With our eyes locked, I dip between her thighs again and swipe my tongue where she's soft and sweet. With Cadence's second moan, I hit the ball out of the park, and I'm off, outlining each fold and flicking her clit before sliding home, my tongue diving into her.

Cadence writhes above me. Her hips gently rocking as I rush to devour her. I slip my hand to her ass and squeeze, tugging her tighter to my face. With her leg over one shoulder and her backside trapped in my hands, she's open and wild on my tongue. Her breath hitches. My name is a soft cry. With a flick of my tongue on that sensitive nub, Cadence grips both my ears and releases a deep, long hum.

"Cow-*boy.*" Her legs slightly stiffen, and I memorize the motion, her sound, and the way she tastes. I'll never be the same.

With her strangled cry, my desire intensifies, and I broadly swipe over her folds once more, before dipping in for a second round.

"Ford?"

"I'm a perfectionist," I mutter to her sweet, wet pussy. "I want another one." I might even demand a third. Or a grand slam of four.

Slipping my hand forward, I use my fingers in tandem with my tongue on her clit. First one finger, then two enter her heat. "Take three."

Cadence whimpers while allowing me to slide three fingers deep, stretching her, filling her. God, I can only imagine what it'd be like to slide my fully hard cock inside her, but I can wait. I want her sounds and taste more.

Within seconds, Cadence is rocking against me again, her body flinching, her sighs a staggered catching of her breath.

I want this woman to fall apart while I'm on my knees. "Break, baby."

For the second time, she does.

Chapter 27

[Cadence]

Just when I think Ford is finished with me, he isn't. He breaks away from my thighs, slick and dripping with the combination of his mouth and my arousal and stands in a rush. Spinning me to face the countertop, I catch myself on the surface. Ford slides his hand around my throat while two fingers on his opposite hand delve back inside me.

"Ford," I cry out, then bite my lip, attempting to stifle the loudness.

"I told you I'm a perfectionist. Let's go for one more."

My legs tremble while Ford's fingers move in a new way, fast and smooth, slick from the wetness he created. Plus, his other hand collars my throat, and while I wasn't into breath play, the sheer possessiveness of his grip has my hips rocking once more. Then, I'm pinned to the countertop with Ford's weight against my back and his firm, stiff length easily distinguished through his thin sports shorts wedged against my ass.

I could make jokes about batting averages but I'm too Ford-dazed to think. He plays my body like a rapid-fire fiddle-rendition of "The Devil Went Down to Georgia." Suddenly, I know I'll sin in any manner Ford demands.

With the right pressure from the pad of his thumb on my already swollen and sensitive nub, a wayward screech escapes me. Ford's hand at my throat quickly coasts up to my mouth, covering it, and I clamp my own hand over his to drown out any other sound that might wake the girls. His rough breaths saw in and out at my ear, stirring my hair. Strained whispers from him urge me on, his words low and filthy as my body slides into another release.

Silver speckles dance before my eyes. I've never come three times in a row.

As I'm floating down from the high, Ford removes his fingers and grips my hips, tugging so I bend in half. With my hands clutching the edge of the counter, Ford grinds against my ass. The thick bulge in his shorts is not disguised in the least. With thoughts of what he'd feel like inside me, filling me, my pussy continues to tingle. Wetness coats my inner thighs.

"Cadence," Ford grunts, digging his fingers deeper into my hips, moving my body how he wishes.

"Just think of what it'd be like to enter me, cowboy," I tease, wanting him to lose control. Wanting to set him free. Just a dip of his shorts and that sweet cock of his would be loose and slam into me.

"Fuck," he groans.

"I'm so wet, Ford," I continue, drawing out the torture, drawing him deeper under the spell of possibility. I could sleep with Ford Sylver and not think twice about it.

But something tells me Ford isn't going to take this moment further than getting off by grinding against me like a randy teen, and with one final thrust, he stills, tugging my hips hard, wedging himself deeper against my bare ass cheeks.

A heavy groan exits Ford, the sound tickles my ear.

Within seconds, his hands release my hips, and his arms wrap around me like the tying of a ribbon. One arm circles my waist. The other wraps over my collarbone. I'm pulled upright and plastered to Ford's chest. His heart hammers against my spine. His breath heats my neck. After the race of lust, Ford surprises me with the softest kiss on my shoulder.

And something inside me breaks in a new way.

Ford eventually drops his arms and lowers behind me. With my hands returned to the counter, I hold steady as Ford helps me step into my pajama shorts and then turns me to face him. He rights a strap that slipped down my shoulder, then rubs both his hands from my shoulders to my wrists, circling them a second. His gaze dips to where his hands hold mine. Dropping one, he starts walking backward, leading me toward the hallway.

"Whatcha doin', cowboy?" I tease, thinking he's ready for round two when I'm still recovering from round one. If he's looking for a doubleheader, I'm going to need a minute.

"I want to hold you."

I stop moving and tug at the hand he's holding. Our eyes meet and while the sharpness in his is brighter than I've ever seen, I'm certain mine tell the truth. "I can't."

Other than rubbing his thumb over the back of my hand, as if attempting to soothe the wild cat inside me, Ford stills. His touch is comforting, reassuring, but I can't cradle. I don't want to cuddle. The idea is too intimate, and I can't do intimate again.

"Why not?"

"Ford," I groan. "Neither of us is in a position for what cuddling means."

"And what does cuddling mean?" The brightness in his eyes dims. He isn't proposing marriage, and I should just drop this, but I'm not getting myself into a sticky situation again. Nor am I willing to put this precious family in one. I won't put Ford in danger. Or the girls. And I'm not going to allow myself to think something is more than it is. The old Cadence returns.

"Cuddling means commitment."

Ford releases my hand, and while I expect him to stagger backward, he stands firm.

"I'm not looking for commitment, Cadence."

"Neither am I," I state, finding I'm the unsteady one. Why can't he commit to me? Why hasn't any man been able to?

Ford watches me a long minute. "Then what was that?" He nods toward the kitchen.

"Fun?" The word tastes bitter on my tongue.

Ford continues to stare at me before swiping his hand down his face. He lifts his hand again, fingers to his nose. "I can still smell you." He sucks the tips. "Taste you. And you want to call that *fun*?" He breathes deeply. "That was fucking amazing. And while I'm not certain about many things, I have no uncertainty about how I feel when it comes to you. I want you."

We continue to stare at one another, my heart hammering in my chest and between my thighs. I want him, too, but I won't admit it. I can't. Despite my reputation, my heart can't take another breakup, and neither can his.

"Ford, we're going to go our separate ways in a few months and this,"—I point between us—"isn't smart. You have the girls and baseball. And I have my music and—" *And what?* It's not like I have someone waiting on me when I return to my career. I'm a one-woman show in that aspect, but I also have people relying on me to come back, to hit the studio, and to produce more songs.

"It just wouldn't be a good idea."

Ford continues to watch me and just when I think he'll turn and leave me standing in the hallway alone, he steps forward, wraps his arms around me once more, sliding one around my shoulder blades and the other against my lower back. Pressed into his chest, I inhale deeply. Leather. Fresh grass. And a twinge of manliness.

Ford kisses the top of my head, then steps back. "Let me walk you to your room." He holds out a hand and I slap mine against his, but he catches my fingers before I can pull away.

And I briefly wonder if Ford could catch me in other ways.

+ + +

Where are you?
You can't hide forever.
Are you with him?

The texts are never ending, and most days, I turn off my phone to avoid them. There doesn't seem to be anything I can do to stop the cyber-harassment; other than change my phone number which I am refusing to do because hope doesn't die easily within me. *Why should I hide?* I want Evan to just stop it. Neither of us needs the scandal of a public broadcast that we'd had an affair.

For now, Sterling Falls is my safe haven.

Zelle, Winnie, and June are an excellent distraction. Our hike the other day had been amazing. Ford is a great dad, although a bit standoffish at times. I suspect he's barely keeping his head above water between his recovery and his girls. I don't push for information about his ex. The girls never receive a card, gift, or phone call from their mother. As far as I can tell, she is completely out of the picture.

While I want to pretend nothing had happened between Ford and me in his kitchen, he has made it impossible to forget. He doesn't bring it up, but he doesn't keep his distance. Little touches against my lower back, a swipe across my hand, or a fingertip along my wrist drives me crazy whenever we are close to one another. The weirder part is how often we are near each other. In the kitchen as I set out dishes for dinner. In the bathroom tag-teaming with the girls. In the family room on the couch.

Ford and I are like magnets, drawn to one another despite my declaration that we are a bad idea.

And if I thought I could keep away from him, I was crazy.

"What are you doing?" Ford whispers as I enter his bedroom a week after our kitchen escapade. With my back plastered to the door, I stare at him as he sits on his bed, arm elevated on a pillow with an ice pack over his shoulder. His back rests against the headboard.

I didn't know what I was doing. I only knew I couldn't stay away any longer. "Sneaking into your room?"

Ford humorlessly chuckles before his expression tightens and his jaw ticks. "Thought you said we were a bad idea."

"Maybe not bad. Just not smart." I was trying to be logical, but logic had gone out the window. I'd seen Ford too often with a towel wrapped around his waist after a shower or shirtless and working his arm. His body is a lean, mean machine and I want to know how it works with mine.

"So, you being in my room is . . ."

"Reckless." My gaze drops to something bright and yellow and sitting on his nightstand. Stepping forward without thinking, I point. "You kept it."

Ford glances at the rubber duck with a baseball cap on its head beside his bed. "It's my good luck duck."

I laugh. "I thought you'd toss it, considering you weren't happy to see me."

"I wasn't happy to see anyone." Ford exhales and hitches up his arm. "Fucking Romero." Ford told me how Romero has returned to the team but not without some hatred from the fans. "But you aren't in my bedroom to discuss Romero, right?"

"Wouldn't dream of talking about him," I tease.

"So what do you dream about?"

I've never been one who had difficulty expressing what I want sexually but for some reason I can't seem to explain myself to Ford.

"You don't want me to touch you," Ford begins.

"I never said—"

"Then touch yourself and let me watch."

Surprised, I stare at him a second, hands forming anxious fists at my sides. "You want me to put on a show for you?"

Ford lifts his good arm and crosses it behind his head. A mischievous grin curls his mouth. "Yep."

"You want me to strip," I flirt, grabbing one shoulder of my tank top and sliding it down my arm.

"Whatever you want, baby."

After reaching for the other strap, I dramatically drag it off my shoulder and tip my head coquettishly. "Whatever I want?"

Ford slowly nods to answer my question. His eyes follow the way I trace my finger over the swell of my breast peeking over my tank top then draw around the curve of the other one. My breasts are still covered but my nipples are clearly outlined, sharp and erect, and pointing through my thin shirt.

"I'll give you a show, but you can't touch yourself. Not yet." I want Ford to myself but first I want him so turned on he can't think.

While Ford doesn't verbally agree, his chest rises and falls once, a calming move while his gaze zigzags over my body. And Ford is looking at me like I lift the sun and sprinkle the night sky with stars.

Slowly, I turn around, giving him my back but looking at him over my shoulder. I tease my shoulder strap up and down before leaving it lowered. Spinning to face him, a sensual song comes to mind, something I'd been working on. I seductively move, swinging my hips side to side before arching my back, emphasizing my breasts. Crossing my hands over my chest, I drag them down incrementally. My palms caressing over my aching swells, catching on hard nipples. Cupping my tits, I pinch the stiff nips a second, before coasting down my belly to the apex of my legs. While I'm lost in my head, I risk a glance at Ford. His hand has dropped to his stomach, his palm flat on his hard abs. I give him a warning glare.

"Tell me, cowboy. Do you touch yourself and think about me?"

With my hands between my legs, I spread my thighs and lean forward, giving Ford a peep show of my breasts. Standing upright, I watch him as he slowly shakes his head.

He hasn't jacked off to visions of me? The thought nearly stops my performance.

"Figured the real thing would be better." His voice is strained. He swallows hard.

I step toward the bed and climb on it, straddling the lower portion of his legs. On my knees, I run my hands across my belly once more and between my thighs again. Slowly, I stroke over myself, pajama shorts saturated, folds swollen against the fabric. Turning my head to the side, I raise one arm to hold up my hair while the other hand rubs circles against my clit.

Ford leans forward, reaching out for me but I arch in a way he can't touch me. "Uh-uh-uh. You wanted a show, mister."

Ford bites the side of his fist and sits back. The ice pack on his shoulder falls to the bed. "I want to see you."

I tug the material to the side.

"No panties?" He groans. I hadn't had any on the other night either.

"No panties," I repeat, and the loose material of my shorts easily slips to the side, allowing Ford a view of what I'm doing to myself.

Ford spreads his lower legs, forcing my legs wider apart until I collapse backward. Seated on my backside, I lift my knees, my ankles on either side of Ford's shins. My center is exposed and on perfect display for him.

"I can smell you from here."

The statement shouldn't be sexy. "And what do I smell like?"

"You belong with me."

"Cowboy." My breath hitches but I tell myself it's only because I force a finger inward and then drag it back out, using the moisture to continue working myself. With Ford watching me, I'm lost in my head. His mouth on me. His fingers touching me. His tongue doing that thing and—

The release hits me hard and I drop my head back as my fingers still. The pulsing continues, though, and eventually, I clap my thighs together, riding out the wave.

Ford's hand cups my ankle and slowly my eyes open to meet his. With a heavy breath, I ask, "So you never touched yourself thinking of me?"

"Didn't want to disrespect you."

I stare at him, not understanding.

"Figured lots of people whack off to a superstar. I was hoping the superstar would give me a private show instead." He nods at my body.

I flip to my knees again, balancing on all fours over his legs. "And what if the superstar wants to take care of you?" I reach for the waistband of his shorts.

"Don't tease me, princess."

"Princess, huh? What happened to songbird?"

"You're more like a siren, those mystical creatures causing sailors to leap into the sea. You're going to be the death of me." Staring at my hands on his waistband, he's breathy, anxious maybe, desperate for me to follow through and please him.

I chuckle, scooting forward so I can tug his shorts to his hips, releasing what I didn't get to see the other night. Ford is long and thick, and my mouth waters as I stare at the tip, seeping with desire. Curling my hand around his cock, I lower for the tip. When I swirl my tongue around the crown, Ford hisses. His breaths become more ragged, like he's trying to control himself. His hand comes to my hair, brushing it back before curling it around his fist.

"Been a long time. I'm afraid I'm not going to last."

How long? I don't ask. I only want Ford to remember me and our time together, so I open wide and draw him to the back of my throat.

"Oh, fuck." His abs flinch. His other hand comes to my head.

Then, I'm working Ford like a candy stick, sucking and licking, and dragging him deep. My eyes water. Ford is bigger than I anticipated but I'm not a quitter. I draw him in until his hips are moving and he's hissing apologies, but I take him until *he* can't take anymore.

"Gonna come, baby."

Three words, and he spills in my throat. I swallow him down until he's releasing my hair. With a kiss to the tip of his dick, I release him.

Ford is pinching his eyelids when I glance at him. "You okay, cowboy?"

When he pulls his fingers back, I've never seen anything like the flames in his eyes. He starts scooting his body lower, sliding beneath me.

"What are you doing?"

"Fuck no touching. Get on my face."

"Ford," I gasp but he wedges himself below me.

"We aren't stopping until you've hit second base and cross third."

I giggle until I feel Ford's finger press aside my silky shorts and his tongue unleashes on me once more. And this center fielder gets his homerun as I come two more times.

Chapter 28

[Cadence]

"We're going out," Ford eagerly announces one night after a week of sneaking into his room. Days with him and his daughters are heavenly. Most of our time is spent orbiting the girls and their activities, plus Ford's therapy sessions and my occasional break to put lyric thoughts to paper.

The nights of touching and discovering one another have been out of this world.

"I'll get the girls ready," I tell him. I've enjoyed every second of braiding the girls' hair in the mornings or making ponytails with extra flare like little twists along their hairlines. I've loved hanging out to play games or giggling at their antics. Bath time. Bedtime. I've fallen into their routines, and it's been a welcome reprieve for me.

"No, just us."

I'd been peeling an apple because June doesn't like the skin on her slices, and I pause, knife in hand, to look up at Ford.

"Ford Sylver, you asking me out on a date?"

"Would you say yes if I did?" His smiles have softened over the weeks I've been here. His eyes still piercing but lighter, playful, warm.

"Quack," I tease.

He chuckles as he approaches me in his kitchen. A shiver runs up my spine every time I think about our first night together, right here near the sink.

"Get dressed. Something fun for you. Something that makes you feel good."

My mouth falls open ready to tell him I feel good in all my clothing but the heat in his eyes stops me. He's telling me to make myself feel sexy. Not so much for him but for me. And he's taking me out.

For a moment, I hesitate. "We might get recognized somewhere public." I've enjoyed our private little bubble here in Sterling Falls where we stick mainly to his house or the homes of his family. The general public doesn't seem to bother us, more star-struck by Ford's return than caring so much about me.

"I've got it covered." He brushes loose hair back over my ear, tickling the backs of his knuckles along my neck. These kinds of touches happen constantly despite our agreement to keep whatever we're doing separate from the girls.

I don't know how I'll leave them when it's finally safe to return to Nashville.

"Where are we going?"

The corner of Ford's mouth crooks upward and he lightly swats at my ass. "It's a surprise. Be ready by seven. Cowgirl hat required."

Now I'm extra intrigued.

After we feed the girls dinner, Violet arrives to babysit, and Ford and I leave.

We travel along mountain roads vibrantly lined in shades of green. A golden cast covering everything as the sun slowly begins its exit on another day. Another day pretending this life, Ford's life, is one I could live every day.

With the window down, I wave my hand through the wind. I'm wearing a lightweight summer dress with my purple swirled cowboy boots and a light brown cowboy hat. I feel flirty and giddy with Ford driving his Cadillac SUV, wearing faded jeans and another of the million worn cotton tees he owns. He's wearing a baseball cap on his head like he often does. He earns bonus points the nights he wears one backwards in bed with me.

I smile at the images popping through my head and Ford's eyes shift, catching me. "What?"

I don't answer him, just watch him drive. His masculine forearm on display. Wrist dangling against the steering wheel. His profile rugged. The tips of his ears turn pink.

"You're so beautiful, Ford."

He risks a quick glance at me, his eyes wide.

"I mean it. Not just your physique." However, there is that. "But the way you love your girls. Fatherhood becomes you."

"I'm trying," he says, his voice tight, panic momentarily etched into his expression.

"That's all any kid can ask."

Ford clears his throat. "How about we don't discuss the girls tonight. No heavy stuff. Just us this evening." He reaches across the seat to take my hand and brings it to his lips.

"Just us," I whisper, wistfully.

When Ford finally pulls off the mountain road, his SUV jiggles and jostles over rutted terrain before he parks amid a ton of other vehicles.

"Where are we?" I ask, eager to be surprised while still curious.

"You'll see." Ford pops open his door and hurries around the truck to help me out. Holding my hand, he leads me to the back of the SUV and pulls out a blanket and a cooler bag. Tossing the blanket over his shoulder, he carries the pack while never releasing my hand. As we walk over the choppy, grassy field mowed down by the number of cars that have driven over the space, Ford leads us to some sort of entrance.

A man wearing a red flannel opened to expose his bare chest greets us.

"Two," Ford says, handing over a hundred-dollar bill.

"Hey, Ford. Rough season," the man says.

Ford only chuckles. "Don't I know it."

When the man looks at me, he does a double take before his eyes narrow. "Are you—"

"Caitlin Calloway." Ford drops my hand and wraps his arm around me, tucking me into his side. "This is Caitlin Calloway," he states again, cutting off the man's inquiry.

"You look kind of like—"

"Caitlin Calloway," Ford says again. "Don't be flirting with my girl, Perry."

With my hand pressed against Ford's chest, I peer up at him. *His girl.*

He's also calling me Caitlin. He's protecting me from recognition. He's downright demanding I'm me. My smile grows wider, and I turn back toward this Perry guy, giving him a wink. "Yeah, Perry. Don't flirt with me in front of my man."

Perry incoherently stutters a second before waving us forward through the makeshift entrance. I flutter my fingers at the poor, confused guy as Ford leads us on and I hear music flare to life.

As we reach the top of a grassy knoll, our destination becomes clearer. The slight incline of the landscape forms a natural amphitheater filled with tons of people. Most are seated on blankets along the dip, while those closer to a stage stand.

"Is this a concert?" My question has an obvious answer from the guy breaking into song, strumming his guitar while his band plays behind him.

"I don't have any idea if this guy is good. Or if the later band is either, but you said you never get to go to concerts as a fan and missed it."

With my mouth agape, I turn toward Ford. "You brought me to a concert." My throat is scratchy. My eyes prickly with happy tears. "This is so . . ." Thoughtful. Romantic. Special.

However, I don't say any of those things. I tip up on my toes, cup his jaw, and bring his mouth to mine kissing him here where we're blocking others from entering the area and making a public scene. The kiss quickly heats. Ford drops the cooler bag, whips the bill of his baseball cap backward and cups my face in return, taking our lips meeting to tongues swirling until I'm leaning into Ford's strength and holding my hat on the back of my head with my hand.

"Let's find a seat," he breathlessly says after pulling away from me too quickly. He grabs my hand again and keeps us at the top of the knoll, leading us toward a stand of trees near stage right. Fewer people sit this high up. Darkness creeps in faster under the shadow of the trees.

Ford stops a safe distance from both the woods and others, spreading out a blanket and tugging me downward. He opens the cooler while I ask, "What is this place?"

"Perry's Field. Every June they host a music festival. Most people are local talent, but sometimes he has bigger names, up and coming groups. I don't know who this is." Ford nods toward the stage. "But later tonight is some guy named Tennessee Hampton."

I pull my gaze away from the stage and blink at Ford. "I've heard of him. He has a song on country radio." And I'm betting he'll have more in the future.

"So he's good?" Ford questions, giving away how little he knows about country music.

Leaning toward him, I bop his nose. "*You* did good, cowboy." He's so sweet and I can't seem to stop touching him. Or kissing him. I steal another one and be quick to draw away. Only Ford catches the back of my neck and brings my mouth to his again. The kiss is slow but no less heated than only moments ago. He takes his time to tug at my lips and suck at my tongue before releasing me.

"I'm promising myself to *be* good, tonight."

"Now, where is the fun it that?" I tease. Ford and I haven't had sex, but we'd done so much else and I'm never disappointed. Our nightly hijinks are more than the act of two people coming together. We're learning what the other likes. We're finding new things to do to one another. The experience has been unlike any I've ever had, and I'm thinking that's because I have real feelings for this man. Lasting feelings that scare and thrill me at the same time.

He isn't Evan. He is just Ford.

We smile at one another with my flirty question before Ford snaps off the cap on a beer and hands it to me. On this warm summer evening, we tap the long necks together and drink. And listen to music echo over the mountains in a little basket of space.

I'm certain I've never been happier.

As the first act finishes, I mention needing a bathroom and Ford leads me to the portable kind set up in long rows. Keeping his arms around me, my back tight to his chest, he rests his chin on my shoulder, knocking into my hat on occasion.

"Hmm. Didn't consider the hat," he mutters against my skin, pressing soft kisses there.

With my hand on my head, holding my hat in place, I smile and shiver. "That tickles."

"I know something else that would tickle." With a slight tilt to his hips, I feel what he means.

"Don't tease me, cowboy."

The line moves, and Ford walks me forward as if we are attached.

"You're the one teasing me tonight, songbird. With this dress." He hums at my neck again. "And those boots." The hum turns to a low groan.

The distinct sound of a plastic portable potty door opening signals I'm up next, and I giggle as I shimmy out from underneath Ford's arms. "Be right back."

I'm still giggling as I do my business and praise the heavenly beings that there is toilet paper and hand sanitizer in the stall. Stepping back out into the now dark night, I quickly find Ford still waiting on me. He takes my hand again and leads me back toward our blanket. Only we hardly stop as he whips off my cowboy hat and sets it down on the cooler bag then guides us beneath the nearby trees.

Seems a few other people have the same idea as Ford, and these are the moments I miss about music fests. The stolen moments on the edge of everything—potentially getting caught while getting frisky.

Ford backs me up against a tree and props his good arm over my head. With my back against the bark and my hands behind me, I tip up my face and meet his eyes.

"You're so beautiful, Caitlin."

Caitlin. Not Cadence. Not the superstar. Just a woman wanting to love a man. *Could this be real?* My throat thickens at the possibility. Words clog my airway.

Then he's kissing me.

I remain with my hands pressed behind my back a second, just melting into the way Ford's mouth commands mine. His tongue demanding. His lips sweet. But after seconds, I cannot resist touching him, and I fold my arms over his shoulders.

Ford leans forward, the length of his body meeting mine as the kiss turns more desperate, hungry even. His hand tugs up the side of my dress and he hums against my mouth. "This dress."

The lightweight fabric slowly collects over his hand as he dips it beneath the material, running his large palm along my outer thigh. His skin is hot against mine and a rapid pulse ratchets up between my thighs, but Ford's hand doesn't wander there. Instead, he curls around to my backside and breaks our kiss before pressing his forehead lightly against mine.

"So fucking sexy," he murmurs, kneading the hint of my ass that has escaped the high cut panty. He runs his fingertips along the swell where my butt meets my leg, then firmly cups me a second, tugging me tighter against his body. "I want to be inside you."

"Yes," I whisper, but I somehow know Ford isn't going to take me against a thick tree trunk just feet from other couples making out and doing other things. I'm not opposed to such an idea, but Ford won't do it. Not yet. Not here.

His mouth is on mine again, hot and heavy, and I fist my hands in his tee, holding him against me as I tilt my hips forward, nudging the hard bulge in his jeans. Ford grinds back as our mouths grow more impatient. His fingers tighten against my ass beneath the skirt of my dress.

And as we make out beneath the dark sky, sheltered underneath trees, I feel myself on the edge of everything in a new way.

I'm in love with Ford Sylver.

The first chord of the headlining band strikes up and Ford pulls back, looking up over his shoulder as if he forgot for a second where we are. I chuckle and drop my head to his chest, and he presses a kiss to my hair.

"Concert's starting." His voice is rough. His palm is still on my backside but holding me more than kneading my flesh.

"I hear that." Stating the obvious, I lift my head and meet Ford's eyes which are illuminated in the sudden brightness of stage lights beaming outward, reaching this dark corner.

Ford kisses the tip of my nose. Then one eye lid before the other. "Let's go listen to the music."

I nod, but I already have a soundtrack playing in my head. One that includes Ford, and his girls, and a life I never thought I'd have, complete with worldwide success *and* stolen moments.

Taking both my hands, Ford lifts them and presses a lingering kiss to my knuckles. "Thank you," he whispers.

Something inside me cracks, and my voice matches the splintering. "For what, darlin'?"

"Just being here with me. With the girls." He looks up at me as he lowers my hands.

"Thank you for letting me crash your party." He'll never know how much it means to me that I was able to escape to this small town and have the good fortune to end up being his roommate.

My good luck duck has been watching out for me.

Ford nods, then slips an arm around my shoulders and leads us back to our blanket. Although Tennessee Hampton's music isn't romantic ballads, more gravelly tomes about heartbreak, Ford wraps an arm over my collarbone, and places the other around my belly, pulling my back to his chest, and we sway to the sound like we're at a private concert.

One where only two hearts sing the refrain, thumping in time to the pulsing beat.

Love. Love. Love.

Chapter 29

[Ford]

When Cadence and I return from the concert, I walk her to her bedroom door and stand outside it, pressing her into the frame while I kiss her goodnight. I want her to invite me in. I want to take her to my room. Most of all, I want her to spend the entire night with me. Because in spite of all the touches and kisses, strokes and licks, one thing remains constant—Cadence does not stay in my bed through the night. Her excuse has been her concern the girls might need me during the night or wander into my room in the early morning hours. She doesn't want to confuse them. Instead, she's confusing me.

Feelings are getting in the way. I hadn't realized how attention starved I'd been, and not for the cheers of a fan-filled stadium, but the one-on-one kind. The kind where a woman craves a man, that man being me. I didn't want to lose Cadence, but I didn't know how to keep her. Her world, her drive, was bigger than the new corner I was carving out for me and my girls. A corner that quite possibly had me not returning to baseball.

When another Sunday arrives, we return to Stone's house for the weekly meal.

Standing in the back yard of my childhood home, I feel off. A hum beneath my skin. I'm restless to play ball again and my eyes keep wandering to the gravel lane leading to the barn. Once upon a time, our mother loved horses and we owned a few. I have hazy memories of entering what is now a weather-worn structure, the scent of long-gone horses still a whiff in the air on occasion. I didn't spend much time in the place once our mother passed, and as my older brothers grew, a punching bag was set up in a stable. The irony that our father never used the thing, preferring his children instead, was never lost on me.

Wandering away from the gathering, I saunter toward the barn but focus on the overgrown meadow surrounded by a dilapidated white fence. Walking all the way up to the fence, I cross my arms over the top rail, plant one foot on a lower one and just stare at the tall grass waving beneath a hot summer afternoon.

"Needs a bit of cleanup." Stone's strong voice has me turning my head but not shifting my position.

My brother stands beside me, lifting a leg like me, staring at the weedy, overgrown field. "Used to have some good times out here," he begins. "Mom had her horses, and Dad just loved to watch her. We strung lights on tall posts." Stone points around the fenced-in yard. "And played whiffle ball one night."

My gaze darts from him to the vacant space. A dusty memory comes to me. I had to be younger than four, no older than June right now.

Standing behind me, helping me hold an oversized plastic bat, a woman's laughter fills my ears as together we swing our arms. When the bat thunks *against the ball, the woman tosses the bat to the side. Behind me, she cheers, "Run, Ford. Run."*

I'm racing toward one of my brothers. One squatting down and waving me toward him, only I decide I don't want to go to him. I veer left and race to a different base, making my own path. Eventually, I'm caught up in strong arms and raised in the air.

"Ford, you're supposed to run to first base," someone laughs.

"He'll learn the rules one day," Dad adds, his voice behind me.

"You did good, Fordie." Feminine laughter follows the praise.

Like a whisper in the wind, I can almost hear the sound. I fell in love with baseball because of my mom. The thought hits me so hard it's like I've taken a fast ball to the chest. But my memory can't be right. I was roughly June's age when my mom passed.

"Think she would have been proud of me?" My voice cracks as I ask.

Stone turns his head. "Definitely." He squints and glances at the field. "But you could have done anything, Ford, and she would have been happy, as long as you were happy." He looks back at me. "Are you?"

Leaning away from the fence, I stretch out my arms, hands curling over the top rail. The pull stretches my left shoulder. The burn has lessened, but an ache still lingers. My range of motion hasn't fully returned.

"I need to play ball," I admit.

"There's a field at the high school. You could probably talk to Tate Haven. He's the athletic director."

"Tate Haven?" I stare at Stone. "I didn't think the family was speaking to the Havens." There was bad blood between my older brother and his ex-best friend, who happened to be the eldest of the Havens. Tate was Cortland's younger brother.

Stone shrugs. "Sometimes you need to be civil." However, his jaw ticks, a trait I'd picked up from watching him bite his tongue and hold his ground against belligerent men.

"Maybe," I sigh, turning my attention back to the field. Playing on the old dirt near my high school certainly would bring back memories, but I didn't necessarily want to hit there.

"I never thanked you enough for all you did." The confession comes decades late, but having my own kids, I can see how parenting will be a thankless job. I want Stone to know I appreciate him, especially since he wasn't my parent, but he made ends meet. He kept us Sylvers together. "You really helped me get where I am. The equipment. The camps. The encouragement."

The corner of Stone's mouth curls. Not a full smile but a hint he's touched by my gratitude.

"I can't take full credit, though. Need to thank Sebastian for a few things, even if he didn't come by it legally."

"What do you mean?" I shift and lean into the top rail, facing my eldest brother.

"Even if his methods weren't legal, I might have turned a blind eye a time or two at first. I wanted to give all of you what Dad couldn't."

"Stone, what are you saying?"

He turns his head, deep blue eyes meeting mine with sympathy and guilt. "Sebastian bought the equipment in the early years. He paid for the camps."

"What? How?" I straighten off the fence.

Stone stares at me long and hard, almost begging me to not make him explain. My brother sold drugs from a young age. Not noble. Not right. But the money helped. Stone wasn't the sheriff then but a deputy, a newbie in the hierarchy of civil servants. The job included a meager salary when he had three young mouths to feed after Knox took off for the Navy. Which meant there shouldn't have been anything left over for the expensive attire needed for a growing boy and the necessary camps to help build his skills.

"Stone? I never . . . I didn't . . ." I turn my head toward the house, not able to see the full family from here but knowing my *younger* brother is in the yard.

"I didn't want to admit it, and sometimes it was extra difficult to accept, but Sebastian was sneaky. He'd purchase the stuff and already set it in the room you shared. He'd register you for camps and sign my permission."

"What is with all the forgery surrounding me?"

Stone chuckles, narrowing his eyes once more toward the overgrown field. "Wasn't malicious then." He turns back to me, looking me right in the eyes. "It was love." He sighs. "Your brother knew you were destined for bigger things. Bigger than this yard." Stone nods at the fenced-in space. "He wanted to give you what he, and I, couldn't afford."

My mouth falls open and I stare back toward the house. "But he's always been a dick."

Stone laughs harder. "And you were the easiest to live with? He had his own demons to wrestle. I think he might have just wanted a little *positive* attention from you."

And sometimes negative behavior is the only way to get attention. Except, I'd ignored Sebastian most of the time, especially when he started selling drugs and I focused on baseball. I'd assumed our separate paths were chosen for us without realizing he'd been nudging me deeper along mine.

"Why didn't you ever tell me?" I glare at Stone.

He shrugs, his mouth crooking up in the corner. "Figured I would when you were ready. You seem ready now to handle the truth. And maybe make amends with your brother."

"Fuck." I swipe a hand down my face, my palm scratching on the growth on my jaw.

"He'd only done it a few times before I caught on. Should have questioned how a twelve-year-old had the money, but I didn't. By the time he reached high school, things were different for me financially. You were on your way to college scholarships, and I'd shut the door on how you'd gotten there." Guilt is ripe in every word, but Stone cannot beat himself up. He'd done the best he could, being just out of boyhood himself.

"Fuck, I'm so sorry, man."

Stone shakes his head before I'm even finished. "Your apology might be better directed to Seb."

I lower my head and sigh, but a firm hand comes to my shoulder forcing me to look up once more.

"And I've never needed your gratitude, although I appreciate it. I'm proud of you, brother. Always have been. Always will be. No matter what." He squeezes once before he walks back toward the house.

His touch punctuated his sentiment.

Whether I played ball or not, *he'd* be proud of me, as long as I was happy.

+++

Over the sound of Chris Stapleton's "White Horse" blaring in my ears, I think I hear someone yelling at me. Turning the corner on the ride-on mower Stone uses to cut the grass, I've cleared half of the fenced-in meadow. But there's no getting around the sudden wall of Sebastian standing in my path.

"What that hell are you doing?" The loud holler resounds over the din of the ride-on.

I cut the engine, turn off the music, and tug an ear bud from my ear. "What?" I shout louder than necessary.

"I said, what the hell are you doing?" He yells louder than he needs to as well before clearing his throat and crossing his arms. My brother is wearing his signature dark T-shirt and jeans. Heavy black boots cover his feet despite the summer heat. He looks more biker than baker and we couldn't be more opposite as I'm wearing loose sports shorts and a sweat soaked tee with the sides cut out. I'd destroyed a handful of shirts to make them easier to get on and off with my fucked-up shoulder.

"I'm mowing." My tone suggests it should be obvious, but I immediately clear my throat, remembering what Stone told me days ago. "I'm cutting the field."

Sebastian glances around us. "I can see that, but why?"

Shrugging, I gaze off to my left, my sight catching on the ugly brown barn. "Thought I'd build a baseball diamond."

"Come again?"

My brother doesn't actually expect me to repeat myself but when I look back at him, his mouth holds firm, as if questioning my sanity. "Is this one of those, 'if you build it, they will come' things? In case you don't remember, this is West Virginia, not Iowa."

I snort, ignoring his sarcasm. "Nah. I don't need others to come here. I'm doing it for me."

"Of course you are."

I could question his tone. The hint of sarcasm. The layer of resentment. But now, I have a better understanding of why my brother talks to me like he does. Although Stone's explanation might not explain why Sebastian and I rubbed each other the wrong way *before* he sold drugs, perhaps our behavior was simply sibling rivalry. The easy kind like Zelle and Winnie sometimes display. Like when Winnie wants the last cookie and Zelle uses her mother hen voice to say she's older and deserves it. But unlike Zelle and Winnie, where Zelle would have broken the cookie in half to share it with her younger sister, I was never like that toward my younger brother. I didn't let him play ball with me. I easily grew frustrated when he did weasel into a game. I acted like he was a pain in my ass instead of accepting him as my brother.

"I'm sorry, man," I blurt without preamble.

Sebastian's head flinches. The slight movement a hint to his surprise but his mouth is still sharp. "What the fuck for?"

"For being a dick most of my life to you."

"Most?" He scoffs but he reads something in my sweaty face before narrowing his suspicious eyes.

"I never knew you bought some of the stuff I needed when I was younger. Always thought it was Stone. Stone led me to believe it was from him, although I'm not faulting him. We all know he did what he could for us." In Sebastian's case, Stone eventually did what he had to do to save our brother from himself.

With a deep exhale, I add, "So . . . thank you." Fuck, if the team shrink heard me now, he'd be so proud.

Stumped, Sebastian lowers his arms to his sides. His body language reads less defensive. He remains speechless, and I'm not certain I've ever known my brother to be at a loss for words when it came to me.

"Maybe you could apologize for that hit the night before your wedding?" I prompt.

"Fuck you," Sebastian retorts, but not an ounce of heat fills his voice. He tips his head back, blinking a second before lowering to face me once more. His crass words in a cooler tone might be all the apology I get.

"What did you need?" I tip my chin at him. Why is he here?

"Wanted to talk to you about Cadence."

"What about her?"

Sebastian's eyes narrow to slits, a warning behind the shutters of his lids. "What's going on with you two?"

"Nothing," I state too fast, too adamant.

"Bullshit." Sebastian waits. "You think I haven't noticed the glances between you two. The way her face flushes and yours just turns red. The way you orbit around her."

"Why would I do that?"

"You tell me. I've noticed all this shit because I know that's how I am with Enya."

Turning my head away from him for a second, I take a deep breath before peering back. "We're both consenting adults. No commitment required, just how *she* wants it."

Sebastian arches one brow but remains silent.

"How did you know?" I've been extra vigilant around Cadence, keeping my distance, and not dragging her off to my old bedroom like I want to, when we are here on Sundays. But I guess I haven't been diligent enough.

"I didn't. But you just confirmed it."

Fuck. I tip my head back before snapping my neck forward. "Then why the fuck did you ask?"

"Because she's a fucking superstar, man. She's out of your league."

"Oh, because I'm not good enough," I counter as if I can't hold my own with someone of her caliber.

"Because she might not be good enough for you."

"She— What?"

"Look, I haven't known Cadence long. I don't interact with her often, but she's my wife's sister so I know well enough that Cadence does not want to be tied down. She has her routine. Guys on the fly until this Evan shit. And you scream stability and commitment and more than one night."

"What Evan shit?" I sit up straighter, hands fisting on my thighs.

Sebastian stands taller. "You don't know about the Evan situation?"

"No." Who the fuck is Evan? *How* did I not know there was a situation with him, especially after the past few weeks?

I suddenly feel sick, my vision blurring. With a shaky hand, I swipe at my sweaty brow.

Is this the same situation I had with Felicity all over again? Is Cadence secretly seeing someone else?

Fuck! My stomach drops. My chest feels like it's cleaving in two.

Is this why she can't commit to me? Won't give me more of her? Cadence, who has taken up full residence in my head and my fucking heart, can't stay the entire night in my bed, because of someone named fucking Evan?

"Sebastian, if there was ever a time in your life to tell me something important, this is it."

"Not my story to tell, man, but you better get it from her." His shoulders lose their tightness. "Especially with your girls."

After becoming a dad, my younger brother has changed once again. He'd be the first to admit his heart expanded in a way he didn't know it could because of Adara, and now that he and Enya have another baby on the way, his heart is going to keep growing, keep opening him up to more love. And more wounds.

Because loving someone eventually can lead to a few punctures, if not an entire break.

And suddenly, I'm worried Cadence's secret is going to ruin us all, my girls included.

Chapter 30

[Cadence]

Today was one of those days where everything had fallen into place and life felt wonderful. I'd spent the morning playing hide-n-seek with the girls. Then Zelle went to a new friend's house. Winnie was at afternoon camp, and June was taking a nap. Ford had physical therapy this morning and he planned to go to Stone's house afterward.

And I was still riding the high of our date the other night.

I was looking forward to a few hours alone to write some lyrics. Ford was my new muse.

Typically, my bedroom door is closed because my favorite Gibson is inside, and I don't want June accidentally playing with the classic guitar I wrote most of my songs with. Exiting the bathroom, I notice my bedroom door is open, though, and inside is Ford wearing a T-shirt with the sides missing, the back discolored with sweat.

With his back to me, he's staring down at my phone set on the nightstand beside my bed. The one he hasn't been in yet as I'm always sneaking into his room. Beside my phone is the small rubber duck he gave me months ago to watch over me. That duck has been damn lucky for me.

However, the hunch of Ford's shoulders and his concentration on my phone suggests he isn't interested in the romantic gesture he gave me.

"What are you doing?" I try to keep my voice on an even keel, but the tone is still hard. I don't want to accuse him of invading my privacy, but *he's invading my privacy* when all he had to do was ask me any question and I'd answer.

Ford picks up the device which has a passcode on it, however, a simple swipe upward reveals the most current message notifications.

"Who is Evan?" His voice is level but accusation rides beneath the surface. Ford slowly turns, holding up the phone and turning it so the screen faces me. "And who is this fucker that wants to know if you're sleeping alone?"

Ford's voice is stone cold. His judgement first; questions second set me on edge.

"You shouldn't be in my room." He'd been very insistent that I could have my own space in this home. A Sylver-free zone.

"It's my house."

The statement is a trigger.

It's my house and if you aren't going to follow my rules then you can leave.

I was seventeen years old. Enya was away at college. Our older brother was God knows where.

I'd countered that threat with my own. *Fine, then I'll leave.*

Don't think you can come back.

My parents never had to worry. I wouldn't. I hadn't. I'd owned many places on my own, but nowhere has felt like a home the way this house has for a few blissful weeks.

What was I really doing here, though? Ford was on the mend. His girls were doing great. Violet, his niece, was helping more often than I was. I didn't have a purpose here, and my production team was waiting.

Stepping forward, I reach for the device, but Ford lifts his arm higher, having the unfair advantage of being taller than me. I might climb him like a tree if I didn't feel the anger vibrating off his body, ruffling his limbs.

"Fine. I'll leave." Turning toward the closet, I take a step intending to grab my suitcases, but Ford catches my arm.

"Talk to me."

"Oh, now you want to talk?" I counter.

Ford collapses on the edge of the bed, not releasing my arm while lowering my phone to his lap. "Cadence," he groans. "Evan. Explain."

With a heavy sigh, and an equally weighted heart, I drop my chin and stare at Ford's bare feet. "He was a mistake. A huge one. One I made long before I met you."

Silence slowly swirls between us as his thumb rubs my inner forearm and my heart thunders. "He was someone I used to know." Sheepishly, I lift my head. "Someone I *thought* I loved."

Ford's face remains stoic. His jaw ticks. His cheeks hollow out sharp and fast, but he stays focused on me.

"It had all been a lie." I close my eyes, roll my lips inward, knowing what I say next changes everything between us. "He was married."

Ford drops my arm like I knew he would, pulling his hand away from me like touching my skin has somehow infected him.

"I didn't know," I quickly defend, the argument sounding weak even to me. How had I not?

"How?" Ford's voice is gritty and eerily quiet but still anything but calm.

"We'd been at an industry party. I'd bumped into someone quite literally and his drink spilled on my dress."

The blame was mine. I'd turned too quickly, caught my heel on the rug, and lurched forward. Evan was in my path, and I reached for anything to break my fall, his arm being the nearest thing. The drink in his hand met my dress. He'd apologized when I'd been the one who tripped. We had an awkward exchange with him trying to dab my dress with a paper napkin. I suddenly looked like a wet T-shirt contestant in a silk gown. Giggles happened. Blushes, too. Innocently enough, he'd offered me his jacket, so I didn't have to exit the place with erect nipples and a giant wet stain.

"I'd apologized for being a klutz. He offered to buy me a new dress, and a drink." I'd thought he was charming. "It wasn't until later I learned who he was and how he was married."

Turned out, Evan Lauer was an English actor invited to be opposite me in a music video. He was tall and handsome, and one thing led to another in the London countryside where we shot the short film.

"He'd been coming out of a London restaurant, her on his arm with a giant ring, and a swollen belly." I mimic the bump over my own stomach. "She was pregnant." She was far enough along for it to be evident it happened *while* I was with Evan. We'd been meeting for months as I lingered in the Box Hill area, an easy commute for Evan to visit me.

"I felt sick," I admit. Bile rushes up my throat once again.

"So he cheated on his wife with you."

There was no denying the truth. I'd been the other woman and I hated myself. The way Ford clarified my position, it was evident how he felt. In a comparison of failed romances, I was the Romero Valdez in my tale.

"I never asked him to leave her," I quantified. "*He'd* told me he would, but I didn't want that. I didn't want him." How had I been so duped as to think he loved me? How could he abandon his pregnant wife? How could I trust a man who had done what he'd done to someone else?

For weeks, I couldn't get showers hot enough, scalding my skin and scrubbing at my flesh. I didn't want a single trace of Evan on me, and after a quick jaunt back to London, abruptly leaving my new-mom sister, I haven't been back to the UK. At that time, Evan contacted my manager, demanding to know where I was, threatening to expose *me*.

Ford stares down at my phone. He'd been cupping the device in his hands while I explained myself. Suddenly, he tosses it to the mattress, like a potato straight from a microwave burning his palm. He rubs his hands down his face and tips back his head, swallowing hard.

"So now what? He's been calling you? Sending texts? I'm assuming Evan is the anonymous person getting through to your number." Ford tilts his head forward, eyes narrowing. "But you said only five or so people know this phone number. Block him. Get a restraining order. Change your number."

"I can't," I snap. I have my reasons for not changing the seven digits. Ford is right, though, in some manner. "I would block the number only Evan keeps changing the phone he's calling from. I do have a restraining order, but it's tricky. Those orders are public record, and in registering one, I had to explain my side of the story. Do you know how difficult it is to be the *clueless* other woman? No one believes that story. *I'm* the seductress." I jab a finger to my sternum. "*I'm* the cheater. *I'm* that woman who doesn't care about other women or values vows. I'd steal any man I want."

There's no denying I'd wanted Evan. His looks. His charming personality. His lies. I fell for it all. He'd known who I was, but it hadn't mattered. He was a well-known actor in the UK. I believed we shared the same dreams, to escape the grind of our grueling industries and the harshness of the media's perception. We talked about living a quieter existence, simplifying our lives, but there was nothing simple about our positions. My giant career and his blossoming one. He was finally getting recognition for his talent, and he had blockbuster after blockbuster headlining his name coming out in an eighteen-month period. But behind the screen, he lived a fairy tale with his wife and their pregnancy. I'd been a dalliance in the countryside, like some historical romance gone wrong.

"Not to mention, I had to prove Evan was stalking me. And with what? A handful of anonymous phone numbers and a few innocuous texts. Not much could protect me other than Evan coming close to my person." I wave a hand down my body. "And actually threatening me."

He'd been close. Too close in Phoenix, but I'd avoided him. He shouldn't have even been in the United States. He's a British sensation, but I quickly learned he'd been filming in the US since January.

"Is he a threat? Are my girls in danger?" Ford stiffens on the edge of my bed.

"No." The answer is instantaneous.

"Are you?"

I shake my head. "Evan is stupid, but he isn't dumb, and he isn't a fighter." He's a fucking weak man with no morals who cheated on his wife, unfortunately with me. "He'd never fuck up his career by coming after me."

Still, he'd pulled that stunt in Arizona. He'd sent me flowers. He'd been seen in Nashville, and that's when I headed here.

"Who else knows about this guy?"

"Enya." She'd been the first person I told after Evan. When I fell apart and he'd gone ballistic last June trying to find me. "Sebastian. My former manager. My new one, Lana. And Stone."

"Stone?" Ford snaps.

"He's the local sheriff. I felt obligated to let him know my situation before staying in town." Didn't want to be the innocent lamb drawing out a big bad wolf, although Evan is the sheep. I am the alpha. He wasn't going to get near me, and he needed to get over himself. His wife had their baby last fall. He should be blissfully happy and move on.

"Who told you?" I'm curious how Ford suddenly knew about Evan other than snooping through my phone.

He turns his head, eyes catching on the rubber duck that I take everywhere with me, and place on my nightstand, so I see it when I fall asleep at night and wake to it watching me in the morning.

Here's to watching over you. As if a bath toy can do that. As if anyone does.

"Sebastian. He came to warn me."

"Warn you about what?"

Ford can't look at me, but I see the uncertainty and distrust in the set of his shoulders. "You."

His words are like a bat cracking in half after connecting with a hundred-mile per hour pitch. Shards of pain erupt inside me. Think before you act, I'd told Winnie. My thoughts were blank. I'd spilled my story, holding nothing back but Ford was like everyone else, making their assumptions, giving into their judgments, and pointing a finger at me.

No tears came to my eyes, only the sting of his rejection and disappointment. I thought Ford would be different, but his unspoken accusation remains. I'm the problem. My new brother-in-law must think the same.

My hands tremble a little with the rush of adrenaline, fight or flight kicking in. Flight always wins. Because now I felt unwelcome in a place I thought might be a home for me. How wrong I'd been again. My heart, already fragile, has been splintered in all the places Ford once healed. His silence does the trick.

There wasn't anything to be done other than pack my bags and leave. Sadly, I couldn't even go to my sister's home, because I'd been betrayed by my new brother-in-law.

Chapter 31

[Ford]

"Cay-Day." June's sleepy cry turns both our heads.

With equal parts uncertainty and anxiety, and unable to look Cadence in the eye, I quickly rise, and head to my daughter's room to get her up from her nap. Holding her tightly to my chest, I spin toward the door to see Cadence standing outside it with her guitar case in hand.

"I'm going to leave." With her head lowered, her voice quiet, something inside me snaps.

"Leave?" A rush of panic races through me. "Where are you going?" How could she leave after the bomb she dropped?

Cadence was the other woman. She was Romero to my Felicity and me.

"I need some space." Defeat I'd never heard was heavy in her tone.

"We need to talk," I rush, stepping toward her with June in my arms.

Cadence steps back. "Later," she whispers, not convincing me in the least she'll be back.

I don't want her to go, I just need a second to think. However, Cadence is gone before I make it to June's open door. Instead of following Cadence, I return to her room, relieved to find her suitcases still in the closet. Ironically, the rubber duck I'd given her is missing. I hadn't given the bright yellow toy a second glance when I invaded her private space. When I didn't even know what to look for. I just wanted the truth.

On one hand, guys were dicks, and I had no doubt any man could sweet talk a woman with a smooth line and good looks into bed. On the other hand, Cadence was smart. She was gorgeous and quirky, and she wasn't the type to fall for a pretty face and a sharp one-liner. *How had she been fooled?* Because deep down, I am convinced . . . I fucking know . . . Cadence had been tricked.

I didn't believe the guy wanted nothing from her other than a simple life in the London countryside. *Come on.* She's Cadence. Then again, what was I doing with her? Or rather, what was she doing with me? I was a single dad, newly divorced, and an injured baseball player with an uncertain future.

Fucking Sebastian. He'd been right. Cadence had a secret. He'd also been wrong. She wasn't cheating on someone else or me. She wasn't disloyal like that, and she wasn't a one-and-done-woman. Case in point was me. We'd been touching and kissing one another every night for weeks. Even if we hadn't had actual sex, I had no doubt we'd eventually get there. We were still learning things about each other, both in the bedroom and outside of it.

Cadence and I had more to discuss. I wanted to understand her position. She'd told me she didn't want fucking Evan. She never wanted him to leave his wife or kid. She hadn't known about them. And I believe her. The conviction in her face. The guilt in her eyes. I believed her. I did.

And I realize her situation was nothing like mine with Felicity.

Hugging June tighter, I stand in Cadence's bedroom doorway and stare at the empty bed. Things are certainly clearer now about Cadence's standoffishness and why she doesn't stay in my bed overnight. She doesn't trust people to love her. Thus, the one-night stands she's told me about. The reckless, short-term relationships, she'd hinted at. She's afraid to commit to someone because when she finally wanted a person, he wasn't available. He'd proven how nonchalantly some people treat their marriage vows, like the Felicitys and Evans of the world. And if Cadence leaves first, she can't be hurt. With this Evan-dick, she'd been burned.

"Daddy swink." June wrinkles her cute nose at my body scent while speaking around her thumb. I really need a shower after this morning's mowing.

No, Daddy sucks. I should have been more understanding, more patient. I'd just needed a minute, and that minute had cost me. In baseball, you don't have time to think. You react on instinct.

Overthinking leads to missed opportunities. Underestimating leads to injury.

My instinct had been wrong, though. I'd fucked up once again with Cadence.

+ + +

"Hey you," I croak in relief when I finally find her.

After Cadence left, I'd called Violet to babysit. That girl was a godsend. Then, I set out in search of Cadence. I hadn't a clue where to look. First, I called Enya and explained what I'd learned. I cursed out Sebastian while also thanking him for giving me the nudge I needed to dip deeper with Cadence. We'd only been scratching the surface, and I wanted to dig harder into an *us*.

I'd sensed her holding back for a while now. She'd erected an impenetrable wall as thick as the ivy in Anchor Field. Perhaps she thought she was protecting us both. However, her bunt, a short swing solution, did nothing to prevent me from rushing home plate. Like on the ballfield, misinterpreting the signs can lead to an unwarranted error. I had strong feelings for her, and I wanted something long term, even if I didn't know what that looked like yet.

The last place I expected to find Cadence was at Stone's house. Vale had called me.

"Did you lose somebody?" she'd teased.

"What do you mean?"

"A very deflated looking country singer just barreled into our driveway, narrowly missing the front porch steps, and then took off on foot down the lane past the barn with a guitar strapped to her back."

The description certainly fit the woman I was looking for, right down to the poor parking job. To Stone's I went, driving down the dusty lane myself until it turned into two tire tracks leading toward a rustic structure.

On the back acre of the property was a cabin I'd forgotten existed. The place hadn't been more than a stone wall with a window in it then.

Now, the front façade looks newly built while the back wall made of field stones remains. A new roof covers the one-room rectangle replicating the original building.

Cadence sits on the low step with the door to her back. She scoots over just the tiniest bit, just a hint of an invitation, and I sit beside her. The neck of her guitar juts over my thigh, and I quietly wait while she plucks at the strings. My outer leg presses against hers, and I take my first breath in an hour.

"Don't run away from me, Caitlin."

Her given name causes her fingers to screech down the strings, the sound harsh and ear piercing.

"I didn't run. I drove." Her attempted joke falls flat, matching the tone of her voice.

"You know what I mean." I shift, bringing her attention to me. "If you need to run, run *to* me." Suddenly, I'm picturing my brother standing at first base, waving his arms frantically for me to run down the makeshift baseline and into his arms. That brother had been Stone. Funny Cadence came here as well but I want her coming to me, or at the very least, not turning her back on me.

"Let me be your safe place. Your home plate." I cup her jaw and draw our foreheads together.

"I can't if you judge me."

I tip back so she can look me in the eye. "I'm not judging you. I want to beat the shit out of him. He hurt you. He *used* you. And then he threw you away."

"I tossed him," she reminds me.

"I don't like it either way."

"You don't have to like it," she tells me, dropping her gaze to the guitar still on her lap. "It's in the past and I can't go back."

She's right. I can't change hers. I can't change mine.

"And no one hates me more than myself."

"Hey," I snap. "Don't say that. You made a mistake. He made a bigger one." Stepping out on his marriage vows. Not disclosing to her he was even married. He's the dick here.

I curl her hair behind her ear and tuck a finger under her chin. I need to see her face. "And I don't want you hating yourself." I press a kiss to her lips, tender and gentle. I want to comfort her, soothe her broken heart, and lingering guilt. Because I'm in love with her and she's going to hate that.

Slowly, I pull back and we stare at one another a second.

"So those messages . . ." I swallow at the thought of this dick getting to her. If not physically, he's been harassing her mentally. "I don't understand why you don't change the phone number. Get a new phone with a new number."

Cadence pulls her head out of my grasp. "It's complicated." She looks down at her guitar and strums against the string in an ominous tone.

"You can tell me."

"I—" She bites her lip hard. Her expression says she can't tell me. She doesn't trust me. Obviously, she doesn't trust me if she didn't tell me about *him* in the first place.

"Who are you protecting?" Did she not change the number because she *does* want him back? No, she was too adamant she does not.

"My heart." Her voice trembles, her lip quivers, and suddenly, she's crying. This beautiful, strong woman who doesn't seem ruffled by anything sobs once, covers her mouth with her hand and lowers her head.

"Caitlin." Her birth name only makes her cry harder, and I remove the guitar between us, pulling her onto my lap and wrapping my arms around her as tight as I can. She leans into me, and I kind of hate myself with how much I need her to do that. How much I want to hold her, protect her.

"How do I keep you safe, baby? How do I help you protect your heart?" I squeeze her once while pressing my lips to the side of her head. My fear is more than watching Cadence walk away from me. My fear is someone might take her from me. Death took my mother. Another man took my wife. I wasn't letting anything come between Cadence and me. Not even her insecurities.

"Just hold onto me."

After minutes pass and Cadence relaxes, her sobs slowing, I whisper to her hair. "Let's get out of this town."

Cadence looks up at me. "And go where? What about the girls?"

"I've got them covered. Violet is spending the night." I hadn't known how long it would take me to find Cadence in Sterling Falls, provided she hadn't left for Nashville, but I'd been prepared to drive all night if I had to.

Now, I had a different plan.

+ + +

With Cadence in my Escalade, her guitar safely stored in the back seat, we drive outside of Sterling Falls. Up ahead, the sign for Randy's Bar illuminates the dark surroundings.

"Taking me out for tequila, cowboy?" she teases, once again becoming the woman I love, full of fiery spirit and take-no-shit attitude.

"Nope," I say, driving past the rundown bar with a bright neon red sign. "Need you lucid for tonight."

"I was lucid back then." She laughs. "You were the one who couldn't handle tequila."

Something tells me I wouldn't have been able to handle her either that night, but I am in a better mental place now. My shoulder is doing better. I have my girls . . . all four of them . . . and I wasn't letting the one sitting beside me go. Reaching for her hand, I bring it to my right thigh and hold it there while I continue to drive us through the mountains to a place outside a small town named Wrightwood.

Cadence sits straighter in her seat, eyes wide, mouth open, reading the motel marquee as we approach. "Mountain Motel."

She'd told me how she'd had plans to stay at this place when she came to Sterling Falls for Enya's wedding back in October, but she'd cancelled her reservation last minute. The motel was rehabbed but still had a vintage vibe. Cadence wanted to check it out because of the history and the potential to make a music video here. The place had a lobby that reminded her of old supper clubs. The rooms each had a theme to them. No two rooms were the same.

When I flip my blinker and turn onto the gravel drive, Cadence side-eyes me. "You brought me to a motel."

After checking in with Violet and saying goodnight to the girls, I made a call to this place. With the summer months in full swing, they only had one last-minute vacancy.

"Not just any swanky motel. This motel." I set the SUV in park and shift in my seat. "We can turn around and head back home. Or we can check in to a room and hang out." My voice conveys how serious I am. I didn't bring her here to only mess around. We could talk. Or I could just hold her. "I just want to pretend I didn't drink too many shots one night. And a beautiful woman didn't take my pathetic body to a random motel to hide me from my daughters. I missed the ball that night."

Cadence chuckles. "No, I missed the ball." She winks.

"Tonight, I want to be the one pretending you are mine." From that night in October, Cadence told me how she acted like I belonged to her to prevent me from getting hit on by some woman in Randy's Bar. Tonight, there wouldn't be much pretending on my part. Cadence belongs with me. She owns me.

We eye one another for a heated second before Cadence opens her door and I hop out the driver's side. She rounds the back of the SUV and I stop her there.

"How do you feel about role playing?"

Her eyes widen once more. The blue of her irises bright in the dim summer night.

"Why, Ford Sylver, what did you have in mind?"

"Let's have you enter the lobby, take a seat at the bar. I'll be the one to rescue you tonight."

"Will we be sneaking into a motel room afterward?" She clasps her hands beneath her chin and bats her eyelashes at me.

"What is it with you and sneaking into rooms?" I laugh at her enthusiasm, then lean forward and give her a quick kiss. She whimpers.

"No more of that until I have you to myself," I tease, then I smack her ass and aim her for the lobby.

"You watching me walk away, cowboy?" she calls over her shoulder, accentuating a Southern drawl filled with seduction.

"You know it, songbird."

She gives her hips an extra sashay. The sundress she's been wearing all day flows back and forth with an exaggerated sway. The back of her toned legs and that firm ass keep me focused. But it's really the whole woman who is blinding me with excitement.

It's time to prove to her she could be mine.

Chapter 32

[Cadence]

With a little extra pep in my step and an additional sway in my hips, I saunter to the lobby doors, feeling the pressure of Ford's gaze on me trickle down my spine, along my inner thighs and against my sensitive bits. My entire body throbs with anticipation.

This is going to be so much fun.

Taking a seat at the bar shaped like a horseshoe, the open end pointed toward the back wall, I order tequila on the rocks. I'd order a margarita to keep my head clear, but this place has mountain cozy with gin-joint vibes happening, and straight alcohol might be more in order. I'm also nervous.

The bartender has a don't-fuck-with-me aura. One that would typically have my mouth watering and my flirt on. With his short dark hair and thin layer of scruff, he looks a little like Ford, but that's where the similarities end.

The lobby isn't full, but people filter through it. A few other stools are taken. A family plays a board game on a low table in front of a large stone fireplace. A woman rushes out a swinging door that must lead to a kitchen area.

"Duke, I owe you," she says, out of breath while addressing the bartender.

"That you do." He gives her an affectionate smile but not one that says they are an item while he continues to wipe glasses behind the bar.

My body hums waiting for Ford to enter this space. The area is dimly lit but not dark like Randy's. Instead of crooner's music like I imagine once played in this lobby, Luke Comb's sings "Fast Cars," a remake of a Tracy Chapman classic. Their combined performance during the last Grammy's was showstopping.

The minutes tick by slowly.

"You good?" The woman asks me, glancing at my sliver of tequila. I haven't touched the drink. Ford says he wants me lucid. I can't wait for whatever he plans although he sounded quite clear that we didn't have to do anything. If I tell him I want to binge-watch *Leverage*, his favorite series, or talk all night, I have a feeling he'll be just as content.

That isn't going to happen, though. I have a few plans for my cowboy as well.

"Yeah." I hardly recognize my own voice when I answer her.

"My name is Lindee, if you need anything." She looks over my shoulder after speaking and exits the bar area, heading toward the front doors.

I feel his presence before I see him.

Ford takes the seat beside me, orders a beer from Duke, then remains quiet. The anticipation is killing me. I smell his closeness. Feel the hum of his body mixing with mine. His leg bounces. He so close and yet not close enough. Not yet.

Finally, he turns toward me. "Do I know you?"

Duke scoffs from behind the bar, as if already sensing our gig before we play it out.

I fight a laugh and turn only my head, giving Ford my best smile. "I don't think so."

His eyes roam my seated position from my hair to my mouth and over my breasts until he's tipping back to check out my legs. If he were any other man, I'd be closing out my tab and walking away. Then again, who am I kidding. He's hot as sin, and with the way he's looking at me, like I'd be his last meal, I won't be leaving this stool until he propositions me.

"Hmm. Swore you looked familiar."

"Doubt it," I play along.

"Maybe only in my dreams, then."

I can't help it. I laugh outright, turning the head of the mother-figure playing the board game.

Tucking my head, so my hair falls forward to shield my face, I finally respond. "Maybe we had the same dream. You look familiar to me, too."

Ford shifts on his stool, his legs spreading, his foot hooking into my high-seat chair. Suddenly, I'm dragged closer to him, wedged between those spread-wide thighs with his knees caging me in.

"Want to get more familiar?"

I chuckle again. "Is this really how you'd pick up a woman?"

Ford picks up his beer and takes a long pull while never looking away from me. After he drinks, he says, "I'm out of practice."

"Maybe I could teach you a thing or two." I tease, leaning my elbow on the bar and twisting my upper body toward him.

"The only thing I want you teaching me is how to be better acquainted with you." His eyes heat. His gaze intense. He's going to incinerate me right here where I sit.

I walk my fingers over his thigh, leading the tips to an area I hope is eager to know me. Ford catches my hand before I get too close to the zipper of his jeans. He's dressed similar to the night we met. Dark denim and a faded gray tee minus the fall jacket and baseball cap. He looks like any other guy when my heart knows, he's not.

"I mean it," he says, lifting my fingers to his mouth, where he kisses the tips but keeps his gaze on me. "I want to know everything there is about you."

My heart hammers. There's so much dirt in my corners and yet something tells me Ford could be the one to sweep me clean of every bad memory.

I clear my throat, falling back into our act. "There isn't anyone I can save you from tonight." I glance around, noting that Lindee hasn't paid Ford any attention, and the mom with her family hasn't looked up again.

"I don't need saving, darlin'."

My head swings back to him with the endearment. *Maybe* I *do.* "Then how are we going to pretend you're mine."

"We aren't pretending." Those eyes of his heat up another notch.

"Ford," I whisper. My love for him frightens me.

Still holding my hand, he says, "Ready to get out of this place?"

I can hardly wait, and I quickly dismiss what he said. For tonight, we will be pretending Ford is all mine.

And I'm all his.

+ + +

On the door of our motel room, a handcrafted sign states the room's theme.

"The Birthday Room?" I question.

"I was told they try out new themes every once in a while. Guess this room isn't terribly popular and that's the reason it was the last room available tonight."

"Well, we can always pretend today is your birthday," I say as Ford opens the door with an actual key linked to a hexagon-shaped fob, the room number etched into the plastic.

I enter the room and immediately start to giggle. The strawberry-shortcake pink and buttercream yellow wall coloring is painted horizontally—pink on the bottom, yellow on top—with a white stripe through the center and white color thickly layered at the top. The design makes me feel like I've entered a slice of cake. A lamp shade that looks like it has candy sprinkles sits on an ice cream cone-shaped base. The bed's cover has raised polka dots in vibrant pastel colors like someone spread Funfetti confetti on the white spread.

Ford stands behind me, quietly closing the door before looking up. "What the fuck?"

I laugh again. "Happy Birthday," I tease, spreading my arms like a game show hostess.

Ford stutters a laugh as well. "Too bad it's really my birthday."

"What?" I turn to face him.

He stands with his hand cupping the back of his neck. His expression one of mirth. "Turned thirty-eight today."

"Ford." I playfully smack his chest. "Why didn't you tell me?"

"Because someone ran away from me earlier." The sudden reminder of how this day shifted presses on my shoulders but Ford grips my hips and tugs me to him. "But we aren't going back to earlier."

"Ford. We should be somewhere special. A fancy restaurant or an elegant hotel, not . . ." I glance over my shoulder at a picture of muted candles over the bed. "Not here."

"But I didn't meet you at some five-star restaurant or upscale hotel. And I wanted to start over."

He suddenly looks so innocent, and I cup his jaw, the stubble prickling my palms. "That's so sweet, cowboy."

He leans forward and kisses me, but this kiss is nothing like earlier. Where that kiss was tender, this one reminds me of that first kiss we shared. When we'd been arguing outside my sister's wedding, and I ordered him to apologize to me. Ford has nothing to be sorry for tonight, though. He's been nothing but good to me lately, and I want him to know how I feel about him.

I'm falling hard for him. And losing him would be so much worse than losing anyone else.

So tonight, we pretend.

Breaking the kiss, I reach around Ford and click off the light. "Maybe in the dark, we won't feel like we're in the middle of a birthday cake."

Ford reaches awkwardly behind his back and flicks the light back on. "But I want to see every inch of you while I devour you."

"Oh, and you think you'll be eating me?"

"Don't lie to yourself. You know you want me to. You know I want to. Your pussy is becoming my favorite treat."

"Well, you sure know the way to a woman's heart."

Ford covers my hammering heart with his flat palm. "Somehow I doubt that's all it takes to get to yours."

"Cowboy," I whisper, but Ford is cutting me off, filling my mouth with his tongue while his lips meld against mine. He presses me to back up and I take the few steps to the bed without breaking our kiss. When my knees hit the edge, I fold to the mattress and stare up at him.

"When you look at me like that . . ." He runs his thumb over my lower lip, tugging it downward.

Any second, we're going to be saying things neither of us might be ready to hear. Or maybe it's that I'm afraid to say those words, so I reach for his waistband and tug him toward me.

Ford stumbles a bit from the force and catches himself on my shoulders.

"Since it's your birthday, I was thinking spankings might be in order."

"You are not spanking me," he threatens as I unbutton his jeans and lower the zipper, giving his thick shaft space.

"I was talking about me."

"Fuck," Ford mutters.

He gently presses at my shoulders, forcing me to fall back on the bed, where I bounce once. With laughter, I scramble further backward on the mattress before Ford catches my ankles and flips me face down. A squeal escapes me. Ford climbs over my body, straddling my thighs while tossing the skirt of my dress above my hips.

"You've been wearing this beneath this dress all day." He growls. There's no real question in the statement, just pure desire as he plucks the thin string of my thong between my ass-cheeks.

Ford leans forward, catching himself on his good arm. "I should punish you for running from me." He lightly taps one bare cheek. "Maybe for keeping secrets, too." He smacks the other a little harder, the sting forcing me to lift my head.

"Do we need a safe word?" he asks.

"I've never done this before."

"Had your ass spanked?" Surprise fills his tone as I glance at him over my shoulder the best I can.

Our reflection in the mirror above the dresser catches my eye. My backside on display. Ford straddling my legs. I want him to take me just like we are, and he must sense my desire because he meets my stare in the mirror.

"Gonna get to all the things tonight, baby. And then we're going to do something else you haven't done." Ford leans forward again, his mouth close to my ear. "I'm going to hold you all night. Spoons. Knives and forks. Whatever utensil you want to call it. You'll be mine. And in my arms."

This turns me on more than it should, and I buck my hips, forcing my backside upward to nudge at Ford. His hand comes harder on my ass in response, and I squeal again, but then his fingers slide between my crease and lower for where I'm wet and ready for him.

Ford tugs the thin material and the fabric snaps. "Better," he groans before slipping two fingers into me. My knees bend but I have nowhere to go. Ford is holding me down and I want to rock.

"Need to move, baby?"

"Yes," I whimper.

"Not yet." He smacks my ass again, pulls his two fingers out, then rushes in again.

I moan at the sensation. Then he's twisting those fingers, and his thumb slips between my cheeks.

"Ford," I whimper, lifting my head again.

"Another something you haven't done?"

I drop my head once more, shaking it against the polka dot coverlet.

"But you like me teasing you, don't you?"

He isn't asking for an answer. He can feel how my body is responding to his fingers inside me, his thumb against the puckered hole, teasing me. I'm grinding into the bed, fighting against Ford's thighs over mine, and yet loving the restraint.

"Gonna come, sweetheart." No question. Pure fact. Within seconds, I'm screaming into the bed cover beneath me as Ford presses harder at my hole and slides his fingers faster into my entrance. I didn't expect to come without clit stimulation, but I'm rubbing against one of those raised dots on the bed in just the right spot, and suddenly, I'm like a firework, exploding in the night.

"Yes," Ford hisses behind me as my body lights up and I let go.

While I'm still in the throes of the high, he removes his fingers and flips me to my back. He presses my dress up above my hips. His eyes focus between my thighs where I'm soaked and dripping, and still throbbing with need.

"Now, I eat cake for my birthday."

My knees are bent beneath his forearms as he scoots back a bit and presses his face between my legs. His tongue laps. His lips suck. He even gives that sensitive spot a nip, and Ford eats like I'm the tastiest dessert ever.

"Frosting," he licks up my slit.

"Filling," he delves his tongue inward.

"Pure sweetness." He kisses me, then starts the process all over again. My legs tremble. Something drips down to my ass. I'm a mess and I'm loving every minute of it, but it's Ford's birthday.

"Need to celebrate you," I remind him.

"We'll be getting to that."

"Gonna let me lick you like an ice cream cone after this cake?"

Ford groans against me, lifts me by my backside, and cups my cheeks like he's holding up a bowl and slurping the contents within. His tongue moves faster. His mouth presses firmer. He flicks my clit and, like a match, I light up again, crying out his name.

He doesn't relent until there doesn't seem to be a spark left in that orgasm. Then, he lowers me to the bed. I'd tossed an arm over my eyes. The room too bright. Ford too much. But he reaches for my wrist and tugs my arm down.

"Ice cream time," he announces. "But first. Get naked."

Chapter 33

[Ford]

Cadence is a fucking vision.

After scrambling off the bed, she stands at the end and unbuttons the few buttons over her chest. Opened wide, her dress easily falls off her body. Next, she removes her bra, holds out her arm to one side, and dramatically drops the scrap of fabric to the floor. Perched up against the headboard, I watch the unveiling, like a slowly unwrapped gift, and slip my hand into my boxer briefs fisting my dick.

After admitting to her I didn't ever jack off to visions of her in my head, she's made me do the deed a few times during our nights together. With her in the room no fantasy is required. Her watching me take myself in my hand and spend while I'm looking at her naked form is pure heaven.

"Fuck, you're going to make me come before you touch me," I warn her.

Tonight feels different. Not only is it my birthday but I have Cadence trapped. Not caged in, though. If she really wants to leave this room and forget the later portion of the evening—cuddling—I'll honor her request. But I'm hoping she'll honor mine. I want to hold her after we do everything this night brings.

For now, I want her mouth on me, and with the gleam in her eye and the way she's crawling up this bed, she wants the same thing. Slipping my arms behind my head, I watch her remove my pants and boxer briefs in one swift move.

"Lose the shirt," she demands.

Three months ago, I would have struggled to tug this thing over my head. Hell, I wouldn't have been able to lift my left arm and hold it behind my head. A pinch in my shoulder reminds me I still can't exactly do either without it hurting but I'd tear this shirt to shreds in order to expose my skin to her.

With my chest bare, Cadence runs her hands over my lower belly and around my dick without touching it. She coasts her palms down my thighs, cupping the backs of my knees, and making them bend a bit to accommodate her between my legs. Then her hands curl around me. Both of them. One cups my balls, the other swipes her thumb over the slit at the tip that seeps with desire for her.

"You're better than a banana split, Ford Sylver." She squeezes at my shaft and tightens her hold on my balls.

"Do not fucking make jokes about ice cream right now."

"Why not? You're my favorite flavor." Her sassy mouth lowers, drawing me between her lips. The first suck always gets me. Cadence goes to the throat before drawing to the crown, swirling her tongue as she glides upward then repeating the motion. Within seconds, I'm ready to burst, but there's something more I'd like for my birthday. A different gift.

"Cadence. Sweetheart." I brush back her hair, which tickles my belly and curls over my hips. "Let me inside you."

Releasing me with a pop, Cadence lifts her head. Her bright eyes meet mine. "I thought you'd never ask."

We'd been exploring one another for nearly a month in no rush to take anything further, but suddenly the weight of time presses on me. I don't want to pass up any more chances to be with her.

I want her to know I'm hers.

Twisting, I grab my jeans which are dangling off the side of the bed and fumble for the condoms in my pocket. We already had the safe sex talk. She's on the pill but condoms are extra protection.

Cadence grabs the packet from me, confidently rips it open, and proceeds to cover me. And every second is an additional tease. I'm so hard I'm ready to combust, and I'm worried this will be over embarrassingly fast.

Once I'm covered, Cadence crawls over me, and holds me at her entrance, swiping the tip through her soaked folds. I'd love to feel her dripping down my dick, want to feel her heat surrounding me, but we aren't there yet.

As she lowers herself onto me, taking just the tip at first, I lose all thought and just watch as I slowly slide into her.

"Cadence. Baby." I'm a stuttering mess. With my fingers on her hips, I dig into her flesh, worried I'll leave a bruise but needing to hold onto something, so I don't surge into her. The gradual way she takes me in is torture and pleasure in a conflicting swirl.

Eventually, I'm seated to the hilt and Cadence pauses a second. We both take a deep breath as she stretches around me.

"Feel so good, baby."

When she's ready, she drags up my shaft and my eyes roll back. "Fuck. That feels incredible."

She drops back down repeating the easy pace until she sets a newer rhythm. Cadence takes the lead, but I charge forward, matching her thrust for thrust, until her breath hitches.

"Cowboy?" The question in my name and the widening of her eyes has me slowing down but Cadence only speeds up. "Cowboy. This. Never."

"Heck yeah. Take it." *Take everything from me.*

As Cadence bounces up and down, her mouth gapes, her hair wild, then she slams down on me and as her channel tightens around me, I go off. Lifting my head, I capture her cries with my mouth, setting off my own as I let go, hard and fast. *This. Never.* I steal her thoughts. Nothing has ever felt like this before.

Cadence collapses over me, her hair fanning out over my chest, and I wrap my arms around her, attempting to hold her tight while my body feels loose and languid.

"Happy birthday, cowboy," she mutters over my racing heart.

"It ain't over yet, baby."

While we remain in our little bubble of spent limbs and galloping hearts, I press my lips to her head. Eventually, she lets me up and I dispose of the condom then return to the polka dot bed.

"We should have a real cake," Cadence whispers, laying on her back, as if anyone else is present to hear her. "And a party. You need presents and—"

I tug her side into my front. "I don't need any of that. I never really celebrate my birthday."

"Why not?" She glances up at her. Her cheeks are still flushed. Her lips swollen.

I shrug. "They weren't a big deal when I was a kid." I don't remember ever having a party or a big celebration. "When I was a teen, and my baseball team often had a long tournament over the Fourth of July weekend, someone's mom always brought a pity cake."

Cadence scrunches her nose. "A pity cake?"

"Yeah, she'd feel sorry for me that I didn't have any family present for most of the tournament." Stone would be there when he could. Clay, too. But I didn't have that constant stream of family like many of my teammates, especially if it was an out-of-town tournament.

Cadence glances back toward the end of the bed. "I always celebrate mine." Her voice remains quiet. "But I'm a Valentine's baby and somehow I always end up with red presents containing pink hearts."

"Valentine's baby, huh?" I chuckle, then realize I'd missed her birthday by a week when she came to Arizona.

She waves out her arm. "I'd have champagne and go to a club." She drops her arm and picks at a polka dot puff. "And it's always lonely."

I lower and press a kiss to her shoulder.

She playfully pouts, "I want a party." Quickly, the sadness in her expression morphs to that shield of protection.

"Next year," I tell her. "Nothing Valentine red. How do you feel about purple?" I tease. "And cake and ice cream."

"Next year." Her voice is wistful, but also hints she doesn't believe in next years. She lives in the present.

Cadence shifts to her side. "You have great colors for your birthday. Red, white, blue."

I snort. "Who knew birthdays were supposed to have colors?"

"Those are Chicago Anchors colors, too." Her voice lifts stronger. "It was fate."

"Speaking of fate, where's my lucky cap?" I'd like to see her wearing the blue cap with a red anchor outlined in white, and nothing else covering her body as she sits on my lap.

"Keeping me lucky." She giggles and the sound goes straight to my heart.

"Well, since it's still my birthday, I have another request."

Her head quickly shifts on the pillow.

"You're always calling me cowboy, which makes you my cowgirl, right?" Maybe she needs a cowgirl hat on her head and nothing else.

Cadence pulls her head back as if to eye me better.

"How do you feel about riding in reverse?"

"Giddy up!" She motions her hand like she's about to lasso me, then presses me to my back proving she isn't opposed to the idea one bit.

+ + +

"I'm going to get us coffee," Cadence murmurs at my ear in the morning. Her body is no longer wrapped beneath my arms but seated on the edge of the bed. A thin stream of light beams through the space where the curtains don't quite meet.

"Why aren't you in bed?" She slept against me last night as I wished. We'd even made a game of her explaining just how the knife and fork work, with her arms tucking against my chest and our legs entwining together. Only being naked, when our fronts met, we were tangled in a new way.

Three times last night we came together. I wanted a fourth this morning.

"We should really get back. Plus, it's a beautiful day." Her voice is too chirpy with the suggestion we return to Sterling Falls.

"Don't tell me you're a morning person." I groan, rolling fully to my back, feeling a twinge in my shoulder.

"Okay, I won't tell you I love the start of a new day, although I'm equally a night owl. *Who-who.*"

I laugh and meet her eyes. "I thought you were a duck." My duck.

"Well, I guess I'm all kinds of birdies." She bends her elbows and flaps her arms, imitating a flying creature and having too much energy for this early.

"I'll go with you to get coffee," I jackknife upright, still feeling a little spent from last night. My dick, however, wants to celebrate a new day.

With a hand to my chest, Cadence presses at me. "Lay back. I'm only going to the lobby. I just didn't want you to think I'd run off." Her eyes soften, reminding us both of yesterday afternoon.

I grab her hand and kiss her knuckles. "No more running."

Slowly, she stands, does a twirl, and curtsies. "I don't run. I flit." She waves out her arms before turning for the door.

Once she leaves, her words settle hard in my chest. I don't want her flitting away from me either.

Quickly, I shower, check in on the girls knowing they're most likely up at this hour, and tell Violet we'll be heading home soon because I'll be bringing Cadence home with me. To my room. To my bed. I'm not ready to burst the bubble of Cadence and me. If only I could convince her, we can have something more. Next year. The year after. I'm not certain how that would look but I am certain I'm not spending another birthday without her as my present.

Chapter 34

[Ford]

"Surprise." The cheer isn't overly emphatic. No one jumps up from behind a couch or stands in a dark room before the lights flip on.

No, my family is lingering in various positions in the middle of the fenced-in field I started mowing the other day which now appears to be a rudimentary baseball diamond. Exactly how I envisioned this land transforming.

A bit tongue tied, I eventually ask, "When did you guys do all this?"

After Cadence and I spent the night at Mountain Motel, we returned to Sterling Falls and took the girls on another hike. Last night, I snuck into *her* room and filled her up again before tucking myself around her in her bed. That way, I spent the entire night with her beside me.

Clay shrugs. "Finished this morning. Had the sand delivered yesterday. Brick and I laid it out with the help of a few guys from the Seed & Soil. Stone counted out the baseline and chalked it."

The lines were perfect even if the running path wasn't. The infield was still a choppy-mowed meadow. The outfield matches the rough-cut grass, but none of it matters.

My family built me a baseball diamond.

"We bought you new bases, too," my nephew Hudson proudly states, pointing to the bright white bags at first, second, and third, and a flat home plate.

I glance from family member to family member, my jaw tense, my shoulders tight. I'm not an overly emotional man but this . . . this is so much more than pity cake for a birthday. And I'd been kind of a shit brother who didn't deserve what I'd been given. Siblings who stood beside one another through thick and thin. I wasn't as tight with each of them as I should be, but I was damn thankful they were my family.

Out of habit, I glance at Stone. "Thank you."

He turns his head and tips his chin at Sebastian. "His idea to finish it."

"Dude," I snap as my eyes start to burn. Then I close the distance between Sebastian and me, startling my younger brother by wrapping my arms around him. Sebastian stands stone still a second before his hands come to my sides where he awkwardly pats me a few times. Stepping out of the embrace, I cup the back of his neck and look him directly in the eye. "Thank you."

Despite wanting to have words with him about Cadence, he deserves my gratitude for what he'd done for me. Again.

"It was nothing." Not used to praise from me or the overshow of appreciation, Sebastian brushes it off while lowering his head and fighting a grin.

"I mean it. Thank you for everything."

Sebastian eyes Stone. I squeeze the back of his neck, drawing his attention back to me, and nod at the field. "You did good."

Almost at the three-month marker from my shoulder surgery, this space is perfect for easy batting practice and the conditioning I want to begin with the heavy metal ball typically used in a shot-put tournament. With my mitt in the back of my Escalade, I'm eager to test my shoulder.

Sensing my anticipation, Clay pulls a ball from his back pocket and tosses it up in the air before catching it with his other hand. "What do you say? Wanna play ball?"

"Hell yeah!" I cheer.

"That's a dollar please," Zelle rolls out her hand like I've seen Hudson do, charging my brothers every time they swear during Sylver Sundays as Cadence has deemed the weekly family meal.

"You've been hanging around your cousin too much," I tease. In the short time we've been here, Zelle and Hudson have quickly formed a friendship.

"Hell isn't really a swear word," Winnie corrects her sister. "It's an actual place."

I do not want to know how Winnie learned such a thing, but I chuckle as I glance at Cadence, who is holding June's hand beside her.

All my ducks, right in a row, and a gaggle of family around me. I'm one lucky man.

"Prepare to go down," I point at Clay. "Who are the captains?" And just like that, I'm ten again on the field near my elementary school.

Clay and I each captain a team, although we don't have enough players for every position, and we'll need to rotate out batters.

Incorporating the second generation, I snag Hudson while Clay steals Zelle.

Sebastian goes with me. Enya with Clay.

"She's pregnant," Sebastian warns our brother.

"I'm not that far along. I'll be fine," she dismisses his concern.

Vale with me. Stone with Clay.

I take Tim. Clay gets Violet.

I take Halle. Clay gets Knox.

Seeing the family is getting unevenly distributed, I ask for Judd who is surprisingly present and while he doesn't have a lick of athleticism in him, he's strong and can run.

"Then I get Cadence." Clay winks.

The sexy superstar walks passed me, pulling my cap from her back pocket and slipping it on her head. She's wearing short white jean shorts and the Anchors tee with my name on the back plus light gray gym shoes on her feet.

"Did you know about this?"

With a mischievous smile, she points two fingers at her eyes, then swivels her wrist to point at me. "I'm watching you, cowboy."

That doesn't answer my question but I'm grinning back at her. She can watch me all she wants. I'll be looking right back.

"Me pway," June whines.

I glance up at Clay. We both know June isn't going to hit a ball, but he nods at me to take her and Clay picks Winnie.

"I always get picked last," she pouts, crossing her arms.

"Saved the best for that position," Clay argues to dispel a tantrum and swoops up my girl.

With the family divided into teams, we play ball, and a teetering whisper in the wind sounds like a voice that's tickled my dreams.

You did good, Fordie.

The rousing game turns into a night of beers and brats in the backyard. A cake in the shape of a duck is brought out and when I cut into the layers, one pink and one yellow, Cadence and I share a laugh. I'm keenly aware my family is watching us, and I don't care.

Eventually, Stone lights the fire pit and Cadence grabs her guitar although I don't remember her putting it in the back of the SUV. My siblings and I are not known for carrying a tune, but Enya and Cadence have everyone clapping in time to "Good Time" by Niko Moon, and I can't remember the last time I was this happy.

Chapter 35

[Cadence]

Whatever it was that Ford and I were doing, I'd assumed he'd want to keep us a secret from his family. We'd agreed the girls didn't need to know anything, which kept our nights interesting as we stifled screams and cut off groans by kissing one another.

But at the impromptu baseball game, Ford didn't keep his hands to himself.

When I scored, he was there to wrap me in a hug and lift me in the air, even though he was on the other team.

When I played my guitar that night, Ford sat close enough our legs touched and he set his arm behind me on my chair.

And in between those times were subtle touches and stolen kisses when we thought no one would see us. Vale was the only one who caught us, giving us a surprised stare before softening her features into a warm smile.

"Knew I liked you, girl," she'd said to me.

Vale's approval also came when she saw how attentive I was to Ford's girls. Zelle, Winnie, and June circled me like the little ducklings I call them, and I loved every minute of it more than I should. They weren't fans of Cadence the superstar. They liked me, the silly woman who waddled like a duck, played hide-n-seek, colored pictures, and could French braid even the shortest hair.

They were imprinted on me as much as their father was becoming.

And that scared the bejeezus out of me.

+ + +

Small towns like to celebrate for any reason, but the Fourth of July was a big excuse, especially when you had someone considered a hometown hero, like Knox Sylver, and a hometown star, like Ford.

The annual parade happened along the main street through the business district, and afterward townsfolk filtered into the common green space at the end of the district. Packed with picnickers, the area was almost worse than the parade, and I held my breath at every encounter when someone approached Ford, afraid they'd also recognize me.

I hadn't received a new text in a few days and the silence unnerved me almost as much as the previously incessant messages. I had a weird feeling in my stomach all day which was high in humidity and sunshine. Keeping my hair tucked into Ford's ball cap, and my roundest sunglasses in place, I did the best I could to hide myself despite being out in the open.

Still, at one point, I was walking toward a small pop-up tent where local high schoolers were selling lemonade to raise funds for the school band when a woman bumped into me.

"Sorry, *Cadence*." Her apology was so quick and her disappearance into the crowd just as fast that I didn't get a good look at who she was. The strangest part was how hard she hit me in the shoulder when there was plenty of space to walk around me despite the crowd.

"Are you okay?" Zelle asks me as I'd recruited her to help me carry cups of lemonade back to my sister. Sebastian and Ford are surprisingly civil with one another as the four of us gravitated together with all the younger girls.

"I'm good." I squeeze my upper arm, roll my shoulder, and offer Zelle a smile before taking her hand again. A little bump is nothing compared to the injury her dad had incurred.

Purchasing the lemonade seemed like it took forever as each kid filled plastic cups with ice, sugar, water, and lemons, shaking the mixture for the best combination of tart freshness. With cups in hand, Zelle and I return to our little sliver of a blanket on the square where Ford is standing upright, hands on his hips and a tight expression on his face.

"What's wrong?" The fine hairs on the back of my neck prickle.

"Was June with you?" Sharp and strong, his voice is like the crack of a bat.

"No." I glance at Zelle as if a now nine-year-old can help me out. "Was June supposed to be with us?"

Zelle shakes her head and glances at Winnie who stands by Ford looking equally concerned.

"What happened?"

Ford tugs off his ball cap and curses before slapping the hat back on his head. "I can't find June." The anguish in his voice says it all as he scans over the crowd, as if hoping a little girl with wild blond curls and her thumb in her mouth will magically appear in the sea of people.

"Where's Enya?" My sister and Sebastian are both absent from our spot along with Adara's stroller.

"They went to search for June. They told me to stay here and wait for you in case June was with you."

"Ford, I'm so—"

Ignoring my apology and dismissing my next question—what does he want me to do—he brushes away my extended hand while reaching for his phone with the other to call someone.

"Stone. I lost June." His voice cracks again as he runs a hand over his face.

I step closer to him, intending to place my hand on his chest. His heart must be racing. But Ford takes a step back from me and I stare at him, telling myself his sudden distance is only because he's lost his daughter.

"I'll go look for her, too." Reaching out for Zelle's hand, thinking it would help to remove her and let Ford concentrate solely on finding June, he grips Zelle's thin shoulders and draws her closer to him.

"Leave Zelle with me."

I scowl, not liking his tone. But again, I dismiss his behavior as concern for June and waste no more time arguing. Gingerly, I step through the seated crowd of people, crying out her name as I move beyond them.

With my hands cupped around my mouth, I call again and again, drawing attention to myself, more than I'm comfortable with. While I never mind the whispers, stares, and pointed fingers, I'm also well-aware

I'm in a sea of people who could suddenly full-on recognize me. The potential of a mob isn't something I can tackle on my own, and I fight off the panic rising in my chest as I continue to call for June.

A few people start to mimic me, crying out June's name as if in response to my call. Knox and Halle are also walking among the crowd asking if anyone has seen my little duckling. After what feels like hours, but might only be minutes, something in the distance catches my eye.

A person wearing a dress and a large floppy sunhat with her back to the gathering is walking away from the square. The same woman who bumped into me. In her arms is a curly-headed blond child, sucking her thumb over the woman's shoulder.

"June!" I scream, then take off running, dodging people like a fish swimming upstream. Every few feet I jump up as best I can, attempting not to lose sight of that hat and June. With my phone in my hand, I try to call Ford, but someone knocks my raised elbow, and my phone clatters to the ground. I don't bother to look for it. Instead, I power through the swarm of celebratory town's people until I'm in the clear.

Then I'm racing down Main Street.

+ + +

FORD

Violet intercepted me at some point and took over with Zelle and Winnie who was crying hysterically that we'd lost June. Despite the frenzy of my search, while attempting not to lose my other girls, and the pounding of my heart in my ears, I'd heard Cadence's scream for June.

When Cadence's head pops up above the rest of the crowd, I try to make my way toward her until she breaks free of the gathering near the entrance to Main Street. Shifting my race toward the intersection of Main and Corner, I lose sight of her. Thankfully, the road is still blocked off from the parade and cars aren't driving toward me as I sprint down the middle of the road.

I nearly passed Corner, focused on the emptiness of Main ahead of me, when something causes me to turn my head. Two women stand near a minivan; June is in Cadence's arms.

Changing direction so quickly, I stumble, trip over my own feet at the change in trajectory, and almost fall to the cement, making an awkward windmill with my arms before righting myself seconds from face planting to the ground. With renewed momentum, I rush down Corner and almost collide with Cadence before ripping June out of her arms and tucking my baby girl into my chest, pacing a few steps away from the two women.

With June's head cradled in my hand, holding her face to my neck, my other arm supports her against me.

"June. June. June." I whimper. My heart is in my throat. My legs tremble from the sprint. My shoulder screams. I don't think I've ever run so fast in my life. I'm also certain I've never been so frightened.

Spinning back toward Cadence, I glance from one woman to the other who has Cadence's full attention.

"You shouldn't be here, Angela," Cadence grits. Her hands are fists at her side.

Taking a step closer to them, I consider calling Stone. I should notify everyone that I found my June Bug, but I'm afraid to release her and reach for my phone. I don't want to ever let her go.

"I couldn't seem to get your attention otherwise," the woman states, crossing her arms. Her tone is off or maybe it's the pitch. Wearing a dress too large for her small frame and a floppy oversized sunhat, she could be anyone. I've been absent from Sterling Falls long enough I no longer know half the people who reside here. But something about her says she isn't a local.

And *what* she just said to Cadence makes no sense.

"You don't need my attention," Cadence counters. "You need to leave me alone."

"Like you left my husband alone?" The tenor of her voice becomes clearer. She sounds like she belongs in the English countryside.

"What the fuck?" I don't care that the four-year-old in my arms hears me. June is crying into my neck, and whether that's her own fear or the fear vibrating off me, I can't be certain. But one thing is for sure, this woman is a nutcase. And she's the wife of someone Cadence once slept with?

"I—" Cadence's knuckles are nearly white with how hard she's squeezing her fists. "I don't think you should be talking to me." Her eyes narrow. "How did you even find me?"

The woman—Angela—glances at me a second before turning back to Cadence. "Not hard to find you when you leave a social media trail."

Cadence's mouth pops open before she spares me a glance. "I have not."

She once told me she doesn't post half of what's on her profiles. As I'm not on social media myself, I haven't checked out Cadence's accounts after my initial investigation.

Did she put my girls on her social media? Am I on there as well? "What the fuck, Cadence?"

She knows I'm protective of my daughters and while Felicity used to dress them up like dolls and parade them over her socials like she was the perfect mother, I didn't feel comfortable posting my girls' images with mine. I was afraid of this very moment. When someone with a loose screw would put two and two together and take one or all of them.

"Oh, so this is my fault," Cadence counters, guilt written in her eyes while her face is stern.

Ignoring her question, I bark at this Angela woman. "Who the fuck are you?"

"No one of consequence to you." Her voice isn't half as strong as she'd like it to sound. I'd never touch a woman, but I could snap her small frame in half.

"You are if you touch my daughter," I roar.

"She's Angela Lauer, Evan's wife."

"Evan, as in Evan Lauer," I state incredulously. Had Cadence told me his full name before? Maybe she did, but I hadn't connected the dots when learning she'd been the other woman in an adulterous relationship.

And now Angela's accent makes even more sense. She's British, like her world famous, action-adventure film star husband.

Addressing Angela, my incredulity grows to full-on anger. "You're pissed at *her*, so you decide to take my kid?" But I'm equally angry with Cadence and turn on her. "I'd asked you once if my girls were in danger, and you told me no." Yet this happens. My daughter is almost kidnapped by a scorned woman because of Cadence and her drama.

Cadence stares at me. Her hands still balled into fists at her side. Her head high, eyes flaming with indignation and shame. I can't deal with her right now.

I want to take June as far away from here as I can but there are consequences to be paid for Angela's actions.

I snap. "Call Stone."

"I can't." Cadence drops her gaze. "I lost my phone somewhere."

This is the final straw. "Maybe you should have disconnected that number like I thought you had. And next time, run a background check on potential lovers."

Cadence gasps, her mouth dropping open and freezing in a shocked expression.

My limbs are vibrating with the rational terror that had another few minutes passed, June might have been gone forever. I don't care what this stranger tells me. What her intentions had been. How she only wanted Cadence's attention.

Using my daughter for such a thing was unacceptable.

I twist and hitch my ass toward Cadence, refusing to move my hands from June's trembling body. "Take my phone. Stone is the first number in my favorites." Actually, Cadence's number is the first, but I don't know where she ranks after this situation.

While Cadence taps my phone, Angela runs around the minivan but there's no chance of escape. I set June on the cement against the building and reach Angela before she can open the driver's door. Pressing her up against the vehicle, I'll worry later about potential battery charges against me. For now, the woman is pinned with her hands behind her back.

Within seconds, Stone arrives on foot and a squad car turns onto Corner Street.

"This was a bad move, Angela," I growl.

"So was *her* fucking my husband."

I agree, but there's someone more at fault here. "Your husband made his choices, lady. Bad ones. And I'm sorry that hurt you but taking my child only made your problems worse."

"I wasn't going to hurt her." She twists in a way to show me her pleading eyes. "I just wanted Cadence's attention."

I don't spare Cadence a glance because I'm too afraid to remove my eyesight from this sad woman but out the corner of my eye, I sense Cadence clutching June to her.

Stone takes over my position and a squad car pulls up behind us. My brother doesn't bother to ask Angela what her intention was. He's reading the bitch her Miranda rights and cuffing her while I return to the sidewalk where Cadence is holding June in her arms, pressing a lingering kiss to her head.

Adrenaline still rushes through my body, so I reach for my daughter and tug her to me, briefly noting the hurt in Cadence's eyes. She releases a whimper when I drag June from her grasp and grip my child to my chest once again.

Cadence's vulnerability makes her raw. However, anger and fear still rage within me.

Beside me, she clears her throat and speaks to Stone. "I think I better come to the station as well."

Stone's gaze doesn't flicker from Angela. He nods once to agree with Cadence. After he places Angela in the back of the sheriff's car, he leads Cadence to a second vehicle that arrived.

And with only an apologetic glance back at me, Cadence is gone.

Chapter 36

[Ford]

I skip the fireworks and take the girls to Stone's house. With six bedrooms, there is plenty of room for us, and I don't want them out of my sight. I also don't want them anywhere near the rental house if the place has become recognizable as where we were staying.

I doubt I'll sleep tonight, and I really wish Cadence was here.

I'd been a total ass earlier. My fear of losing June got the best of me, causing me to lash out at Cadence, blame her. I need to apologize. I need her with me. She'd raced after my girl as if June were her own, and I needed Cadence's forgiveness. I want her to know I hadn't meant whatever I'd said. I can't even recall what I said, but I'm certain I said something, because I remember the pain suddenly piercing Cadence's expression. A look that reeked of hurt, caused by me.

When Stone finally arrives at my childhood home, he looks exhausted.

"Where's Cadence?" I rush from my seat at the kitchen table to stand, glancing around my brother for her.

Stone gives me a puzzled look before announcing, "She's going back to Nashville."

"What?" The pit in my stomach that had been growing for the past few hours was the size of the New River Gorge. Once the adrenaline dissipated, the cocktail of anger and fright lessening, guilt and shame over how I'd treated Cadence settled in. I'd been nauseous while anxiously awaiting her return.

Only, she's leaving? Why didn't she come back to me?

Both my questions can easily be answered as I've had time to reflect on how I behaved earlier. How my fear for June made me irrational. I'd been harsh, cutting even, in how I'd spoken to Cadence. How I'd blamed her for something beyond her control. She didn't make Angela Lauer do what she'd done. Hell, Cadence had even been a victim herself of

Angela's crazy. Stone watches me for a long minute before turning toward Enya. Cadence's sister has been frantic with concern for her, and Sebastian is equally upset that his wife is so worked up. "She said she'll call you when she gets home."

Home? For weeks I've considered the rental Cadence's home, but hadn't I told her just the other day that the place was *my* house? My emotions had been zinging in different directions when I learned about Evan. Jealousy. Upset. Judgment. And I'd done it again even knowing the truth.

Cadence did not want Evan. She made a mistake with him. He'd duped her, used her, and she'd been targeted by him and then Angela.

I could learn a lesson from Cadence's words to Winnie at Art's Studio. Think before you act, and I hadn't. I'd gone with my instincts, but they were wrong. Again.

"What happened to Angela?" I ask, sliding my hands into my back pockets, sounding rational when I'm feeling anything but. At this point, I'm assuming Stone knows all about Cadence's history and connection to Angela Lauer. I need to know Cadence is safe from her. That my girls and I are safe from the off-kilter woman.

"Seems Angela Lauer's husband left her after all. After she'd just had his baby."

Vale has been lingering in the kitchen as well, and gasps at this news before covering her mouth. This explanation might hit a little too close to the chest for her.

Stone continues. "Between the loss of her husband and post-partum depression, she became fixated on Cadence as the cause of her marriage falling apart."

Maybe Cadence was the reason. But most likely she wasn't. While Felicity had stepped out on me, and I wanted to fault Romero, our marriage had been dissolving long before Romero came to Chicago.

"Ball's in your court about pressing charges." Stone nods at me. "Attempted kidnapping?"

"Fuck yes."

"Angela Lauer will also have a battery of charges from Cadence. Cyber-harassment being the most prominent. She already has a restraining order against Evan. He threatened her last summer with bodily harm but hasn't made an appearance again."

The idea of anyone physically hurting Cadence knocks the wind out of me. I can hardly breathe with the thought. She told me she couldn't get Evan unless he came close to her in person. Unless he violated that restraining order she set in place. I didn't want him anywhere near her.

I glance at Sebastian, his head bowed. *Had he known?* My girl was in danger, and yet he came to warn me about *her*.

Stone says something to Enya, but I don't hear him over the ringing in my ears. Cadence *was* in danger as well, and now she is leaving.

Enya and Sebastian leave the house. Vale says she's going to check on all the kids.

I remain still, the pressure in my chest feels like a boulder pinning me in place.

Stone remains as well, standing at the opposite end of the kitchen table, where he sets his hands on the back of a chair. "Heard you blamed Cadence for this."

My head pops up. "I—" I swallow hard recalling the fear associated with June's disappearance. "I lost my head a bit."

My brother stares back at me a long minute. Those blue eyes are often compassionate, but I'm well aware they can display disappointment, and he's truly disappointed in me right now. I'm upset with myself, too. I'd blamed the wrong person.

"Understandable." He means my fear over potentially losing June. "But let me tell you something you aren't going to like hearing."

Stone continues. "Today could have happened to any parent at any time. Glance away for a second in a crowd and your child could be gone."

I hang my head, knowing he's right. I'd been focused on Winnie, watching Cadence with Zelle, and thinking June was right behind me. When I twisted around, I didn't see her. I remember standing, casually looking around, scanning faces, and glancing over seated bodies. Panic took over like the slow leak of sand in an hourglass. My brain couldn't compute fast enough that my daughter was missing.

Sebastian and Enya had been talking to someone they knew when I clutched my brother's shoulder and he turned. Something in my expression had him asking me a question I could barely hear over the buzzing in my head. I couldn't form an answer. I couldn't admit what my brain already knew but my lips didn't want to let pass.

"June," I'd whispered. The truth was unbearable.

Immediately, Sebastian started probing around us like I had, by calling out her name until eventually, he and Enya took off with Adara, telling me to stay put in case June only wandered away. She'd know where to return, although that was a lot of faith to put on a now four-year-old. Still, I did as they suggested hoping June had wandered after Cadence, as my willful child had a mind of her own. However, I could see Cadence didn't have June with her.

"June is trusting," Stone states as if reading my thoughts. "You've said so yourself how you worried she'd easily go to any woman because of Felicity."

My ex-wife. The mother of my children. My girls were scarred by her. Starved for positive, adult, female attention. Attention they fully received from Cadence.

Who was leaving us.

"And if Cadence was at fault . . ." Stone pauses. "Why would she race after June? Risk exposure of who she is, and corner a kidnapper, when she herself is a victim here?"

Because she loved my June Bug.

I hate that Stone is the voice of reason.

"Did you drop Cadence off at the house?" I mentally calculate time and distance, then add an allowance for the minutes Cadence would need to pack her bags before leaving for Nashville.

The corner of Stone's mouth quirks up. Not a full smile but a subtle stamp of approval. "Dropped her there and came right here."

Roughly thirty minutes have passed.

I'm hoping I still have time to catch her.

+ + +

CADENCE

The slam of Ford's front door makes me jump. The sudden sound accentuates my already fragile nerves and the tremor in my hands as I race to finish packing my three suitcases. He calls out my name as he thunders toward my room. Blindly tossing items into the last case, I don't stop moving.

"Cadence," he whispers behind me. His voice sounds relieved while breathless. Keeping my back to him, I sense him step closer to me. His once comforting scent invades my nose, sparking the tears I've been fighting for the past few hours.

"Please. Don't go." The anguish in his plea does nothing to quell the ache in my chest.

"Why, Ford?" I spin toward him. "So you can point a finger at me again? Pass judgement on me once more?"

With my palms pressed together as if in prayer, begging him to spare me, I unleash. "You shredded my heart today, Ford." Taking a deep breath to stave off the sob threatening to crack my voice, I continue.

"Do you have any idea how afraid I was for June?" My voice cracks as the visual I'm certain will haunt me for years continues to play on repeat in my head, as it has all day.

June being carried away by Angela.

The anguish that I might not be able to get to June fast enough. The unbearable fear I couldn't stop Angela before she drove off with that precious child.

I'd never forgive myself. I already can't, and the last thing I needed earlier was Ford stabbing my guilt deeper into my chest.

Ford's head lowers. His eyes close as if he sees the same thing that is burned into my memory.

"I love your girls, Ford. *I. Love. Them.* I would never, ever do anything to put them in danger."

"I know." His head snaps up and he steps closer to me, reaching out to touch me, but I hold up my hand to protect myself and step back, bumping into the bed.

"But you don't believe that," I remind him. Jabbing a finger to my chest, I add, "You blamed *me* for putting June in danger."

"I know." He exhales, exasperated with himself. "I'm sorry."

I'm already shaking my head. "For once, Ford, your apology won't work on me. You don't have my trust."

"I know," he repeats. His face stricken. "I'm sorry. Tell me what to do."

"I can't." He needs to make his own decisions.

"Please," he begs. "I overreacted. I panicked." The truth lifts his voice, and he grasps my wrists. "I was so scared today. I'm constantly afraid I'm not doing a good job, being a good dad. I don't want to do this alone. I want you with us."

My foolish heart leaps with his last sentiment, but I crush the hope buoying up in my chest.

"Understandably, your fear was rightfully for June. You were upset. Your girls are your world, as they should be. I'd just thought I was a sliver of space within that stratosphere, but I now see I'm a splinter instead."

"You're not." His hands slide to my upper arms, his tone desperate. "You're everything to me. To us."

Shaking my head again, I continue. "There's always going to be some creep out there, Ford. Someone thinking they can get to me, and potentially get to your girls, if we were together. I'd never jeopardize them. And you've proven you think I'm a threat. Instead of having my back and protecting me, keeping me safe like you asked how you could, you lumped me with my stalker."

Ford lowers his head. His eyes closing while he licks his lips. "I didn't mean it."

He might not have but he still flung those hurtful barbs at me. Implied I needed to run a background check on lovers and disconnect phone numbers. Those damning words were the final blow.

"This is for the best, Ford. You've hurt me." The dam breaks and the tears I've fought finally spill. "I care about you so much." *I love you.* "And I don't want to put anyone in jeopardy again."

"You won't. I'm here and—"

I cover his mouth with two fingers. Swallowing hard, uneasy with the words I say next. "It's time for me to go."

Am I flitting? Am I in flight mode? Nope. This is pure self-preservation because I can't be around Ford if he doesn't trust me. If he can't protect me. If he can't love me.

And the way he acted today spoke volumes.

I'd been fooled once by another man.

Now I was simply ashamed that I'd let it happen again.

"Please," Ford begs, pulling me closer to him and lowering his forehead to mine. "I don't want to lose you."

I could argue Ford never had me but that would be a total lie. I'd been his from the moment I pretended he was mine to save his ass in a shady bar.

"I'm not lost, cowboy. You are." I tip up and press the lightest kiss to his lips, struggling to hold back and not kiss him harder, demand he kiss me back.

I can't command Ford to apologize to me, knowing if he truly wanted me, he'd be begging me to stay with sincerity, asking my forgiveness without prompting.

Chapter 37

Mid-season

[Ford]

I let Cadence go because I couldn't keep her.

For once, I listened, heard what she said, and with a heavy heart, I gave her the space she needed. *Think before you act*, she'd said. She took my heart with her.

When I told Stone what happened, stating Cadence leaving might have been for the best, he had final thoughts on my relationship.

"Losing Felicity was for the best. Letting Cadence go is just a loss."

He wasn't wrong. My losing streak seemed to continue.

And after I canceled my rental and moved in with Stone and Vale, I'd decided to stay in Sterling Falls for the remainder of July. Sylver Sundays carried on but without their typical flare with the absence of one superstar.

One afternoon in early August, as I near the four-month marker for my recovery period, I'm ambushed by my brothers Knox, Clay, and Sebastian. The three of them are practically giddy as they force me into one of Clay's Sylver Seed & Soil trucks and we head away from Sterling Falls.

"You three aren't taking me somewhere to plant trees or build a patio, are you?" I had enough of that shit as a kid, always worrying I'd injure my arms working odd jobs for cash for the family business. Most times, I got out of manual labor because I had school, practice, or games, but occasionally, I'd be recruited especially when Clay was trying to rebuild the business our father had let fall apart.

"Nope," Clay counters, popping the *-p* like he's cracking bubble gum. "Even better."

I'm not trusting this outing.

"It's a field trip," Sebastian states and suddenly I'm thrown back to when Cadence lived with me and took the girls and me to the actual falls.

I clear my throat, fighting the question that's been burning my sternum for weeks. *How is she?*

Sebastian would know but he's been especially tight-lipped about his sister-in-law. Maybe, it's guilt because he warned me about her. Maybe, it's compassion because he saw me with her. Neither instance would be her fault.

I'm the one who fell for her. And I'm the one who let her go.

As we hit the highway for a short stint, and then pull back off, driving along mountain roads, I have a vague sense of where we are. Eventually, we pull onto a gravel drive. Overhead the entrance, a sign reads The Duck Inn.

"You've got to be fucking kidding me," I murmur, as the name alone sets off more memories of Cadence.

I still have the duck she gave me, staring accusatorily at me each morning and night, reminding me I'm an idiot.

Cadence has had communication with my girls. Three stuffed yellow ducks arrived at Stone's one afternoon.

To watch over each of you. Love, Aunt Cay-Day.

My heart cracked open like a freshly laid egg. Explaining Cadence's absence had been only slightly easier than explaining Felicity's. At least with Cadence, I could say she was off writing new songs and making a new album, which prompted Zelle to ask if we could attend her next concert. Still, I hadn't been able to explain Cadence's sudden disappearance without saying goodbye to the girls.

How could I tell them I'd pushed her away? Because I'd been the one to let Cadence slip through my fingers. Unlike the night I wedged her fingertips through mine, like fork tines spearing fruit, I let her go back to her life while making mine miserable.

I should apologize for what I said, but how many times can you tell a woman you are sorry for being an idiot before she accepts you really are stupid. The question was rhetorical. I'd already had my three strikes with her. I was back to sitting on the bench, possibly permanently.

Which brought my attention back to the old single room cabins and an empty in-ground pool on The Duck Inn property. A lake was somewhere beyond the woods behind the cabins. The Duck Inn had been a hunter's retreat decades ago but now sat vacant. To my surprise, Trudy Wallace was present. Although a local realtor, and one of my mother's best friends from their childhood, I only saw Trudy in passing during the Fourth of July Parade.

"What are we doing here?" I duck my head to glance out the side window taking in the state of disarray.

"*We* have an idea," Knox says, pushing open his door and stepping out of the truck. Sebastian and I follow, and Clay joins us as we stand among the weed-infested gravel that might have once been a parking lot.

"Boys," Trudy says, her voice loud but kind. She tried to help our father when our mother first passed away, or so I'm told, but Dad wouldn't have anything to do with the woman who eventually raised her nieces, nephews, and a handful of foster kids. A round of hugs occur with Trudy before the four of us line up like we're standing on a base line waiting for the National Anthem to play.

Clay begins, "You're not going to be able to play baseball forever."

"Thanks a lot," I quickly snap.

"And we'd like to have you closer to home," Knox adds. He returned to Sterling Falls three years ago after a long career in the Navy.

"Don't know if you've considered coaching," Clay continues.

I shrug. I had been thinking about it and Ross even suggested maybe I could rejoin the team early, though I wouldn't officially be off the injury list. I could work with the other outfielders, like a consultant to the coaching staff. He even hinted that if I ever wanted a permanent coaching job in the future, he'd help me find a team.

But with the girls, I wasn't certain I could continue the rigorous demands of a professional baseball schedule. Hardly any nights at home. Most weekends away or home games taking up hours of those days. A season that ran from February through November if a team was lucky to make it to playoffs. The missed time wouldn't be fair to the girls who needed me more than ever.

I'd grown weary of the number of nannies I'd been through and how none of them compared to the attention Cadence had given my girls. *I* needed to be there for them. I wanted to be present.

"I don't know yet what I think about coaching, but the professional level isn't an option."

The largest college in West Virginia was WVU in Morgantown, three hours from here. That left the local high school.

"I could always ask Tate Haven about a job," I say recalling he's the athletic director at the high school.

"Fuck no," Sebastian counters. "This is better."

Trudy Wallace has remained suspiciously silent, letting my brothers do all the talking and I'm still wondering why she's present.

"What's better?"

Sebastian points at the set of weather-worn cabins and the pool with a ripe stench coming from the muddy water within it. "This."

I'm still missing something.

"*We*," Knox starts again. "Thought maybe you'd consider starting a baseball camp here." He nods toward the cabins again. "Or even a general sports camp." He'd told me how Tim had to go all the way to Charles Town where his dad lives for soccer camp last summer.

"The land is cheap," Clay continues.

I snort. "It should be. These buildings look like shit." I send an apologetic glance to Trudy, who simply smiles at me, as if silently agreeing.

But slowly, I see the one room structures fixed up and made into mini-bunkhouses, maybe four guys to a cabin. The pool could either be restored or filled in, but swimming was good conditioning to keep arms loose. To the left of the immediate gravel lot was an open field. Was it big enough for a diamond, or two? Or maybe an indoor facility could be built?

"I—" My tongue ties. I don't remember what I was about to say. I don't know what to ask. This came out of left field, every pun intended.

"A baseball camp," I whisper. Suddenly, my mind is reeling with the idea of scholarships for kids like me who need the place and the means to get ahead. Who knows what kind of talent might come here? Or what an experience here might lead kids to do? Sports weren't only about being on a national team but being a member of something, learning teamwork, strengthening determination, and building pride even with a loss.

Clay adds. "Lucky for you, you have cheap labor to fix this place up."

"That was not part of *our* deal," Sebastian counters, glaring at Clay. Trudy chuckles.

"Why do you guys keep emphasizing *we* and *our*?"

Knox looks off to the right. Sebastian lowers his head. Clay stares past me.

"Alright, assholes, what's going on here?" I glare at each of them as they ignore me, giving them each a second to spill before turning on my heels. I don't need this shit. I have enough on my plate even if these jerks have planted the seed in my head.

Could I run a baseball facility?

"Okay fine," Sebastian calls out.

"Seb," Knox warns.

"Fuck it," Clay adds. "If a woman looked out for me like she's looking out for him, I'd worship at her feet."

"What woman?" I spin around, narrowing my eyes at my brothers.

They all know about Cadence and me by now because tequila and my tongue are enemies. One night, I told them how I first met Cadence, what she did for me. I added how she came to see me in Arizona, which they knew, and rushed to Chicago when I was hurt, which they also knew. What I tried to keep to myself was how we'd fallen into bed together and I'd fallen in love with her, but I'm certain that spilled out as well. I've been a grumpy ass since Cadence's absence.

With more staring off in different directions from Sebastian and Knox, Clay meets my gaze head on.

"You know which woman would be looking out for your future and your girls. She figured a camp would bring you closer to us, and we could help with the girls because we're family," Clay emphasizes. "You'd be available to Zelle, Winnie, and June all the time."

He sighs like he's read my mind about wanting to be more present for my daughters. Running a hand over his short gray hair, he adds, "Look, this is only contingent on you *not* returning to the Anchors, and even if you did return, we can start this project now and have it all set to open next year. Or the year after. Just think about it."

I didn't have to think too hard. The place is perfect, and I glance at Trudy, suddenly understanding why she's present.

"What did she do?" My throat is thick. Did Cadence buy this land already? What was she thinking?

Trudy straightens her shoulders. "Nothing other than find the property and propose an idea. The rest is up to you, Ford. What is your heart telling you to do?"

Run home, Fordie. Rapid clapping and cheerful laughter whispers around me, and I glance at the trees assuming it's only the leaves rustling in the wind. Then I look back at that empty field.

"Is there something in it for her?" I counter, squinting off into the distance. Would she come back to me, to us, if I did this?

"You're a dick." Sebastian lifts his head and glares at me.

"You're the one who told me to stay away from her." I point at him. Our relationship might be better but there's always going to be a thread of tension between us.

"I never said that." His eyes widen. "I wanted you to be careful because I could see how you were getting with her."

"Oh? And how was I *getting*, Sebastian?" I snap, daring him to say something negative.

"You were falling in love with her." Then he chuckles softly and rubs at the back of his neck. "There's just something about those Calloway girls."

"And loving her would be a bad thing?"

Sebastian's expression hardens. "Loving her is exactly what she needs."

"I—" Fuck, he's right. He knows he's right, but I let her go. She said it was for the best. Frustrated, I ask, "What do you want me to do, Sebastian?"

He glances up at me, long and hard for a second. "You're a baseball player, man. You swing. You miss. You swing again. She's your endgame. Your homerun."

Knox slaps Sebastian on the shoulder and swipes beneath his eye like he's wiping away a tear. "That was fucking beautiful, *man*." He coughs like he's trying to pull himself together.

"Fuck you, you love sap," Sebastian grouses. "You're the one all goofy for Halle, and you know I'm right."

Trudy chuckles, addressing me. "It might be difficult to remember the good times with your parents, but your mama had a vision once. Wanted to open that Seed & Soil, and your daddy made it happen for her. Love leads us in odd directions. Once you hit the ball, Ford, you know you have no real control over where it lands. In a mitt. On the field. In the stands. But a small adjustment can land that ball outside the stadium." Trudy arches her arm and whistles to imitate the whizz of a ball. "Grand slam." She smacks her hands together once and smiles.

"Just what are you getting at, Trudy?" Bringing up the happier times of our parents feels out of place here, although I appreciate her baseball analogy.

"Pay attention, Ford. Grand gestures are a result of the smallest actions."

Like a yellow rubber duck for protection.

"Someone's looking out for you," she adds in her all-knowing voice.

Did Trudy mean an angel up above? Or a superstar in the present? My thoughts return to my earlier question. What was Cadence thinking? Does she miss me like I miss her? Has she thought of those good times with me, or only the mess I made in the end?

I nod once and avoid Trudy's soft stare by tugging my ballcap from my head then quickly putting it back in place. "As long as you're here, want to show me the place?"

Trudy smiles wide, a spark in her dark eyes like she already knows which direction my love is leading me.

Run home, Ford. And that home is a woman always taking care of me.

As I step toward Trudy, Knox speaks up. "She did have one thing she thought you should consider." He softly chuckles, clapping my good shoulder. "She thought ducks would make a nice mascot for the camp."

I laugh, the sound genuine for the first time in a month. "Of course she did."

Chapter 38

[Cadence]

Of course it was my fault. It was always my fault.

I felt sick over what happened to June. The situation could have been so much worse, and yet, it was still bad enough. My June Bug had to have been so scared but when I talked to Stone days later, he assured me she was doing well. Enya backed up that assessment, along with asking me to return to Sterling Falls.

I couldn't. Too many heart-filled moments and heartbreaking ones marked the small town, and just like London, I didn't think I'd ever return.

Guilt was permanently my middle name. I'd felt awful for Angela Lauer although she had no right involving June. The woman needed help. She'd been wronged by her husband and struggled after having a baby. I took responsibility for her and paid for treatment, even though the reciprocity was nothing compared to the anguish she'd been through from losing Evan. One day, she'd realize he wasn't a loss.

My suggestion for Ford's future baseball camp was also partially born from guilt. I went to Clay first. He'd been the one to turn an empty field into a baseball diamond with the help of his family. A financial estimate of supplies and labor, plus a timeline, were needed. The project would not involve me. I just wanted facts, weighing the merits of such an undertaking, before Clay pitched the idea to Ford. There was only one condition; I needed to remain anonymous. I'd been thinking of his girls. His daughters needed him to be present and supportive of them. He was probably financially set for life, but I didn't want anything to take away from their futures. Colleges. Weddings. Whatever they needed. Plus, Ford should be near his larger family. Sterling Falls was home even if Chicago had been for a little while. He needed his siblings, and he was fortunate to have so many.

Finally, Daggett Ryan called in that favor I owed him. He needed a replacement act on his tour. Just a short stint of shows from August to November. The timing was uncanny. The surprise announcement that I'd accepted the gig had fans going wild. With the new productions nicely coming together, my followers deserved a sample of what was in store for the future of Cadence. There would still be songs of heartache and breakups, but I was ready to change the tune a little bit. An epic love song was itching to be written, even if I didn't have love in my life. I knew what love had felt like.

Unfortunately for me, the first stadium Daggett and I are scheduled to play is Anchor Field. I love outdoor concerts. The open air reminds me of country music festivals, like the one Ford took me to, now etched into my memory as a precious moment in time. Facing this baseball field only brought up further memories of Ford. Especially when the management gave me a complimentary jersey with my own name on the back. It hadn't exactly been the name I was hoping to wear here, but I'd been foolish to ever think Ford Sylver could be mine.

A sharp rap comes to the door of my bus as a signal it's time. The stadium doesn't have much of a green room and it's part of the appeal to play this iconic ball field. The visiting team's locker room is tucked behind the laundry room and hosts most of the warmup singers.

As I slip from the bus and onto a golf cart that whisks me into the underbelly of the field, my gaze quickly catches on a trophy case, and I wonder if Ford has anything of significance behind the glass. We whizz past the display too quickly for me to read a thing. Through the tunnel we ride, before popping out behind the stage set up in the center of the outfield, right where Ford would stand during a game.

Enya told me he hasn't returned to his team yet. Only a few days have passed since his brothers shared *their* baseball camp concept. I didn't have any hint if Ford liked the idea or hated it. I was told he had thoughts and was mulling it over.

"Cadence?"

I turn toward the person who hooks up my mic while hair and makeup touch-up my head and face. The night is warm, like Midwest

August can be. The stadium is pumped for country music despite the location in a major city. I love this place even if I'm not a baseball fan. Or wasn't until Ford.

Shaking thoughts of him, I take the stage and wave while the riotous roar of fans erupts. I love a crowd, but I'm missing one man.

Forcing a smile, I greet the stadium and remind myself this is what I do best.

Back to business, Cadence.

+ + +

When the concert ends, I'm led back to the golf cart where I'm whisked off to meet with those who have backstage passes. For years, I held my breath thinking my parents might appear, using the concert tickets I sent them along with the passes giving them access to me after a show. The dream included them congratulating me with hugs and flowers, telling me how proud they were of my accomplishments. Over time, the fantasy dimmed and while I no longer believe it would ever happen, I still always do a precursory glance through the hallways and in the appointed room out of habit and false hope.

So, I do a double take when I see someone I fully recognize leaning against a wall toward the back of the crowd.

Lana and her new assistant are good at moving people through the meet-and-greet while security stands nearby, not taking any chances with me after all was revealed about Evan and Angela. Not that everyone needed full disclosure, but my bodyguard deserved the truth. I didn't fear for myself anymore. I didn't really fear for Ford or his girls either, especially since the threat—*me*—had been removed from their lives.

As the line dwindles and people are led into a separate room for after concert drinks, my heart begins to race anticipating a greeting with the last people in the room.

"Ford," I whisper his name, afraid if I say it louder, he might disappear. Or be part of my imagination.

At his name, Lana's head pops up. She glances between us and before I speak, she clears the room except for David, my personal bodyguard on this tour.

Ford stands with his hands in his front pockets, his shoulders hitched high. The tee shirt he wears is one of those soft, worn cotton ones I love on him. His eyes are bright but cautious. He looks both tired and terrific. His jaw ticks before he clears his throat. "Great concert."

"You saw me?" Of course he did if he attended, but I have a bigger question that I am afraid to ask.

"Perks of knowing the field management." He chuckles, scratching underneath his chin a second. His smile is timid, but his gaze never leaves my face.

"Are you back in Chicago for good?"

He slowly shakes his head. "I had some unfinished business here." A spark fills his eyes. "A post-surgery evaluation." He lifts his shoulder. "I'm doing good but not great. Not well enough to return."

With another weak smile, he lifts his hands and spreads them wide like a headline. "Breaking news in sports. Ford Sylver retires early."

"Oh, cowboy. I'm so sorry." I know how important his career is to him. How much he loves the game. We've talked about how baseball is all he knows. And it's another reason I suggested the camp.

Ford shrugs. "I have other plans." His smile grows crooked and mischievous. I recognize that look and my heart hammers.

"Nice outfit." He softly chuckles, tipping his chin at my dress.

The vibrant purple costume looks like a 1920s flapper dress minus the middle section. My midriff is covered in opaque, nude-colored material with the occasional sequins for glitter.

"It's my signature color," I remind him, doing a half curtsey.

"It's my new favorite."

My mouth falls open then shuts. We stare at one another a long minute before Ford clears his throat.

"About July."

I hold up a hand, cutting him off. "It was my fault." The easiest out is taking the blame even when I felt Ford was in the wrong. He didn't need to be so harsh with me, but I've forgiven him over and over because of June. I'd been equally scared out of my mind about her.

Ford is already shaking his head. "It wasn't. I was wrong."

The air rushes from my lungs, especially when Ford steps closer to me. "I'm here to apologize." The corner of his mouth ticks up. "And you didn't even have to prompt me this time." He reminds us both of how many times I demanded he do such a thing.

He reaches out and strokes around my ear although not a hair is out of place on my head. Too much spray holding it together.

"The fear of losing June . . ." He shakes his head and drops his hand. "It was too much."

"I totally understand. I don't think I've ever been so scared in my life." Talking about that day is no less unsettling and yet I feel calm discussing it now with Ford.

His mouth curls wider but his expression remains sad for a second. "You were in danger as well and I didn't understand the full extent."

I harrumph. "Me? In danger? Never."

Ford steps even closer. "Do not dismiss your safety." He catches my wrist, the one naked of beaded bracelets. "*I* want to watch over you."

David coughs from somewhere behind me. I turn only my head and wave with the back of my hand. Ford is not a physical threat. Only my heart is triggered to burst.

The thundering in my chest returns my focus to what Ford said. "You've apologized. I accept." I gently tug at my arm because even the light touch of his fingers circling my wrist is too much contact. My heart can't handle another eruption from Ford. He hurt my feelings more than anything else.

Almost reading my thoughts, he says, "I hurt you. And I'll never forgive myself. Because what I want to do is love you."

My gaze lowers. My heart rate spikes. My voice isn't more than a croak. "Ford."

He tips up my chin with his other hand, so I look him in the eye. "I know about the camp. What you did. What you continue to do for me." Ford holds my gaze. "This could have been the worst year of my life, and yet at every difficult turn there you were, a shining star. You saved my ass in a random bar. You came to cheer me on for spring training. And you dropped everything to visit me when I got injured."

Ford twitches his shoulder again. "And now the camp. You're always looking out for me." He pauses and exhales. "And I've done nothing to deserve you, but I want you. I want to be the one to protect you. To keep you safe. To be your home base." He leans closer. "I don't want you running from me but toward me like I told you earlier this summer, and I'm sorry I made you doubt you could do that. That I made you question how I felt about you. Because I love you, Caitlin."

My vision blurs with tears. My tongue is thick within my mouth.

"So, I have some questions I'd like you to consider." He playfully jiggles my wrist still circled by his fingers. His voice lightens, hopeful but still hesitant. "Will you have dinner with me? Will you sleep with me? And will you live with me?"

My brows crease, his questions rather abrupt.

"No more pretending in any manner. I'm yours. Will you be mine?"

Another, softer cough comes from behind me. "Cadence." Lana's voice is patient, almost apologetic, but the show must go on, and I'm the show.

"We need to keep moving," she adds.

A change of clothes. A walk through a bar. A late-night arrival at my hotel. Then back on the road tomorrow to do it all over again.

"I need to go," I whisper to Ford.

He nods once. His jaw ticks but if he feels defeated, he holds his emotions at bay. As for me and his declaration of love, I don't trust myself to respond. My pulse thumps in my throat. My body trembles.

"I have something for you." He pulls a small purple fabric jewelry sack from his pocket and holds it out to me. "The girls said this is a thing."

After taking the sack from him, I tug the thin ribbons of the closure and peek inside. A set of handmade, plastic-beaded bracelets are within.

Friendship bracelets go back some fifty years or more, but the new beaded ones are popular to exchange during concerts. I didn't start the trend, another more famous-than-me pop singer did. However, I wear a few of my own on my wrist but they aren't available for trading.

Slowly, I remove the bracelets made in bright colors from the violet-shade bag. Three fluorescent bracelets made with a range of colors represent each of the girls. A tear trickles down my cheek and I lift my other wrist.

"I already wear one for each of them."

Ford's finger presses at the bracelets, spinning them to read the names. Zelle. Winnie. June.

"I wanted them with me." I shrug, feeling awkward that I'm wearing his girls' names as my talisman, similar to Ford having the girls' initials inked on his skin.

"Songbird," he whispers, noticing a fourth bracelet says Ford.

"Cadence," Lana calls again and I close my eyes, but another tear slips free. Ford catches it with the pad of his thumb. Then he kisses the corner of my mouth.

When my eyes spring open, Ford pulls another bracelet from his pocket. He takes my bare wrist and slips the handmade jewelry over my hand.

"Figured you probably lost my number. Again." The lilt in his voice suggests he's teasing. He was the one always losing mine, or so I thought. When I lost my phone, I finally got a new number.

Glancing down at the bracelet, I comment. "It's very pink."

"*It's pink. And I think. Could she love me?*" Ford sings the lyrics from one of my hits, and my head pops up. My mouth falls open, but I don't have time to speak before Lana calls my name once more. I recognize that tone. I don't have another second to spare.

"That's your call, superstar." His half-mast smile doesn't reach his eyes. He lifts my hand once more and kisses my inner wrist just above the bracelet he made. Too quickly, he releases me, offers another patient smile, and turns to walk away.

As he exits the room, I glance down at the single set of beads, noticing a series of seven numbers among the pink plastic baubles.

And a yellow duck charm dangling from the band.

+ + +

An after-midnight phone call to my sister isn't ideal, especially when she has a one-year-old, and she's pregnant, but Enya always answers her phone for me, and I need to talk.

Quickly, I explain Ford's appearance and his three random questions.

Enya groggily chuckles. "Aren't you the one who announced one of those questions at a Sylver Sunday?"

"I did not," I counter.

"Ford Sylver, are you asking me to move in with you?" My sister mimics me with an exaggerated Southern drawl.

I could argue again that I never said such a thing, but I slowly remember that I did. I'd also teased Ford once about him asking if he could sleep with me and suggested he was asking me over to his house for dinner.

The questions finally make sense. "But what do they mean?

"Maybe he's saying he wants dinner with you, wants to sleep with you, and wants you to live with him." Enya wistfully sighs. "It's a grand gesture."

My breath hitches. "I've never had one of those." My voice isn't louder than the wind outside my window. A sudden thunderstorm struck the area. Lightning brightly flashes over Lake Michigan, cracking open the dark sky like the splintering of an eggshell. My gaze leaps to the duck on the hotel nightstand.

I want to watch over you.

"He said he loved me. Do you think he meant it?" I can't bring myself to speak louder, afraid of the answer.

"Why wouldn't he love you? You're amazing with his girls. You take care of him. And he wants to take care of you. He's sorry, Cadence. He really is."

"I know," I whisper once more. His reaction wasn't about me but his fear for June. "But he didn't chase after me."

Enya softly chuckles. "The man might be known as The Streak because he's able to run fast but he's slow on the uptake of his feelings. And he's chasing you now."

Enya squeaks through the phone and I picture Sebastian poking her in the side.

"Do you think I should call him?" It's late, but he gave me his phone number on a pink beaded friendship bracelet.

"I have a better idea."

Chapter 39

[Ford]

The day after Cadence's performance, the field is vacant of the stage like a concert never happened. The Anchors have an afternoon game having just finished a three-game away series.

Like I told Cadence, I'm in Chicago for a post-surgery checkup on my shoulder, but I also had a meeting with Ross Davis. Both purposely coincided with her concert.

Before the medical report was given, I'd known the discouraging results. While my shoulder mobility was good, it wasn't great. I'd regained a decent range of motion, but I still couldn't arch my arm backward in a manner that I could throw a ball with any strength or speed. I no longer had the ability to perform at a professional level. I was fucked.

But I wasn't as deflated as I thought I'd be. Ross Davis told me my body needed more time to heal. Jokingly, he reminded me I am not as young as I used to be, and my arm has been through the wringer with a lifetime of throwing. While early retirement once felt like a no-win situation, I no longer felt that way.

The idea of the baseball camp solidified my decision. Cadence had done that for me.

When I went to her concert, I'd been hoping for more of a reaction from her, especially since I laid myself out last night.

I love her. I want her to be with me and the girls. I want us to be her home.

Then again, I understood time has passed. Was I too late? My questions were my intentions, but they might have been over the top. But like Sebastian said, you swing, and swing again, always with the hope of knocking the ball out of the park.

I wanted Cadence to know how I felt, and I didn't want more time to pass before she belonged to me, because she did belong with me, and my girls. *We* loved her.

The afternoon after her concert I'm standing in the press box above home plate in Anchor Field, waiting to be called up to sing the seventh inning stretch, a tradition in this stadium. An announcement will reach the press later today if it hasn't already.

I'm out for the season and taking an early retirement.

Bowing out before my contract was finished, I struggled that it meant I was quitting. What would a woman like Cadence want with a man who gave up?

Stone had been the voice of reason again, reminding me I'd never quit anything in my life. Not my determination. Not my dream. Not even my dismal marriage. And definitely not my girls. My future was them.

The only thing I'd be abandoning was a chance at love if I didn't take the swing, and risk a miss, by laying out my feelings to Cadence. The ball had been hit. I'd only been hoping she'd catch on to all that I wanted from her.

I was not so patiently waiting to hear from her, but I *would* wait. Giving her my number on that beaded bracelet felt a bit risky, not to mention adolescent, but the girls insisted I make a bracelet for Cadence as well as the ones they made for her. They'd be tickled to know Cadence already wore bracelets with their names on them. Mine too.

I just wanted them with me.

Fuck, I love her.

The girls were not happy I was going to see Cadence without them, but I promised they could make her more jewelry and give her the pieces next time.

Because I was still hopeful there would be a *next* for us.

As I'm waiting for the seventh inning, a media commercial timeout is taken, and the cameras span the field. A Cadence song is played, and the sound feels like a spike to my heart.

What if she doesn't call me? What if I really fucked up this time? There was no fourth or fifth strike in baseball.

Anxiously, I stand in the press box, watching the cameras' focus reflected on the jumbotron located between left and center field. Suddenly, the camera pauses and holds.

A woman wearing an Anchors baseball cap is holding up a poster with hand-painted royal blue and red lettering.

Hey you.
Ford Sylver.

When it's clear she has the cameraperson's attention, they zoom in. Despite the cap and large sunglasses covering half her face, I recognize the shape of a body I'm *very* familiar with.

The Cadence song continues. The camera zooms closer. And Cadence flips the sign.

I have answers.

What the— I narrow my eyes wondering just where in the stadium she is until I realize she's right below the press box. Rushing to the open window, I lean over the desk to get a glimpse of her standing in the middle of a vacant row, holding up the sign with her back to me. Seeing me on the supersized display, my body hanging out the window, she twists to glance up at me.

She drops the sign and cups her hands around her mouth. "Quack, quack, quack, cowboy."

Rumblings occur around me mingled with snickers and puzzled 'what the fucks', but I don't need an interpretation.

"Caitlin Calloway, get your ass up here." Only, I don't wait, I scramble out of the press box, and turn the corner on the lower walkway as Cadence rounds the stairs to this upper level.

Instantly, she's in my arms. Someone mutters near us, and without releasing her, we're ushered into the privacy of a hallway accessed mainly by the team owners and other special guests to the stadium.

Within seconds, we're given privacy as her bodyguard blocks one end of the entrance and field security blocks the other.

"What are you doing here?" I cup her face then remove her sunglasses so I can see her eyes.

"Figured you might want your lucky cap." She grabs the bill but tugs the cap downward over her eyes. Then she tips her head back to see me better and smiles.

"So, your answers?" She'd been quacking like a nutty duck, but what did that mean?

"If I'm reading you right, you want to have dinner with me."

"All the dinners."

"And you want to sleep with me."

"Every night."

"And you want me to move in with you."

"Yes." I exhale. "I know you live in Nashville and I'm going to be setting up in Sterling Falls."

"You're building the camp?" Her voice rises with excitement. Her hands tightening in my shirt.

"I am. So, I don't know how this will work for us." The whole living arrangement part. "But I don't want to be without you."

Her smile grows wider.

"I want sneaking into bedrooms, but preferably sharing one. And birthdays. We can pick our own color scheme," I tell her.

Cadence starts to laugh while tears fill her eyes.

"And maybe, possibly, we could work on that pregnancy thing we told your dad about."

Cadence laughs harder but a sob also escapes, and she covers her mouth with her hand.

Concern sets in. "Or not. *We* have the girls. I'm fine with that, too."

But Cadence is already shaking her head, slipping her hands to cup my jaw. "No. No, I want all the babies with you. I love you so much, Ford."

"I love you, too."

Our mouths meet and I'm pressing her into the cinderblock wall at her back, wanting to get started right here, right now on making a baby with her.

When we finally break apart, we're both breathing heavily, but her hands are in my hair and mine are cupping her backside, keeping her close to me.

"So new birthday colors, huh?" She teases. "How do you feel about purple?"

"I'm becoming partial to rubber duck yellow."

Cadence tips back her head to laugh but that crazy snort comes out instead, and then we're both guffawing like silly fools.

Fools in love with each other.

"Ford," echoes through the cavernous space open at each end, and I turn toward the media specialist frantically waving his arm. "The seventh inning stretch."

"Oh shit. I need to go sing."

Cadence chuckles. "You don't sing, though."

"I know. But it doesn't have to be perfect." The fans will enthusiastically stand and join in singing "Take Me Out to The Ballgame," a tradition established by a sports commentating legend who often sang the song with a few beers in him.

I take Cadence's hand and lead her toward the exit. "Sing with me."

She wraps her hand around my bicep and tips her head against my good shoulder. "Whatever you ask."

"Whatever I ask." I stop short of the entrance and spin to face her. "So if I ask one very big question one day, will your answer be more than a quack?"

"How about a resounding yes," she whispers, shy and flushed while the largest smile I've ever seen crosses her mouth.

"That's a word I plan to hear more often. Tonight even."

"And every night?" she questions but I don't want there to be any doubt.

"Every night, baby. Someway, somehow."

I lead her to the press box where I count down the baseball classic and the fans sing. Cadence takes over while I wrap my arms around her middle until the song finishes and a roaring cheer goes up for the Chicago Anchors.

"I love you, Chicago," I cry out over the mic, knowing I'm going to miss this city, these fans, and my team.

"I love you," Cadence draws my attention, reminding me I love her and my girls more.

And then, I kiss her in front of a stadium full of baseball lovers, dispelling any rumors by letting the world know Cadence is my girl.

+ + +

After Cadence and I collapse in my bed, exhausted but sated by makeup sex, we curl toward one another. We don't have much time before she catches a last-minute flight to meet up with her band and continue the impromptu tour.

"It's only until November," she reminds me, her voice quiet while I tuck back her wayward hair.

"Then it's the holidays in Sterling Falls."

"I haven't celebrated family-style in forever."

She's told me how she used to spend her time, but the future will be different.

"And now you'll have forever to celebrate with a family."

She softly smiles before suggesting, "We should probably talk about Nashville."

I shake my head, cupping the back of hers. "We don't have to figure it all out tonight. Just promise me you'll come back to me. No flitting."

"Promise me you'll be waiting?" Her eyes suggest she's still vulnerable, but she'll learn. My feet are firmly planted. My stance solid. She's the swing I'm not going to miss taking.

"Absolutely." I kiss her once more for reassurance. "Call me any time. Day or night."

Cadence lifts her wrist displaying the four beaded bracelets I gave her yesterday. "Nice grand gesture." She winks.

"You didn't do so bad yourself." I swipe her nose and inhale her grapefruit scent, a fragrance I've missed for the last month. I'm going to miss her again for the next few. "I love you."

She sweetly claims, "I love you, too, cowboy."

Pulling back, she looks up at me, and we kiss again like we won't have enough time before she leaves.

Then I think of something. "I'll need your new number unless you kept it the same as the one on the phone you lost."

Cadence slowly rolls her head on the pillow and lowers her gaze, toying with the bracelets on her wrist. "I changed it."

Tipping up her chin, I force her to look at me. "Explain to me the significance of the old one."

"My parents had it." She shrugs, keeping her eyes dipped despite her face pointed at me. "I never wanted to change it in case they decided to call." Her voice drops quieter with the explanation.

"I'm sorry, Cadence. They suck."

"They weren't ever going to reach out, but a girl can dream." She finally peers up at me. "A daughter can hope."

I nod once, my jaw tightening for the vulnerable little girl deep inside this beautiful woman and the hurt her parents have caused her.

"How about this then? When your husband calls, you answer."

"Husband?" She chuckles, the playful mood restoring. "Ford Sylver, are you asking me to marry you?"

"You promised to say yes when I do," I remind her.

"That I will." She leans into me, and we kiss again with our future clear.

She is mine. And I am hers.

Chapter 40

Offseason

[Cadence]

I never consider concerts grueling but the time ticking for this one to finish was brutal. Lana and I had a long talk while on the road about what might have happened back when Ford called me from Arizona. How she answered my phone and been the one to tell him to lose my number, not knowing it was Ford. Her romantic heart was full of guilt. We also discussed how adding on these concert dates had been a rash decision and I needed a break. I wanted to focus on the remixes and producing a new album, but the drive to perform live needed a rest. However, I had concerns about slowing down.

"Why? You're the boss, Cadence. It's your business, and no one else's."

In theory, I knew this but hearing her spell it out, it finally sank in. *I* controlled my future.

"You can do what you want, when you want." Essentially, my time was my own and I was giving it to Ford, Zelle, Winnie, and June. And they were giving it right back to me.

Lana's support meant everything to me, and her encouragement came with a compassionate smile. She wanted whatever would make me happy.

Ford was my happy place.

He and I talked every day and night.

Sometimes the conversations included Facetime with the girls. Ford told me how he'd talked to them about me living with them.

"I thought Cadence already was," Zelle had replied.

"Can she braid my hair every day?" Winnie wondered.

"My woom," June asked again.

Ford told the girls that he and I would be sharing a room together, and that one day soon, I'd be joining their family as his wife. I wanted them to accept me as a loving, supportive female role model who they could come to as a friend and rely on like a mother. Not their mother, as she was gone.

And I couldn't wait to get home to Ford and the girls.

Home. A once foreign concept that was now my future.

I was giddy every time I considered how Ford and I worked out that Sterling Falls would be our home base. Ford found an old farmhouse to renovate and suggested we build a recording studio for me on the property. My production company will stay in Nashville, and I'll plan trips accordingly, but my schedule will center around my family. Separating at times wouldn't always be easy, but we'd make it work. He didn't want to stifle my active career and he was looking forward to being a more interactive father, available for the girls while building his own future with the baseball camp.

I missed him so much, especially on nights when our conversations were private and then turned to dirty whispers and acting out how much we loved one another, trusted each other.

It had taken some time for me to feel comfortable trusting Ford again. He'd made promises he broke in the past, but he'd been proving himself every day as we talked and learned more about each other. We accepted that love sometimes has field errors, like a dropped ball or a missed hit, but together we could play the game any way we wished.

Together, we were a winning combination.

+ + +

After the final concert, I land in Charlestown, West Virginia's airport, where I'm greeted by four smiling faces and four sets of hands holding up signs. All my darling ducks are in a row.

Zelle smiles knowingly wide while holding her little poster.

Winnie bounces on her toes, gripping her sign between clenched fingers.

And June drops hers to run toward me.

But I'd read the words.

Will. You. Marry. Dad.

The final sign is held by Ford, and after scooping up June, I spin us around and set her on the ground so I can rush Ford, leaping into his arms and crushing the poster between us.

"Quack," I cry out, tipping back my head before lowering my feet to stand and look directly into Ford's eyes. "That's duck speak, for yes, yes, yes."

Ford laughs, his head tilted back before he reaches into his pocket and lowers to one knee. With a giant square-cut solitaire diamond on a white gold band, Ford stares up at me. "I planned to do this later, but the girls wanted to be part of the asking."

"As they should," I turn to them, hardly noticing Ford slipping the ring on my finger. But when he lifts my hand and kisses my knuckles, I'm drawn back to him.

"I love you," I tell him as I say every day.

"Love you, too, Cait." He's taken to calling me by my given name to remind me he isn't in love with a superstar, but a woman who loves to sing, and does pretty well at it. He isn't in love with the mogul running a production company or the bad ass taking back her music. He loves me. The woman who loves him and his girls.

He stands and kisses me, not a care that the girls are watching. We want them to see what a loving relationship should look like. Too soon, we break apart, and Ford slides his hand into mine. I hold out my other arm for the girls.

"I need some Sylver duckling hugs, ladies."

They clamber into me, a mob of an embrace, and the feeling is better than being center stage under bright lights in front of thousands of fans.

This four-pack is my family, and they'll be the center of *my* world from now on.

Epilogue

Retirement

[Ford]

There are two sports' seasons: baseball and the offseason. I'm happy to discover a new season in my life.

Family time.

I've been surrounded by mine for months, cleaning up, repairing, and rebuilding the space around Sylver Sports Camp, home of the Metallic Ducks. Cadence and I had a slight disagreement, as I didn't think bright yellow was the best color for our camp mascot. The duck is a mix of purple and silver, instead.

In addition to having my siblings around me, sometimes more than they should be, I had Zelle, Winnie, and June enrolled in the local school, and they are thriving in our new home. If I ever had concerns that they'd miss city living and Chicago, there wasn't a hint of it among them.

Zelle was secretly giving some boy in her third-grade class Jolly Ranchers every day, instead of the other way around.

Winnie was making friends and protecting those without any.

June was in pre-school half the day.

And Cadence was splitting her time between production in Nashville, perfecting our new home, and building her new studio in the barn behind our house.

Life was good.

Entering the barn, I see the red light off outside the glass enclosure to her studio. She's started filming herself and posting videos from her new space, encouraging young musicians, and speaking about simplifying her life. She's still a force but not quite the storm she used to be. More like a steady stream of controlled chaos.

When she sees me standing outside the enclosure, she waves me into the booth. I hardly have the door closed behind me and her hands are coasting up my chest, her arms suddenly around me, and her mouth on mine.

"Well, good morning to you, too," I jest, breathless from the way she kisses me.

"Hey you," she whispers, blue eyes lit up. She has all these looks about her.

When she's concentrating on new lyrics.

When she's watching our girls.

When she's looking at me as I enter her.

"How was June?" Cadence asks.

"Eager to go to school, as usual." I take the girls to school every morning and June loves to act like the older girls, bringing a lunchbox with her even though she doesn't eat at preschool.

Cadence hums, tugging the baseball cap off my head and setting it on hers. Then she tips on her toes again to kiss me.

I chuckle against her mouth. "You seem extra feisty this morning."

"Make love to me, cowboy."

My girl doesn't need to ask me twice.

Backing her further into the studio, I start by removing her sweater, finding she isn't wearing a bra beneath it. She tugs my flannel shirt down my arms, but I do the rest to remove it. Our mouths hardly leave each other.

Love has never felt like this. This excitement to see every inch of her, although I know her body inside and out. The wonder every time I touch her, kiss her, hold her, that she is mine. And while she has thousands of adoring fans, I'm the person she loves the most.

Within minutes, my jeans are off, her leggings, too. We tumble to the floor of her studio which is covered in a collection of thick rugs for comfort and sound absorption. I've learned more than I ever thought I would need to know about making music.

When the final layer of clothing is out of our way, I make love to my fiancée. With Cadence on her back, I slide my hands to her wrists, lifting her arms over her head and dipping my fingers between hers. Forking, she calls it.

Clasping onto one another, my tip at her entrance, Cadence moves, and I easily slide inside her, finding her already wet. We've been going without birth control for a while now and nothing has felt better.

"So ready for me, songbird," I tease.

"Always want you." Her head tips back, her eyelids lowering as I rock into her. With her legs raised, one wrapped around my lower back, we move with ease, familiarity, and love.

"I love you," I whisper.

Her eyes snap open, meeting mine. "I love you, too, Ford. So much."

There's something in the serious way she says this, the gleam in her eye one I haven't seen before, and sparks something inside me. I thrust deeper in long, drawn out pushes and lingering pulls. Cadence's fingers tighten within mine. She tilts her hips and a soft, sweet gasp escapes.

"Right there," I strain.

"Right there." Our bodies take over, our breathing ragged as I move within her at a measured pace until she's begging me to hurry.

Releasing her hands, I press over her, watching where I disappear inside her, where we become one. Her fingernails dig into my biceps. My dick is slick from her.

"Ford," she whimpers.

"Break, baby."

She arches her back, and this look is my favorite of her expressions. One of pure bliss and calm, awe, and love.

"Ford, Ford, Ford," she sings.

With her channel clenching, I slide home, holding out as she comes undone around me until I can't take it anymore, and I'm releasing in her with the hope to plant my seed.

We both want that to happen.

As stars dance before my eyes, I keep still, holding myself inside her. This moment feels different from the way we've made love before. We've had sex in a dozen different positions, and I marvel at how each time feels so right.

Cadence's half-lidded eyes open and the brightest blue stares up at me.

"I think I got you pregnant." This is a joke we started saying as soon as she was home in November, and we stopped all birth control. A throwback to her father's nasty words about getting her pregnant after one night together. We've discussed how there is no rush to have a baby. When it happens . . . if it happens . . . it happens. I don't want her to feel pressured in any way. She's already an amazing mother to Zelle, Winnie, and June, and if the girls are all we ever have, they are more than enough.

I withdraw from Cadence, and fall to my side, placing my hands between her thighs and finger any wetness remaining, pressing it back inside her.

She rolls her head, eyes still bright and watching me. She likes how I touch her even after we're spent. How I tease her with the release still dripping from her.

"Actually," she whispers, her gaze focused on me. "I already am."

My fingers stop tracing over her soft, slick folds and my head snaps up to look her directly in the eyes. "What?" My throat clogs, causing the question to croak.

Chewing at her lower lip, she reaches for my jaw, running her fingers along it. She tells me I have this clenching thing I do that she finds both attractive and worrisome.

Slowly, she nods, confirming what she already said.

"What? When? How?" I bring my hand to her lower belly, covering it with the expanse of my palm, and staring at her smooth stomach.

"Well, Ford, when two people love each other . . ." She giggles when I look back at her face and narrow my eyes.

"And we love each other," she continues.

I take her chin in my fingers. "We do."

"And we want this together."

"Hell yes," I interject.

"I'm pregnant." Her voice isn't more than a whisper before a tear spills from the corner of her eye.

Concern sets in. "What's wrong, baby?" I swipe at the tear, scanning her face for signs of distress.

"I'm just so happy. But frightened."

"Oh, songbird," I softly chuckle. "You're going to be perfect. We got this."

"Together," she says, eyes still watering as she focuses on me.

"Together, baby."

We're having a baby, and I can't wait for our family to grow.

Leaning forward, I cup her face and rub my nose against hers. "I love you."

"I love you, too, cowboy."

And as I roll back over her, and slip inside her once more, I feel like the luckiest man alive. A man on a winning streak . . . of love.

+ + +

Thank you for taking the time to read this book.
Please consider writing a review on major sales channels where ebooks and paperbacks are sold and discussed.

If you want a small snippet of more Ford and Cadence, scan here.

BONUS: Sterling Streak

Up next in Sterling Falls – sick/comfort, crush revealed, close quarters in *Sterling Clay*.

Sterling Clay

Turn the page for an early sample of *Sterling Clay*.

Sterling Clay

Chapter 1

[Mavis]

"What the hell are you doing?"

The gruffness in his tone was the last thing I expected, although I'm familiar enough with his voice to know he sounds like he smoked a pack of cigarettes when he doesn't smoke.

"I—" I blink, stunned as the heavy downpour hammers at my skin.

For late September, the weather has been unpredictable, and this sudden deluge came out of nowhere. I hadn't been to Sterling Falls since summer a year ago—nearly fifteen months—but I needed to be here. While I no longer had a home, I wanted to be somewhere more welcoming than where I'd been.

This was no pleasant greeting, however.

I'd debated even stopping. The mountain was dark, the hour late, and the trees around us drenched in rain emitted an ominous atmosphere. Witnessing a pickup truck pulled off to the side of the road should have meant nothing to me. I was a single mother with my six-year-old child in the backseat of my car. But when I saw the side of the truck, read the logo branded on it, and then noticed the hood popped upward with a man bowed underneath, I pulled over.

With my hazard lights on and a quick check of Dutton sleeping in the backseat, I'd set the parking brake and exited my warm, safe, *dry* vehicle to see if the man needed assistance.

Now, piercing blue eyes narrow at me. Eyes like ice when they'd been nothing but kind over the last five years. His silver head of hair is plastered to his face, jet black from the wetness of the rain. His leather jacket reflects how soaked the material is, suggesting he'd been out in the storm for a while. Standing here only seconds, the rain has already seeped through my own layers of a heavy sweater and long-sleeved tee, plus my jeans.

"I thought you might need help," I call out over the thundering rain shower, my voice rough and sheepish. I hate this about myself. Hate how I cower. How anxious he makes me.

I wasn't afraid of him. No, Clayton Sylver—Clay—would never harm me physically.

What frightened me was how attracted I'd been to him from the moment I first met him. A kind smile once upon a time. A friendly greeting whenever I entered his local business. The teasing banter he expressed among his employees, reminding me his jovial behavior was nothing special toward me. His attitude was simply who he was.

So, his rough sound and sharp words throw me off like the onset of this September storm.

Clay glances over my shoulder, the light from my hazards blinking red behind me. "You're getting drenched. You shouldn't be out here."

Does he mean in the rain? Or simply out in the openness of the late-night road? Or maybe he even means I shouldn't be returning to Sterling Falls after all that happened.

However, I'm doubtful I've ever made an impression on Clay Sylver. I've simply been a customer over the years. A woman who thought she was decorating a house to make it a home. A woman designing a backyard for a child to roam. A woman duped by the wrong man when the right one didn't know I existed.

Yes, I'd been crushing on Clay Sylver for a while now.

"I thought you might need help," I repeat, a little stronger, forcing myself to hold my head a little higher. My cold fingers are clasped together before me, tightened until they feel like they might crack. The rain is nearly painful, pelting my face and continuing to make me blink. My own hair is plastered to my cheeks like Medusa's snakes, but I don't reach for the strands. Instead, I stand stone still staring back at Clay.

I only want to help.

Holding my breath, I wait for him to tell me he doesn't need me. Whatever caused his vehicle to be pulled to the side of the road, hood up, isn't my concern. Considering a flashlight is propped up near the engine, though, the situation doesn't look good for him.

Clay slowly turns his head, glancing back at his truck. Swiping a hand over his hair, which does nothing to remove the water in the continued downpour, his shoulders fall, and he gazes back at me.

"I guess I could use a ride to town."

I nod once. "Need help with anything in your—"

A sudden hand, held upright, palm outward cuts me off. "Just get back in your car. I'll be right there." Frustration fills his voice. Maybe even defeat. He sharply turns back for his truck, and I watch as his broad back hunches. He hitches up the collar of his leather jacket as if that could prevent any further rain from hitting his body.

I spin away from him as well and briskly walk back to my SUV. Once inside, I shudder and glance in the rearview mirror to check on Dutton again. Still asleep. Lucky little man.

Reaching for the thermostat, I crank the heat and gaze through the side mirror to check on Clay's progress. The hood of his truck is closed. The brightness of my hazards flash in measured time, flicking across the slick dark road and colliding with the front of his vehicle.

While looking to my left, the passenger door to my right opens, and I let out a squeak as I shift in the driver's seat. Clay's eyes crash with mine. Bent forward, he has a hand on the top of the passenger door. His other arm rests on the roof of the SUV.

"Are you sure about this?" he asks, eyeing me, noting my surprise. As if I hadn't asked him if he needed the ride.

"Get in," I state quietly, quickly darting a glance to Dutton once again.

Clay tilts his head, door still open, rain hitting his back, and catches sight of Dutton in the backseat. My son's head is tipped to the side, leaning awkwardly on a bed pillow pressed against the window. His mouth hangs open, gently snoring.

Clay's eyes drift back to mine. He pauses another second as if contemplating something but when a clap of thunder rustles through the trees and a sudden bolt of lightning cracks upward from the street before us, Clay settles into my SUV. He slams the door then shifts once more to check on Dutton.

"Sorry about that," he mutters, side-eyeing me. He shudders once while facing forward then sets his fist to his mouth and coughs. A sharp, barking kind of cough that wracks his entire body. He bends forward as if curling into himself as the hacking continues harsh and deep. Once the spell passes, he sits upright, swipes at his mouth, and tips his head back. He closes his eyes a second.

"Are you sick?" I question.

"Just a cough," he mumbles, his voice still rugged and rough. He swallows hard, and I watch his Adam's apple roll along his throat.

"I work at the Sylver Seed & Soil," he states, like I don't know, muttering the address just outside of Sterling Falls. "You can drop me there."

I silently nod, turning off the hazards, and releasing the parking brake. Giving another quick glance at Clay, his tense body remains rigid in the passenger seat.

"I'm making a mess of your car." His voice scratches while his eyes remain closed. He smooths his large hands down his thighs, covered in soaked denim. His body shudders once more.

"No worries," I whisper, not half as concerned for my front seat as I am for the man sitting beside me. In the darkness around us, the glow of dashboard lights offers the only illumination, making it difficult to determine if Clay is sicker than a simple cough. The roughness of the barks suggests otherwise.

I glance over my shoulder once more to check on Dutton. He'd recently gotten over the flu and I don't want him sick again.

"I can call one of my brothers." Clay's voice has me turning my head, meeting those icy blue eyes once more. His pinched expression suggests he'd rather not call one of them, though.

I don't know a lot about Clay, but I know his older brother Stone is the local sheriff. One of his younger brothers, Knox, is a firefighter. Unfortunately for me, I've been acquainted with each of them through their professions, not as a neighborly citizen of Sterling Falls. Clay also has a brother who owns the local bakery, and a sister named Vale.

"No. I'll drive you wherever you need to go." Placing the car in Drive, I cautiously roll onto the mountain highway, curious what Clay was doing out here near midnight. Glancing through the windshield at the slick pavement, I wonder if I should be worried about black ice as the temperature outside has dropped considerably. Or maybe concerned another strike of lightning will burst before us.

"I'm Mavis, by the way." I clear my throat noting it isn't half as strong as the woman making a rash decision to pull over to the side of the road and help a stranded male driver. "Mavis Grant."

The use of my maiden name with him feels foreign on my tongue when it shouldn't. I hadn't been married. Not like everyone thought.

"I know who you are." His voice is quiet but no less rugged. The tone implies more than recognition of a repeat customer to Sylver Seed & Soil. He knows about my past, or at least the local lore of fifteen months ago.

With Clay's head tipped back while he spoke and his eyes closed, I want to shut my own as if they can hide me. As if it will make the past disappear and protect me from the blaze of history I'm rushing toward.

I shouldn't be returning to Sterling Falls, but this was my home despite all that happened. Deep down in my gut, I once sensed I belonged here. Not on the run. Not hiding. Dutton and I have been hidden for long enough.

My parents encouraged me to move on. Start somewhere new, somewhere fresh. That newness meant remaining in Florida with them. But amid the told-you-so speeches, and the pitying looks, I couldn't continue there any longer. We'd overstayed our welcome. It was time to return to the only other place I'd known.

I can only hope Sterling Falls is forgiving and forgetful, unlike the man seated beside me.

+ + +

I don't take Clay to the Seed & Soil. With him practically passed out in my front seat, mumbling on occasion, and coughing sporadically in a way that made his entire body tremble, I drove him to his house. I shouldn't know where he lives. It made me appear like a stalker that I did but in a small town, it isn't unlikely to know where people reside in and around the town limits. Clay owns a sprawling ranch that looks like it is tucked into a hill. Taking the winding gravel drive, now pocketed with puddles, my SUV jostles cautiously toward the single-story home.

Stopping at the end of the drive, marked by a line of railroad ties, I turn my head to notice a singular light illuminating the front door and a wall of windows facing us. Somewhere within another light glows and a strange thought hits me.

Does Clay have someone in his life?

He didn't have a wife or steady girlfriend as far as I knew, but a lot can change in a year. I'm hopeful many things are different about me. Still, the light offering a soft beam from behind the windows has me second guessing my decision to bring Clay here.

Glancing back at his slumped body, head resting against the cool glass in a similar fashion to Dutton in the backseat, I argue that I've made the right choice.

Clay Sylver is sick.

Unbuckling my seatbelt, I hesitantly reach for Clay, gently placing a hand on his shoulder and jiggle him.

"Clay." My voice is too soft, and not enough to rouse a waking man. "Clay, hon—" I quickly cut myself off from continuing the gentle endearment, as if *we* are more familiar with one another.

Giving Dutton another glance in the backseat, I shake Clay more firmly and strengthen my tone. "Clay."

A smug smile quirks one corner of his mouth higher than the other. A damn dimple pops out, nearly blinding me. "In a minute, baby." His muttering suggests he's dreaming of someone. Someone clearly not me.

The sobering thought has me pushing harder at his shoulder. "Clay," I snap sharply, sparing Dutton another glance, torn between waking my son and needing to wake the sick man happily fantasizing beside me.

Clay's eyes ping open, staring straight ahead a second. His gaze appears unfocused. Those icy blue eyes cold. Then his forehead furrows, deep creases forming as recognition slowly takes place. His rugged voice harshly whispers, "I'm home."

"No place like it," I softly tease.

His head shoots upward, those piercing eyes locking on me. His expression suggests he isn't certain who I am, despite claiming he knew me earlier, or how he got here. In my SUV. At his house.

His hand slides to the handle, and he pops open the passenger door, awkwardly tumbling out of it before catching himself with one foot. Twisting his body without a second glance at me, he slips from my car and blindly presses on the door to close it behind him.

With the way Clay sways forward, staggering side-to-side before reaching his front door, I'd think he was drunk if I didn't know better. He still doesn't look back and I watch with bated breath as he types in a code on a keypad to open his front door. As the door swings open, I tell myself I'm only waiting for him to enter the house. Make certain he's safely inside. Then I'm leaving his apparently ungrateful ass behind.

Through the floor to ceiling glass panels, I watch the outline of Clay moving inside the immediate entryway and into what I assume is a living space.

Then I watch him stumble, pitch forward, and land on the floor face first.

Continue reading *Sterling Clay*.

Sterling Clay

More by L.B. Dunbar

<u>Sterling Falls</u>
Seven siblings muddling their way through love over 40.
Sterling Heat
Sterling Brick
Sterling Streak
Sterling Clay

Parentmoon
When the mother of the groom goes head-to-head with the single father of the bride.

<u>Holiday Hotties (Christmas novellas)</u>
Holiday novellas certain to heat the season.
Scrooge-ish
Naughty-ish
Grouch-ish

<u>Road Trips & Romance</u>
Three sisters. Three destinations. All second chances at love over 40.
Hauling Ashe
Merging Wright
Rhode Trip

<u>Lakeside Cottage</u>
Four friends. Four summers. Shenanigans and love happen at the lake.
Living at 40
Loving at 40
Learning at 40
Letting Go at 40

<u>The Silver Foxes of Blue Ridge</u>
Small mountain town, silver foxes. Brothers seeking love over 40.
Silver Brewer
Silver Player
Silver Mayor
Silver Biker

<u>Sexy Silver Foxes</u>

STERLING STREAK

When sexy silver foxes meet the feisty vixens of their dreams.
After Care
Midlife Crisis
Restored Dreams
Second Chance
Wine&Dine

Collision novellas
A spin-off from After Care – the younger set/rock stars
Collide
Caught

The Sex Education of M.E.
The original sexy silver fox.
When a widowed professor decides she'd like to date again, and a local
fireman volunteers to give her lessons.

The Heart Collection
Small town, big hearts - stories of family and love.
Speak from the Heart
Read with your Heart
Look with your Heart
Fight from the Heart
View with your Heart

A Heart Collection Spin-off
The Heart Remembers

BOOKS IN OTHER AUTHOR WORLDS
Smartypants Romance (an imprint of Penny Reid)
Tales of the Winters sisters set in Green Valley.
Love in Due Time
Love in Deed
Love in a Pickle

The World of True North (an imprint of Sarina Bowen)
Welcome to Vermont! And the Busy Bean Café.
Cowboy

L.B. DUNBAR

Studfinder

THE EARLY YEARS
The Legendary Rock Star Series
A classic tale with a modern twist of rockstar romance and suspense.

Paradise Stories
MMA romance. Two brothers. One fight.

The Island Duet
Intrigue and suspense. The island knows what you've done.

Modern Descendants – writing as elda lore
Magical realism. Modern myths of Greek gods.

About the Author

www.lbdunbar.com

L.B. Dunbar loves sexy silver foxes, second chances, and small towns. If you enjoy older characters in your romance reads, including a hero with a little silver in his scruff and a heroine rediscovering her worth, then welcome to romance for those over 40. L.B. Dunbar's signature works include women and men in their prime taking another turn at love and happily ever after. She's a *USA TODAY* Bestseller as well as #1 Bestseller on Amazon in Later in Life Romance with her Sterling Falls, Lakeside Cottage, and Road Trips & Romance series. L.B. lives in Chicago with her own sexy silver fox.

To get all the scoop about the self-proclaimed queen of silver fox romance, join her on Facebook at Loving L.B. or receive her monthly newsletter, Love Notes.

+ + +

Connect with L.B. Dunbar

 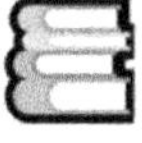